# LET IT SNOW

BETH MORAN

Boldwood

First published in Great Britain in 2022 by Boldwood Books Ltd. This paperback edition first published in 2023.

1

Every effort has been made to obtain the necessary permissions with reference to copyright material, both illustrative and quoted. We apologise for any omissions in this respect and will be pleased to make the appropriate acknowledgements in any future edition.

A CIP catalogue record for this book is available from the British Library.

Paperback ISBN: 978-1-78513-795-2

Hardback ISBN: 978-1-80280-640-3

Ebook ISBN: 978-1-80280-643-4

Kindle ISBN: 978-1-80280-644-1

Audio CD ISBN: 978-1-80280-635-9

MP3 CD ISBN: 978-1-80280-636-6

Digital audio download ISBN: 978-1-80280-637-3

Digital audio MP3 ISBN: 978-1-80280-639-7

Large Print ISBN: 978-1-80280-641-0

Boldwood Books Ltd.

23 Bowerdean Street, London, SW6 3TN

www.boldwoodbooks.com

MIX
Paper | Supporting
responsible forestry
FSC® C171272

# 1

---

'To summarise, Poppy Walton, you can tell Mum that a new sledge will definitely come in handy tomorrow afternoon. Maura Kelly, I'd hold off on booking those ferry tickets home, you'll be struggling to reach Holyhead by Christmas Eve. And for everyone who's asked, I'm not a betting woman, but even I'd be tempted to stake my stocking on the snow lasting until Christmas. So, get your shovels ready, allow extra time on the roads and keep an eye out for each other. I'm heading home for the holidays until the twenty-ninth, but you'll be in Summer Collins' capable hands until then. This is Bea Armstrong wishing you all a magical, merry Christmas.'

I kept my smile in place for those awkward few seconds until the camera cut, at which point my forehead immediately furrowed at the reminder that I'd be spending Christmas with my family. Don't get me wrong, I love Christmas. I love my family more than life itself. But combine the two together and, well, let's just say that I'd be packing my migraine medication.

As I approached my desk a few minutes later, the phone began ringing right on cue.

'Mrs Lewinski,' Sondra, the receptionist, said in the exact same drone she used every day at six forty-five.

'Mrs L,' I chirruped. 'What can I do for you?'

'Good evening, Bea,' the reedy voice rasped. 'A lovely broadcast as always. However, I'm a little concerned about my parsnips...'

Today it was her vegetables, yesterday it was whether she needed to ask the 'nice young man' next door to de-ice the garden path. Mrs Lewinski phoned the television studio most days at six forty-five on the dot and asked for her own personal weather report. I was happy to give it to her. Not just because part of my presenting style included answering individual questions from the viewers at the end of each broadcast, or because I knew I might well have been the only person she'd spoken to all day. But also because the weather was quite simply my obsession, and I would willingly talk about it in great detail to anyone who'd listen.

As soon as I'd ended the call, another one came through. Walter Pirbright.

'You got it wrong again.'

I paused, the phone tucked under my chin so I could pack up my things at the same time. 'Oh?' Walter was a local farmer. He contacted me no more than once a month, every time to correct what he considered to be an inaccurate forecast.

'The snow'll be here tonight. A couple of hours, I'd say.'

Various arguments popped into my head about why he was wrong, and the data clearly showed that the snow wouldn't reach Nottinghamshire until the early hours of the morning. I bit my tongue. In two years, Walter had been wrong once.

'How bad?'

'If you're planning on getting home tonight, I'd not hang about, and if you've plans for tomorrow, cancel 'em.'

The phone rang off before I had a chance to reply. I was mulling this new information over while checking my desk for anything I might have forgotten when Jamal sauntered over. Jamal was a broadcasting engineer and my closest friend at work. 'Great forecast. Letting all your obsessed fans know where you'll be for the next week.' He assumed his usual position, compact frame perching on the corner of my desk, hands pushed into the pockets of his skinny chinos.

I rolled my eyes, pulling a turquoise duffel coat over the Fair Isle knitted jumper dress I'd worn to embrace the festive season. 'Telling viewers that I'm going home is not quite handing out my address.'

'It's not hard to find out where your parents live.'

'Maybe by "home" I meant my own home, where a gorgeous partner, adorable twins, and stinky dog will ensure a perfect Christmas.' I leant past him to pick up my travel mug.

Jamal smiled. He was the one with a stunningly beautiful wife, four-year-old girls, and a perfectly groomed Pomeranian called Stinker. 'I think it's pretty obvious you live alone.'

'What?' I paused to look at him. While I was proud of how much I enjoyed living alone, I wasn't sure Jamal was paying me a compliment. 'How is it obvious?'

He shrugged. 'If you shared with someone they'd never let you leave the house wearing those tights.'

'Oh, shut up!' My tights were covered in glittery snowflakes and I loved them even more than the matching earrings now tangled up in the dark bob brushing my shoulders.

We were both still laughing when the air turned frigid, which usually signalled – somewhat ironically – that Summer had arrived in the vicinity.

'Ooh, care to share the joke?' she trilled, popping out from behind Jamal with a flick of her blonde extensions.

'Just general merriment at the knowledge that I won't be spending Christmas here for once.' I grinned back.

'Gosh, Bea. I really admire how you manage to feel so secure in your career! If it was me, after so many performance hiccups I'd be terrified that abandoning my fans on such a crucial weather week would risk having no job to come back to in the new year. Your confidence is amazing!'

'With popularity ratings like Bea's, I don't think she has anything to worry about,' Jamal said, assuming a blandly pleasant expression as he pushed off from the desk and walked away.

As the main weather presenter for our local, East Midlands news, I covered most of the lunchtime and early evening news programmes as well as updating the website and apps and writing any additional weather-related stories. When a few months ago Summer had joined the team straight out of drama school, I'd imagined we'd develop some sort of mentor-mentee relationship where I passed on my meteorological expertise, gained from an environmental studies degree, a year training at the Met Office, and a lifelong passion.

She'd be grateful for the time and investment I was willing to offer, and we'd swiftly become friends. Fellow women cheering each other on in the cut-throat world of broadcasting.

That wasn't quite how things had turned out.

While I wanted to blame Summer's passive-aggressive snarkiness on her five a.m. starts, I suspected it was more of a basic personality trait than unsociable work hours.

And as for the recent performance 'hiccups'? They were nothing to do with my ability to provide weather reports. My aim was to make people feel as though I were a friend who'd popped round to tell them exactly what they needed to know about the forecast, and my popularity ratings showed how much viewers appreciated my answering their queries live on air. But after I'd broken up with my boyfriend Adam in June, my organisational skills had taken a hit. I'd missed a couple of important meetings and got the wrong deadline for a feature on local flooding. While my producer had initially been understanding about my eleven-year relationship coming to an abrupt end, I had been firmly informed last month that I had Christmas week off to rest with the proviso that I'd be returning back to my 'old self'.

While no one who'd met my family would consider a week at Charis House anything close to restful, someone did once say that a change was as good as a rest, and it was certainly nothing like my usual life.

'I guess you'd better be off, then,' Summer said. 'Wouldn't want you to get caught in the snowstorm.'

'The snow won't hit us for at least a couple of hours,' I said, deferring to Walter's prediction. 'Why are you here, anyway? Didn't you leave straight after lunch?'

It was then that I noticed her outfit. While I tended to push the boundaries of the dress code with fun, personal touches like flowery headscarves or, as in today's case, the snowflake tights, Summer stuck to shift dresses and suits. This evening she was in a silver sheath dress with a neckline that dipped below her ribcage in a sharp V and a hemline revealing several inches of toned thigh. Because I tried to avoid looking her in the face, I'd also not spotted the sweep of dark eyeliner and fake lashes, or the scarlet pout.

Before she could answer, there was a general straightening of postures and quietening down of conversations as Mike Long, the studio head, strode through the newsroom doors. Summer immediately glided over to him. For a stunned second I thought they must have a date. I would have considered that none of my business except that our main newsreader worked on Reception until Mike took a fancy to her, and Summer's comment about my job security came back to slap me in the face.

'Right, I've not got long but this one has persuaded me to buy the first round,' he boomed across the room before throwing a

wink at Summer. 'So are we ready to hit the town and party like it's
almost Christmas?'

There was a flurry of laptops being signed off and coats and
bags grabbed as my colleagues, who all seemed to know what was
happening, hurried to join Mike and Summer by the entrance.
Jamal wandered back over to my desk. At some point in the past
few minutes he'd slipped into a smart jacket and added a reindeer
tie.

'Ready?'

'Ready for what?' I asked, a snowball of dread gaining
momentum as it rolled through my intestines.

'Christmas drinks.' Jamal frowned. 'With the boss.'

'I... I wasn't invited.'

'Bea, everyone was invited. Part of the whole new team-
building strategy. We had a reminder email this morning. "Do not
forget. We expect to see all of you there. No excuses."'

'What?'

As unrealistic as it was to assume that the entire newsroom was
invited apart from me, the main weather broadcaster, who people
seemed to mostly get along with, old habits die hard. The sight of
everyone gathering without me sent a hundred horrible memories
stampeding through my brain, crushing my self-esteem underfoot
as they went.

'Don't tell me – another missing email?' Jamal flashed a look at
Summer, currently linking arms with Mike as she threw back her
head and laughed in full flirt mode. Jamal had a theory that
Summer was sabotaging my calendar, intercepting my emails in an
attempt to get me fired so she could slither into the top job. I
preferred to believe that my head was still recovering from the
roller coaster that was my love-life, rather than anyone I worked
with being capable of something so malicious. My upbringing at
Charis House had instilled in me the need to see the best in every-

one, even when they failed to see much at all in me. Besides, I was pretty sure Summer barely knew how to send an email, let alone hack into one.

'Well, you can still come along, no harm done.'

'Except I can't. My train leaves in an hour.'

'So catch the next one.'

'The next one is at ten. If I wait for that I'll miss the last bus to Hatherstone.'

While in some ways I agreed with my parents that Charis House had the perfect location, our family base being in the heart of Sherwood Forest had its drawbacks, especially when I didn't have a car. It was yet another reason to put off my visits home.

'Couldn't you get a taxi?'

'I'm not sure it's worth it.'

'It can't be that much?'

'I don't mean the cost. Although finding someone to drive me out there would make a serious dent in my budget.' I grimaced. 'Mum's organised a big family meal for this evening. She's checked a dozen times that I'm not going to cancel. If I miss it she'll be furious, Dad will start crying, and my brother won't let me hear the end of it. I can't do that to them.'

Mike Long waved at us impatiently. 'Jamal, Bree? Come on, the complimentary canapés are waiting.'

'Yes, do stop standing around making everyone wait for you, *Bree*,' Summer added, gleefully reminding us all that after four years my boss still couldn't remember my name.

'Just come for one drink,' Jamal said quietly. 'Disappointing your mum has to be better than snubbing the boss.'

'Easy for you to say,' I mumbled, looping my scarf around my neck as I started walking to join the rest of the team. 'You've never met my mum.'

* * *

I was forty-five minutes late by the time the taxi finally pulled away from my garden flat in West Bridgford, a popular suburb in south Nottingham, and therefore the opposite side to where I needed to be. I'd followed Jamal's advice, staying at the bar long enough to ensure that Mike registered my presence before slipping out through the increasingly raucous crowd. Having jumped on the next bus home, I'd stuffed a suitcase full of the nearest clothes and other essentials to hand and grabbed the bulging bag of presents waiting by the door on my way out.

We were still sitting in the clog of city-centre traffic when my phone rang.

'Beatrice, where are you?'

'I'm sorry, we had a thing at work that I needed to stay for, so I missed the train.'

A sharp intake of breath.

'Don't worry! I'm in a taxi, on my way. I'll be there in about...' I did some mental calculations, winced internally and adjusted them to prevent a Mum-meltdown '...half an hour.'

'Well, I hope you've had time to get changed! You know this is a special evening. I did request that you look nice.'

'Don't I always look nice?' I asked, tugging on my woolly dress.

'Well, yes, but we are entertaining guests, so I want everyone to look their best.'

'I'd hardly call Jed, Mia, and the kids guests.'

'It's your first Christmas at home in years.'

'Mum, my home is in Nottingham. And there hasn't been a single Christmas I didn't see you.'

'Dropping in for an hour on Boxing Day hardly counts.' She paused, no doubt to crank up the guilt-o-meter. 'I just don't want you to feel out of place or underdressed.'

'If only you'd decided that twenty years ago.' My childhood wardrobe had been somewhat unusual to say the least. I would describe it as home-made, but it was worse than that. Charis House was an alternative provision school. It specialised in teenagers with behavioural issues and a whole host of challenges that meant they needed more time, flexibility, and expertise than mainstream schools could provide. That was all well and good and amazingly noble, but one of the subjects was fashion design and textiles, and to provide extra encouragement to the students, whilst teaching the wider lesson of 'waste not want not', our family ended up wearing their projects.

Mum ignored me. 'Did you get the itinerary? I emailed and shared on the Armstrong WhatsApp.'

Unfortunately that hadn't been one of the emails that mysteriously failed to appear in my inbox.

'I haven't had a chance to read it yet.' If 'had a chance' meant 'summoned the mental strength'.

'I don't want any grumbles that you weren't aware of the schedule.'

'It's my first Christmas off in four years. Maybe I'd rather not have to follow a schedule.'

'Then how will you know what's happening? If this is a twice-a-decade event, we need to ensure you don't miss out on anything.'

*That really wouldn't be too much of a problem...*

'Hang on, wait. Your dad wants a word.'

Taking a fortifying breath, I steeled myself for parent number two.

'You are going to join in with everything, Sweet-Bea? There are lots of people looking forward to seeing you.' Dad already sounded distraught at the very thought. 'We've missed you being a part of Christmas so much. Your mother has worked very hard planning it all so we can make the most of this one.'

'I get that, Dad, but please bear in mind that this is my holiday. I'm actually pretty knackered. Unless the itinerary includes reading, snoozing, and lazing-about time, I might have to duck out once or twice.'

'Of course it does! Your mother needs a rest, too. She's not a robot.'

'Are you sure about that?'

We finished the call and, with my stomach sinking into my furry boots, I looked back through the messages to where I'd previously scrolled past Mum's 'Armstrong Family Christmas Itinerary', this time opening the spreadsheet.

It took a few seconds, but I found it eventually. In between eating, rehearsals, seeing wider family, and other activities spanning this evening, the twenty-first, right through until New Year. A luxurious two-hour slot on the twenty-seventh: Free time.

It was going to be a long week.

## 2

The first flakes had started to fall as we left the city behind, the taxi now racing along the open road towards the forest. After a few miles we made the sharp turn onto a country lane and within seconds we were surrounded by trees. The only light was the glint of windows from the occasional farmhouse until Hatherstone village appeared up ahead, the yellow lamp posts competing with the reds, blues, and greens of Christmas lights spread between the cottages and adorning the oak trees lining the main road.

Just before the first house we turned off onto an even narrower, twistier lane, bumping for nearly a mile over potholes and loose stones until reaching the towering iron gates bearing the sign 'Charis House' in slightly wonky lettering thanks to another school project.

'All right if I stop here?' the taxi driver asked. 'I want to get back before the snow settles.'

I feared he was too late for that – the headlights revealed a shimmering layer of white that already made it difficult to spot where the road ended and the forest began. While I didn't relish the prospect of dragging my suitcase up to the house in a blizzard, I wasn't about to force him to tackle the long driveway. Especially when I could navigate it with my eyes closed, whatever the weather.

I pulled my hood up, wound my scarf up over my nose, took a deep breath that I instantly regretted thanks to the sub-zero temperature, and headed for home.

The last time I'd been back was in May, seven months earlier, for my niece Elana's tenth birthday. I know, it was terrible, but after Adam and I broke up, I simply couldn't face going home. By the time I was halfway to feeling myself again, work had flipped from a dream to a constant stress. In the past few weeks I'd forfeited most of my days off as I tried to find my feet again. In between that, I'd been applying to other weather forecasting roles, wondering if a completely new start was the answer.

I trudged past the main house, keeping my eyes firmly on the ground in front of me. A large, white building that had once boasted twelve bedrooms and a ballroom, it had been my mum's family home since 1842, and became a school after she'd inherited it on her thirtieth birthday. It had been where I'd met Adam, where we'd flirted and fallen in love and stolen our first forbidden kiss. In amongst the thousands of memories swirling alongside the snowflakes was the bittersweet pang of teenage passion that held so much hope, only to end up crushed so many years later.

Continuing on past the workshop and the vegetable gardens, I automatically diverted from the path that led around to my parents' front door, instead leaving a trail of footprints as I cut across the sports pitch to the high hedge that separated the Coach House from the rest of the school. Typing in the security code that opened the wooden gate, I gave it the little shove to the right that enabled it to skim over a wonky paving slab no one ever bothered to fix, and slipped through.

Immediately the back of the house lit up in a blaze of light, accompanied by the anti-burglar alarm that was my parents' two black Labradors – their frenzied barks were always intended to welcome any visitors, rather than scare them away.

Wow.

Mum had not been exaggerating when she'd said that she'd made an effort.

The six trees that proudly lined the two sides of the garden stretching towards the house were covered in icicle-shaped lights, underneath one of which stood the statue of a doe and her fawn. Beside me, in the furthest corner from the house, the fir tree that stood fifteen feet high was decked out in more finery than most indoor counterparts, with lights, shiny ornaments, and dozens of silver bows drooping under half an inch of snow.

The footpath leading from the gate to the back door was marked with lanterns, and the door itself displayed a giant wreath in the shape of a star. The patio was dotted with pots of evergreen bushes covered in more tiny lights, and while on any other day it might have looked overdone, with the snow falling it was enchanting.

The back door flung open as I approached, the dogs rushing out only to skid to a stop two feet away and offer me a paw. Mum and Dad always had dogs as emotional support animals for the school, so while they might bark if someone came to the house, they were unfailingly polite in person. These two were officially called Dumbledog and Kardashian, as decided via student vote. Thankfully, they had soon been shortened to Dumble and Dash.

'Hello there!' I gave them the fuss they deserved before letting them bound off to enjoy the snow. Turning back to the house, I was unsurprised to see Mum standing on the doorstep flapping a tea towel.

'Come on, then, we've delayed things long enough thanks to your *work thing*. Nana Joy is almost asleep at the table.' She softened her scolding with a brusque hug and practically pushed me into the kitchen. 'Oh dear, you are a mess. Were you planning on changing when you got here? There's a hairdryer in your room if you want to take fifteen minutes to sort yourself out.'

'I thought I'd delayed things long enough?' I asked, flipping back my hood so that a clump of snow plopped onto the tiled floor.

She glanced up and down, face scrunched in dismay. 'I think we can make the sacrifice.'

'Is she here?' Dad's voice drifted through from the hallway, his head appearing a second later. 'Sweet-Bea!' His eyes lit up, mouth open as if I'd returned from a polar expedition unannounced, not spoken to him on the phone mere minutes earlier. 'Come in, come and sit down, let me take your coat. It's so wonderful to have you here. You getting the week off work is the best Christmas present we could have hoped for.'

He hurried across the room and flung his arms around me, managing to lift me about a millimetre off the floor before his back made a disturbing crack and he quickly plonked me down again.

Still handsome at fifty-eight, at six foot he stood an inch taller than me and Mum, though he was brawny where Mum's love of sport kept her lithe (and I was somewhere in between). In contrast to Mum's sudden interest in my looks, neither of my parents usually cared much for outward appearances. Dad's silver hair had never found a comb it could agree with, and Mum's ash layers framed a face permanently devoid of any beauty products beyond a quick smear of moisturiser. Workdays and weekends Mum wore athletics gear, stretching to a smart pair of trousers and shirt for a special occasion. Dad lived in jeans, moth-eaten jumpers, and the worst of the fashion students' projects.

Today he wore a suit. His tie matched Mum's claret cocktail dress.

What on earth was going on?

'Come on, let's get you seated.'

'Jonty!' Mum hissed, grabbing the arm that had started to propel me towards the dining room. 'She can't go in looking like that!'

Dad stopped, as if bewildered. I knew how he felt.

'What are you talking about? She looks captivating.' Dad reached up to brush another smattering of snow from my hair.

'She looks like she rolled down the drive!'

'Um, excuse me, but I am standing right here. A grown adult. Who can decide for herself how she wants to look. I don't know what's got into you both, but I can go in looking however I want, and I will!'

With a good shake of my sopping-wet hair, ignoring how the damp sheen of melted snowflakes was smearing my day-old make-up, I thrust my coat at Dad, kicked off my soggy boots, and marched to the dining room.

I say marched. I'd forgotten how slippery the tiles can be, especially in tights. It was more of a skid than a march, but I felt as though I'd made my point.

'Auntie Bea!' A chorus went up from my nieces and nephew, producing a warm glow that I knew was completely undeserved considering how long it had been since I'd seen them.

'I'm so glad you're here, we were almost starving to death!' Frankie, who was seven, said, jabbing his fork in the air. 'Grandma said we weren't allowed any more bread until you finally bothered to turn up.'

'I honestly thought she might *explode* if you didn't get here soon,' Elana added, her dark eyes serious. 'Things were getting quite stressful.'

'Bea,' my brother, nearest to the door, stood up and gave me a peck on the cheek.

'Auntie Bea, you look very messy,' my youngest niece

announced. 'Your hair is all wet and tangled and there's black marks down your face.'

'Shhh, Daisy!' Jed's wife, Mia, said. 'That's rude.'

'It's not rude it's the truth!' Daisy shrugged, her blonde curls bobbing. 'And it's not fair because you said that we had to look pretty and smart and that's why I had to brush my hair and wasn't allowed to wear my Rudolph onesie even though it's nearly Christmas and you said it was rude to look like a scruffpot for Grandma's special dinner so Auntie Bea is the one that's rude not me!'

'She's got a point,' Elana said, adjusting her glasses.

'Well, excuse me!' I retorted, hands on my hips as if genuinely offended. 'I fought through a snowstorm to get here, arctic gale whipping at my face, skin turning to ice, wolves chasing me through the woods, a goblin jumping out at me from behind a bush... let alone the town-centre traffic! So excuse me if I don't look as perfect as all you gorgeous people. We can't all be stunningly beautiful as well as charming and intelligent!' I squeezed down the gap between the enormous dining table and the sideboard as I spoke, kissing each of the children on the top of their head. 'Besides, I'll have you know that this is all the rage for weather presenters these days. Scruffpot chic, we call it! So there.'

I stopped at the final chair on this side of the table, where Nana Joy was sitting, her blue eyes looking far from sleepy as she twisted around to face me. 'Oh, now look at this! It's...'

There was a momentary pause.

'Beatrice,' I finished for her, the ache of grief burning behind my eyes. Nana Joy was eighty-seven. She'd first starred in a West End show at seventeen, and had gone on to appear in movies, record chart-topping albums and enjoy the well-earned accolade of National Treasure. Since retiring from the spotlight aged seventy-five, she'd moved to Charis House and taught drama, dance, and music until she started to forget pupils' names and get muddled about the timetable. While she could still sing every word of *Guys and Dolls*, she spent most of her days lost in memories of a more glamorous time. I felt a stab of shame that I'd left it so long. She seemed so much smaller than last time I'd been here, in every sense of the word.

I bent over and gently gave her a hug. 'You look beautiful,' I whispered, pressing my face against hers.

'Well, yes, I'm quite the talk of the town, don't you know,' she tittered, arching her eyebrows suggestively. 'That young man is quite taken with me.'

She nodded across the table, and for the first time I realised that there was another person here.

It took me three thumping heartbeats to recognise him. By the fourth, everything made sense.

'Hello, Beatrice,' he said, with the same frown he'd used to address me the handful of times we'd unfortunately been forced to converse thanks to our parents being best friends.

'Um, hi.' I continued to stand there, behind Nana Joy, waiting for someone to tell me why Henry Fairfax was at my family pre-Christmas dinner.

'Well, I was expecting a warmer welcome than that for one of your oldest friends,' Mum said, having entered the room with a large dish of steaming vegetables. She took a step closer to Henry, lowering her voice to the kind of whisper that people can hear from several feet away. 'I think she's a bit flustered. Give her a moment.'

*Flustered?* That was not how I felt. Annoyed? Embarrassed? Already driven to banging my head against the wooden panelling a few times?

She plonked the dish on the table. 'Are you sure you don't want to take a moment to freshen up?' Her eyes slid over to Henry and then back to me.

'Yes. I'm sure.' I reiterated my point by moving around Dad's place at the end, past Henry to where a crayoned place card indicated my seat.

'Uggghhhh!' Frankie groaned. 'Can we please eat now?'

The obvious thing to do would have been to offer Henry a few polite pleasantries, then become fully engrossed in conversation with the person sitting on the other side of me. As if anticipating this tactic, the person sitting on my left was my mother.

'So, Henry,' her initial onslaught began. 'Why don't you tell Bea why you're here?'

My stomach clenched in protest. Whatever flimsy excuse Mum might have concocted, we all knew the reason he was here.

One summer when Henry and I were about six, our two families had gone camping. Jed, twelve at the time, had spent most of the holiday mooning after teenage girls in the park. Henry's sister had been a baby, and therefore of limited interest to both of us. Through lack of alternative options, Henry and I had ended up spending the two weeks playing together. One evening, no doubt fuelled by one too many glasses of rosé, our mothers had declared how excellent it would be if Henry and I ended up as a couple. For the remainder of our childhood, for some excruciating reason I had yet to fathom, they had refused to let the dream die.

Seemingly, being in the same year at school and both liking science was enough to ensure a perfect match.

The fact that by the time I'd reached secondary school I had decided Henry was a tedious, unbelievably annoying super-nerd with the worst haircut known to man was immaterial in their grand schemes.

As was how Henry regarded me with the general air of smug disdain he reserved for anyone who failed to understand the depths of particle physics or wear their perfectly ironed school tie a precise three centimetres above their elasticated trousers.

Henry cleared his throat. 'I'm starting as a science teacher here next term. Mum and Dad are visiting Polly in Singapore, so your parents kindly invited me to join them for Christmas.'

'Henry will be moving into the stable apartment,' Mum said. 'It needs a fresh coat of paint, so he's staying with us until the decorators are finished.' She paused, eyes gleaming. 'He's in the spare room.'

'Right.'

'So, how's things with you?' Henry asked, and when I turned to face him he was almost smiling. 'Have you still got the garden flat in West Bridgford?'

Ugh. I hadn't seen Henry in years, but thanks to the parental gossip-line he probably knew everything about me, including my latest break-up with Adam. I'd had to sit through enough of Mum's ramblings about Henry's amazingly successful career and how he was inexplicably still single.

'Yes. I really like it there. And it's so convenient for work.'

'Ah, yes. You're doing the main news now.' Henry stopped, his eyes darting anywhere but at me. 'Mum told me. Of course.'

'Of course.'

I probably should have asked him a question back, out of Christmassy politeness, but I was home for the first time in months and I wasn't about to spend it making monotonous chit-chat with a possible cyborg when I could be having fun with my family, who I actually liked. I leant towards Elana and asked her about the new play she was starring in at her drama school, ignoring Mum's irritation as her well-thought-out plan began to shrivel.

It was harder than it should have been to ignore the man sitting next to me, however.

Henry still seemed a bit odd, and still wore a perfectly knotted brown tie over a beige shirt that looked as stiff as his shoulders, but there was a reason it had taken me a moment to recognise him.

'You look different,' I blurted, after the kids had got distracted with a debate about who got to sleep on which identical inflatable mattress.

He paused, a fork bearing a cube of carrot hovering in mid-air. 'It's my hair.'

It *was* partly his hair, which instead of resembling a Lego helmet had now been cut much shorter at the sides than the top. It had darkened over the years, too, from a mousy brown to rich chestnut.

'You're right. I think one of them might actually be out of place there.'

He automatically reached up and ran a hand over the top of his head before realising I was joking. Giving a short shake of his head, he almost smiled again, his gaze pointedly resting on my own matted mess.

'And the contact lenses,' he added, after a strangely lingering moment.

'Yes, of course.' For the first time since I'd arrived, our eyes met. I'd probably never seen him without a pair of enormous, ugly glasses on. If asked, I'd have guessed his eyes were the same nondescript sort of brown as his hair, but in fact they were a startling shade of blue – almost aqua – and framed by the type of thick lashes that some women paid good money for.

'The new look's nice. A definite improvement.'

Henry's eyes widened for a split second, the tops of his ears turning pink as he acknowledged the compliment with a nod before quickly turning all of his attention to his meal.

If I'm honest, nice was an understatement. I felt relieved when Mia leant past Mum to ask me how work was going, so I had an excuse to turn away again. The hair and the contact lenses were only part of Henry's transformation. A round baby face had sharpened to reveal cheekbones and a firm jaw smattered with stubble.

Somehow, through some bizarre quirk of fate, he'd ended up not bad-looking.

It was most disconcerting, and perhaps Mum wasn't so wrong about me being flustered after all.

## 3

Once pleasantly stuffed with Mum's beef and butterbean stew, I took the opportunity to clear some plates and hopefully my head at the same time. It was far too hot in the dining room, packed with so many of us, and I needed fresh air and to be somewhere I wasn't continuously trying not to bump elbows with the person next to me.

'Hey, sis.' Mia was right behind me. She dumped a stack of serving dishes on the enormous kitchen table and pulled me in for a huge hug. 'It's so good you could get the time off this year.'

I squeezed her back. I loved my sister-in-law. I was thirteen when she first started going out with Jed, and while she'd never quite lost that allure of being older than me and therefore cooler and infinitely more worldy-wise, over the years we had also become genuine friends.

'What, so I could dilute the Mum-factor?' I said, laughing as we broke apart.

'She's gone full Armstrong this year. I don't think I could get through it without you,' Mia replied, her face deadpan until suddenly breaking into a wicked grin as she pointed at me. 'And now your childhood betrothed is here, I can properly sit back and relax. She probably won't even notice if I skive Christmas dinner.'

'You could have warned me he'd moved in.' I opened the fridge and took out the cheesecake Dad had prepared for dessert. While my mother insisted on wholegrain and home-made, Dad occasionally managed to sneak in a treat that contained refined sugar.

'Then you might not have come home.' Mia's eyes shone with glee as she picked up an enormous bowl of fruit. 'Besides, I think your mum could be right on this one.'

'Um, excuse me?'

'You two can barely look at each other.'

'Yes, because we can't stand each other!'

'You're very flushed for someone who's only had a small glass of wine.'

'I'm wearing a lot of wool. Plus, I had a cocktail before I came here. Have you been scrutinising my every move?'

'Of course I have! I was dying to meet this mystery man who's apparently so perfect for you. You can't blame me for wanting to see if there's any chemistry.' Mia waggled her eyebrows suggestively as she left the room.

'Well, I hope your curiosity has been satisfied. Sorry to disappoint you, and everyone else.'

She twisted her head to look at me over her shoulder as she went, her fair hair gleaming in the fairy lights shining through the kitchen window. 'Oh, I'm not disappointed.'

\* \* \*

Every muscle in my neck and shoulders was aching with pent-up tension by the time we finished eating. However the torture was far from over. Once we'd cleared up and put the kettle on, any hope of escaping upstairs was quashed by Mum's guilt-tripping comments about the itinerary.

'Jed and Bea, will you make hot drinks? Everyone else find a seat in the living room and divide yourself into pairs.'

'I bagsy you to be my pair,' I told Jed while we waited for the coffee to brew.

'I reject your bagsy. No way I'm unleashing the wrath of Principal Armstrong this early in the celebrations,' he replied, patting me on the head as if that made his betrayal okay.

'If you're colluding in this ridiculous conspiracy to match me up with Henry then I henceforth disown you as my brother.'

'I'm not colluding.' He paused, tossing decaffeinated teabags into Mum's giant teapot. 'Just remaining neutral.'

I scowled. 'You're either for me or against me.'

'Would you like some older, wiser, brotherly advice?' he asked, his voice softening with affection.

I thought about that while I poured boiling water into four mugs of hot chocolate. 'I suppose so.'

'Just roll with it for a week. Let Mum pair you up with Henry, smile, be friendly, pretend it doesn't bother you. You'll have a much better time than if you try to fight her on this. What's the worst that can happen?'

'I have to spend Christmas being forced into close proximity with someone I don't like, instead of my family, who I thought I unreservedly loved with all my heart until this conversation?'

'Come on, Henry's not that bad. I know he used to be a bit of a geek, but he's a really decent guy.'

'If you like androids who think they're better than everyone else just because they know the circumference of Neptune.'

I pulled open the kitchen door to find the android standing on the other side of it. I could have pretended he hadn't heard, but the look on his face proved otherwise. It said a lot about our history that the immediate thought to pop into my head was, *Wow – he has feelings!*

'Cora sent me to see if you needed a hand.' Henry's voice had taken on the robotic cadence that I was used to, and out of nowhere a tiny idea broke through my bitchy, schoolgirl attitude. Was Henry so stiff and irritatingly precise because he was *shy*?

'Great, grab this, will you?' Jed intercepted, handing Henry the coffee pot before casually sauntering off with a tray of mugs.

'I... um...' I, um, had no excuse.

'It's 155,600 kilometres.'

'Pardon?' As I stood there shrivelling with embarrassment, Henry leant past me, grabbed a jug of milk and *winked*, before heading back to the living room.

I took another few moments to try to defluster, picked up the teapot, and followed him.

\* \* \*

'Right, this is the deciding round!' Dad said, doing his best imitation of a quiz show host. We'd completed five rounds, including Disney and Pixar characters so the kids had a chance to shine, and a musicals round, where, instead of writing them down, Nana Joy chose to give us a mini rendition of each answer. She put on a fabulous show, with the added bonus that everyone then got full marks. After a science round, sports, and popular culture, Henry and I – paired up as predicted – were neck and neck with Jed and Daisy.

'Feeling confident?' Henry muttered, sitting beside me on one of the giant sofas, the knuckles of his clasped hands glowing white.

'Of course.' My eyes narrowed as I sized up the competition. In twenty-odd years of Armstrong Christmas quizzes, the best I'd achieved was second place. 'I can't wait to wipe the smug smile off Jed's face.'

'Hasn't he won once or twice before?' Henry asked, his face blank.

I looked at him, the corner of my mouth curling up in surprise. 'Maybe you should ask him.'

Jed had repeatedly announced to no one interested that he was the reigning champion, having won a total of twelve quizzes.

'Right, here we go.' Jed smacked his fist into the other hand, like a bully preparing for a punch-up. 'Prepare to meet your doom, Astro Quizicists!'

'Yeah, Astro Quizitist! You're going DOWN!' Daisy yelled, jumping about on her sofa.

'Oh, button up, Rainbow Mermaid Warriors!' I jeered back. 'You're all talk and no trousers. It's not over until the fat lady sings!'

'Nana Joy isn't fat!' Frankie squealed with gleeful horror.

'I wasn't talking about—'

'Who said I was fat? Was it that good-for-nothing reporter from that trash magazine again? He's always spreading wild rumours about me. Barely half of them are true!'

'I have got trousers but Mummy said I had to wear a pretty dress. I did told you this already, Auntie Bea!'

'Can we pleeeeaaaase get on with it? I've got tons of lines to learn before the show.'

'*Quiet!*' Mum barked. Once she'd given us all her best head-mistress glare, she nodded to Dad to proceed.

'This vital round is on...'

'Dinosaurs!'

'Chipmunks!'

'Chipmunks? Daisy, you're so strange. You know nothing about chipmunks.' Elana rolled her eyes.

'I know lots about them! Mummy, Elana said I don't know nothing about chipmunks but I do! I know that they live in America and live under the ground and eat nuts, berries, insects, frogs and—'

'Hey, if you aren't quiet we won't get to hear what the topic is,' Mia intervened.

'Well-then-Elana-shouldn't-have-said-that-I-don't...      sorry, Mummy.'

'It's on an even better topic than dinosaurs or chipmunks... the Armstrong Family!' Dad announced with a flourish.

'Not fair!' Elana grumbled. 'I've only been in the family for ten years.'

'Well, it's a good job you're on my team, then,' Mum said, patting her quiz partner's hand.

'And what about Henry?' Frankie said. 'He's not even in the family so Auntie Bea will have to answer all those questions.'

'Ooh, I don't know about that,' Mum smirked. 'Let's wait and see.'

'Right. Question one.'

By the end of nine questions, we were still matching Jed and Daisy point for point.

'Last question!' Dad announced.

'This has to be about you,' Henry said, leaning closer so that our competitors couldn't hear. 'We've had a question on everyone else. It's a slam dunk, surely.'

We all leant forwards eagerly.

'What song did Beatrice Armstrong perform in the Charis House Christmas Spectacular ten years ago today. I'll give you a hint...'

'No!' I shouted. 'No hints! You didn't give us a hint for Daisy or Jed's question.'

'Challenge the quizmaster again and he will automatically deduct you a point.' Dad peered at me over the top of his reading glasses. I kept quiet. On second thoughts, never mind Jed; I could do with a hint.

'The theme of that year's show was Let It Snow. You have thirty seconds to write down your answer.'

I did some quickfire calculations. 'Okay, I'm pretty sure it was this.'

I wrote down 'Winter Wonderland' on the answer paper so our rivals wouldn't catch a whisper of the answer.

Henry shook his head, took the pen from me and scribbled it out, writing 'White Christmas' instead.

I hunched over the paper, frowning.

'Fifteen seconds!' the quizmaster called out.

'No. I'm pretty sure I did that one the year later. I'd just got back together with Adam, and it was his favourite Christmas song,' I whispered hurriedly.

Henry shook his head. 'It was this. You wore a shiny white dress with loads of snowflakes dangling off it and had a cloud on your head. You started crying right after the last verse.'

A vivid memory flashed up: me and Adam, backstage, arguing because he'd turned up stinking of beer and he was supposed to be coming back to the Coach House for drinks and mince pies after-wards. He made a cruel joke about needing to self-medicate before spending the evening with the principals – the kind of comment he'd never make if he was sober, and I was furious.

'Time's up!'

'Dammit!' Jed growled, prompting a stern reprimand from his wife about behaving like a good sportsman in front of his children.

'DAMMIT!' Daisy echoed, proving Mia's point.

'Rainbow Mermaid Warriors?' Dad asked.

'Winter Wonderland.'

'Astro Quizicists?'

I took a deep breath. 'White Christmas.'

The tension in the room was thicker than the snowstorm whirling outside the window.

'The answer is...'

*'Please, please, please, please...'* Daisy muttered, eyes closed and hands clasped as if she was praying. I felt a pang of regret that I might be about to crush her hopes. Then I saw my brother glaring at me across the room, and the regret morphed into cut-throat ambition.

'Mother, if you would be so kind?'

Nana Joy pressed one hand against her chest, raised the other aloft, took a deep breath and sang the opening line.

'YES!' Henry and I sprang to our feet, grabbing each other's arms and doing a victory dance in time to Nana Joy, who was still singing.

'How did you know?' I muttered in his ear, not wanting to reveal that I'd have got the answer as wrong as my brother.

He dropped my wrist. 'Android brain. Never lets me down.' He shrugged, head bent as he sat back down and started readjusting his shirt cuffs, his eyelashes casting a perfect semicircle shadow on his cheekbones.

'Impossible question,' Jed grumbled once the celebrations had died down and Henry and I had been awarded the old vase that we used as a trophy. 'Who could remember that apart from Bea?'

'I remembered,' Dad replied, with a patient smile.

'Okay, so who could remember apart from someone so full of sickeningly, soppy love for her that he files away every minute thing she does?'

It took every ounce of will I possessed, but I managed to avoid glancing at Henry as I made my excuses and went up to bed. Partly because I was so embarrassed by Jed's declaration. Partly out of worry that there might be a hint of truth in it, and I might see something in Henry's reaction that would make the next few days even more awkward than I feared.

# 4

It was inevitable that being back in my childhood bedroom would throw up a thousand memories. It was so long since I'd been up here, even climbing the steep staircase to where my room was tucked up in the eaves of the Coach House generated a flashback to the countless times I'd scampered or stomped up there before. The smell hit me as soon as I opened the door – wood and a faint whiff of varnish, blended with the lingering trace of the perfume Adam had bought me for Christmas one year.

The room had barely changed. Mum and Dad had offered me the polite ultimatum that any items uncollected a year after moving to my new flat would be disposed of as they saw fit, so it was far sparser than when I'd last stayed. However, Elana usually slept up here when the children stayed over, so the rows of shelves were still full of children's books and games. The curtains and bedding were the same mint-green stripes that I'd chosen for my thirteenth birthday, and the knotty, multicoloured rug that some enthusiastic Charis House pupils had created still took up half of the modest floor space.

I brushed my teeth in the tiny porcelain sink, changed into my warmest pyjamas, and slipped into bed, wincing as I remembered quite how icy it got here in winter. And then, cocooned in the familiarity of home, I let the memories wash over me, the tears following closely behind.

* * *

*Christmas, twelve years earlier*

For the first time ever, I wasn't dreading the Charis House Christmas Spectacular. Jed was planning something with his new wife, Mia, and so instead of us being cajoled into a cringe-worthy duet, I was going to ignore all parental pressure and perform something authentically *me* for the first time ever. At fifteen years old, this meant reciting a spoken-word poem I'd written about how Christmas had been hijacked by capitalism. It would surely be lauded as ground-breaking creative genius by all who heard it. And if anyone thought it was depressing twaddle that didn't even rhyme, that merely showed up how little they knew about true art.

Even better, the new boy would be coming. He'd agreed to play lead guitar in the school band, and I couldn't wait to have a legitimate reason to stare at him for a full three minutes. I'd first spotted him at Charis House eight days earlier, and had thought about little else since. He'd been chopping wood outside the workshop – one of the activities Dad used to help pupils channel aggression – and despite the temperature being close to freezing, he'd removed his jacket and jumper and revealed a non-regulation sleeveless top that showcased his flexing muscles with every stroke of the axe.

While I'd had a chance to observe him as I approached, lumbering slightly from the weight of a giant cake tin, once I got closer I instinctively dropped my eyes, focusing on the path ahead.

'Hey.'

I took another few tentative steps. Surely he wasn't talking to me?

'Hey, girl with the massive tin,' he called again, and I was compelled to stop and swivel around to where he now stood, leaning on the axe with one hand, sweeping sandy, chin-length hair off his face with the other.

My heart scrabbled about in my chest like the dogs when they heard the postman approaching.

I was several metres away, but even from this distance his gaze was piercing, sending electricity crackling through my nervous system.

He was the most beautiful person I'd ever seen. Like an angel. Yet, something in his stance, the glint in his eyes, the crooked smile, gave the warning that he was far from holy.

'Are you going to come over and say hello, then?' he asked, his voice carrying a hint of gravel that made my breath stutter.

'Um...'

He arched one eyebrow, almost daring me to approach, and as if sucked in by a tractor beam I couldn't resist walking back until close enough to see the life-sized tattoo of a beetle crawling out of the top of his T-shirt.

'I've not seen you before. Are you even newer than me?' he asked, those dark eyes seeming to bore right into the depths of my befuddled brain.

'No. I don't go to school here.'

He watched me for another long, heart-trembling moment. 'You aren't old enough to work here.'

I was indeed old enough, having been roped in more times than I could count to scrub desks, file reports, and tackle any other odd jobs that needed doing when there was no one else around to do them, but not in the way that he meant.

'I'm fifteen.'

He nodded once, as if satisfied that his estimate had been accurate.

'So-o-o-o... are you the Christmas fairy? Or just lost on your way to Grandma's cottage?'

He smiled then, jerking his chin at my red duffel coat.

I really didn't want to tell him who I was, but it would only be a matter of time until he found out anyway.

'I live in the Coach House. The principals are my parents.'

'Oooh, ouch!' He winced. 'That must be interesting.'

I shrugged. 'Not quite the word I'd use.'

'Why are you here, then? Are you home-schooled?'

'I had a dentist appointment.' Again, I cringed inwardly at having to reveal something so mundane to this boy. If my brain hadn't turned to mush in his presence, I'd have come up with something glamorous like I had an interview with a modelling agency or I'd skipped school today because I'd been out partying all night.

Mercifully, he didn't seem put off. 'What's in the tin?'

With clumsy fingers, I prized off the lid. Mum had agreed to me not going back to school for the final lesson on the basis that I spent the time learning a new skill. While I'd made plenty of cakes before, this was my first attempt at piping icing, and I'd been feeling quite pleased with the result until now, where I became suddenly racked with anxiety at my wobbly letters.

'Looks great,' the boy said, leaning closer.

'I don't know. It was my first go at writing on a cake. Next time I'll try not to make so many blobs.'

'Don't knock yourself like that,' he said, looking up at me, his forehead creasing. 'Why focus on the one small thing that's not perfect, when the rest is so good?'

'Um...'

I fidgeted about for a couple of seconds, lost for words and now sweating profusely underneath my hood.

'Are you taking it over to the school?' he asked, face hopeful. 'Is it some kind of Christmas goodwill gesture – the principal's daughter bakes for the delinquents?'

'Well, I thought you deserved a change from gruel and stale crackers, seeing as it's Christmas.'

'How very kind, miss. We do so appreciate your thinking of us like this.' He tugged at a lock of his hair.

'If I were you I'd finish chopping that wood before the other reprobates have eaten it all.'

He hefted the axe high above his shoulder, then slammed it into the block of wood that he'd been splitting the logs on. 'I'm done here. Your darling dad said I had to keep chopping until I'd stopped wanting to punch a hole in the wall.' He pulled a baggy grey jumper over his head. 'I think I've found something that works even better. Next time I need to calm down, I know who to look for.'

I was trying to remember how to breathe when the moment was totally ruined by my mum bellowing from the main house doorway. 'Beatrice, is that you? Please stop dilly-dallying and bring that cake inside.'

I could see her peering closer to identify who had caused my delay, her tall frame stiffening when she realised it was a male, probably even more so because it was this particular male. 'Now!'

I hurried down the path, barely noticing how Mum watched my every step from up ahead, her opinion fading into irrelevance compared to that of the person following behind.

Over the last few days of term, my initial attraction rapidly evolved into obsession. It was as though everything about my life before had been pointless and petty. I finally understood all those poems and plays, had indeed written more than a few verses myself, and felt sure I would be consumed by this strange fever burning through my bloodstream, if I didn't get a chance to do something about it soon.

Every afternoon I raced home from school on my bike, torn between hurtling up the two flights of stairs to my attic, where I could style myself into the kind of person people like him were attracted to, or heading straight for where the Charis House Christmas Spectacular rehearsals were in full swing in the old ballroom, now repurposed as the school hall, so I could spend as much time as possible in the same room as him.

Mostly, I made do with pulling on a hat and throwing on the fur-lined bomber jacket that, after I'd found it in a charity shop, was now the coolest item I owned.

The boy, who I now knew was called Adam, had spoken to me six times, not including the quick hello he usually offered when I showed up in the hall. Not that he said 'hello', of course. More like, 'Hey there,' or, 'good evenin', milady.'

He seemed to be taking the rehearsals as seriously as the rest of his bandmates, most of whom had been coming to Charis House for at least a year, and so knew that the Spectacular was well above your average school show, with the potential to snag a gig in the Hatherstone pub or, even better, at the Robin Hood Festival in August. However, I couldn't help noticing that, while riffing through the two songs or quietly strumming as the rest of the band worked out a bridge intro or tricky chord progression, he spent an awful lot of time looking across at me.

There were other girls for him to stare at. A group of year

elevens practised a dance routine while others decorated the hall or sat clustered in one corner waiting for their turn on stage.

I felt sure that Adam liked me. There was only one giant problem. He asked me about it on the second-to-last time we spoke before the day of the show.

'Principal Armstrong doesn't seem very happy about me coming over to talk to you.'

'No?' I asked, sounding as though my scarf were wound too tight.

'Every time I say hello I can feel her death stare scorching my skin.'

I glanced to the side where Mum was indeed standing there, hands on hips, glaring at us with as much venom as if she'd caught us vandalising her Christmas Spectacular banner.

'Yeah.'

'So is it me in particular, or does she take issue with her daughter fraternising with riff-raff in general?' He looked at me, brow furrowed, and my heart swooned inside my chest.

'You must have had some conversations with her?'

He nodded. 'I do football and running. Plus, the big welcome speech.'

'Then you know she doesn't consider any of the students here to be riff-raff. Or delinquents.'

He nodded. 'So why the devil eyes?'

'She also wants the best for every student here. That's not a hollow speech. It's genuinely her life's work. This was her family home and instead of lazing about in luxury she invested everything into welcoming kids that everyone else has written off and giving them a chance to be all that she believes they can be.' I pulled a face. 'She won't allow that to be jeopardised by unhelpful distractions.'

He looked at me steadily for a long moment. 'I can understand that. You're very distracting.'

As a respecter of science, I refused to believe in love at first sight. But at seventh sight? I had the evidence to prove it.

* * *

I'd promised myself more times than I could count that I was going to stop doing it. I knew it would be about as pointlessly painful as stabbing myself in the face with a fork, but churning up these memories made the temptation to stalk irresistible. I went for Adam's Instagram first, both his personal account and the one for his latest band. Scouring through the images, I scrutinised every photo and comment for evidence that he'd moved on – or hadn't. There was no sign that he was dating anyone. Or, perhaps more importantly given the reasons we'd broken up, that this band was any more of a success than the previous three. His other social media channels were much the same. Seeing his face instantly brought back the familiar ache that had accompanied our many break-ups over the years.

*Did his life feel emptier, smaller without me, as mine did without him?*

*Was this actually how our story would end – heartbreak and disappointment and a mountain of broken promises?*

How long did you wait for the love of your life to finally change? To grow up?

I had thought eleven years was more than enough, but it seemed incomprehensible that this was it, Adam was just carrying on without me, and would keep on doing it for as long as we both shall live.

And that, I reprimanded myself as another tear plopped onto

my phone, was the reason I'd banned myself from non-weather-related social media.

I pulled the duvet over my head, reminded myself about what happened last Christmas, and eventually tumbled into a fitful sleep.

# 5

'Ah, there you are,' Mum greeted me with an exaggerated glance at her fitness watch. I was a grand total of eleven minutes late for breakfast.

'Mum's eggs, my pancakes, or both?' Dad asked, turning around from the hob to give me a kiss on the cheek.

'I'll just get a coffee,' I mumbled, shuffling over to the machine.

'Nonsense, you can't embark on a six-mile walk with only coffee swilling about in your stomach,' Mum said.

'In that case, maybe I'll skip the walk.'

'Skip the walk?' Daisy looked up, syrup dripping off the pancake clasped in a sticky hand. 'I'm good at skipping. Grandma, can I skip the walk with Auntie Bea?'

'An excellent idea!' Mum replied. 'Skipping is highly beneficial for physical and mental health. Perhaps I'll join you.'

'I'll have a pancake.' After twisting about in my duvet all night, I simply didn't have the energy to rebel today. Instead, I took my coffee and slid onto the bench beside Elana and Frankie. A solid warmth settled on my feet, and I bent down to see Dash curling up on my woollen socks.

'Where's everyone else?' I asked, leaning back as Dad placed a thick, steaming pancake on the table.

'Mia is with Nana Joy in the living room and Jed and Henry are clearing the snow off the drive,' Mum said.

'Have you seen the snow, Auntie Bea?' Frankie asked, his face beaming. 'It's like the North Pole!'

I twisted around to take a proper look out of the large window. Frankie wasn't exaggerating; the entire garden was covered. Only the tops of the patio pots were still visible, and the poor fawn was up to his belly.

'How are we going to walk six miles in that?' I asked, continuing to examine the snowfall. 'It's higher than the kids' boots. The temperature is minus three. With the wind chill it'll feel like the air is turning to ice crystals inside our lungs.'

'That's a little dramatic, Bea. We live in the middle of Sherwood Forest. How do you think Robin Hood got about every winter?'

'He probably stayed holed up in the Major Oak when the snow was this bad.'

Mum carried on, ignoring me. 'Let alone five generations of Armstrong! How would we have survived one hundred and eighty years, if a little bit of snow could defeat us?'

'There's no way we can walk in that,' Jed announced, bursting through the kitchen door with a blast of bitter air. 'It'll be up to Daisy's armpits.'

'Oh, poppycock!' Mum barked.

'He's right,' Henry added, following immediately behind him. 'It took us a good fifteen minutes just to get to the end of the drive.'

Mum shifted her gaze to Henry, her scowl instantly softening. 'Well, if that's your scientific opinion?'

Henry threw me an awkward look. A dark-red, woolly hat with earflaps was pulled low over his forehead, framing his face in the exact same way that his old haircut had done, making it far easier to see him as the old, super-nerd schoolboy who always seemed to know better than me.

'Henry is an astrophysicist, Mum,' I snapped. 'I'm a professional meteorologist!'

'I think I'll count the opinion of someone who's actually been outside above that of a local weathergirl, given the BBC's usual level of accuracy, if you don't mind.'

'Now, now,' Dad soothed. 'It doesn't matter whose opinion counts for more, since you all agree.'

'Not true!' I retorted, still smarting. 'And I do mind whether you take me seriously, Mum, however hard I wished I didn't. I might not be turning around the lives of vulnerable children, but what I do means something to a lot of people. And I happen to be damn good at it.'

'Please don't swear again in front of your nieces and nephew.'

There was no risk of that because I'd slammed out of the room and was halfway up the stairs before she'd finished the sentence.

I flung myself onto the bed, determined not to cry about such a pathetic little spat, but I was hurt and angry. Not only about Mum's attitude to my career, but also how she'd belittled me in front of everyone, especially Henry.

This was another reason I'd stayed away for so long, despite the guilt. I knew that beneath the bluster, Mum meant well, and in this instance had only meant to compliment Henry. The problem was, I'd spent an entire childhood seeing my mother devote herself to building up other people, while enacting this twisted notion that, thanks to my privileged circumstances, I had no excuses not to attain her lofty standards as a matter of course. The only way I'd learnt to live with that was by limiting my exposure.

I groaned, collapsing on my bed and pressing both arms against the beginnings of a migraine throbbing behind my skull. Looking over, I saw my open suitcase, imagining how easy it would be to cram the contents back inside and escape back to my non-judge-mental, memory-free flat.

There were two things stopping me. One: I wasn't prepared to upset everybody's Christmas, even if it ended up being a torturous time for me. Two: I had no car and no taxi driver would risk coming to fetch me in this weather. Despite what my mother might think, I knew full well that the snow was here to stay at least until Christmas Day, which meant that I was staying too. I popped open my medication and consoled myself that at least I wouldn't have to go on the walk now.

\* \* \*

I woke with a start to hear my phone ringing right beside my ear, where it must have fallen when I'd drifted off. Taking a moment to clear the sleep from my throat, I registered the unknown number and made a split-second decision to answer it anyway.

'Bea Armstrong?'

'Yes.'

'This is Melody Briggs, calling on behalf of Bigwood Media'

'Hi.' A prickle of something akin to excitement fluttered in the bottom of my belly. A month or so ago, in a moment of despon-dency about missing yet another meeting, I'd applied for a job with a major national news channel, BWM Today. I'd half-heartedly flung a showreel together and sent it off with a basic CV, so hadn't been surprised when I'd not heard anything back. But if they were calling me now, surely that wasn't to tell me I'd *not* got any further in the process?

'I'm sorry to disturb your Saturday, but Baxter was so keen to take you further in the process he wanted to find out why you hadn't replied to his email, with the hope he could persuade you to reconsider.'

'Um...' *Excuse me? Baxter Bigwood, reclusive billionaire and founder of Bigwood Media, had asked her to call me?* Thank goodness this wasn't a video call, so she couldn't see me gaping like a fish. 'I never received an email.'

'Yes, we sent it... one moment... on the third of December. We have a notification to confirm that you both received and read it.'

'No, I really didn't. I'm so sorry, I've been having a lot of problems with my emails lately,' I garbled, almost drowning in dismayed panic. 'The tech team think my account has been hacked, so that might explain it.'

'Right.' There was a brief pause. 'So does this mean you would like to participate in the next stage of the selection process?'

'For the national weather broadcasting role?'

'The job you applied for, yes.'

'Yes! Absolutely, definitely, yes!' I paused to wade through the frantic thoughts whizzing through my brain for the right response to this bombshell. 'Can you send me the email again? I'll give you my personal address, so there's no risk of it getting misplaced this time.'

I reeled off my email address and she gave me her phone number, just in case I didn't receive it.

'I'll get that over to you now. Baxter will be delighted to see you this evening.'

I hung up, every cell in my body buzzing with adrenaline. This was unbelievable. It was a Christmas miracle! *Baxter Bigwood* was *so keen* about me interviewing for the job that he'd asked this person to call me on a Saturday morning to try to change my mind!

This was the answer to so many problems. A chance to get away from the issues at work. I could prove to my parents that I was more than a local weathergirl; I was a national broadcaster with the respect of Baxter Bigwood.

One other potentially monumental thing: the job was based in London.

Three stops on the Underground from Adam's flat.

I'd checked as soon as I'd seen the job advert.

And I couldn't help wondering if this could solve all our past relationship problems in one, fabulous swoop.

Only – hang on a moment – had she said *this evening*?

\* \* \*

*Christmas, one year earlier*

'I'm sorry, Bea, it was organised last minute. I can't let the band down.'

'So you'll let me down, instead?'

'Well, this way I'm only letting one person down, not four.'

'That's not how it works, Adam! One girlfriend should count for more than four "mates".'

He gave an exasperated huff down the phone. 'Be reasonable, please. You're working Christmas Day, anyway. Do you seriously expect me to bail on our best chance of a record deal in months to sit in your flat by myself all day?'

'I finish at two! We can spend the evening at home and Mum and Dad are expecting us for dinner on Boxing Day.'

'Dinner with your parents? You're not making this decision any harder for me.'

'What if I came down to see you?'

'Look, I'm sorry. We'll be rehearsing non-stop. Twig has offered us his parents' place in Kent for the week. You know what it's like. I can't think about anything other than the music when I'm rehearsing.'

'I'm not sure it's any different when you aren't rehearsing.'

Ugh. I hated sounding like the sulky girlfriend, but Adam had promised, multiple times, that he would definitely be coming up on Christmas Eve, which was tomorrow. I'd asked him over and over in the past few weeks, until he'd got angry and started ranting about trust issues. Since he'd moved back to London in January I'd seen him five times, four of them when I'd gone to visit him. This Christmas trip was to make up for cancelling all the other times he'd promised to come up to stay. One of them he'd only phoned when I'd already stood waiting at Nottingham station. Apparently he'd lost track of time in the studio and they'd been on the brink of finishing a new single; he could hardly have got up and walked out then.

'Come on, love. We agreed that taking this last shot was too good to miss. That means I have to be where the band needs me.'

'We said we'd give it a year.'

There was a hard silence.

'Yes, but you can't expect me to pull out now, when we're so close. Honestly, Bea, I can feel it this time.'

Adam had 'felt it' so many times before I'd lost count.

'That last show, with the exec watching, it was magic. We're finally finding our sound, making music that really means something...'

He went on, babbling about how this was surely the break they'd been waiting for, how our dreams were about to come true. I didn't bother correcting him that these were his dreams, not mine.

I finally interrupted with a weary, half-hearted question about when he could come instead.

'Ah, that's hard to say. If we get spotted, things could happen fast. I don't want to let you down again. I'll be in touch after the gig, let you know what's happening.'

'Right. Well. Happy Christmas. I hope it goes well.' That wasn't a complete lie. I knew how much this meant to him.

'Thanks, Bea. You too. Say hi to everyone for me.' There was a brief pause. 'You know how much I love you, right? You're my inspiration. Every time I pick up the guitar I'm thinking of you. I promise it'll be worth it in the end: all the sacrifice, all the waiting. Just a little bit longer...'

'I love you, too.'

For the first time I realised, with an overwhelming rush of dread, that love wasn't going to be enough.

While the thought of living without him ripped my guts apart, this pretence at being with him was killing me one excuse at a time. I let things drag on until June, when I finally admitted that it was never going to change. Chasing the dream was Adam's first love; I was merely the mistress waiting on the side.

## 6

I read the email, my heart plummeting into my slipper socks.

*This evening.*

I'd assumed that the 'this evening' comment must have been either rhetorical, or a slip of the tongue, but the email made it very clear that this assumption had been incorrect.

The interview process started with a welcome drinks reception at 6 p.m. this evening.

It concluded with lunch and the 'grand announcement' two days later, on the twenty-fourth – who in their right mind held a residential job interview on Christmas Eve?

I devoured every word of the email with an urgency that I hadn't felt in a long time. I had to be at that interview.

Clicking up the Armstrong Family Christmas Itinerary, I skim-read the activities for the next couple of days. This afternoon was rehearsals for the show, followed by a trip into Hatherstone for the Christmas market and dinner at a local restaurant. I couldn't see any trips into the village happening in the next few days.

Sunday the twenty-third was a champagne brunch, afternoon

board games, and a walk to Hatherstone chapel for the carols by candlelight, finished off with a singalonga-Christmas film.

Christmas Eve carried on in much the same vein, with an Armstrong Family Buffet in the evening that included Mum's four cousins plus assorted partners, children, and their families.

Mum would be gutted if I missed it. If I was honest, I didn't want to miss it. Then again, that still left four days to go full Armstrong, including the Spectacular on the twenty-sixth. I decided that if I could find a way to get to the interview, and then back again for the Christmas Eve buffet, I would take that as a sign that I was meant to go.

If the local weathergirl was to believed (and I had it on good authority that she knew her stuff), there would be no trains running today. I wondered whether once I navigated the drive, I'd find the roads outside the forest were clear. My weather apps confirmed that the snow fizzled out at the southern border of Nottinghamshire. So, all I needed to do was persuade someone to lend me their car, and get it the short distance to the main road.

This could be doable after all. Hope began to accelerate through my bloodstream.

When I checked the exact address so I could estimate the time it would take, it screeched to a stop.

While the job would be in London, the interview was at Baxter Bigwood's country retreat.

In Scotland.

With a reluctant finger I typed the address into my maps app.

Six hours, in normal traffic.

I checked the time. Five past ten. So, if I allowed an optimistic hour to get down the drive and all the way to the main road, that gave me thirty minutes to pack, convince someone to lend me their car and listen to everything Mum had to say on the matter, plus a quick stop halfway there for a wee and a coffee.

It would take a serious dose of Christmas magic for me to stand a chance of making it on time, but compared to the alternatives, it was a chance worth taking.

Right: the first thing to do was pack.

It should have been a relatively simple task, given that most of my things had never left the suitcase. However, as I stuffed my pyjamas and other bits and bobs back in I realised that, partly due to the haste with which I'd packed the night before thanks to the surprise drinks party, I hadn't brought the kind of outfit suitable for a job interview. Especially when interviewing for a job where appearance mattered.

I was sitting on the floor, back against the bed, eyes squeezed shut in the hope that a solution might somehow appear by the time I opened them again, when there was a knock at my bedroom door.

'Oh, great.' My first reaction was to pretend I was asleep, or somewhere else. But then I remembered that I needed a car. And also to let my family know that I was abandoning them for a couple of days.

'Come in.'

I expected Dad bearing tea and a sneaky mince pie. At a close second, Mia or one of her girls. Last on my list (besides Nana Joy, who couldn't manage the steep climb any more) was Henry.

'Um, hi. Hello.' He'd pushed open the door tentatively, as if half expecting to find a wild animal on the other side. He had a mug in each hand. 'Mind if I join you?'

'Has Mum allowed you a break?'

He frowned ruefully. 'Instead of a walk we've had a snowman competition, which lasted about ten minutes before turning into a snowball fight. I pleaded an injury and ducked out early.'

He bent his head to show me an angry red mark on the side of his neck.

'Ouch. That looks nasty.'

'Elana had a pebble inside one of her snowballs. I'm sure it was an accident.'

I couldn't help smiling. 'Ha. I wouldn't be at all sure about that. Not if there was some sort of competition involved.'

He wrinkled his nose. 'Losers had to finish clearing the drive. I think I prefer being hit in the neck with a rock.'

Henry stood just inside the doorway, his whole body hunched to avoid banging into the eaves. He'd changed into a cream Aran sweater, which contrasted with his chestnut hair.

'When did you start wearing jeans?' I asked, getting up to sit on the bed and indicating that he could take the small chair.

'What?' He glanced down at his legs, as if only noticing for the first time. 'I got changed because my trousers were soaking.'

'No.' I took a sip of tea, surprised that he'd remembered to add a quarter of a teaspoon of sugar. 'When did you first ever wear a pair of jeans?'

The whole time I'd known Henry, he'd worn school trousers (often on the weekends) or cotton trousers with a sharp crease down the front. Once, on holiday, he'd worn knee-length shorts, though his socks had been pulled so high up his shins it hadn't been that much of a difference.

I watched with interest as the tips of his ears turned pink again. Henry had always seemed so self-assured, as if he'd made the logical, rational choice and therefore no one else's opinion was relevant. It was so intriguing to see him ruffled.

'I had a girlfriend who liked fashion. She bought me them.'

'*What?*' I nearly choked on my tea.

'It's that much of a shock that I've had girlfriends?' he asked, the tips of his mouth curling up.

'Girl*friends*? Yes! Mum never told me there were women fighting over you, revamping your wardrobe.'

'Do you think that could be because she never knew about them, because I was sensible enough not to tell *my* mum?'

'Oh, now *secret* girlfriends are even better!' How had I never realised before that teasing Henry was so much fun? 'Were they physicists? Did they complete maths puzzles with you? Ooh – did you go on dates and spend the whole time correcting grammar?'

'Of course. Once we'd read each other our favourite quotes from the latest journal of *Astroparticle Physics*.'

'I love this new information about you.'

'Just because I'm not some leather-jacketed, bad-boy musician, it doesn't mean that no other women want to go out with me.'

'I know, I know. I'm just fascinated because I didn't know.'

There was a pause in conversation for half a minute or so while we sipped our tea. Henry broke the silence.

'Speaking of new information, I'm guessing this was your childhood bedroom?'

'Well done, Sherlock.'

He nodded graciously in mock-acknowledgment of the compliment. 'While I could see Jed reading *Malory Towers*, I'm not sure he'd be interested in *The Secret World of Weather*. And I can see why you would like to be tucked up in the attic.'

'I can't deny there was a bonus to being as far as possible from the rest of the house.'

'Is that your suitcase all packed?' He nodded to where it sat, zipped up and ready to go. 'I know what Cora said was upsetting, but I honestly don't think she meant...'

'I have a job interview. I can't go, though, so I might as well unpack again.' I blew out a shaky sigh, trying to keep my emotions in check.

'Why not?'

I closed my eyes. 'It's a two-day residential interview. In Scotland. I only just found out that I'd been invited thanks to a problem with my work emails. Besides which...' my voice was getting higher and faster as I tried to finish speaking before bursting into tears '... I have nothing to wear, because I'm here and not at home and I packed in a rush to get here so I didn't miss one second of Mum's stupid itinerary.'

Henry handed me a tissue, waiting for me to take a shuddery breath, wipe my eyes and blow my nose before he spoke. 'What's the job?'

'National weather reporter for BWM Today.' I gave a watery smile. 'Baxter Bigwood got someone to call me because he was so impressed with my application.'

'Wow.' Henry nodded. 'It sounds like you need to be at this interview.'

'Yeah. Maybe if I ask him nicely, Baxter will send a helicopter to pick me up. We could stop off via a John Lewis on the way.'

'Or I could drive you.'

My head jerked up so sharply that I nearly spilled the remains of my tea. 'It's two days. In Scotland.'

'I love Scotland.'

'The roads are impassable. We'd probably get stuck in a snowdrift.'

He shook his head. 'Once we got out of the forest, the main roads'll be clear. Ish.'

'Is that a scientific term?'

Henry said nothing, waiting for me to accept his offer. I gave another long sigh. 'You must really want to avoid more Armstrong Christmas.'

'Not at all.'

I raised one eyebrow.

'Okay, I accept it can be... a lot. But I'm very grateful to be here rather than on my own somewhere. However—'

'Really?' I could easily imagine Henry spending Christmas

alone, planning his own little traditions with scientific precision. 'I'm not going to drag you away on a three-hundred-mile slog for my sake, then.'

Henry frowned. 'What I was going to say is, *however*, despite appreciating being here – especially Cora's rigorously detailed itinerary – I like the sound of a cross-country adventure.'

I frowned, about to come up with another reason why I couldn't accept his offer. Not least that I wasn't at all sure if I liked the sound of a cross-country adventure with *Henry Fairfax*.

'Bea, this is too good an opportunity to miss. I won't be able to enjoy Christmas knowing you're here, when you should be there, and I could have helped.' He paused to look me right in the eye. 'Besides, I think it's about time I repaid my magical debt. I still owe you a big one, remember?'

I shook my head, but couldn't help a tiny smile. 'How could I forget? They've only just stopped calling me Henry's glamorous assistant.'

He winced. 'You have to let me repay my nine-year debt and drive you to this interview.'

When I thought about it, six hours in a car with Henry was a minuscule price to pay for a fantastic new job, fifteen minutes away from Adam. And he did owe me big-time.

'On one condition.'

He widened his eyes in surprise. 'Which is?'

'You come with me when I tell my parents.'

\* \* \*

*Christmas, nine years ago*

It was my first year studying at Durham University, and a whole term away from Charis House had been fabulous and terrifying in equal measure. I'd been desperate to break away from the shadow of my family and had done my best to embrace my new-found freedom. However, it was harder to leave behind my insecurities and lopsided self-image than I'd thought and, for such a country girl, even a small city like Durham was overwhelming. The main thing I'd learned, on top of a whole load of fascinating environmental study, was that my family were even more peculiar than I'd thought.

A major event of the term was breaking up with Adam, again. I'd barely heard from him for weeks, and when he cancelled coming to visit me for the second time, I declared that I was done. Partly in the hope that he'd then turn up on my doorstep to change my mind, but he'd been asked to join a new band on tour, and I knew in my heart that was wishful thinking.

He'd arrived back in Hatherstone on Christmas Eve, but so far I'd resisted his pleas to meet up. It was now Boxing Day, the night of the Christmas Spectacular, and I was keenly aware that Adam's band were backstage waiting to perform later in the show. In a moment of mid-term homesickness, I'd agreed to accompany Nana Joy on the piano, but was at least avoiding having to sing or otherwise embarrass myself for once.

That was, until I spotted Adam sauntering down the corridor, causing me to duck through the nearest door to avoid him, which happened to lead into a store cupboard.

'Ouch!' I stumbled over a stray mop – the first sign that something was amiss; the Charis House cleaner would never dare leave anything out of place – and fell directly into something solid that turned out to be a someone.

'Oof.' Two hands jerked up and caught hold of my shoulders, preventing me from knocking us both over, and with a prickle of annoyance I recognised the smug tone instantly. What did catch me by surprise was the rock-hard torso I'd smacked into. It appeared Henry Fairfax had spent his first term at Cambridge in the gym.

'What are you doing in here?' we asked at the same time.

'Hang on,' Henry added, before a second later the cupboard filled with the glow of his phone torch.

'Hiding from someone?' he asked, squinting at me in the sudden light.

I gave a curt nod. 'You too?'

He glanced down at his outfit, which was more than a sufficient answer. Henry wore a shiny blue magician's robe covered in silver stars and a matching pointy hat.

'You look ready for World Book Day.' I couldn't help grimacing in sympathy. 'Did your mum make that?'

He nodded, face drooping with uncharacteristic misery. 'She signed me up as the Great Henrico. Thought it would be fun to have me take part this year, get me more involved seeing as I've been away.'

'Why a magic act?'

'It felt less humiliating than singing. That is, it did until I saw the costume.'

'You could just wear your normal clothes.'

'I could. But it would hurt Mum's feelings. That's not the only problem, either.'

'Oh?'

'I mistakenly believed that learning a decent magic trick wouldn't be that hard. I've watched enough Spectaculars to know that the standard is generally, well, spectacular. My trick isn't. I don't want to embarrass anyone.'

I leant back against a shelving unit, fascinated at this glimpse of the man behind the mask. Henry had never expressed anything close to embarrassment or dread. He assessed the options, selected the most appropriate, and proceeded accordingly. No emotion necessary.

'Since when did you worry about that?'

He shrugged awkwardly. 'Polly's brought her friends from school along, thanks to Mum bigging me up for weeks. They're expecting David Blaine.'

I did a quick calculation. Henry's little sister must be around thirteen. A precarious age when it came to friendships.

'So, what, you're going to hide in here?'

He shrugged, mournfully. 'I just needed somewhere quiet to come up with a solution.'

'Which is?'

'I haven't come up with it yet.'

I checked the time on my phone. 'The show starts in ten minutes. When are you on?'

'Second.'

'Ah.'

He tugged on his robe in the ensuing silence, as if a straight hem would make things any better. It was when I spotted his hand trembling that I realised he was on the brink of a panic attack.

'It's not too late to duck out. Tell your mum you have a stomach bug, or something.'

'I can't lie to her.'

I'd have argued that extreme circumstances justified bending his strict code of honour, but I knew that was a literal statement. Henry couldn't have produced a convincing lie if his life depended on it.

'So you're going to go on, wearing that, do a rubbish trick and embarrass your sister in front of her friends.'

He took a shaky breath. 'It would seem so.'

I could already imagine how the scene would unfold. I really liked Polly.

'Then how about I join you?'

'What?'

'I'll come with you on stage, deflect some of the attention and make it look like it's me who messes up. Our parents will be so excited to see us paired up together, they'll gloss over the disastrous performance.'

'I can't let you do that.'

'What, humiliate myself on stage? I've done it every other year. It's something of a tradition. It wouldn't feel like Christmas unless I've disgraced myself in public.'

'Who are you hiding from?' he asked after a few seconds of silence.

I ducked my head. 'No one.'

'Your boyfriend?'

'He's not my boyfriend. Stop changing the subject. You've only got a few minutes to fill me in on what I'm supposed to be doing.'

Henry stared at me for a long moment. I suspected various options were being rapidly processed behind the blank expression.

'I'll only let you do it if I can buy you a pizza afterwards.'

'Perfect. Come on, then, Great Henrico, our audience are waiting.' I snatched his hat and stuck it on my head as we walked out.

He was right, the trick was terrible. Fortunately, I was even worse, so most of the attention was focused on me, as planned. I pretended to fluff my lines, tripped over the robe that I'd donned, leaving Henry in plain black trousers and a white shirt, and blew the big reveal. From our point of view, it was a complete success.

'I owe you a pizza and a stiff drink,' he whispered, appearing out of nowhere after I'd gone on to play piano while Nana Joy sang and then found a discreet spot at the back of the hall. 'Mum said I can borrow her car and drive us into Mansfield.'

'Okay.' I didn't especially want to go out for pizza with Henry

Fairfax, but I was still intrigued by this new side to his personality, and I also didn't want to hang around here.

'To be honest, I probably owe you a full three-course meal...'

Before I had a chance to answer that no, a pizza and a pint of cider would be fine, we were drowned out by the sound of the audience clapping and the first few strums of a guitar. The stage lights went up to reveal Adam, looking every inch the rock star, his old school band in the background. My heart leapt.

He then began to perform a new song that I'd never heard before. It was called 'Wannabe idiot' and the lyrics were all about how he'd been an idiot by putting fame above the girl he loved. Bea rhymes with a lot of different words. I think he managed most of them.

It was a lovely song. Just right for the evening – heartfelt yet upbeat, not taking itself too seriously but full of real emotion, and Adam sang it like a pro. During the last chorus he ditched his guitar, jumped off the stage and started walking straight down the centre aisle to where I stood, every nerve trembling. When he dropped to his knees, begging me with the final line to give him another chance, the crowd erupted.

'Hey.' He offered a sheepish grin, one hand pushing the chin-length hair off his face.

'Hi.'

'I missed you.'

I took a deep breath. The crowd were still clapping, so no one could hear my reply. 'I missed you too.'

'Wanna get out of here?'

The second I nodded he stood up, grabbed my hand, gave the rest of the room a wild wave and dragged me out of the doors and off into the night.

And that was the last time I'd seen Henry until the Coach House dining room the night before.

## 7

I found everyone in the kitchen, warming post-snowball-fight hands on mugs of hot chocolate and devouring home-made raisin toast dripping in butter.

'Ah, Bea, how lovely of you to join us,' Mum said, with a brusque pat on my arm. 'It looks as though you were right about the snow.'

That was as much of an apology as I would get, but, given what I was about to say, I accepted it. Bracing myself against the worktop, I got straight to the point.

'I have some news.'

Mia gasped. 'You're pregnant?'

'You're not ill?' Dad asked, his face turning pale.

'Have the BBC let you go?' Mum said. 'I know you've not got the allure of that morning girl, but honestly, I don't know what things have come to when a national institution opts for beauty over brains.'

'No!' I cried. 'To all of them! Why on earth would you think...? This is *good* news!'

'Then why are you doing that face?' Daisy asked, pulling her mouth down and lowering her eyebrows in a comically exaggerated frown.

'It's good news for me, but means some slightly not-so-good news for you.' I straightened my shoulders, trying to force my eyes to look at Mum before giving up and opting for Dad instead. 'I'm going to Scotland for a couple of days.'

'What?' Everyone stared at me, open-mouthed. I might as well have told them I was off for a ride on Santa's sleigh.

I briefly explained about the last-minute email, before adding a deliberate deflection.

'Henry's driving, so you don't have to worry about me getting there safely.'

'*Henry?*' Mum glanced at where he stood in the kitchen doorway. I had hoped her delight at me and Henry spending so much time together would override the upset at it not being here.

I was wrong.

'Henry's going too?'

'We'll be back on Christmas Eve, Mum. It's only two days.'

'You promised you'd be here for Christmas this year!'

I expected Mum to be annoyed, but she was distraught, twisting a tea towel up in her hands, her eyes filling with tears. I couldn't remember the last time I saw my mother cry. I waited for Dad to dispel the tension with a warm comment about me knocking Baxter Bigwood dead, but instead he came over to Mum and put his arms around her.

Turning to Jed and Mia, thinking that they would surely have something rational to say, instead I found my brother glaring at me, Mia's mouth a thin line.

'Really? You think I should stay here, play board games, and watch films we've all seen a hundred times before?'

'It's more than that, Bea, and you know it,' Jed retorted.

'More than the job opportunity of a lifetime?' I snapped back. 'Are you serious?'

'Actually, yes. Very. Armstrongs don't put their jobs above family.'

'Well, that's very easy to say, when all of you already have your perfect jobs!' I tried to keep from raising my voice in front of the children, but I was livid. With every second I was more determined that I was going to this interview, no matter what my family thought.

'I'm so sick of you not taking my career seriously. I know you don't get why I would want to work in forecasting, but I wouldn't be going if this wasn't really important to me. Why can't you try to understand that?' I sucked in a fierce breath. 'Why can't any of you, just once, try to understand *me*?'

'No, Bea,' Mia said. 'You're the one who doesn't understand.'

'Mia,' Jed replied in a warning tone that sent my heart galloping.

'Doesn't understand what?' I was virtually yelling now. 'That you rate not disrupting the ridiculous Armstrong Family Christmas for a couple of days above my career, which happens to be every other day of the year? It's Christmas, for goodness' sake, there'll be another one next year.'

'That's the point, though, isn't it?' Mia said. 'There probably won't be!'

'No Christmas?' Daisy and Frankie squealed in horror.

'What are you talking about?' I asked, even as Mum, Dad and Jed started to protest.

'You might as well tell her,' Mia said, waving her arms about. 'She's already spoiled your perfect plans.'

There was a charged silence. Mum leant on Dad's shoulders, a tear trickling down one cheek. Jed's face was solid concrete. Nana

Joy sat at the table and sipped her hot chocolate, surreptitiously sliding the last piece of toast onto her plate.

'Will someone please tell me what's going on?' I asked, voice trembling.

Eventually, Jed spoke. 'We might have to close Charis House.'

'What?' I sank back against the worktop, my brain refusing to compute this information. Jed should know though – as well as teaching English and performing arts, he handled all the school finances.

'Two more major donors have died in the past couple of years. Another one went bankrupt.'

While the council provided funding to run an alternative provision school and my parents sourced additional income where they could – for example the Christmas Spectacular – it wasn't enough. Without generous regular donations from a group of Nana Joy's old showbusiness friends, Charis House could never have opened, and certainly wouldn't have survived this long. The emphasis was on 'old', though. Every time one of them either passed away or had to cease giving for other reasons, it left a bigger hole in the budget.

'We need a new roof, and the heating system isn't going to last much longer. With ongoing maintenance, it'll cost hundreds of thousands just to keep the main house open. Let alone run a school on top of it.' Mum's shoulders slumped in defeat for what was probably the first time ever.

'There must be other people you can ask.' I looked desperately to Dad. 'Aren't there trusts and places where you can apply for grants?'

'We've tried,' Dad said. 'No one thinks that spending all that money on a roof is a good use of funds.'

I didn't even suggest they look for a more economical, robust location. Charis House was the Armstrong family home. Without the house, there would be no school. And then what would my parents do? The thought of Mum living in the Coach House while the main house stood empty was too awful to contemplate.

'What's going to happen?'

'We don't know yet,' Jed replied. 'We still have a couple of avenues to explore. But, well. It isn't looking great. If it comes to it, if we can sell the house then at least it won't fall into ruin.'

Dad rubbed Mum's back as she stifled a sob.

'Why did nobody tell me this?'

'This is why,' Mia said, gesturing at Mum and Dad. 'Cora wanted one last, perfect Christmas to remember. Not hushed conversations and everyone feeling sad because we might never get to do this again.'

Now it all made sense. The itinerary, the compulsory participation. Every spare minute crammed with Christmas.

'And I thought all this fuss was because I'll be dead next year!' Nana Joy announced, around a mouthful of toast.

'Mother!' Dad exclaimed, before faltering over what to say next.

'Nothing lasts forever,' she added, pointing the remaining chunk of toast at each of us in turn. 'Each for its own time. We've lived our dreams. It's Bea's turn, now. Give her your blessing for this interview. Why should she stay here pretending not to be miserable, just because you lot are?'

I scanned the faces of my family, hoping that they would tell me to go and give it my best shot, even as I wrestled with wanting to stay for solidarity's sake.

'And if this handsome young man is driving – well! If she doesn't take him up on the offer, I might have to instead!'

\* \* \*

We were forty-five minutes behind schedule by the time we left. It had been all hands to the shovel to clear the end of the driveway.

Thankfully, Henry's car was parked by his flat, on the far side of the main house, leaving a much smaller area to clear than if we'd set off from the Coach House.

We dumped our suitcases in the back of his Honda along with winter-weather supplies including blankets and a torch. Mum handed me a bag with enough 'wholesome' snacks to get us to the North Pole, and a flask of tea. Dad gave me a hug and told me to just be 'your wonderful self, Sweet-Bea,' and I then found myself sitting in a car with Henry Fairfax, with the disconcerting knowledge that I was going to be in this position for a long time.

'Ready?' he asked, slipping on his anti-glare glasses.

'As I'll ever be.'

Five minutes later I was feeling a lot more ready, as the car inched around the curve of the driveway.

'On second thoughts, maybe I should walk. It'll definitely be faster.'

'But also colder,' Henry replied, eyes fixed on the icy gravel. 'And not so safe on the motorway.'

'Okay, fine, but can you speed up *at all*?'

'Would you like to drive?' he asked, face an innocent mask.

Deciding to call his bluff I said yes, and to my amazement he stopped the car (it didn't take much) climbed out and walked around to the passenger side.

I could hardly back down now, so I slid across to the driver's seat and started the engine, wondering whether I should mention that I hadn't sat behind a wheel in years.

Two minutes later, as we skidded across the last few feet of the driveway, spinning in a slow arc until lurching to a stop facing back up towards the house, I blurted it anyway. 'I'm so sorry, I haven't driven in years!'

Henry said nothing, instead clambering out of the car and walking carefully back to the driver's seat. I slunk back into my rightful place, waiting for the smug recriminations followed by a maths lecture about the impact on stopping distances per millimetre of snow. Instead, he steadily manoeuvred the car around, before turning to me and saying, 'Full speed ahead?'

Once we'd crunched down the forest lane, with no further protests from me about how slowly Henry was chugging along, the main road was, as we'd predicted, much clearer.

'Some music?' I asked, not sure how else we were going to pass the ensuing hours. Henry clicked a button on the steering wheel and the car filled with classical music.

'Or not,' I added, after a full twenty seconds of one lone clarinet's mournful toots, plugging my phone into the music system.

'Please, no.' Henry grimaced over the first few bars of Wizzard's Christmas hit. 'Anything but that.'

'Anything but this song, or anything but Christmas songs?' I might have chosen my Christmas Classics playlist as another test of Henry's current state of Henry-ness, but if he'd been prepared to participate in an Armstrong Christmas, he couldn't possibly hate all seasonal music.

I flicked onto the next song, 'Merry Christmas Everybody'.

'Anything but these types of Christmas songs,' he not-so-helpfully clarified.

'What does that mean? Happy ones? Ones that mention Christmas?'

'Ones that any old chump who picks up a guitar can thrash out and end up winning a talent show.'

I looked at him, taken aback. 'Are you making a dig at Adam?'

He continued to face straight ahead, making it hard to discern his expression, but the tips of his ears were definitely tinged pink. 'I sat through enough Charis House Spectaculars listening to teenage boys destroy the same three chords to never want to hear them again. Although Adam was the exception in managing to make them sound half decent.' He paused to check the rear-view mirror. 'When it comes to talent it was nothing compared to, say, someone playing an original piano piece in the key of F minor.'

'You think I should have beaten Adam that year?' Henry's robot memory was disturbing. I couldn't even remember the key that song was written in, and I was the one who wrote and performed it.

'Yes.'

I shook my head. 'Adam's band were incredible. I was surprised to come second.'

'Adam's band were good.' Henry slowed to a stop for a red light, giving him the opportunity to glance over at me. 'You were better.'

He picked my phone up from where it rested between the seats and started scrolling through the playlist, selecting a song just as the lights changed and he needed to start moving again.

'Really?' I asked as the opening line of 'White Christmas', the song that won us the quiz, wafted through the car. 'This is what you like?'

Henry said nothing, but as he gripped the steering wheel in the exact ten-to-two position, I could see the hint of a smile twitching at his lips.

\* \* \*

'I need to talk to Jed,' I announced about half an hour later. I'd been trying to focus on preparing for my interview, which so far had consisted of eating two banana oat bars while wittering about whether we could make it to Scotland on time. However, it was impossible to concentrate on my ideas for how to take weather presenting into the digital age when the bombshell about Charis House was still rattling about in my head.

Henry must have pressed something, because the music faded to a faint background murmur.

'How bad is it really?' I asked, once Jed had answered his phone.

There was a slight pause. 'Remember Dad's patchwork dungarees?'

'How could I forget?'

One of our students had produced the most horrific outfit in their fashion design class, which Dad then insisted on wearing almost constantly as a means of encouragement until it mercifully fell to bits due to the poor construction.

'It's that bad.'

'And there are really no other options?'

His reply was thrumming with frustration. 'If there were, don't you think we'd have come up with them by now?'

'I can't believe it.' I had to force the words past the lump of dismay clogging up my throat.

'We knew we couldn't rely on Nana Joy's contacts forever. She's barely left the house in the past few years.'

'What about Mum's family? Some of the Armstrongs must be rolling in it.'

'Even if they were, Mum inherited all the land. The rest of them don't feel especially inclined to help pay for its upkeep.'

'They never did like her converting the ancestral home into a school.'

'Her cousin Tildy offered us a cricket set and a chipped microscope.'

'What about Dad's family?'

'What about it?' I could hear Jed's frown. 'You know Nana Joy's family had nothing.'

I hesitated for a moment. 'But what about his dad?'

Jed was silent.

'There's a chance he could be somebody.'

'There's a far bigger chance that he's not alive any more, even if he was.'

'You never know. She always did love a younger man.'

Joy Papplewick had been associated with many a leading man in her time, the majority of them several years younger than her. She had always refused to name the father of her child, insistent that she wouldn't drag him into the scandal of an illegitimate baby. This had led to wild paternity speculations ranging from Elvis to a seventeen-year-old theatre usher. While it was a forbidden topic of conversation whenever our parents or Nana Joy were around, Jed and I had debated every possibility from a doomed affair with a married man to her simply not knowing for sure. In all likelihood, our unknown grandfather was probably an actor or musical director who Joy hadn't wanted to be tied down to.

'Is it worth trying to find out? If Dad's dad is a famous actor, then he might want to help. Especially as he's never contributed a penny to his son's upbringing.'

'I don't know, Bea.' Jed sighed. 'This isn't our secret to uncover. There's a reason Nana Joy never said who the father is. And if it does turn out to be someone with the means to help out, are we really prepared to turn an elderly man's world upside down – along with whatever family he might have – to pay for a new roof?'

It was a fair point, but saving the school wasn't the only reason to find out our grandfather's identity. If Mum's legacy was going to crumble, then Dad's family could turn out to be something of an anchor in the ensuing storm. Dad had taken on the Armstrong name partly to escape the glare of the Papplewick limelight, but also as a commitment to Mum's heritage. We'd been born and raised Armstrongs, but maybe it was time to find out who else we were, too.

'Is it worth a try, though? An initial poke about?'

Jed hummed and hawed.

'How will you feel when Charis House closes, if you didn't even try?'

'Let me think about it. Maybe talk to Mia. In the meantime, you could always see if your new billionaire boss fancies throwing a few thousand our way.'

'As soon as he's my actual boss, I'll demand he open his wallet.'

'Perfect.' When my brother spoke again, his voice was softer. 'Seriously, sis, I hope you smash it. We are really proud of you, you know?'

I sighed. 'I don't, especially. But thank you for saying it.'

## 8

'Why the change in career?' I asked, once we were safely on the motorway.

'Mine?' Henry said.

'Well, unless there's someone hiding on the back seat who's also recently ditched a high-flying job to work for my parents.'

'My job wasn't high-flying.'

'By that do you mean you didn't fly in an actual aeroplane? Because you won't be able to afford a car like this on a teacher's salary.'

Henry glanced over, and I caught the hint of a smile. Maybe the robot had a sense of humour in there after all.

'It paid reasonably well, but money isn't everything.'

'How about having people respect your work, rather than throwing things about and swearing in your face when you try to help them?'

According to the Fairfax-Armstrong grapevine, Henry had received multiple accolades for his work investigating supermassive black holes.

'I got bored.'

'*You* got bored? Of *physics*?'

There was that tiny smile again.

'I was in a meeting listening to my supervisor babbling on about gravitational waves and binary systems, and I suddenly thought, I don't care. I could spend every day of my life slaving away, trying to find information that might help us come up with a theory about a tiny fragment of time at the start of the universe, and for what? What difference will it make to anyone's actual life now? So, I decided to start doing something that might help someone. I don't know anyone who's made more of a genuine difference than your parents.'

'Wow.'

'I know it won't be easy. It won't be a case of waltzing in with my noble intentions and seeing all these young people's lives turned around by the end of term.'

'I can guarantee it won't be that.'

'But there might be one, or two, every now and then, who... I don't know, realise they can do something they didn't think they could. Or start to believe they aren't a hopeless case after all. Or manage to learn that e equals m c squared.'

'Or master the correct use of apostrophes. Nothing worse than an incorrect use of "you're" on a toilet wall.'

Henry jerked his head in surprise. 'How did you know about that?'

I laughed. '*Everybody* knew about your graffiti editing.'

His forehead wrinkled. 'And I used to wonder why I didn't have many friends.'

'That wasn't the main reason.'

'Still,' he mused. 'It was weirdly satisfying, wielding war against illiteracy with my black Sharpie.'

'Weird being the operative word, here.'

'*I* was weird? You're the one who brought in cabbage crisps for the end of year party.'

'Which is why I *never* wondered why I'd hardly any friends.'

'They didn't taste as bad as everyone thought.'

'You ate one?'

He shrugged. 'I'm a curious person.'

'Speaking of which, Mum has generously packed up several tasty home-grown treats.' I picked up the bag and peered inside. 'We've got beetroot crisps this time, flavoured with cinnamon for a seasonal twist. Roasted chickpeas, two more banana bars, and some blobs that I think mostly contain peanut butter.'

'I'll have whichever one you don't want.'

'That's all of them. I'm buying some fat-, sugar- and chemical-crammed snacks as soon as we take a pitstop.'

A few minutes later, Henry pulled off into a service station. We'd been driving for three hours and since leaving the snow behind had made good time, so could squeeze in a late lunch stop. It felt extremely odd, standing in the Costa queue with Henry Fairfax. I was still trying to reconcile this man with the socially impaired boy I'd emphatically ignored in the school canteen queue.

Loaded up with drinks, toasties, and a box of Krispy Kremes for the car, we found a table away from the chill of the entrance.

'Is it worth you booking a hotel while we're here?' I asked, once we'd got settled.

Henry nodded. He'd refused to take up any time before we set off looking for somewhere he could stay, insisting that he'd sort something later.

'We're coming back Christmas Eve?' He opened his phone and started typing in the search engine.

'I was going to mention that. I think you should head back tomorrow morning, leave me to find my own way home.'

He squinted at the screen. 'Why would I do that?'

'There's going to be heavy snow in the north tomorrow. It'll hit eastern Scotland by lunchtime and it's not going to stop for at least twenty-four hours. If you make an early start, you should be able to miss it. Otherwise, you might end up stranded.'

'Which would leave you stranded. With no transport.'

I pulled the crust off my toastie and poked it at a blob of melted cheese. 'I'm willing to take that risk, considering what's at stake.'

Henry's face switched to android mode. 'So am I.'

'I can't ask you to do that.'

'Then don't. I'm doing it anyway.'

I shook my head, frustrated. 'I don't want to be responsible for you spending Christmas alone in the middle of nowhere in some cheap hotel.'

'I'll find a nice hotel, and once the interview's finished you'll be with me.'

I started to protest, but he interrupted, his reddening cheeks the only indication that he was growing annoyed. 'Bea, I'm not going to leave you in Scotland so I can go and spend Christmas with your family. Even if I was that selfish, I'm not that brave. Can you imagine what your mum would say if I arrived back without you?'

'But—'

'Would it be easier if I just lied and told you I'll go home tomorrow?'

'Okay, fine.' It was more than fine; I was incredibly relieved. The thought of trying to fight my way home on public transport didn't bear thinking about. 'Make sure it's a very fancy hotel, though. And I'm paying. In fact, I'm going to book it for you so you can't argue.'

We sat eating and scrolling through our phones for a while, before reaching the same conclusion at about the same moment.

'There's nothing!' I lowered my phone, seeing Henry about to do the same.

'There's a couple of places in Glasgow.'

'That's miles away, and a long stretch of the road will quickly become impassable if the snow's bad. There's no point you staying so far away that you can't come and get me.'

'What about an Airbnb?'

We had another search, but it was the week before Christmas and the select number of places near the Bigwood estate were all booked up.

'There's this cottage.' Henry slid his phone across the table so I could see. 'Cottage' was pushing it. A more accurate description would have been 'shack'.

'It's how much? Three hundred pounds a night?' I peered closer. 'I don't know how they have the gall to charge more than three pounds.'

'It's better than nothing.'

'You cannot stay there!' I put my hand over the phone to prevent him from booking it anyway. 'Besides, it's too far south.'

He sat and watched me patiently, happy to finish his coffee in the knowledge that I couldn't hold onto his phone forever.

'You'll have to stay with me at the mansion instead,' I blurted, before my rational brain could stop me.

Henry frowned. 'How would that work?'

I thought for a moment. 'We could pretend you're my agent.'

'Do regional weather broadcasters have agents?'

'Maybe ones who have grand ambitions about becoming TV celebrities do.'

'And they'd bring them to a two-night job interview, without mentioning it in advance?'

'Maybe, if they only found out about the interview an hour before they had to leave and they were all flustered.'

'Or, how about we say that I gave you a lift, there are no rooms available anywhere nearby, and I want to stick around to ensure you can get home in time for Christmas?'

Given that my next suggestion had been to pass Henry off as my 'emotional support person', we decided to go with his idea.

'We'd better get going,' I said, the second our plates and cups were empty.

'Yeah, I won't be long.'

Henry got up and hurried across the building, presumably towards the toilets. However, when fifteen minutes later he still hadn't returned, I started to wonder whether the thought of gate-crashing Baxter Bigwood's house had been too much, and he'd done a runner back to Sherwood Forest.

I gathered my things, tucked the box of doughnuts under my arm, and continued anxiously scanning the service station, which was bustling with pre-Christmas weekend travellers. My initial relief after hurrying outside and finding his car still there soon switched to more confusion as I tried to think where he could be. Surely he hadn't been in the bathroom all this time? I would have called him, only I didn't have his number.

After another five minutes worrying that something awful had happened, I decided to wait at our original table. Almost the second I sat down, I spotted a man striding through the building, followed by a uniformed woman yelling at him to stop. Another man was pulling at the woman's arm, trying to pull her back. The first man, who happened to be carrying a waist-high rubbish bin, was Henry.

Open-mouthed, I watched him march out of the automatic glass doors, move to a nearby patch of grass, and tip the bin upside down, scattering the contents. The employee did her best to hurry after him, dragging the other man behind her, but came to an abrupt stop when she saw Henry wade into the pile of rubbish and start pawing through it.

Grabbing all our stuff, I rushed outside.

'What the hell are you doing?' I screeched as Henry dropped to his knees in the filth.

'He's breaking the law, that's what!' the woman retorted, her complexion a worrying shade of purple. 'Is this man with you?'

Henry stood back up then, stepping out of the mess and holding out his hand as the other man rushed towards him. 'Is this them?' he asked.

The other man, slipping on a greasy burger box so that Henry had to grab his arm to prevent him from falling over, cried, 'Yes!', as Henry gave him the contents of his hand. 'Thank you so much!' He then promptly burst into noisy tears.

'Police are on their way.' Another employee rushed up, panting. He looked about fifteen, his eyes alight with excitement.

'Go!' Henry said, encouraging the sobbing man with a gentle hand on his shoulder.

'Fleeing the scene of the crime!' The woman spun around, pointing at the man as he staggered towards the direction of the car park.

'Shall I go after him, Ange?' the teenager asked. 'I reckon I could take him down, keep him restrained until the coppers get here.'

'Let him go, Bob. He's small fry. Stick to the brains behind the crime.'

Henry was now scooping up clumps of rubbish and putting them back in the bin, using napkins as makeshift gloves.

'How long until backup arrives?' Ange asked, her bravado evaporating now that Henry was right in front of her.

'They said seven minutes. Ten at the most.'

At this news, Henry froze, mid-scoop. He glanced at me before giving a visual sweep of the car park, robo-Henry computing the data before coming to a split-second decision.

Dumping a handful of old drinks cartons in the bin, he sprang to his feet, grabbing my hand as he dodged past the employees and started racing back to the car, me stumbling behind him.

'Henry, what the hell?' I gasped as he yanked open my door, bundled me inside and then skidded around to the driver's side, diving in and slamming the door shut just as Bob flung himself against it.

Jaw hanging open, I wrangled my seat belt on as Henry accelerated away, barely missing several bystanders as he veered for the exit.

It was only once we'd joined the motorway that I regained the ability to form a coherent sentence.

'Please tell me that there's a rational explanation for what just happened, and I'm not trapped in a car with a deranged hooligan.'

Henry inhaled a couple of times, his chest shuddering as he fought to regain his composure.

'I apologise, I really shouldn't have manhandled you like that. But if the police turned up, we'd have been forced to hang around for ages, and that would make you even later. If they wanted to question me at the station, you'd have had to drive the rest of the way yourself, and I think this morning demonstrated that this was a safer option.'

'While I accept your apology—' I opened the box of doughnuts and took a fortifying bite of a caramel iced ring '—that's not really what's bothering me! You disappeared for twenty minutes and then turned up with a stolen bin.'

'Diego's wife is in labour.'

'Oh, that explains everything, subject closed.'

'He was on his way home from work, stopped at the fuel station to grab a secret KFC because he's supposed to be on a low-salt diet, when his mother-in-law called to say the baby was on its way. When he got back to the car he couldn't find his keys. I spotted him tracking back and forth looking stressed so I went to ask if he needed any help. The obvious thing to do was retrace his exact steps. Once we'd done that, the most likely explanation was that he'd dropped them in the bin when he'd dumped the zinger burger in a moment of guilty panic. It would have been a health and safety risk if I'd emptied it inside, and Diego didn't have time for me to be careful.'

I was flabbergasted.

Not at Henry's story – it all made plausible sense. But the fact that while talking to me about potentially getting stuck in a blizzard, trying to figure out where he was going to sleep that night, Henry had not only noticed a man looking stressed, and then bothered to go and offer help. *He'd rummaged through the contents of a service station bin.*

Spending time with Henry was only reinforcing my belief that he wasn't normal. But I was starting to appreciate that he was abnormal in some of the best ways.

## 9

'Do you think they've taken down your number plate and the police are in hot pursuit as we speak?' I asked, two doughnuts and thirty miles later.

'I'd hope the police have better things to do. I did put most of the rubbish back.'

'I wouldn't be surprised if Bob and Ange decide to go rogue and bring you down themselves.'

Henry twitched one eyebrow. 'Ange wouldn't know what to do with me if I drove back and handed myself in.'

'Looks like we've made it to the border, anyway. Home free.' I nodded at the 'Welcome to Scotland' sign up ahead, the turn-off for Gretna just beyond it.

'Two hours to go.'

'I'll call and let them know my driver will be requiring a room,' I said, putting on a frightfully posh accent that did nothing to disguise how uncomfortable I felt. To my great relief, Baxter's assistant, Melody Briggs, didn't answer the number she'd given me. Rather than garbling a message, I decided the best (least scary) thing to do was to leave it for now.

I put the phone down and settled back into the heated leather seat, closing my eyes and trying to focus on what questions Baxter Bigwood might ask, and how I could answer them in a way that portrayed me as the perfect combination of red-hot television personality and expert meteorologist.

When a ping startled me out of my snooze a while later, night had fallen, as had the first dusting of fresh snow. Thinking it might be Melody, I hurriedly rummaged about in the darkness until I found my phone in the footwell.

One word flashed up on the screen.

Hey

I pressed the phone against my pounding chest as various potential responses raced through my head. Henry adjusted his position, rolling his shoulders, and the reminder that I wasn't alone was enough to stop me giving in to temptation and immediately calling Adam. Instead, I took a deep breath and went for the safer option.

Hey

A second later, he replied.

You busy?

Henry had his eyes firmly on the road. At some point while I'd been sleeping we had left the motorway and were now on a winding lane.

Not especially

I was thinking how this will be our first Christmas apart

*Well, not really, Adam,* I thought, but didn't type, given that last year he'd bailed on me for a gig. Before I had a chance to come up with an actual reply, another message appeared.

Will you be at Charis House or are you working?

I have a job interview but I'll be home on Christmas Eve.

That's great! What's the job?

I didn't know if entering into a conversation with Adam was a terrible idea. This was how we'd ended up getting back together every other time we'd broken up, one of us tentatively reaching out with a message, the other replying in the guise of a friendly chat that both of us knew would soon lead to us tumbling back into a whirlpool of passion.

My trembling fingers kept on typing anyway.

He responded to the news that I could be moving to London with an immediate invitation to meet for a drink. I ignored the hope fluttering in my stomach and made a bland comment about how that would be nice, at the same time knowing he wouldn't be fooled for a second by my innocuous answer.

'Brace yourself!' Henry barked, jerking me away from the screen as the car screeched to a halt, coming to a stop about a foot away from the huge tree trunk blocking the road. After blinking a few times, which was probably about as panicked as Henry Fairfax got, he switched off the engine. 'I'll see if there's any way we can get past. Can you check for an alternative route?'

Nodding, I waited until Henry had got out of the car before quickly sending one last message.

I have to go

Okay, hope it goes well!

I held back from opening the map app up when three dots appeared signifying that Adam was sending something else. After an agonising wait as they disappeared then almost instantly reappeared again, the message finally pinged through.

Just be yourself and they won't be able to resist loving you x

The interior light flashed on, causing my eyes to automatically screw shut as Henry opened the door and climbed in. 'Any joy?'

'Um...' I hastily clicked open the app. 'Not yet. The signal's rubbish.'

'We're going to have to turn around and go back the way we came. Hopefully it won't end up wasting too much time.'

*The story of my life,* I thought. Yet again, one brief conversation with Adam felt as if it had flipped my heart inside out.

\* \* \*

In the end, we found an alternative route less than a mile back down the road. It was twenty past six when the sign for the Bigwood estate loomed out of the darkness. I had tried calling Melody Briggs again to let her know there'd been a delay, but there was no answer – probably because she was currently hosting a drinks reception for the candidates who had managed to arrive on time. When we pulled up at the giant gates and pressed the intercom buzzer, a man's voice crackled back, asking if we could hold up a piece of identification at the security camera.

'I'm Bea Armstrong, and this is my driver,' I chirruped once I'd brandished my driving licence, as though this were the kind of thing I did all the time. The only response was the gates gliding open, so I assumed we passed the test.

We crunched up a curving drive lined with trees on either side, their boughs dusted with snow. Above our heads was a sparkling canopy of Christmas lights, strung between the branches. After about a quarter of a mile, we rounded another bend to see what appeared to be a floodlit castle up ahead. In front of the stone building the drive opened up to a wide, circular space in the centre of which stood an enormous Christmas tree covered in red and gold lights. As Henry pulled around the tree to a row of parked cars, about a dozen, three-foot-high, animatronic figures waved, bowed, or spun around to offer us a present.

'They're elves!' I exclaimed, slightly creeped out by their grinning faces leering through the shadows. Pausing with one hand on my seat belt, I looked at Henry. 'Do you think they might start following us if we get out?'

'Don't worry, someone's keeping an eye on them.' Henry nodded to where a wooden structure sat on a patch of lawn. An enormous star on the roof lit up the nativity scene below, and the sombre looks on Mary's and Joseph's faces were somewhat reassuring. We climbed out, limbs stiff from the long journey, and I creaked around to where Henry was unloading the boot.

'It's like someone exploded a Christmas bomb,' I whispered, spotting more figurines, lights and other decorations every time I looked in a new direction.

'This must be what Christmas looks like when you're a billionaire.'

I shuddered. 'Either that or he needs to sack his decorator.'

We walked over to the wide steps leading up to enormous wooden doors painted red. The stone pillars either side of them were covered in ivy dotted with more lights, overshadowed by the huge silver faces of what I presumed to be angels, glowering at us from the undergrowth at the top of each one.

Before we had a chance to find a doorbell in amongst the ivy, the door swung open, revealing a short, curvy woman wearing a red Mrs Santa costume trimmed with gold. She would have looked quite glamorous if it weren't for a green blob in her blonde hair, and the white stain on her chest.

'Bea, please do come in. I'm so glad you made it. The others have told us about the fallen-down tree holding everybody up.' She stepped back to allow us to come inside. 'I'm Melody, Baxter's assistant. Oh, and this is Betty.' She spun around to reveal a sling on her back containing a sleeping baby in a reindeer outfit.

'Let's get you checked in. We're starting off in the library, but we'll sort your bags for you, and the cloakroom is here, behind me, so you can freshen up.' She walked over to a walnut desk on one side of the enormous room, getting the passcode on an iPad wrong twice before closing her eyes and muttering, 'Not Benji or Bobby's, can't be Betty's so must be Billy's. Was he the sixteenth or seventeenth...? No, the fifteenth!' Jabbing her fingers in triumph, she unlocked it and started typing.

I took the opportunity to have a good look at the entrance hall – wooden-panelled walls, the kind of staircase that was made to be swept down, with a banister smothered in greenery and crimson berries. Another tree stood in one corner, with a whole army of beady-eyed drummer boys dangling from the boughs. Every wall was covered in oil paintings of people with expressions ranging from infuriated to disgusted.

'This is your driver?'

'Um... yes.'

'If you can provide your car registration number and name, Security will buzz you straight in on Monday. Bea should be finished by four, but if she's not quite ready just come in anyway and I'll find a spot for you to have a drink and something to eat. Don't wait in the car. The cold is bad enough but I'm pretty sure those elves are plotting something.'

'Actually, I did try to speak to you about that earlier, but there was no answer.'

'About the elves?' Melody's eyes went round with alarm. 'I've barely had a chance to glance at my phone all day. Is there a problem?'

'No, not the elves, about my driver – Henry – picking me up. Um, if you remember I didn't see the email until this morning?'

Melody nodded, looking visibly relieved.

'So it wasn't until we were halfway here that we had a chance to find a hotel for Henry.'

'Well done!' She shook her head. 'You've usually as much chance of finding a room around here this close to Christmas as Mary and Joseph in Bethlehem. The weather must have put people off.'

'Yeah. No. It didn't.' I fumbled with the strap of my bag, the embarrassment burning my cheeks.

'We couldn't find anything closer than Glasgow.' Henry spoke for the first time. 'Bea is concerned about the increased risk of me having to drive up through the snowstorm before picking her up and then heading back south again.'

'I have to be somewhere Christmas Eve night.'

'With your loved ones, I'd hope!' Melody smiled sympathetically, showing a smear of red lipstick on her tooth, and the tension in my shoulders dropped a couple of inches.

'It's the first Christmas I haven't worked in years and my parents would be devastated...'

'So you don't have anywhere to stay?' she asked Henry.

'Not unless there's room for one more in the stable.'

'Again, far too close to the elves.' Melody checked the iPad, jigging up and down slightly as Betty started to stir. 'Okay, so I don't know how to ask this discreetly, but we have quite a few people who bring staff with them, and they are more than just staff, if you know what I mean, so maybe I should just be up front about it because we haven't got any extra rooms.' She looked up. 'Are you happy to share a double room? As in, the same bed?'

'No, definitely not!'

I spoke way too loudly as Henry politely replied, 'That wouldn't be appropriate in this case.'

Melody ducked her head, and for a moment I thought she was trying to hide a smile.

'Right, let me think... I could do a swap and put you in a twin, Bea, so Henry can have your room. There's another candidate about to arrive, so she won't know that she was supposed to be on her own. Ooh, hang on.' She peered at the screen. 'I think you must know her!' She gave a couple of taps, beaming now. 'Perfect timing!'

Melody hurried over to the front door, presumably alerted by a security camera. I tried to figure out who the other job candidate could be. I was friends with a few fellow forecasters on social media, but surely that depth of information wasn't stored on Melody's iPad.

Unless...

As the door swung open a horrifying revelation dropped into my head, nearly knocking me over.

'Hi, please come in.'

'Thank you, and I'm so terribly sorry I'm a little late.'

I swung around to face Henry. The panic must have shown on my face, because a tiny crease appeared between his eyebrows.

'I can't share a room with her.'

'Why not?' Henry bent his head closer as Melody chatted to the new guest.

'I'll explain later, but I would honestly rather share with the elves.'

Before I could say any more, Melody was back at the desk. Forcing my jaw to unclench, I turned to face Summer Collins clicking across the chequered tiles in gold stilettos, shaking out her hair as she unbuttoned a red trench coat to reveal a gold jumpsuit beneath.

To her credit, she only faltered for the briefest millisecond when she saw me standing there. No one would have detected the wobble in her smirk if they hadn't been looking for it. Sashaying up to the desk, she placed one hand on her hip and switched to the hundred-watt smile that had won her fans across the East Midlands.

'Oh my gosh, if it isn't Bea Armstrong. I would not have expected you of all people to turn up at an opportunity like this. Aw...' She turned down the corners of her mouth in mock sympathy. 'Didn't you get the information about the dress code? I know gold might be a stretch, given your whole cutesy, homespun thing going on, but you must have something red. A Nottingham Forest shirt, or a pinafore dress?'

'Hello, Summer.' I ignored the comment about the red and gold dress code for the evening, which had also stated 'Max Glam'. I had read it, and would be adhering to it, but I had chosen not to go Max Glam in a car with Henry for six hours.

'And he-e-el-l-o-o-o... whoever *this* is!' Summer added, giving Henry an objectifying once-over.

'Shall we get you checked in, Summer?' Melody asked, her tone clipped.

'Um, before you do,' I interrupted. 'That question you asked me, just now, about the room, which I said no to. Due to a change in circumstances, the answer is now yes.'

Melody swivelled her eyes to Henry and back. 'To clarify, you're referring to the one that your driver said would not be appropriate?'

'Yes.' My cheeks were so hot they'd have no problem adhering to the dress code.

'Would you like to take a moment to discuss this with your driver?'

'What Ms Armstrong is trying to explain is that we would prefer the twin, leaving the other room free for anyone who hasn't checked in yet,' Henry said, giving a subtle nod in Summer's direction.

'Okay, one moment, please.'

While Melody disappeared into a side room, Summer cranked her smile back up. 'I didn't know you had a driver, Bea. How on earth can you afford that?' She tittered, patting Henry's arm to let him in on the joke. 'I had to get the train and then a taxi, like any old bod! If I'd known you were coming I'd have asked for a lift.'

'He works for my parents.' Years of broadcasting experience meant there was no way Summer could outdo me when it came to being faux-friendly. 'I don't have a car at the moment and there's a 70 per cent chance that the trains won't be running on Monday. If I'd known *you* were coming, I could have offered you one. As far as I was aware, you were working all week.'

Summer shrugged. 'An unavoidable emergency came up, so the late-night guy is covering for me.'

'Right.' Melody reappeared, ready for business. 'The boys will take your bags to your rooms. Henry, Baxter says he's happy for you to join the others in the library, no bundling the staff off to the servants' quarters at Bigwood. But you will need to wear this.' She held out a gold jacket. 'Bea and Summer, you can freshen up in here.'

I followed Summer into a bathroom that was larger than my living room and kitchen combined. Ducking into a cubicle, I quickly stripped off my turquoise coat, stripy jumper, and Mom jeans, stuffing them into the oversized shoulder bag that Mia had lent me. I then slipped into the slinky red dress that also belonged to my sister-in-law. To finish off, I swapped my boots for a pair of glittery gold heels and draped a thin matching scarf around my neck, trying to copy how Mia had shown me.

The outfit was like nothing I'd ever worn before, but circumstances – and Henry – had pushed me into it. Somehow I'd ended up donning a floor-length satin dress with a slit up to my hip and a back that skimmed the top of my sensible knickers. I took a deep breath, adjusted the spaghetti straps, and opened the door. I'd decide whether or not to blame Henry or thank him once I'd got this evening over with.

* * *

It had been a strange conversation, huddled on my bed that morning. Once I'd accepted Henry's offer of a lift, that had left the issue of what I would wear. In addition to this evening's Max Glam dress code, the email had instructed the candidates to pack clothes that 'best expressed their vision for the role'.

'I've got nothing suitable for a job interview. My priority when packing was not freezing to death in this attic. I have no idea what my vision for the role would be, but I'm pretty sure it doesn't include corduroy dungarees or an oversized sweatshirt.' I pulled at my fluffy cardigan in frustration. 'I've not got time to go home and grab something. The best I could hope for is Min Glam, even if I did.'

'Could you borrow something?' Henry asked.

'You think Mum might have a gold tracksuit stashed away somewhere?'

A brief smile flickered across his face. 'I was thinking more of Mia.'

That was how fifteen minutes later I found myself wearing a fake leather trouser suit that barely reached my ankles and stretched an inch too tight around my torso.

I took a look in the mirror and tried not to cry again.

'I spent my whole childhood dreaming about dressing in outfits like this. Actually feeling cool for once, rather than the strange girl with the terrible clothes.'

'Some of your clothes were so strange they cycled all the way around to cool again. Only a highly cool, confident person could have got away with that dress you wore to the prom.'

'If you genuinely believe that, it only shows that you were even less cool than me. But thank you for trying to make me feel better about it.'

He shrugged. 'I liked your clothes.'

'That's not a compliment. I hated them.'

'You like this more?' He nodded at my interview suit. 'Because the fact that you never wear things like this suggests that the uncool, quirky Bea might be the real you. Your work outfits are hardly conventional weather-presenting garb.'

I tugged at the leather jacket, trying to get it to sit right across my chest.

'You should wear your own clothes for the interview.'

'What?' I shook my head in disgust. How on earth had I ended up listening to fashion advice from a man who tucked his trousers into his socks when it was raining? 'One of the reasons I want this job is so I can start again, be a new me. One who is, as I said—'

'Cool.' I could see him studying me in the reflection of the mirror. This must be how the supermassive black holes felt.

'I think the coolest thing you can do is be yourself.' He paused, coughed, shrugged. 'I always admired that about you.'

I was so stressed out I forgot to be shocked that Henry said he admired me.

'I've spent years trying to not be that person.'

'And how's that working out?'

'Well, I guess I'll find out on Monday.'

While Henry had gone to pack, I'd conceded defeat with regards to the leather suit. I could barely breathe with the trousers done up, let alone sit down. However, the red dress was another matter. The only red or gold item I'd brought was novelty red underwear covered in snowmen, so I didn't have a lot of choice.

When it came to the outfits for the rest of the interview, I had to admit that Henry had a point. If I did have a vision for my future role, it would include the relaxed, chatty presenting style that my viewers loved, earning their trust through being myself, not what an outdated dress code dictated. If Baxter Bigwood was looking for the most attractive or charming person to advise his audience on whether they needed an umbrella, I couldn't compete. If he wanted someone relatable, who genuinely cared, I might stand a chance.

## 10

I wobbled out of the cubicle to find Summer adding another layer of scarlet lipstick, an array of bottles and brushes strewn across the sink. I gave my hair a quick tidy and left her to it.

Back in the hall, Henry was standing by the desk in the gold jacket. I was about to exclaim something not very kind about quiz-show hosts but he appeared engrossed in something on the stairs, his face wincing.

Moving around to join him, I saw three boys of varying ages but none of them old enough for secondary school, lugging our cases up the top few steps.

'She said the boys will take our bags up,' I gasped, quietly so they didn't hear me.

'I think this must be Billy, Bobby, and whoever the other one was,' Henry whispered.

'Well, at least Betty wasn't roped in, too.'

We watched the eldest bump Summer's enormous case up the final stair, before hopping down to help his brothers. 'Is this classed as child labour?' I wondered. 'Do you think it's legal?'

'It's only illegal if I pay them money,' Melody said, bustling down the hallway, bouncing Betty in her arms this time. 'Ice cream and the latest Marvel film don't count.' She paused, frowning. 'I don't think. Anyway, it keeps them out of trouble. Always the preferable option.'

She craned her neck towards the stairs. 'All right, boys?'

'Benji made me carry the second biggest one even though I'm the youngest!' one of the boys called.

'Well, you're bigger than Bobby, which counts for more than age in this case,' Melody called back.

'Yeah, but—'

'Did he tell you that you get to choose your ice cream in order of how big a bag you carried?' she said, her smile cracking as Betty grabbed her nose and yanked on it, hard.

The boy, who must have been Billy, pushed his mouth to one side as he thought about this. 'Is there a chocolate one with toffee lumps?'

Melody nodded, somewhat frantically.

'Fi-i-i-i-ine.' Billy continued his slow climb. Immediately, his mum turned to us. 'Ready to meet Baxter?'

'Absolutely.'

She took a few steps down the corridor before stopping and spinning back around.

'Bea, please don't be offended by me commenting on your personal appearance, but if you could manage not to be so terrified, you'd look stunning. I told you this morning, Baxter loves your work, you've really no need to panic.'

'I'm not panicking,' I said, now panicking at how panicked I must look.

'Okay. Maybe tell your face that?' Melody said, with an apologetic scrunch of her nose.

Henry turned to me, his face so serious it made me feel even worse. 'She's right. You look beautiful.'

'Even though I'm not dressed like the real Bea?'

He swept his eyes up and down my whole body, and for a second I felt an inexplicable zap of electricity. It had been a while since someone had looked at me like that, and it only made me feel even more ruffled. Until, that was, his gaze came to rest on mine. And then I remembered it was Henry, who had known me forever and in all that time had never once lied to make me, or anyone else, feel better.

'You look like Bea. Just a Bea that we don't get to see very often.' He crinkled his eyes. 'Party Bea.'

He then crooked his elbow in invitation like the elderly gentleman he'd always been, and when I slipped my quaking arm through his and he patted my hand, murmuring, 'You've got this,' I decided to try my best to believe him.

\* \* \*

'Bea Armstrong!' The familiar voice boomed across the library, causing the handful of people perched on futons and leather sofas to twist their heads around as one, reminding me of the elves outside.

Baxter Bigwood didn't leave his position, propped against a grand piano, but he did open his arms and wave them at me, like a rancher gesturing to a timid horse.

'See this, swanning in nearly an hour late as easy as you please!' He stopped waving and jabbed a finger at me. 'That's the kind of confidence that puts you top of the leader board, before we've even started. Melanie!' He scanned around, as if searching for a lost pair of glasses, despite the fact that Melody was walking right beside me. 'Update the rankings immediately!'

'Yes, Basil.' Melody arched one eyebrow at her boss as she handed Betty to Henry, who was too startled to object, took the iPad out of a hidden pocket in her Santa skirt and started tapping.

'Oh dear, did I get it wrong again?' Baxter rubbed a hand against his round head, which was mostly bald except for the odd patch of grey hair sprouting like scrub on a wasteland. He was by far the tallest – and broadest – person in the room, and despite the craggy face and saggy stomach, he radiated the kind of energy that commanded attention. Unlike the rest of us, he wore a white dinner jacket and trousers, with his only acknowledgement of the dress code a red bow tie.

'Don't worry, lots of us struggle to remember the name of someone we've worked with on a daily basis for eight months.' As Melody spoke, a huge screen above the opulent fireplace lit up. On it was a table similar to that used to rate competitors in sporting events, and as we watched the top name – Calvin Cotton – swapped places with the second name – mine.

I was still trying to absorb this bizarre scenario when Baxter bellowed again.

'Who's this?' He squinted at Henry, who was grasping a squirming baby while adopting a blank expression that I guessed meant he was fighting the urge to turn and run. 'He wasn't on the shortlist.'

'This is Bea's driver. You said he should join us.'

'Ah, the driver! Yes. Very good.'

'Henry Fairfax.' Henry stepped towards Baxter, wedging Betty on one hip so he could offer a handshake.

Baxter shook his head. 'I don't do touching and I've already forgotten what you said, but do join in the fun. Add Driver to the board, please, Melinda.'

'Um, what?' Several people in the room murmured their objection. Others looked positively appalled. There were now nine names on the board, but surely with Henry included this couldn't have anything to do with the job interviews?

Once Summer had joined us a minute later, causing Baxter to announce that she was 'last, but not quite least!', he demanded more drinks before the 'formal proceedings commence'.

Melody disappeared, taking a fretful Betty with her, and Henry and I had found a spare sofa to perch on when she reappeared, two boys trooping behind her carrying trays of champagne flutes that wobbled so precariously I had to sit on my hands to stop me from jumping up and helping them.

'Am I getting older or are the staff around here a lot younger than they used to be?' Baxter asked, giving a nod of thanks to Benji as he helped himself to a glass.

'This is what happens when you grant the regular staff a Christmas night out without checking the diary with me first,' Melody said, busily handing out glasses. 'I can't do everything.'

'I thought your capable husband was working.'

'Oh, so Denzel can cook a buffet for ten people, sort rooms for nine, clean up, and serve drinks as well as take care of four children?' She threw Baxter a pointed look. 'He's more than capable, but that's pushing it.'

'Well, you boys have done an excellent job.' Baxter nodded. 'If you ever need a reference, let me know.'

The drinks were followed by platefuls of finger food deposited on a long sideboard. Baxter took a seat in the chair beside it, giving Henry and me a chance to catch our breath and wonder what on earth was going on.

The library was, as its name suggested, lined with floor-to-ceiling bookshelves on three sides, one of which was interrupted by two full-length windows. The fourth wall contained the fireplace and two doors, including the one leading back into the hallway. Aside from the piano, the rest of the room contained various seating flanked by end tables and the odd footstool. Unsurprisingly, it looked as though the Christmas tornado had also swept through. Garlands criss-crossed the ceiling and framed the fireplace, which also hosted a row of giant stockings. Red and gold floral decorations graced the larger tables, and dotted about were several life-sized geese wearing Christmas hats and scarves while glaring ominously at us through their monocles.

'Do you know anyone here apart from Summer?' Henry asked, after carefully selecting a plateful of food and coming to sit back down.

I nodded. 'That's Lincoln Kim. We've met a few times. He's on one of the local ITV news teams. The other woman is Cynthia something-or-other. I've done some training with her at the Met Office. And, I might be mistaken but isn't that bloke from *Love Rivals*? Jordan Jones?'

'I wouldn't know.' The corners of Henry's mouth quirked down in distaste.

'I don't watch it either, but he did an interview with us about a charity endurance event last year. I have no idea who the other three are.'

We sat and observed while we ate. One of the men was making nervous small talk with Cynthia. Three others seemed to be playing a game of conversational one-upmanship, braying at each other's jokes as their gesticulating grew more vigorous. Jordan Jones and Summer were both sitting on a sofa directly opposite Baxter, straining forwards as they nodded and smiled and flicked their hair about.

'Are interviews for TV jobs always like this?' Henry asked, as the boys brought in more drinks and the volume of chatter subsequently increased.

'The closest I can think of was when a radio station offered me a piece of flapjack.' I scanned the room, still trying to take it all in.

'This is terrifying. It's like an evil genius took an Armstrong Christmas, ramped it up to Max Glam, and then invited some random strangers along. The only thing stopping me from asking you to drive me straight home is that I'm currently top of the leader board. It also doesn't hurt that Summer is second to last.'

Henry shook his head. 'How did I end up higher than her?'

He was currently seventh out of nine.

Before we could begin trying to figure that one out, Baxter heaved himself to his feet and called for everyone's attention.

'Now, as delightful as this soirée is, you are all here for a reason. That being to impress, hoodwink, or bewitch me into offering you a job. You have until Monday to convince me that you are precisely what BWM Today needs to replace the usual boring banality with five minutes that every viewer will soon consider a highlight of their day.' Without pausing to take a breath, he then pointed at Cynthia and said, 'Cynthia Burrows, your five minutes to wow me with tomorrow's weather starts now.'

Cynthia mouthed the kind of word that wouldn't make it past the BWM Today censors, before spluttering and stumbling about the forecasted storm. A minute in, Baxter held up a hand to stop her.

'Cynthia drops to bottom place, please, Melania. Calvin Cotton, where in the UK do you recommend I spend New Year's Eve, if I want a clear night for fireworks?'

'Norfolk,' I couldn't help muttering under my breath. It was impossible to be sure this far in advance, but that was as good a bet as any.

Calvin waffled a couple of sentences about how he of course couldn't be sure, but generally speaking this time of year the south and east were likely to have less cloud or precipitation.

'PATHETIC!' Baxter boomed, causing one of the men to drop

his blini. 'Eighth place. Lincoln Kim, have you a chance in hell of getting back to Cardiff ahead of Father Christmas?'

To his credit, Lincoln offered a competent, if guarded, prediction of the travel situation for Christmas Eve.

'Ugh!' Baxter groaned, rolling his head from side to side. 'I stopped listening and switched to my weather app three words in. Summer Collins, what the devil should I pack for my Boxing Day trip to Riga?'

Summer placed a hand on one hip, held her champagne flute aloft and looked Baxter Bigwood directly in the eyes. I held my breath, certain that she was as clueless about this as all the other questions.

'Well now, that depends if you want to spend it shivering outdoors, or cosied up inside with a spicy drink, warm fire, and even hotter company. I'd suggest that a man of your means can pack whatever the hell he likes and make the location work for him, not the other way around.'

'Utter nonsense, but thinking outside the box. I like it. Up to second place.'

And so it went on, through the remaining candidates. I was oscillating between freaking out at the hideousness of the group interrogation, and a growing sense of anticipation. I was a woman who knew her weather. I'd spent a good hour in the car updating myself on the latest data. I had a confident answer for every question, even if that was explaining how and why an accurate response was impossible. More of an issue was *how* to answer. But Henry's advice way back in Sherwood Forest echoed through my brain. Baxter Bigwood liked me. I would do my best to present my vision for the role, and that meant being my unintimidated self.

Second to last was Henry's turn. The other candidates turned towards him like a wolf pack.

'Driver, where's the closest place I'll be able to ski on Christmas Day?'

Henry shrugged. 'I have no idea, I'm the driver. I don't know anything about forecasting weather.'

'Honesty, I love it!' Baxter chortled, to everyone else's dismay. 'A man who knows his limits. Some of your competitors seem to be severely lacking in this area. Sixth place.'

'What?' Cynthia exclaimed, still languishing on the bottom.

'Bea Armstrong. Your opportunity to retain pole position by showing the underdogs how it's done is now. Keeping to the five minutes, if you will, please summarise a correct answer for every question I've asked so far.'

'This is a joke,' Cynthia sputtered, before plonking her glass on a coffee table and stalking out of the room, pausing in the doorway to sneer, 'You can stuff your job. I'd rather not work for a mad megalomaniac.'

As Baxter nodded to Melody, who wordlessly made Cynthia's name vanish from the board, I took a millisecond to steady my nerves and recall the questions, eons of practice automatically sorting the answers into geographical and date order suitable for a weather report. I took a deep breath, stood up and summoned up my best Bea Armstrong smile.

'Hey, everybody, I hope you've had a great Saturday, got done what needed doing and remembered to have some fun in the process. And if you didn't, well, there's always tomorrow, right? Why do people keep asking if we're ready for Christmas when there's three perfectly good days still to go? Anyway, let's get down to business. I know you people are itching to know how the weather's going to affect your plans for a merry Christmas. So, starting with the Highlands...'

I whizzed through the other eight answers, keeping it short and sweet, and throwing in the odd joke.

'That's all I can tell you for now, but you know that because I'm obsessed with the weather, you don't have to be. Enjoy the rest of your night and I'll be sure to keep you updated.'

I stopped, took in the room of stunned faces and wondered if for a second I'd got it horribly wrong. Then Baxter Bigwood did his final finger point of the night, said, 'That's how to stay top of the leader board,' before turning on his heel and disappearing through another set of doors.

As soon as Baxter had gone, Henry broke into a giant grin.

'I can't believe you had the gall to brand *me* a nerd.'

'Excuse me?' I almost choked on the restorative gulp of bubbles I'd just swigged.

'Sir Henry of Nerdville?' He arched one eyebrow. 'All algebraic equations must bow before his geekdom?'

'The fact that you can remember that only proves that you're the nerd. It was a throwaway comment after you'd beaten me in the maths challenge by one point.'

'Some might hypothesise that only a fellow nerd could score within one point of Sir Henry.'

'I think I just proved how great a nerd I am.' My smile was almost giddy. Having the approval of a man like Baxter Bigwood was intoxicating.

'Bravo, Bea,' Lincoln said, walking over. 'That was... incredibly sexy, actually.'

'Behave.' I rolled my eyes, cheeks colouring. Lincoln had a husband back home, but I still didn't know how to handle comments like that, even when the person clearly didn't mean it.

'No, I'm serious. There is nothing more attractive than competence, wouldn't you agree, Driver?'

Henry coughed and blinked before switching to robo-Henry mode. 'Well, I don't know...'

'Apart from looks, money, and power, I suppose.' Lincoln

winked. 'Seriously, you smashed this evening. If the rest of us don't up our game, we might as well hitch a ride back with Cynthia.' He paused to check his watch. 'Which is why I'm heading off to get some sleep. Great to see you. Unless you continue to thrash me, in which case I'll wish you were never here.'

'Shall we go?' I asked Henry as the others settled down with a fresh bottle of fizz. We were heading to the door when Summer appeared out of nowhere.

'Congrats, Bea. That effortless girl-next-door presenting style proved why you're the main forecaster and I'm stuck in the milkman slot.'

'Thank you.'

'Let's hope Baxter is still so impressed by a girl when tomorrow he gets to see a real woman in action.' She threw a smouldering look at Henry. 'Sweet dreams, Driver.'

'That's an illogical argument.' Henry frowned as we made our way along the hallway. 'He saw her this evening and ranked her second.'

'She's drunk. And infuriated that I'm here.' I started pounding up the stairs. The fury was mutual.

'I try to give her the benefit of the doubt because she's so young, and beneath the bluster she's insecure and intimidated. But that doesn't mean she can stomp over me in this imaginary fight to the top.' I paused to catch my breath. These stairs went on longer than I'd expected. 'My work friend Jamal thinks she's been hacking into my email account.'

'Which would explain why you didn't get the email about this.'

'I'm going to ask him to start digging. He knows the tech guys and I trust him to be discreet.'

We reached a door labelled 'Bea, Henry, and Rudolph' in childish scrawl, with a picture of a reindeer drawn in crayon. I stopped, my anger evaporating in a sudden fog of awkwardness.

'I know I've dragged you away from your Christmas break into this preposterous situation that I'm afraid will only get worse, but I'm so grateful you're here. I'm even more grateful that you didn't make me share a room with Summer.'

Henry blinked. Just before he did, I thought I saw a glint of warmth in his eyes. 'You're welcome. I was dreading the singa-longa-Christmas film.'

'Film*s*, plural,' I said, as if taken aback by his ignorance. 'You think Joy Papplewick would settle for anything less than three festive-themed musicals?'

'Even more reason to be here, competing in an outlandish tour-nament for a job I'm not qualified for and don't want.'

He opened the door, to signal that the conversation was closed, and gestured for me to enter the room.

'Yowzers!' I instinctively jumped back again, bumping into Henry's chest before scrambling behind him.

'I thought you were being polite allowing me to go in first, but you suspected something like this, didn't you?' I asked, once I'd crept in after him.

'*No one* could have suspected this. Even with the clue on the door.'

The room was the size of a standard hotel room. The two single beds were positioned a few feet apart, opposite an old-fashioned wardrobe, chest of drawers, and a bookcase. There was a door on the far side of the room that I hoped led to an en suite.

Taking pride of place between the beds and the window stood a reindeer.

Not a nice little Christmas decoration reindeer.

A life-sized reindeer, either stuffed or a replica so good that it might as well have been.

Reindeers are *big*.

This one glowered at us with all the menace of a large mammal that had been killed, stuffed, and stuck in someone's spare bedroom with baubles dangling from its antlers and another one stuck on its nose.

'Come on.' Henry took hold of the haunch, nodding to indicate that I should grab an antler.

'I don't think he wants me to touch him.' I let my hand gingerly hover about an inch from its head.

'I don't think he wants to stand here all night watching us sleep, either.'

Eventually, sweating, dishevelled and sporting at least two new bruises, we left Rudolph to enjoy the peace and quiet of the corridor. After insisting that Henry went in the bathroom first (no more surprise roommates loitering in the shower) I quickly changed into my cosy pyjama bottoms and jersey top, and tried distracting myself from the fact that I was sharing a bedroom with my childhood nemesis by checking my phone.

There were messages from my parents, both asking whether we'd arrived safely and hoping that the evening had gone well. I shook my head, unable to resist smiling as I imagined Mum's response if I told her my sleeping arrangements. Instead I typed a quick reply letting them know that I was fine, and the interview was going okay.

Jed had also sent a message to say that he'd managed to sneak Nana Joy's scrapbook of press cuttings into his bedroom and while pretending to wrap presents he was going to try to find out what she was doing in the months prior to Dad's birth.

Any luck?

I waited only seconds before he replied.

Nine months before Dad was born she was in between plays. There's nothing to say where or what she was doing. Dead end I'm afraid.

I went over Jed's message while I brushed my teeth. Something was niggling at me, but my exhausted brain couldn't quite grasp it.

'What time do you want to set the alarm for?' Henry asked, once we were both in bed pretending not to feel excruciatingly uncomfortable. 'Breakfast is from eight until nine, but I'm guessing you'd rather be early.'

That was when I remembered. 'Dad was early!'

'What?' Henry looked up from his phone, understandably confused.

'Nothing, ignore me. I was thinking about something else. Um, is seven okay?'

I didn't really listen to his answer, already messaging Jed again.

Dad was six weeks early, remember? Nana Joy has that story about how her waters broke onstage in the middle of her big number. Try a month or two later.

I was lying in the dark, thoughts about Nana Joy and Charis House jostling up against the absurdity of my current situation, when Henry spoke quietly into the darkness.

'I have to confess, I did not expect to be sharing a room with you again.'

I was starting to recognise the slight rise in tone in his voice that meant he was smiling.

'Excuse me, didn't we make a pact never to speak of that night?'

I heard a definite chuckle now.

'I thought you meant to other people. I hadn't realised it applied to each other. We both know it happened.'

'That being so, we made that pact because we wanted to forget it ever had.'

There was a longer pause before Henry answered. He wasn't laughing any more.

'One of us made it for those reasons. The other person did it because he'd have said anything to make her happy.'

I almost sat up in shock. Hugely grateful that we were in complete darkness, I allowed my jaw to hang open as I scrambled for a reply.

'Goodnight, Bea. Try not to worry too much about tomorrow. You're top of the scoreboard for a reason.'

*Try not to worry about tomorrow?*

After that revelation, my mind was nowhere near tomorrow. Instead, it was firmly in the past, replaying every distant detail of a night eleven years ago and wondering if everything I'd assumed to be true about Henry Fairfax was wrong.

# 11

## CHRISTMAS, ELEVEN YEARS AGO

It was three in the morning when I arrived back at the house. Not the Coach House; the Fairfaxes were having a mammoth party two days before Christmas, and, along with various other friends and relatives, our family had been invited to stay over rather than trying to find a taxi that would venture this far out into the Nottinghamshire wilderness.

The five-bedroom, brand-new eco-build had been packed to the solar-panelled roof with guests, with more of them spilling out into the freezing-cold patio area surrounding the pool.

The children and teenagers had been allocated the summer house, which was equipped with board games, video-game console, CD player, and a mountain of snacks. It also contained the crate of beer that several of the older kids had stolen from the house when the adult guests were tipsy enough to neither notice nor care.

Slipping two of the bottles into my backpack, I snuck away as soon as I could get away with it. I used the spare keys that I'd pilfered earlier to retrieve my bike from the boot of the car, having told my parents that some of the kids might be going on a bike ride in the morning. It only took me twenty minutes to cycle into Hatherstone, which was totally worth it.

Adam's parents were out for the evening, taking his younger sisters with him. There was no way I was hanging out in Henry Fairfax's summer house when I could be here.

Only it didn't turn out quite as I'd expected. I'd been looking forward to cosying up on the sofa with Adam, eating pizza and popcorn and watching films, kissing and talking and exchanging gifts. The kind of properly romantic date that I'd longed for but rarely managed due to any relationship with Charis House students being strictly forbidden.

Adam had something else in mind. I'd turned sixteen a few months earlier, and at times it seemed as though he only ever had this on his mind.

'Come upstairs,' he murmured as we kissed on his sofa. 'It's more comfortable up there.'

'We haven't finished the film.' I giggled, twisting my head to look at the screen.

'We can watch the film later,' he said, bending down to press his lips against my bare neck, one hand snaking up inside my hand-knitted jumper.

I wriggled back up against the sofa arm, pushing my hair out of my face. 'You said you'd give me time to think about it.'

Adam grinned. 'Think about what? I just asked if you wanted to come upstairs where it's more comfortable.'

His face was flushed, a chunk of floppy fringe hanging over one eye as the other one glinted at me. For a hot, mad second I wanted to grab his hand, race upstairs, and let him do whatever he wanted. But I was still sober enough to know that I wasn't ready. I didn't want a spur-of-the-moment, hurried fumble on his bed, one ear listening for his family to arrive back home. If Adam loved me as much as he said, then he would respect that.

'What if your parents come back?'

'So what if they do?' He shrugged. 'We don't need to keep this a secret from them, Bea. They aren't the ones who veto who their kids get to go out with.'

'You wouldn't be embarrassed if they came home and found us... upstairs?'

He shrugged. 'It wouldn't be the first time.'

Seeing the look of shock on my face, he reached out and grabbed my hands, leaning his forehead against mine. 'Sorry! That was a joke, I'm sorry. Not funny. I'm a stupid idiot who is so in love with you I can't think straight, let alone talk any sense.'

'Okay.'

'Okay, you'll come upstairs?'

I tried to ignore how his whole face lit up.

'Okay, I forgive you.' I sat up straighter, tugging my jumper back down and disentangling myself from him as I pretended to be absorbed in *Pirates of the Caribbean*.

Adam waited a couple of minutes before gently entwining his fingers around mine. 'There hasn't been anyone else,' he muttered. 'I mean, you know I've had girlfriends before. But none of them ever came to my house. I never invited them.'

He crept an inch closer. 'None of them took my breath away, or made my heart pound. I didn't think about them all the time, or miss them every time we weren't together. I didn't love them.'

'Are you still going on about your ex-girlfriends?' I said, elbowing him in the ribs as he slid back up against me.

'No.' He slipped off the sofa, coming to kneel in front of me, eyes imploring as he rested his chin on my lap. 'I'm talking about you. Wonderful, amazing you. I love you, Bea Armstrong.'

'I love you, too. Can we please watch the rest of the film?'

Apparently not. Fifteen minutes later Adam's parents came home and plonked themselves down on the other sofa, the only acknowledgment that I was there a quick 'All right?' followed by a request for us to make ourselves scarce. So, I ended up in Adam's bedroom anyway.

'I'm sorry, I'm sorry,' he whispered, his breath hot against my skin as I batted his hand away for the second time. 'You're irresistible.'

'What's that supposed to mean?' I asked, pulling back.

'It means you're so beautiful, I just want to touch you.' He ran one finger across the skin above my jean waistband, causing goosebumps to spring up like ripples in his wake.

'And kiss you.' He pressed a soft kiss just below my ear.

'And you want this more than you want to respect me?' I asked, the pressure making my voice brittle.

Adam was the one to pull away this time. He sat up, running one hand through his messed-up hair as he leant back against the headboard. 'If I didn't respect your boundaries we wouldn't be together.'

He looked down at me in a way that made me feel like a child.

'You don't respect *me* when you don't trust me to kiss you and touch you without tensing up because you think I'm trying to trick you into something I know you don't want.'

I couldn't speak, because I knew if I opened my mouth then I'd start crying, and I'd feel even more like a stupid girl who couldn't handle a serious relationship.

'I wish you could stop believing what your parents think about me and make up your own mind.'

'That's not fair!' Too late, the tears came anyway.

'Really?' He arched one eyebrow. 'Because I'm getting kind of sick of being judged for something I've not done.'

'My parents don't judge you. The dating rule is because they care about you.'

'I wasn't talking about them.'

'Then I don't know what you're talking about!'

'I'm talking about you not taking us seriously. Not taking *me* seriously. I'm used to everyone else thinking that I'm some kind of deadbeat who can't be trusted. I wanted to believe you were different.' He shook his head. 'Like, I hate this sneaking around, not being able to tell your parents we're together. But maybe for you that's a really convenient excuse to keep us a secret, because you're ashamed of going out with a dropout.'

'That's not true!' I curled away from him, wrapping both arms around my knees. How had he flipped from being so nice to sounding as if he couldn't stand me? 'Why are you taking this personally?'

'Because it is personal!' he said, almost shouting now. 'We both know they aren't worried about you not being good enough for me! This isn't a schoolkid crush, Bea. I love you and I want to be with you forever and I want the whole world to know about it. It kills me that you don't feel the same way.' His voice dropped. 'I want you to be proud of me.'

The pressure of those words made it impossible to breathe or think straight.

'I can't tell them yet. Don't ask me to, please, Adam. A year and a half and we'll have left school. I'll tell them then.'

'A year and a half?' He screwed up his face.

'It's not that long if we're going to be together forever.'

'Easier to say when you're not the one made to feel like crap.'

'I'm sorry,' I whispered, reaching for his hand.

'Yeah.' He shook his head. 'It's getting late. You'd best go.'

'I... don't have to?' I said, clutching his hand tighter. 'I could stay, and we could just...'

'I don't think so. We don't want to risk your parents finding out.'

Thanks to my heart feeling as though it had been smashed into pieces, and the lanes being iced over like a toboggan run causing me to crash into a ditch, it took me forever to get back to the party. The entire place was in darkness, and when I crept up to the front door, it was locked. After tramping around the back doors and the summer house, I decided to try the garage. I knew that Henry's dad had a workshop above it, which would hopefully be warmer than outside. I ventured over to a set of metal steps, my stiff, bruised limbs struggling to climb up to the workshop door, tears of misery freezing on my face.

To my enormous relief, it was unlocked, and made only the faintest creak as I pushed it open and slipped inside.

'Halt!' A hoarse cry stopped me in my tracks.

Three seconds and the sound of a water glass being knocked over later, a torch switched on, aimed right at my face so I couldn't see who was behind it.

I had a good idea, though. *Halt?*

There was the sound of a throat being cleared. 'The light switch is left of the door.'

The torch beam shifted to a spot on the wall, and I quickly turned on the light, which wasn't much brighter than the torch but at least the dim glow was now spread across the room, rather than concentrated on me.

Henry was sitting up against one of the bare concrete walls, a sleeping bag pooled around his waist. He wore a fleece and a bobble hat, which he quickly pulled off before grabbing his glasses from a neat pile of items on the floor and slipping them on.

'What are you doing here?' we both asked, at precisely the same time. It might have been funny, except that I was freezing cold, beyond exhausted and desperate to find a quiet corner where I could sob my wretched heart out.

Henry pulled up his knees and rested his elbows on them. 'I thought there was a better chance of getting some sleep in here rather than the summer house.' He looked at me. 'Didn't you go home?'

I shrugged, fiddling with the toggle on my duffel coat. 'No.'

He continued examining me until his logical brain had pieced it together. 'Oh. You went to see your boyfriend.'

'The house is all locked up.'

'Right.'

I took a tentative step further into the room.

'Would you mind if I…?'

Henry sighed, starting to wriggle out of the sleeping bag. 'It's not very clean.'

'No!' I held up one hand in protest. 'I didn't mean that, I just meant is it okay if I stay in here? I'll… um…' I looked around at the metal shelving units and piles of equipment before sitting down on a bare patch of concrete and leaning clumsily against a plastic crate that slipped back several inches before bumping up against something else. The floor felt even colder than me, and as the heat of the bike ride began to recede my muscles shivered. Pretending this was all perfectly fine, I closed my eyes and attempted to snuggle down as if on the verge of falling asleep.

My chattering teeth gave me away.

'The whole point of me being in here is to get some sleep. If you think I can do that while listening to you sink into hypothermia, then your opinion of me is even worse than I thought.'

'I'm very sorry, I'll try to freeze to death more quietly.' I huddled into a tight ball, pulling my beret down as low as I could on my forehead.

After a long moment, Henry spoke again, his voice quiet this time. 'Don't be an idiot, Bea. It's not contagious.'

'What's not?' I asked, opening my eyes.

'Whatever it is that makes you want to stay as far away from me as possible.'

As my retinas adjusted to the light again I saw that he'd unzipped the sleeping bag and opened it up, so it was nearer the size of a double duvet. Underneath was a single blow-up mattress that looked luxuriously comfortable in contrast to the floor.

'Are you sure?' I asked, even as I unfolded my creaking limbs and prepared to join him.

'I mean about us sharing a bed, not you being contagious,' I added quicky when I saw the look on his face, only to realise the connotations of that statement when his face flushed scarlet.

Deciding to ignore the awkwardness that followed, I edged through the junk and sank down on the furthest end of the mattress, tentatively climbing under the cover. I curled up so that my legs were mostly off the concrete and only the top half of my face was exposed, while taking up as little of the sleeping bag as possible and, most importantly, making sure there was absolutely no risk of accidentally brushing up against my bedmate.

Henry had wriggled back down so that we now lay a foot apart from each other, both of us facing the ceiling, every tiny rustle echoing through the tension. When Henry suddenly jumped up, for a second I thought it had all got too much and he was about to bolt, but instead he flicked off the light before returning to the makeshift bed again.

I released a slow, silent sigh of relief that it was so dark, even if I couldn't get to sleep, at least I didn't need to worry about Henry watching me. Unfortunately he didn't need to see to know that I was still freezing. The thin mattress, which was a woeful barrier against the cold seeping up from the floor, was practically vibrating thanks to my violent shivering.

'Okay, so now you're just shivering right next to me. That's not really resolved the me being able to sleep issue.'

'You're the one who told me to come over here!' I burrowed

even further below the sleeping bag, so only the top of my head was poking out. 'I'll warm up in a few minutes.'

Henry inched across the mattress until the side of his arm pressed up against mine. 'Does that help?'

I almost groaned out loud, it helped so much. His whole body radiated heat, and I couldn't resist wriggling in a tiny bit closer. In one sweeping motion, Henry lifted up his arm, firmly wrapping it around me as I nestled into the side of his chest.

'Better?'

'Yes. Thank you.'

'Not too weird?'

'It's excruciatingly weird.'

'On balance, it's less weird than waking up to find you've died of hypothermia while in the same bed as me.'

'That would definitely be worse.'

'Note to self: contrary to previous statements, Bea considers touching me to be preferable to death.'

I lifted my head up an inch as if to look at him, although all I could see was thick blackness. 'For a scientist, you're a total drama queen.'

'I'm not the one who said she'd rather die than hold my hand.'

I felt a quiver under my cheek that might have been Henry suppressing a laugh.

'How on earth do you remember that?' I asked, as a faint memory of our parents trying to force us to dance together at a previous Christmas party flashed into my mind.

'It's the kind of insult that leaves a scar.'

'Oh, shut up! You were equally repelled by the idea.'

Henry said nothing, but his chest rose and fell with a long, slow breath. His fleece smelled smoky from the evening's fire pit, with the faintest trace of perspiration. It was the scent of a thousand childhood memories, overwhelmingly familiar and strangely comforting despite the awkward situation.

If it had been any other boy, I would have felt highly dubious about their motives, or the message I was sending by being here. But this was Henry, and, however annoying he might be, I knew he'd treat this with the detached logic he applied to every situation. I also trusted him, absolutely.

'Do you want to talk about it?' Henry asked, his quiet rumble interrupting the silence.

I waited while a few of his steady heartbeats thumped against the side of my head before answering. 'About what?' Honestly, I was half afraid to ask.

'You were crying. When you came in.'

*Oh.*

'No, I really don't.' One of the hardest things about being with Adam was that I didn't have anyone to talk to about him, but if I did decide to talk, Henry would be the last person I confided in. My abrupt answer had stirred up some of the previous tension, however, and I needed to find something to say to settle it back down again.

'So... *halt*?'

Henry froze.

'For a second there I thought I'd stumbled across a highwayman's secret lair.'

'I think you must have misheard. All I said was... cough. I coughed.' He did a strangled cross between a cough and the word 'halt' as if to prove it. 'See? An understandable error, given the circumstances.'

'Oka-a-a-ay, that explains it, then. When you said "halt"—' I coughed this, in an exaggerated imitation '—I thought you said "halt".' The second time I repeated it in exactly the same way. 'My bad.'

I could hear Henry rubbing his head with the hand that wasn't resting on my arm, as if trying to fire up his brain.

'If you could programme a robot to make your Christmas better, what would it do?'

'What?' I had to laugh at this totally Henry-ish change of subject. 'I have absolutely no idea. But I've a funny feeling you've thought long and hard about it.'

'I'd get it to wrap presents.'

'Seriously? Not find a way to provide gifts for children in poverty or convert all the waste generated into renewable energy? All the brilliant things it could do, and you want something to wrap presents.'

'Well, obviously those things are far better if the robot was making Christmas better on a global scale, but the question was on an individual level.'

'Oka-a-ay... so how about doing that vile homework Mr Bennet set?'

'How do I benefit from a robot hijacking my education?'

I tipped my face into his chest and groaned. 'Well, even if you couldn't bear to let a machine steal your homework fun, surely there are way bigger things than wrapping presents. That's hardly a major life hassle.'

'Speak for yourself,' Henry huffed. 'I wasted the whole afternoon wrestling with Sellotape, when I could have been researching the essay. Plus I now have a paper cut right on my pen finger, which makes writing it a lot harder.'

'Well, that's settled, then. What more could you want?'

'You can judge, but I don't hear you coming up with anything better.'

Right. That was a challenge I had to accept.

'And you can't say anything about homework. We've already covered that.'

'Well, that's totally what it would be. But if you're insisting on a different answer, then... um... a robot that could take my designs and convert them into actual clothes, so I could have some decent Christmas outfits for once.'

'Really?' Henry sounded bewildered. 'That's going to make your Christmas better? As long as they are functional and comfortable, who cares what clothes look like?'

'Well, clearly not you!' I retorted. 'Clothes are an expression of who you are as a person. They tell people what you're like, how you see yourself.'

Henry snorted. 'Mine don't.'

'For example,' I went on, speaking over him, '*yours* say that you don't care what anyone thinks about you.'

Henry was quiet for a moment. 'You think I don't care about that?'

I shifted underneath the sleeping bag, not sure how to respond to hearing Henry sound almost human. 'You don't exactly try to fit in with the crowd.'

'Refusing to change who I am for the sake of being popular doesn't mean I don't care what *anyone* thinks.'

Wow. I genuinely would not have guessed that.

'But this is your robot, not mine. If you want to design some snazzy Christmas outfits, then go for it.' His voice dropped as he went on. 'Personally, I think it's great how you always look different.'

'Not that my appearance matters, of course.'

'Of course.' Henry coughed again. 'So, that's Christmas sorted. What about a summer-holiday robot, what would they do?'

As we carried on talking, the pain of the argument with Adam slipped away into the shadows, and I gradually stopped feeling so uncomfortable, simply because Henry was as matter-of-fact and as calm and composed as he always was.

At some point, I must have dozed off, because a flurry of pings jerked me awake to find my head still resting on Henry's chest, one arm and a leg entwined with his. At some point we'd adjusted position so that we were both lying full-length down the mattress, tucking the sleeping bag around us, so as I hastily scrambled away I ended up back on the concrete, the blast of icy air ensuring I was now completely awake.

Pulling my phone out of my coat pocket, I found several messages lighting up the screen.

I'm sorry

I love you

I wish you were here

Please let me know you got back OK

And that you don't hate me

And that I can be your secret boyfriend for as long as it takes xxx

'Everything all right?' Henry asked, voice rough with sleep.

I smiled as a wave of happiness flooded my chest. 'Yes.'

Adam sent one more message after I'd replied to let him know that I was fine, and sorry too.

Sleep well. I'll be dreaming about you xxx

Tucking the phone back in my pocket, I crept back under the sleeping bag and lay straight as a board, ensuring that not an inch of my body now touched Henry's. I suspected that if Adam knew who I was sharing a bed with he'd be amused rather than jealous, but I wasn't going to risk telling him. Henry had done a nice thing in letting me sleep here and I didn't want Adam turning that into a snide joke.

'Goodnight, then,' Henry said, his voice as soft as the shadows.

''Night. Thanks again for not letting me die.'

'It's the least I could do for my childhood betrothed.'

'Okay, so now you've made it weird again...'

Except it wasn't weird. Or rather, the only weird thing about me sharing a bed with Henry was how utterly normal and non-weird it felt.

I still spent the rest of the school year ignoring him. Which on reflection, as I lay in the creaky old bed in a Scottish castle eleven years later, was probably one of the stupidest and meanest things I'd ever done.

# 12

After a night of twisting about in tartan blankets while trying not to disturb my roommate, I hauled myself out of bed just after seven and had a lightning-quick shower. By the time I emerged, dressed in my interview outfit of calf-length tea dress covered in robins, Henry was looking out of the window dressed in jeans. a thick jumper, and his boots.

'The snow's arrived,' he said, nodding at the thick layer now covering every surface of the gardens beyond the window.

'I could have told you that.' I went to confirm that my forecast of at least eight inches was correct.

'I thought I'd go for a quick walk, give you some space to get ready,' he said.

'Okay, great.' I checked the time, grateful for his tact. 'I won't need more than fifteen minutes.'

When he arrived back, I was primped, preened, and replying to one of my social media regulars, a young man who was house-bound due to ill health, but who contacted me every week or so asking about the weather for imaginary trips he'd plan from his sofa.

I quickly pressed send, shut down the myriad weather websites I'd been scouring in preparation for the day ahead, and went to find some breakfast.

'Good morning, I hope you had a restful night.' One of Melody's boys bowed as he opened a gold door leading into a dining hall.

'Thank you, sir,' I replied, giving him a nod and a wink as I walked past.

Inside the hall was a long, dark table that must have been able to seat twenty at least. There were currently four of my fellow candidates clustered at the far end, while another two stood at a side table, helping themselves to food. All the decorations in this room were silver, including a galaxy of stars covering the high ceiling, and pots containing large, spray-painted branches lining the walls. I got a jolt when I glanced at the large wall of windows and saw several snowmen pressed up against the glass, their beady eyes and wonky smiles looking decidedly sinister.

Another boy handed me a plate, and as soon as I'd sat down with my smoked salmon and eggs, a third one offered me a hot drink.

'I hope you boys haven't been working all night,' I said, sitting back to allow him to pour me a steaming mug of tea.

'We were meant to be sledging today but then most of the actual workers phoned to say they're too poorly to come in,' he replied with a shrug.

'Well, that's very noble of you to step in at short notice.'

'Mum said if we don't grumble and do a good job we get to open two Christmas presents early, *and* have pizza for tea and chocolate for breakfast.'

'Sounds like a great deal. Can I get a job here, too?'

He grinned. 'There's not enough chocolate.'

'Fair enough. I'll try to get the weather job instead.'

The atmosphere was cautiously friendly, with a simmering undercurrent of tension. Calvin Cotton was poring over a laptop, while a woman, Fenella, sat opposite me jabbing her half grapefruit over and over with a spoon while not actually eating any of it.

'Are you okay?' I asked.

'I'd be a lot better if I wasn't below your driver on the scoreboard.'

Ah, yes, Fenella had ended the night in bottom place.

'It's all a bit unconventional, isn't it?'

She grimaced. 'That's one word for it. To be honest, if his plan was to weed out the weaker candidates then it's working. I think I'm done here.'

'Really? Are you sure? With Baxter there's no telling what will happen next. You could be on top by lunchtime.'

She stabbed the grapefruit one last time, leaving the spoon sticking out of it like a flagpole. 'That's the crucial factor, though, isn't it? I don't want to be in a job where I never know where I stand.'

I took sip of tea while I thought about this. 'I take your point, but I can't imagine Baxter having much to do with things day to day, once this part of the process is over.'

'Maybe not. But don't you think it's telling that there are no producers or any other people from the newsroom here? The whole thing gives me bad vibes. Even if he offered me the job, I don't think I'd take it.'

Fenella got up, took one last swig of her coffee, and walked out.

Two down, seven to go if you counted Henry.

A minute later Summer arrived, Jordan Jones right behind her. From the way they giggled and nudged each other at the food table, I wondered if Henry and I weren't the only people who'd shared a room last night.

By the time Henry arrived a short while after that, everyone was reading through notes, perusing the online weather data or, in the case of Summer and Jordan, taking snaps and posting them on Instagram.

'Okay?' he murmured, coming to sit beside me with a bowl of porridge.

I nodded. 'I'd be better if I knew what was coming next, but I feel as ready as I'll ever be.'

At nine, Melody led us all back into the library. This morning she was dressed in a light-blue suit, on the back of which someone had taped a piece of paper with 'poke here for a stinky fart' scrawled on it. When she stopped to allow us to go past, Henry managed to discreetly tug it off and stick it in his pocket. Baxter was already standing in front of the fireplace, looking uncannily like one of the geese on either side of him in a tweed waistcoat and enormous cravat. Once we'd all trooped in, Melody invited us to take a seat.

'The scoreboard, if you please.' Baxter nodded at his assistant.

After the screen above his head lit up, he waited for what felt like an age but was probably less than a minute, his gaze slowly scanning from one side of the sofas to the other.

'You all know where you stand. Two have already crumbled under the pressure. How many will still be here tomorrow? How far are you prepared to go to win a life that without me you could only dream of?'

Henry glanced at me. I focused on breathing normally and not letting my inner distaste leak into my TV smile.

'This morning, the real fun begins.' Baxter paused for effect but every person there knew that the only one who'd be having fun today was Baxter. 'A weather hunt!'

'Ooh, sounds intriguing,' Summer managed, nervously smoothing her hair.

'It is!' Baxter barked. 'A treasure hunt, but with weather-based clues. This will test not only your meteorological knowledge.'

Jordan shifted uncomfortably.

'But also your determination and passion for this role. How badly do you want this? Candidates, we are about to find out.'

At that, he swept out of the room, tweed jacket flapping behind him, and left us all sitting there wondering what on earth was about to happen. Melody soon filled us in.

'Okay, so there are several clues in containers like this.' She held up a silver tube which at a guess her kids had made out of an old kitchen roll wrapped in foil. 'They also contain seven tokens, one with each of your names on it. All clues can be found within the estate grounds. None of them on the upper floor, in Baxter's private wing, or any other areas that are locked. It's a straightforward race, the only rule being that you must not move or remove any of the containers, clues, or tokens apart from your own. The first clue will appear on the screen shortly. I'll hopefully see you all back here in time for lunch.'

She turned to go before coming to a sudden stop and spinning around again. 'Oh, wait, I can't believe I forgot this. Baxter has assigned you teams. Hang on.' She tapped on her iPad a few times. 'Here we go.'

The group glanced around at each other anxiously. It was probably fair to say that no one wanted to be paired with Jordan Jones in a weather hunt. Personally, I'd choose Henry's brains over any of the weather presenters', but failing that would be happy with Lincoln or basically anyone apart from Summer.

'Lincoln Kim and Calvin Cotton.'

Lincoln and Calvin gave each other a high five while the rest of us sagged with disappointment. Those two would make a strong team.

'Jordan Jones and Ben Adibisi.'

'Ah, crap,' Ben blurted, before catching himself. 'No offence, Jordan.'

'No worries, mate.' Jordan shrugged it off. 'I'm sick at finding things. We'll smash it.'

That left me, Henry and Summer. For a moment I wondered if Henry would be allowed to sit it out. This thought was immediately followed by the hope that he'd come with us anyway, because I was starting to realise that was how kind he was.

But no, it wasn't to be.

'Driver and Summer.'

'What?' Summer asked, her smile freezing on her face. 'He's not even a candidate. How is that fair?'

'Sorry.' Melody didn't look very sorry. 'You might have worked out that Baxter's not a big fan of fair.'

'Um, so what about me?' I asked.

This time Melody did manage an apologetic nose wrinkle. 'Top of the scoreboard competes alone.'

'Ooh, bad luck!' Summer said, suddenly appearing much happier.

Before I could gather my wits, Baxter's face appeared on the screen above the fireplace. Ben quickly held up his phone to record it, prompting the rest of us to follow suit.

'Congratulations on making it this far. It's by the red one.'

'What?' Ben exclaimed, the rest of us looking to Melody for some sort of explanation.

'Good luck.' With another quick smile, she turned around and left.

'This is a joke.' Summer screwed up her face in disgust. 'He's insane.'

'Probably just wants to force us into tramping around aimlessly until we all give up one by one,' Calvin said.

Lincoln, however, looked far less annoyed than the rest of us.

He nudged Calvin. 'I'm going to change into my boots. Meet me in the hallway in five?'

Calvin and Lincoln strolled out of the door, leaving the rest of us waiting to see who would make a move next.

'Sounds as good a start as any.' Ben shrugged.

'No secret weather code for a red one?' Jordan asked, skimming through his phone as they walked out.

Summer watched me, eyes narrowed. It wouldn't take a genius to predict that she was going to play this game using underhand sneaking about rather than skill. I racked my brains as to the tiniest hint of what the clue might mean. It might be that I'd only be able to decipher it once I found the 'red one', but I had a strong suspicion that Lincoln had already detected something helpful in Baxter's words.

Deciding that boots, a coat, and hat were a good idea, I hurried off to my room, the clue circling around in my head yet still coming no closer to land. Once safely in the room I played the clip of Baxter's video back while I bundled up in my outerwear, certain that I must have missed a vital clue. It was on the fourth replay that I found it.

It sounded as if Baxter had deliberately rushed the sentence to make it harder to hear, but when I focused on each individual word, I couldn't believe I'd missed it:

*Congelations* on making it this far.

Not congratulations, *congelations*.

The transparent ice that's often known as black ice when it forms on smooth water.

The Bigwood estate was on the edge of a small loch. Zipping up my coat, I grabbed my shoulder bag and hurtled out of the door, only to smack straight into Henry about to walk in.

'Woah.' He grabbed both my elbows to stop the rebound knocking me over.

'Sorry.'

'I take it you've figured it out, then?' he asked, a glint of hope in his eyes.

'I have. If you don't mind, I'm already a good ten minutes behind Calvin and Lincoln.'

He stepped to the side to allow me past, but five steps down the corridor I came skidding back. 'Wait, have you?'

Henry pulled a face as he tugged his coat on. 'Why would we bother finding out the clues when we can simply follow everyone else?'

'You can't win that way.'

'We can come second. And then trip up or otherwise delay the team we're following so that we pip them to the post.'

'That's horrible.'

'It is.' He put on his hat and shook his head. 'She's lurking in the hallway waiting to skulk after whoever sets off first.'

'You're going to do your best to sabotage her sabotage, aren't you?'

Henry grinned. It was so rare to see that it sent a rush of warmth through my chest.

'That may depend on who's in front.'

'Well, may the best team win.' I couldn't help but grin back. If Summer was fixated on another team, I might just slip past them both.

'You won't win standing in the doorway talking to me.'

Without another word, I turned and raced to the stairs.

## 13

Stepping outside was like walking into a freezer. The snow had stopped but the wind was fierce, whipping up drifts and whistling into every centimetre of exposed skin. Despite being the middle of the morning the sky was gloomy with the gunmetal grey that signalled more snow.

A quick check on my phone map showed the loch half a mile away behind the house. Trying to keep to where there might be paths hiding beneath the snow, I dodged past a trio of elves and trudged towards a row of trees.

The snow was shallower beneath the pines, but that was about the only thing that made it less of a slog than the open ground. Having found no obvious way in, I had started pushing between the trunks, crouching low and ducking to avoid the low-slung branches. It felt as though the wind had rubbed the top layer of skin off my face, and despite thick boots my feet were completely numb. A couple of times I thought I glanced the flash of bright coats up ahead and to the left of me, but in the shadows of the wood it was impossible to be sure. More than once I felt the sting of a twig scratching my cheek, and I was starting to seriously reconsider how much I wanted to work for Baxter Bigwood.

Just as I'd about decided to give up and head back to the real world, where job interviews consisted of people answering questions in a warm room, I spotted a lessening of the grey up ahead, and a few spiky metres later burst out of the tree line.

The loch was right in front of me, the water lapping at the shallow slope of a pebble beach. Across the water, mountains encircled the far shore in a tapestry of dark greens, browns and purple. It was stunning, instantly dispelling the discomfort I'd endured to get here. I could have stared at it for hours, except that further along the shoreline was a row of boats, each one painted in a different colour. It was easy to spot the patches of ice dotted about the surface of the water, and even easier to see Calvin and Lincoln sprinting away around the edge of the loch, Summer stumbling after them in her ankle boots.

She stopped only a short distance beyond the boats, so that as I hurried closer I could hear her yelling into her phone. 'They've gone around the lake and back into the trees. I'll drop a pin in the map so you know where to head them off. No, I haven't got it yet. I'll look now.'

She turned to find me climbing into the red rowing boat. I'd scanned the ice within reach of the shore and seen nothing. The only other way to find a clue would be to risk stepping onto it or look from within the boat. It didn't take long to spot a small wooden box tucked up beside the bow.

'Oh, brilliant! Well done.'

I jerked in surprise as Summer peered over my shoulder, having somehow sprung up beside me without me noticing.

'What does it say?'

'Why do you want to know? You're only going to let someone else work it out and then sneak after them.'

'What, and you didn't get here so fast by following me?' She pulled the kind of soppy pout that might work on our boss but made me want to slap her. 'Don't be a spoilsport just because I have Driver. What happened to us weathergirls sticking together?'

Ignoring her, I snapped a picture of the clue, grabbed a token, was about to dump the box back on the ice and then decided that Summer was right. If I was sticking to my interview strategy of being myself, I wasn't about to be petty. Instead I handed Summer the box, clambered back out of the boat, and headed off in the direction I'd seen the other team leaving a few minutes earlier.

I didn't see Summer again for nearly two hours. To be honest, there were times she might have been nearby, but with my eyes firmly fixed on the treacherous ground right in front of me, I'd have missed anything smaller than a woolly mammoth.

I made it to three more clues in that time, all written on card and stuffed inside the kitchen-roll tube containers, the first two were straightforward to anyone who knew anything about meteorology, however the third had me stumped until I realised it was an anagram.

The weather hunt might have felt like an adventure had I been working with someone else. Stumbling through the snow, searching behind a cluster of compost heaps and in amongst soggy tree roots by myself was more like a bad dream. The edge of the storm had begun to whip through the estate, shaking the trees and tossing about stray twigs and other debris.

I started to imagine that the other candidates had finished ages ago, and were laughing and joking over hot drinks and crumpets in the library wondering whether to send out a search party for me. That was, until I rounded the corner of a decrepit outbuilding and came across Ben, huddled on a rusty bench.

'Bea, hi!' He tried to smile but it turned out more like a sob.

'Are you okay? Where's Jordan?'

'Jordan?'

'Your partner in the hunt.'

'Oh, yes... Jordan. He gave up hours ago.'

'We've only been out here for a couple of hours.'

'Really?' Ben grimaced. 'My phone died back at the third clue.'

'Have you found the fifth one yet? I thought it must be somewhere by this building.'

He shook his head. 'I forgot what it said, and with no phone I couldn't take a picture or even work out where I was. I've been wandering around for ages, and then thought I'd wait here and hope someone found me.'

'It's a nightmare, isn't it?' I went to sit next to him. His lips were tinged an alarming blue, fingers curled into stiff claws.

'Yes. This is a literal nightmare. It's my first time in Scotland and my second time seeing snow. I did not know that any place on earth could be this cold.'

'The best way to warm up is to start moving. Give me a minute to find the clue and we can get your blood pumping.'

In the end it was two minutes before I found the shiny container under an upturned flowerpot. To my amazement, all the tokens were still inside, meaning that I'd somehow overtaken the others. I guessed the anagram had stumped Lincoln and Calvin, too.

'Can you work it out?' Ben asked, flapping his arms against his sides.

'It's not cryptic, just says to head straight to the library and use the password, the other term for "pyrocumulus".'

'If only there *was* a fire cloud around here. It might warm us up a bit!' Ben glanced around. 'I have no idea which way is back to the house.'

Just as I pointed in what I was fairly sure was the right direction, Calvin and Lincoln sprinted around the side of the building, chests heaving from exertion.

'Please tell us there's a clue here somewhere.' Lincoln gasped. 'You don't need to be specific, but I can't take much more of this. We've been looking in a fountain and I'm so numb I can't even tell if it's still cold.'

'Look.' Calvin pointed at where I still grasped the container, seemingly unable to wheeze out any more words.

Glancing at Ben, who gave a firm nod of agreement, I handed the container to Calvin. Ben and I had just turned to go when two more people staggered into sight.

'Grab it!' Summer shrieked, launching at Lincoln, who was closest to her. As they both tumbled into the snow, struggling to untangle themselves, Henry merely stood there, arms folded, while Calvin read the clue, took his token, and started hurrying away, throwing the container into a holly bush as he jogged past it.

'What the hell, man?' Lincoln yelled after him.

'Only one winner!' Calvin called back. 'I need this job.'

'You should try to catch up with him,' Ben said, as Summer yanked Lincoln onto the ground again using the back of his trousers. 'You can still win.'

'Calvin did the dirty on his own team member.' I shook my head. 'That's not fair.'

'Baxter doesn't do fair,' Ben reminded me.

'Maybe not, but I do.' I approached the holly bush, scanning around for a big stick to knock the container free until Henry reached past me into the branches and pulled it out.

'Yes!' Summer cried, elbowing Lincoln in the stomach as she pushed past him to get to Henry. Her teammate merely waited until she was two paces away then ducked past her and threw it to where Lincoln had finally managed to right himself.

'Cheers, mate!' Lincoln said, looking astounded.

'Traitor!' Summer screeched, giving Henry a solid shove before she spun back around to where Lincoln had already grabbed his token and started off after Calvin, dropping the container as he ran.

Henry, who had absorbed Summer's shove like a crash mat, looked at me and Ben. 'Time to get back in the warm?'

'Please, yes!' Ben shivered. 'Lead the way.'

We half stumbled, half jogged for a good fifteen minutes until the house suddenly appeared in the distance around the corner of a high hedge. Ben had urged us to go on without him several times, not wanting his slow pace to ruin our chances of catching up with the others. However Henry assured him that he'd not bothered picking up any tokens so had no chance of winning anyway, and I was equally far too disillusioned with the whole farce to set out across the open snowscape in a gale without the two larger men to prevent me from blowing away.

I'd glanced behind us a few times to see Summer, hobbling in her pointy boots, hair whipping across her face.

'I think we'd best wait for her,' I said eventually, as she tripped and fell into a snowdrift. 'She's going to end up injured or with hypothermia otherwise.'

'She'd leave you out here without a moment's pause,' Henry replied, his eyebrows raised as if questioning whether I was sure.

'She'll wait for us to reach the front door then push us down the stone steps,' Ben added.

I took a deep, sub-zero breath. 'I know.'

The second I'd spoken, Henry plodded back to help pull Summer onto her feet. At first she batted him away until he leant closer to speak to her, after which she allowed him to link arms with her as they started battling their way to join us.

As Ben and I reached the front door, Summer pulled Henry to a stop two steps behind. 'You can let go of my arm now. Look at me. I was well beyond trying to win about three snowdrifts ago.'

Henry gave her a mild smile. 'I'm not the kind of man to leave a job unfinished.'

It was a sorry clump of bedraggled, ice-cold candidates who stumbled up to the library door. Gasping in response to the blast of warmth in the hallway, residual snow dripping off our coats onto the flagstones, Ben and I knocked on the door at the same time.

'Flammagenitus!' We called out, Summer shouting even louder while Henry looked as though we must be delirious.

Melody opened the door, a large grin on her face until she saw the state of us. 'Ah. It's still a bit blowy out there, I see.'

'If you'd asked us,' I groaned, 'we could have let you know the storm would be here by noon.'

'Right, well, huge congratulations for making it back,' she said, a tinge of concern behind her bright smile. 'The boys will take your coats, and there's soup and fresh bread in the dining hall. Are you quite all right, Summer?'

'Mmmf!' Summer groaned in frustration as Henry refused to budge, still holding onto her arm so that Ben and I could enter first.

It was something of an anticlimax, striding into a library at the end of our epic quest to find no one there except for Billy, Benji, and Bobby. But I have to say, when we'd joined Calvin and Lincoln in the dining hall, that first mouthful of spiced parsnip soup was the finest thing I'd ever tasted.

Baxter appeared once giant slices of apple cake had been followed up with tea and coffee. It had been a subdued meal, Calvin in fresh, dry clothes keeping his head down, eyes on his food, the rest of us too cold and tired to bother making conversation, Jordan Jones noticeably absent.

'Congratulations, all of you!' Baxter boomed, as a screen lowered from the ceiling behind him and flickered to life. 'Six of you completed the weather hunt. This is how things lie as we head into the penultimate challenge.'

'There's two more of these?' Ben said, sounding on the verge of panic.

'Um, excuse me but why am I last?' Calvin asked, sounding well over that verge and into the ditch.

Baxter looked at him, face impassive. 'Because you were disqualified.'

'What?' Calvin's eyes darted around the rest of the table, his cheeks flushing with anger.

'No, nobody snitched on you,' Baxter said, in a bored drone. 'I'm a billionaire recluse living in the middle of nowhere. Do you really think I wouldn't have cameras in every corner?'

'But...' Calvin spluttered.

'But. There was one simple rule, clearly explained to you in advance. Don't move or remove the containers.'

'So why is Bea still at the top?' Lincoln asked, not adding that if Calvin was disqualified he should be in first place, not third.

'Lincoln Kim, it is bold of you to question the rankings, given that you also did not replace the container in the right place. I'm overlooking this because you didn't deliberately *mis*place it. However, this is a job interview, not a game show. I want team players in my newsroom. Bea competed as an individual yet showed more team spirit than the rest of you put together. Driver, I appreciate that in your case integrity and working with your team-mate were in direct contradiction of one another, however, I can't overlook your absence of tokens.'

Henry gave a small shake of his head, as if wondering for the hundredth time that day what he was doing here.

'Summer, before you ask why you're second to last, while I appreciate your ruthless determination, you were dangerously ill equipped for the task in hand. A mistake which I can't tolerate in

Bigwood Media Anyone else like to challenge my decision? No? Very well. Be in the library in one hour.'

I was half expecting to find someone else had dropped out when we regathered in the library, showered, changed and hair no longer resembling stale candy floss. I was a quarter expecting that person to be me. Maybe we all thought that having survived the morning's ordeal it was silly to drop out now. Or perhaps whatever we faced in here it had to be less gruelling than the storm now blowing full pelt outside.

'Time to get serious,' Baxter announced from his armchair. 'You have fifteen minutes to present your ten-year vision for the role. You were briefed in the email so my expectations are correspondingly high. Reverse order. Calvin Cotton, your time starts now.'

I wasn't sure if going last was a plus or a negative, as all of the others (apart from Henry, of course) worked their way through presentation slides covering how weather was likely to change over the next decade, the potential for weather broadcasters to help support environmental issues, the move away from traditional television to online apps. There was some level of repetition, but even Summer managed a competent job of exploring how becoming a social media influencer could benefit BWM Today.

When it came to my turn, I knew that what I had to say could either lead me to the role of national weather presenter, or straight to the bottom of the scoreboard. There was only one way to find out.

'We've heard a lot this afternoon about how the weather is changing. We've heard more about how we can play a part in helping address the horrendous catastrophe that we as meteorologists have been forecasting for decades. Thanks to Calvin and Summer, we've also had a masterclass in how we can best convey this vital information due to even more rapid changes in media and technology. But I wanted to talk about one thing that never changes. People. And how people love to connect with other people. We are built for community. The only way to tackle this momentous challenge is *together*. Whether we find that community when chatting to our neighbours over the garden wall, or via a Twitter hashtag, we all need it.

'So, I'm not a futurist, I can't tell you with any certainty how we will be connecting in ten years' time, but I can tell you that we will be connecting, because that's what people do. And I don't see why the weather should be any different.

'This is Walter Pirbright.' I clicked to an image of Walter, squinting at the sky. 'His family have farmed the same eighty hectares for over two hundred years. Walter can tell you with 98 per cent accuracy if it is going to rain tomorrow, as well as what time and how hard. He could have told me that we'd have a white Christmas back in October. I know this, because he did. My viewers love Walter. I get engaged couples messaging to ask him what the weather's going to be for their wedding. When we showed photographs of his new calves, the website was inundated. He's inspired farmers across the region to adopt methods of sustainable farming, because they know he knows what he's talking about when it comes to the earth beneath our feet and the air above our heads.'

I clicked on to the next slide.

'This is Byron. He has a debilitating condition that means leaving the house just for an hour is a journey of epic proportions, so most days he stays at home, alone. But every month he plans a fantasy trip to a far-flung probably quite dangerous part of the world, and as part of that planning he asks me what the weather will be like. Since I've started including my answers in my broadcast, others have been getting in touch to suggest activities he might like to do while he's there, local food and similar tips. Byron has stopped being an invisible part of the community, and now has people who care about him, who share a common interest, even if his is purely in his imagination. Some viewers have visited him in person, and started helping him get out and about.'

My next slide contained a whole array of different faces.

'My vision is Mrs Lewinski, wondering if she needs to bring her patio pots in for the winter. It's Barb and Mick, who, after debating whether they'd need a gazebo for their golden wedding anniversary party, got offered a discount from a local marquee company. It's the local rock-climbing group, the ramblers and the sailors. It's the village fair and the sports days and the street parties. It's making the people who tune in know that they aren't alone, because those day-to-day things that matter to them matter to me too.

'Whatever the future of forecasting, I know that, for me, people are the heart of it. And that's why they'll watch BWM Today rather than click on to the weather app. Because people will always need people.'

There was a long silence. I scanned the room of blank faces, not daring to look at Baxter. At the moment that I thought I might just melt into a puddle of mortification right there on the antique rug, Lincoln muttered, 'The rest of us might as well pack up and go home, then.'

I released a huge breath I hadn't realised I'd been holding, and the five other candidates offered a smattering of applause that was just warm enough for me to chance a peep at Baxter.

His one, decisive nod would have been enough in itself, but when he added a wink it was all I could do not to jump up and down on the spot.

'That was incredible,' Henry whispered as I scuttled to sit back next to him. 'I knew you would be good, but that was... perfect.'

He looked at me, brilliant blue eyes shining, that rare grin brazenly taking up the whole of his face, and my heart twisted inside my chest. I had spent years believing that Henry and I loathed the very air each other breathed, and now here he was, in Scotland, two days before Christmas, cheering me on with nothing but pure intentions. What a pathetic, wretched waste of a childhood friend that had been.

## 14

Melody informed us that dinner was at seven, to be followed by the final round of the interview. That gave us two hours to chill out, fret, or cram in some last-minute prep, depending upon our personality. All of us except for Lincoln, that was. Now sitting at fifth place, he decided it was time to head home.

'Do you think it's safe to leave now?' I asked, once he'd made his announcement.

He shrugged. 'I'll be careful. Even if I end up having to stop somewhere, at least I can tell my husband I tried.'

Henry, who had no reason to do anything other than relax, decided to stay in the library and read a book he'd found on ancient astronomy. I, on the other hand, wanted to lie down with my shoes off and check my phone. If I squeezed in a restorative snooze, so much the better.

While I was catching up with my social media community, a message arrived from Jed. I'd asked him for an update straight after lunch, but had anticipated that it might take a while for him to reply.

Some progress

I sent a brief reply.

And???

I held my breath while waiting for him to send a follow-up.

1 minute

Three endless minutes later, he called.

'Sorry. We were about to leave for the carol service. I had to pretend I forgot my wallet.'

'So?'

'Right, so I've found a programme for the play Nana Joy was in when she must have got pregnant, *A Murder in Paris*. I've started working through the cast and crew for potential fathers. It was a small production, which means fewer options but also less-well-known ones, so some of the names are a dead end.'

'Anyone promising?'

'A couple of maybes. But remember it might not even be someone from this play. It could be a friend, or a neighbour. Someone she met at a party.'

'I know, but this is still before the swinging sixties. She might have been out and about with different men, but I don't think she'd have gone to bed with just anyone.'

'There was a lot of media speculation at the time. If it was easy to work out, then one of those journalists would have cracked it. If it was a full-blown love affair, Nana Joy succeeded in keeping it a secret.'

I thought about that. 'Someone must have known. A best

friend. Or her agent. The cleaner. Do we know who any of those people are?'

'Bea, I'm not going to be able to find out who Nana Joy's cleaner was from sixty years ago. Even if she is still alive.'

'No, but maybe Nana Joy would tell you, and then you could contact her daughter, who she'd revealed the secret to before she passed away...'

'That's a lot of work to find out the name of someone who is probably also dead, and if not is highly unlikely to have the funds to keep Charis House going, even if they wanted to.'

My stomach clenched in a horrible knot at the reminder of why Jed was chasing down these flimsy leads.

'I know. But miracles have a much higher chance of happening if you try.'

Jed blew a long sigh down the phone. 'Okay, I'm not giving up yet.'

'Once I'm back, you know I'll help.'

'How's the interview going?'

'You wouldn't believe me if I told you.'

'That bad?'

'Well, I'm top of the scoreboard, so not that bad, no.'

'The scoreboard? Oh, hang on a minute.' There was a pause while Jed had a muffled conversation with someone else. 'Okay, Mia says hi and she hopes you're smashing it but we really need to go.'

After that, it was almost impossible to drag my mind away from what was happening at home. Whether or not I changed jobs seemed insignificant compared to losing Charis House. When my parents first started plans to open an alternative provision school, they were met with a torrent of local protest from Hatherstone residents concerned about the impact of inviting 'those kinds of children' into the local area. Mum and Dad worked tirelessly to show that 'those kinds of children' deserved the right kind of chance, inviting anyone who'd listen to summer picnics, sporting events, and the Christmas Spectacular. The work experience programme became so successful that there were soon more offers of placements than there were pupils to fill them.

Inevitably, some kids never overcame their issues. There were the heartbreaking stories of those who ended up in prison, homeless, ricocheting from one bad decision to another. Others we never heard from again. But they were the exception. Two walls of the principal's office were covered in photographs of prom nights, college graduations, and young adults proudly wearing the uniform of their first job. You could find Charis House alumni working in local supermarkets, the animal rescue centre, and the hairdresser's. Even our GP was an ex-student.

The thought that all that might come to an end was like a shard of ice in my chest, turning my blood cold. However far-fetched our plan, it had to work, because the alternative was quite simply unbearable.

After a good cry and a few more minutes staring into space, I decided that it was time to pull myself together and regather my focus, and the best way I could think of to do that was to find Henry.

'Okay?' he asked, looking surprised when I came and plonked myself into the seat next to him.

'Why, can you tell I've been crying?' I whispered. There was no one else in the room, but Baxter had made it clear that there were cameras everywhere.

'No.' Henry sat up and gave me that look that made me feel like a scientific specimen. 'Why have you been crying?'

'I spoke to Jed.'

'Oh. Bad news?'

I shook my head. 'No news to speak of.'

'I see.'

He really did.

'Worst Christmas present ever?' he asked a moment later.

'Given or got?' I asked, pulling my legs up onto the sofa as I swivelled around to face him.

'Got, surely? Why would you give someone a bad present?'

'Lack of ideas, time, or money? Revenge? Because you were broke and desperate so you baked your whole family cookies using the block of chocolate found in the back of a random cupboard and didn't bother to read the label first?'

Henry's mouth twitched. 'Okay, given, then. What's the story?'

I grabbed a cushion and buried my head in it. 'It was Dad's chocolate laxative. End of story because the details aren't for sharing.'

Henry winced, and then grinned before wincing again.

'Your turn.'

He thought about this for a minute. I knew he'd found an answer when his ears started turning pink.

'Spill.'

He coughed, looked down, glanced at me out of the corner of his eye, and then gave in, twisting around so that we were facing each other.

'Concert tickets to see The Last Loris.'

'What? That's an amazing present! I was obsessed with that band. How can that possibly be your worst present?'

'Because the person I got them for made up with her boyfriend about an hour before I had a chance to give them to her.'

My heart hovered between beats for a second.

'I ended up going with my dad. Not quite the same.'

The air in the library had become very still.

'You could have given them to her anyway.'

'Really?' Henry raised one eyebrow. 'How do you think that would have gone? Worst-case scenario, she'd have laughed in my face and all my fears about how she genuinely hated my guts rather than simply pretended to in order to save face would be proven right. Best-case scenario, she'd have taken the tickets and gone with her boyfriend.'

'How is that the best case?'

'Because then she'd have got to see her favourite band.'

I picked at a loose thread on the tapestry cushion. It took a few more pounding heartbeats to find the courage to look at him, but I managed it. 'Have you always been this nice?'

'I was trying to make the girl I was infatuated with happy. Some would say my motives were purely selfish.'

'And then there are some who actually know you.'

'Best ever present?' Henry asked, just as the crackling silence became almost too much to bear.

'Sounds like my best ever present was stolen by your dad.'

He broke into a full-on blush then, ducking his head, mouth curled in embarrassment.

Before I could do anything to lighten the tension, my phone beeped.

How did it go? Are we going to be neighbours? X

So now my heart was thumping for a whole other reason.

I quickly turned forwards on the sofa again and typed a brief reply.

Going well so far, but won't know outcome until tomorrow lunchtime

I paused before pressing send. Kiss or no kiss?

One kiss. I wasn't a monster.

Except that my quaking fingers accidentally added four and I automatically pressed send before my brain could process it.

Sorry about all the xxxxs! My hand slipped!!

Adam replied instantly

No need to apologise. I'm hard to resist

He added the laughing emoji but his next message didn't feel like a joke.

And I've missed your kisses xxxxx

Crap.

How did I let myself end up back here again? I knew that we couldn't be trusted to stick to a simple, friendly 'how are you?' I should never have replied to his first message. I'd opened a door that only led in one direction: to more sadness and crying and feeling as if my heart had been ripped out and stamped on.

I needed a short, sharp reply to shut this down.

Only my traitorous brain refused to come up with anything, instead reminding me of how lovely Adam could be. I'd tried to walk away from him so many times, and every time we couldn't resist returning to each other, like homing pigeons or those penguins who mate for life. Maybe I should simply give in and accept the inevitable. He was my person, for better or worse, and it was time to stop fighting it and find a way to live with the worse. Getting this job would be a good start.

*No! No, no, no! Stop this now!* I gave myself a mental slap around the face. *There was a reason you broke up with Adam, and that's not changed.*

*But remember all those amazing times we had together?*

*Remember all those amazing times you DIDN'T have, because he forgot to turn up, or yet again decided his music came first...*

*Yes, but if I lived in London it would be different! Or at least, it might be? Isn't it worth a try?*

'It's seven.' Henry mercifully interrupted my frenzied internal debate.

I decided that not replying to Adam was probably the wisest option for now, instead following Henry into the dining hall where the other candidates already sat waiting.

'Great, that's everyone,' Melody said, tapping on her iPad.

Two minutes later, Baxter strode in and took a seat at the head of the table, with Summer on one side and Ben on the other. I was initially relieved to be sitting furthest away where I could avoid his scrutiny. However, by the time we'd finished the scallop starter, this time served by two adult waiters, it was clear that Summer saw things very differently.

If she'd spent the meal flirting with Baxter I'd have felt justifiably irked. Watching her engage him in animated discussions about media and other current affairs, ensuring he virtually ignored the rest of us, was a genius move. Rather than the slinky dress she'd worn the previous night, she had on a sophisticated black suit with a cream camisole. Her hair was perfect, her make-up understated, and she looked every inch the national weather presenter.

Ben and Calvin both tried valiantly to wheedle their way into the conversation, but Baxter was having none of it. Ben eventually gave up and started chatting to me and Henry about other things. Calvin merely sat in silence, giving the ivy centrepiece such a death stare I half expected it to shrivel up and wither before our eyes.

The veneer of a pleasant dinner party cracked as soon as the desserts arrived. When Melody clicked the scoreboard that lit up on a screen behind Baxter's head, Calvin dropped his spoon with a clatter and Ben gasped.

Henry, presumably emboldened by having nothing to lose, asked the question the rest of us were thinking but didn't really want to know the answer to.

'Why has Summer moved to first place?'

Baxter threw him a look of mild amusement. 'I changed my mind. A vital business skill, knowing when to overturn your own decision.' He took a large spoonful of raspberry posset. 'Another vital business skill is being able to accurately assess the competition and hone in on their weak spots. Your final task is to do just that. We'll start with Bea. Calvin, kick us off. Why shouldn't I give Bea the job?'

'What?' Calvin looked horrified. The rest of us did, too. Me especially.

Baxter shovelled in another spoonful while he waited.

'She's... not very professional.' Calvin shrugged. 'That whole cutesy, pinafore, "let's all be friends" thing is all well and good for a local news programme, but can it work on a national scale?'

'Anything else?'

Calvin shook his head, his gaze fixed on his own plate.

'Ben.'

'Um... Bea is great but I'm not sure how much she wants this. Is she going to give it everything she's got? Today's weather hunt suggests she'll be offering your competitors tips, not poaching their viewers.'

'And?'

Ben screwed his face up to deliver his final blow. 'She can be a bit irritating.'

Ouch.

Baxter jerked his chin at Henry, who merely shook his head in disgust.

Without waiting for her cue, Summer reached across the table and patted my hand. 'You appreciate that this is a job interview. I fully expect you to maul me to shreds when it's my turn.' She then turned to Baxter and let rip.

'She's more than a bit irritating. Several of her colleagues have complained that she's unpredictable and difficult to work with.'

'That's not true!' I couldn't help blurting.

'Not your turn,' Baxter barked. 'Continue, Summer.'

'Is it true that you've missed numerous important meetings, failed to meet deadlines, and basically stumble from one disaster to another? Behind the camera, she's a liability. She applied for this job because she knows she's on borrowed time. I agree with Ben. She doesn't want it. More to the point, she's not capable of doing it. For goodness' sake, she didn't even get organised enough to know about this interview until the actual day!'

I blinked furiously, tears smarting behind my eyeballs. But there was no way I was about to start crying in front of Baxter Bigwood. Or Summer Collins. Instead, I straightened my shoulders, lifted my wobbling chin and ate my delicious dessert. Screw what Summer said. I was a damn good weather forecaster.

'Duly noted. Let's move on to Summer. Bea?'

I was very aware of Henry sitting next to me, who I felt sure would have passed even if he wanted this job. But then I thought about how much I did want it. I thought about living so close to Adam and my parents finally taking me seriously and getting away from all the crap that had been going on at work, and how Summer was probably to blame. Even if she wasn't, she'd given me permission to maul her. All I needed to do was be honest. It wasn't hard to come up with one or two faults I could mention.

'Summer is...'

Then I looked across at her, caught the flash of fear beneath her flawless eyeliner, and that was enough. I remembered my vision for this role was being myself. And that didn't include slating anyone, no matter what they might have said about or done to me.

'She's charming, and charismatic, and the viewers love her. She joined the weather team straight from drama school, and has done really well in getting to grips with the forecasting and data side of things. I know she'll give this role her all.'

Baxter raised one eyebrow. 'Bea, the team task was this afternoon. This is not some sort of trick, where I'm going to reward you for supporting your competition. I'm giving you one more chance to do what I've asked and tell me why Summer shouldn't have this job.'

'I'll pass, thanks.'

'Excuse me?' Baxter's tone hardened like quick-drying concrete.

I looked him right in the eye, ignored my thundering heart and repeated myself. 'I'll pass. Thank you for the opportunity, but I'm going to leave you to it.'

With that, I pushed back my chair, fumbled to my feet, and walked out, praying that no one could spot my legs trembling. Thankfully, I made it all the way to my room before they gave way altogether.

## 15

Henry was not far behind me.

'Wow,' he offered, leaning back on the chest of drawers.

'Yeah. It looks as though I've wasted two days of your time. Sorry.'

'No apology necessary. I'm impressed you lasted that long, but if you're sure you made the right decision that's what matters.'

'I'm not at all sure,' I replied, sniffing back a sob. 'I really want that job. If I'd thought about it I could probably have found some-thing bad-but-really-good to say about everyone, like, "they have terrible work-life balance, always in the office" or "they're massive nit-pickers who won't leave a stone unturned". The whole thing just felt wrong and mean. No wonder he has no HR staff or producers at these interviews.'

'Definitely a case of power having obliterated any sense of reason or perspective.' He grimaced. 'Summer wangling her way to the top spot proves that.'

'It does potentially solve one of my problems, though. If I'm right about her messing with my calendar and emails, then if she gets this job I can start turning up for meetings again.'

'So, what's the plan, boss? Should I fire up the engine?'

I shook my head. 'Lincoln might have pipped the worst of the storm, but it's going to be horrendous overnight. First thing in the morning we'll be chasing its tail, with far less chance of getting blown off a bridge.'

'Although a decent chance that the snow will have made some of the roads impassable?'

'Better to deal with that in the daytime, though.'

He folded his arms. 'Sure you can stand another night in the same room as Sir Henry of Nerdville?'

I rolled my eyes, but couldn't help a smile. 'As long as you don't blab to anyone.' I shuddered. 'Especially not my family.'

I didn't mention that by now there would be plenty of spare rooms, thanks to four of the candidates' early departures. I also didn't think too hard about why I kept quiet about it. It certainly had nothing to do with Henry's earlier story about how he'd been infatuated with me.

* * *

Ducking out of the last task did mean that we had an evening to fill. I didn't fancy venturing downstairs and risking bumping into Baxter, but Henry was happy to go on a scouting mission, returning with a chess set in a fancy wooden box, on top of which were balanced two mugs of tea and a packet of chocolate digestives.

'Melody intercepted me in the hallway. The security camera must have spotted me stealing the game.'

'Perfect.'

I wasn't a terrible chess player, but twenty minutes in I was ready to throw the board out of the window.

'You do remember that we said we'd head home first thing?'

Henry glanced up, brow still furrowed in concentration. 'Hmmm?'

We'd set the game up on the bedside table in between the two beds. I leant back against my headboard, groaning in frustration. 'If you carry on taking this long we won't be finished by then.'

'Chess is a strategic game. That's how you win, by strategizing.'

'No, that's how you make it completely boring. In which case, nobody wins.'

'I'm not bored.' His hand hovered over a pawn for a few seconds before moving away again.

'Because I don't make you sit there for five minutes when it's my turn!'

'I'm not stopping you. You can take as long as you like.'

He finally picked up the pawn and moved it a space forwards. 'There, your move.'

It was at least two minutes before he realised.

'You're just sat there waiting for me to get bored, aren't you?'

'How do you know I'm not strategizing?'

Henry narrowed his eyes, but I could see a glimmer of amusement in the depths, appearing almost teal in the lamplight. 'Fine. Strategize away.'

I waited another two before realising that I was never going to beat Henry at either chess or the waiting game. It seemed petty to concede, however, so I picked up the nearest piece and plonked it down a few squares away. Henry instantly leant forwards, his frown deepening.

'Do you think I did the right thing?' I asked, eventually.

'I have no idea,' he said, scouring the board. 'I can't figure out your tactics.'

I blew out a big enough sigh for him to look up, and then keep looking as he realised I wasn't talking about chess. Sitting up, he moved to adopt a similar position to me, leaning back on the head-board, arms resting on his bent knees.

'It might depend on how you look at it,' he said. 'Some would say that such a huge career move is easily worth a few comments about three other people's flaws. Especially considering they'd already done the same to you. Do what needs to be done, move on. No big deal.'

'That's not what you'd say though, is it?'

'It's not me who has to live with the decision.'

'But?'

Henry was quiet for a moment. 'I'd say that if your family taught me anything, it's the value of authenticity. Being true to yourself and what you believe to be important in the small things as well as the big ones.' He held my gaze, his voice dropping to a soft rumble. 'I'd say that you're an extraordinary woman. I'm proud to call you my childhood betrothed.'

'Thank you.' I ducked my head, cheeks flushing.

'There'll be other opportunities. Ones that don't include working for Baxter Bigwood. You've proven yourself this weekend to be a first-rate weather forecaster. Those other candidates couldn't come close.'

There was another long silence, Henry's compliments hovering between the beds.

'Best ever Christmas memory?'

'Oh, now that's a tough one.' I pulled one of the pillows into my lap, resting my chin on one hand in a thoughtful pose. 'You know the Armstrongs make a lot of those.'

Although, after swapping stories and reliving our shared history of the over-the-top celebrations our families had colluded in over the years, when I lay in bed later on, all I could do was keep thinking about how, looking back, those memories appeared so different now.

We were packed, ready to go, and sneaking past the angry elves as soon as the first light appeared over the tops of the pine trees. The wind had eased to a soft moan, and the sky was now full of stars, the air crisp and clear.

Snow lay several inches thick upon the top of the car, but Melody had sent her husband, Denzel, and the boys out to clear the driveway.

'This is childhood slavery!' one of them grumbled, stopping to lean on his shovel. 'Excuse me, miss, can you please call the police and tell them that children are being forced into labour?'

'Shut up, Bobby. Slaves don't get paid!' the eldest, Benji, jeered. 'If she calls the police then how do we get McDonald's?'

'Duh, even slaves get given food!'

'None of you will be getting anything if you spend the whole day arguing,' their dad interjected. 'Don't forget, it's Christmas Eve. Not too late for Santa to make a few edits to the naughty list.'

'I bet Santa doesn't agree with child slavery,' Bobby huffed, making another half-hearted stab at a lump of snow. 'Elf slavery, maybe.'

In unspoken agreement, Henry and I each took a shovel off the youngest two children, soon creating a patch around the car that would enable us to at least make a start.

'You owe us a cheeseburger next time we're up.' Henry smiled as he handed the shovel back. 'Oh, and one of the elves asked me to give you this.' He pulled three five-pound notes out of his wallet and gave one to each boy. 'A Christmas tip.'

'Thank you!' The boys grinned as we climbed into the car, attacking another pile of snow with renewed enthusiasm.

'That might be sooner than we'd like,' I suggested, squinting as the rising sun bounced off the gleaming white driveway.

'No chance.' Henry shook his head determinedly as he started to creep forwards. 'I promised your parents that I'd see you safely home by Christmas. I fully intend to keep that promise. Besides, I'd rather stay in the shack we found online than crawl back to Baxter.'

* * *

'I think it might be time to revisit the shack.'

Henry peered through the windscreen, his face grim. We'd been driving for four hours and had so far covered the grand total of thirty miles, thanks to snowdrifts, two more fallen trees blocking different roads, and stopping to check that no one was in the car we spotted hanging out of a ditch.

We'd been banking on the A road we were aiming for being a little easier, but, approaching the junction, we could see a line of cars inching along so slowly that a child had time to jump out, lie down and make a snow angel, then hop back in again.

'Hang on, let me see if there's an alternative route.' I scanned through my various apps as Henry crawled through the slush. 'No. This is definitely our best bet. The further east we go the worse it's going to be. The options are a huge pile-up, a closed bridge, or joining the traffic jam. At least here the cars are moving. And just to be clear, the shack is not an option.'

Right on cue, the cars up ahead rolled to a stop. Henry joined the queue, waving his thanks to the man who'd held back to allow him in. The man gave an ironic, 'what can you do?' wave of his chocolate bar and settled in behind us.

Half an hour and three hundred metres later my fretting started ramping up to panic.

'We aren't going to make it home in time.' I clicked frantically on the apps, but nothing had improved in the last thirty seconds. 'I promised I'd be back for the Christmas Eve buffet.'

'We've still got hours until then. Things will get better the closer we get. Won't they?'

'I need to call Walter.'

A brief and jarringly frank conversation with the only person I knew who knew more about the weather than me, and I slumped back into the seat, pulling my bobble hat down over my face.

'Ungh.'

'Okay. How bad is it?'

I reluctantly pushed my hat back up. 'So, there's this shack...'

Once the decision had been made, there was no pressure to hurry. Walter had assured me that the storm currently settled over a wide area stretching from Yorkshire to Nottingham wouldn't be budging until it had blown itself out in the early hours of the morning. Driving through snow was one thing. Skidding along icy roads in a raging blizzard was plain foolish. Having finished the flasks that Melody had refilled for us, along with the pastries she'd packed us for breakfast, we decided to find somewhere to stock up in preparation for a long day and potentially longer night.

Another treacherous half-hour later we pulled into a service station crammed with other seasonal travellers sheltering from the horrendous conditions. I headed to the shop first, rejoining Henry in the coffee shop queue just in time to hear they'd run out of coffee.

'Peppermint and liquorice tea are the only hot drinks left,' the frazzled barista snapped, eyeing the long snake of people still behind us.

'Fine,' Henry replied, holding out our flasks. 'We'll take as many as you can fit into these.'

We queued at another outlet for two shrivelled-up baked potatoes with grey chilli. Failing to find an empty table, we chose a spot in the far corner away from the worst of the chaos and sat on the floor using our coats as a picnic blanket.

'Bit of a change from last night's dinner,' I said, picking out a chunk of undercooked onion.

'I think I prefer the company,' Henry replied, focused on trying to chop his cremated potato skin.

'At least we're warm and managed to get something hot to eat.'

'Hot?' Henry eyed my cardboard container.

'At least we managed to get something lukewarm to eat.'

'What's the plan, then, boss? Do we hang out here until morning?'

'Seems like the best option.'

At that moment, the double doors opened and what must have been a coachload of men streamed in. They were all wearing football tops and around half of them were carrying cans of beer. They moved like a swarm of flies towards the long-since-sold-out burger outlet, but once they heard the bad news they began breaking off into smaller clumps, odd couples staggering about in circles with their arms around each other singing. Another group started working their way around the tables asking if anyone had any beer, whisky, food, or weed.

'Come on, yous lot!' a particularly red-faced older man

shouted. 'It's nearly Christmas, let's have that festive spirit. We're all in this together, might as well make the most of it!'

He then started singing 'Wonderful Christmastime', only he couldn't remember any of the words beyond the first line, so he sang that over and over until one of his companions swore at him to shut up and gave him a shove into a Christmas tree. Both the tree and the man ended up knocking over a young woman, and things only got worse from there.

Henry did a quick search on his phone. 'Then again, that shack is only three miles away.'

And so it was that after a grovelling phone call by me, followed by Henry phoning back to do some bargaining in his rigid robot voice, we found ourselves taking the next exit off the motorway and crawling along relatively empty roads to the 'enchanting cottage' in the absolute middle of nowhere.

It was now early afternoon, dusk would be settling in a couple of hours, and all I wanted was to be somewhere warm and dry, with a chair to sit on and no drunk men demanding I join their conga line.

The shack was dry, I had to give it that.

There was also a whole sofa.

No drunk strangers – always a bonus.

I did, however, realise that there were a few more things I wanted after all.

We pulled up outside what I supposed was built to resemble a log cabin, but in reality, as we'd seen on the photos, looked more like a tumbledown shed. Apart from another, smaller wooden structure to one side, it was surrounded by snow-coloured fields and not a lot else. The rental agent who we'd managed to get hold of had given us the code for the key safe, which was helpful. Less helpful was finding the key safe empty.

After a few fruitless minutes searching the overgrown front

garden for another one, or any other place where a key could be hidden, we walked around to the back to find that this side of the building didn't even have a door.

'I'll call the rental company back.' Henry hung up a few seconds later. 'The office is closed until the twenty-eighth. Not to worry though, because in case of emergency we can contact the owner via the number in the information folder conveniently located inside the property.'

'We could try next door?' I nodded towards the other building, where an enticing yellowy glow now beckoned us over from a downstairs window.

Henry wasn't happy. 'We can't go knocking on some random person's door on Christmas Eve.'

I gave him a sideways look. 'Surely that's the best day to do it? It's the season of goodwill.'

'Alternatively, those windows look flimsy enough to jimmy open.'

'Not happening.' I started walking over to the other house. 'Not unless we need to, anyway. We're paying enough for this dump without adding on the cost of a broken window.'

It took three drawn-out knocks on the door before it finally opened. I would have gone for the breaking and entering option after knock two failed to get a response, except that would mean losing face in front of Henry.

''Yes?' A deep-set eye peered out at me through a tiny crack in the door.

'Hi!' I gave a little wave. 'We've rented out the cottage next door but there's no key in the safe as promised. I don't suppose you have a spare one? Or the number of the owner?'

'Yes.' The face nodded.

'Um... which one?'

'Both. I took the key to clean the house.' The door opened an inch wider, revealing part of a wrinkled cheek and a hooked nose. 'No renters this week, so I did not put the key back.'

'Right, that makes sense.' I kept smiling. 'We have an email from Dream Cottages to say that we've made a last-minute booking. Here.' I opened up my phone to show her the screen.

'The cottage has not been cleaned.'

'That's okay, we're stranded because of the weather so just need somewhere dry and warm.'

'You will wait here while I clean.'

'No, honestly, it's Christmas Eve, you really don't have to do that...'

The door flung wide open to reveal what at first appeared to be one of the roundest women I'd ever seen. It was only when she stiffly stepped back to let us past that I realised most of the roundness was in fact several layers of thick clothing.

'You wait here,' she barked, fiercely enough that I was inside before I could think about where this might end. 'You, tall man. Come inside.'

Henry, presumably not wanting to leave me alone, promptly joined me in what turned out to be a one-roomed glorified shed. One corner could loosely be described as a kitchen area, including a mini fridge and a two-ring hob sitting on a table in between a kettle and a microwave, and in another was a single bed. The room appeared clean despite the shabbiness, and relatively tidy. The only sign of Christmas was a bunch of fir branches arranged in a jam jar.

'Sit!' The woman growled, pointing at a sagging brown sofa. We immediately obeyed.

'I'm Bea, by the way, and this is Henry.'

'Hmm.' She gave us a good looking-over. 'You can call me Beyoncé.'

'Your name's Beyoncé?'

She narrowed her dark eyes at me. 'You think I couldn't have that name?'

'Um, no. I just... thought there was only one Beyoncé. I didn't realise it was an actual name.'

Especially not a name for middle-aged women with a Russian accent.

Henry nudged my knee with his and nodded at a letter on the rickety coffee table in front of us. The name at the top was Polina Ivanov.

'Right, well, this is very kind of you but we don't want to take up any more of your time.'

'No problem. I have plenty of time.'

She began slowly lowering herself onto a wooden chair, but the layers of clothes she had on underneath her pleated skirt brought her to a stop about six inches above the seat.

'It's very cold in here.' Henry, his scientific assessment of the situation now complete, spoke for the first time. 'Is your heating working?'

She pursed her lips. 'Electric heaters are too much money. I wrap up warm, it's not a problem.'

'What about the fire?'

There was a fireplace built into the wall opposite us.

'I am too old to figure out how to light that stupid thing. My knees can't take it.' She scanned the room as if trying to remember what was happening. 'Ah yes, I will clean the house. You look like people who appreciate a nice, clean place. First, I will make you coffee.'

'No, please, don't worry. We have hot drinks here.'

'You have coffee?'

'Tea.'

'Tea!' She screwed up her face. 'You need good coffee. I promise you have not had coffee like this before.'

'Well, that would be lovely, then, thank you so much.'

Henry glanced at me out of the corner of his eye as she lumbered to the kitchen area. His shoulders were stiff, hands placed in perfect alignment on his thighs.

'It's Christmas Eve!' I whispered. 'She's stuck here on her own. It's not like we've got anything better to do.'

'You still need to call your parents, let them know what's happening.'

'Ah, crap. Yes. I wanted to wait until I was somewhere safe so they had one less thing to freak out about. Once she's gone to start cleaning I'll call.'

Henry turned to look at me properly. 'I'm not sure she's *ever* going to start cleaning.' He swallowed, picking at a non-existent piece of fluff on his jeans. 'I'm also not sure that you're somewhere safe.'

'Here you go.' Beyoncé/Polina handed us two steaming mugs. 'Try it.'

I took a tentative sip, followed by a much larger one. 'This is amazing, thank you.' I nodded at Henry to give his a try. Unfortunately, as he pressed the mug to his lips there was a loud clatter from behind us, causing him to slop a good mouthful down his jacket.

'Ah, Ivan is waking up. I will fetch a cloth for your coat then you can meet him. I have to see to Ivan, then I will go and clean.' She passed Henry a damp dish cloth then started towards a door set into the back wall. I'd presumed it was a cupboard, but perhaps there was more to the dwelling than it seemed.

'No, wait, first I must hide his present!' Polina attempted to hurry back, picking up a woollen item from the table. 'Look, it is not quite finished, but I think he will like it.'

She held up a tiny sleeveless jumper, knitted in green and red stripes.

'Is Ivan a baby?' I asked, my stomach lurching at the thought of a baby living here.

'No, he's twenty-three years old!' she said, with a proud tilt of her chin.

'Right.' I nodded and smiled and tried to pretend that it was perfectly normal for someone to knit a six-inch-wide jumper for a grown man. Or could it be a doll? A dog?

Before I had the chance to find out, my mum called. Promising Henry that I'd be back in a minute ('You'd better be...' was his mumbled reply) I ducked outside to break the news.

'Bea, that weatherman standing in for you was correct for once. The roads are a nightmare! None of the cousins can make it. Margo suggested riding here, but it hardly seems sensible to force a horse into this white-out. What about you and Henry? I really can't see you making it back today. And while I don't want to be the one to say I told you so, if you recall I did query whether once again your job would stop you joining us for Christmas.'

'I'm going to be there for Christmas!'

'Christmas is more than just one day. Anyway, you'll have to stay in Scotland for now.'

'Sweet-Bea!' Dad interrupted. 'Are you okay? Somewhere safe? Are you and Henry taking care of each other?'

'We're fine. We tried to make it back down but didn't get far before realising it was a mistake to keep going. We've found a little cottage to stay the night in, and will be back for Christmas dinner.'

'Humph!' Mum snorted. 'Once upon a time you were going to be here for the week. Then it was back for the buffet! We don't need any more rash promises, thank you. Jonty, you speak to her. I need to check the ham.'

'I'm sorry, Sweet-Bea, she's just upset about having to cancel the party, and she's missing you. It's not the same without you here.'

'No, Dad, *I'm* sorry. I should have stayed with you like I

promised. Mum's got every right to be angry. I feel awful for not being there.'

Dad was quiet for a moment. I could picture him blinking back tears. 'She's not angry. She knows you made the right decision. And you'll be here soon, that's what matters.'

It was my turn to try not to start crying. 'She didn't ask how the interview went.'

'She spent most of this morning baking you a congratulations cake.'

'What?' It took a few seconds to process that. 'She made a *cake*? Do you mean one of those fat-and-sugar-free imposters that she used to make for my birthday?'

'It's chocolate and caramel. Real chocolate and real caramel. With congratulations written on it in Maltesers. She really is very proud of you, Sweet-Bea.'

'That sounds lovely. But you might want to pick off the Maltesers. Or rejig them to say "commiserations".'

'Oh, I'm sorry. We were so sure.' Dad sounded devastated. 'That Bigwood fellow is an idiot who doesn't know a good thing when he sees it.'

'Thanks, Dad. He actually thought I was great until I decided to pull out of the final round.'

'Well, I'm sure you had your reasons.'

'I did. Very good ones. I'll tell you about it when I get back, and I promise you'll be more proud of me than if I'd stayed and got the job.'

'I couldn't be more proud of you no matter what you do.'

'Thank you. Now you need to stop crying and go and find a way to cheer Mum up. I have to get back to Henry.'

'Ooh, yes, Henry! How are you two getting on? Is it—?'

'Bye, Dad!'

I was so distracted by the cake that after going back in the house it took me a good few seconds to notice Henry.

'*What?*' My post-parental mood instantly dissipated. 'Wait, don't move. I have to get a picture.'

Before I could take a photo, the enormous parrot that had been sitting on Henry's head shot into the air, swooping about three inches above my head as it squawked, 'Intruder! Intruder!'

'Ivan, behave!' Polina scolded from where she appeared in the far doorway carrying a box of cleaning products. 'This is no way to treat our guests.'

'Sorry, Beyoncé,' he muttered, returning to land on Henry's head. If a parrot sitting on Henry's head wasn't delightful enough, this one wore a knitted Christmas pudding jumper including a hood and holes for his grey wings.

'That's better. You be friendly while I go and clean.'

'This is really not better,' Henry said, his face a blank mask that I was learning hid a myriad different emotions, in this instance, none of them good.

Too late, Polina had gone.

'How is she going to clean in all those clothes?' I mused, watching her waddle across the garden.

'Not the top question in my mind right now,' Henry replied through gritted teeth.

'Oh?' I sat down on the chair, unable to hide my smile. 'What would that be?'

'That would be how have we managed to end up in an even worse situation than the last one?'

'It's Christmas Eve. Embrace the adventure.'

'If it craps on my head, I'm blaming you.'

# 17

An hour or so later, to our relief, Polina returned. She'd removed at least a few of the layers, and was overjoyed to discover that she wouldn't be needing to put them on again, thanks to Henry having started a fire once he'd persuaded Ivan to relocate to a more suitable perch on the end of the bed.

'A Christmas miracle! You are an angel sent from God himself. Please, sit back down and I will get food.'

'Really, that's not necessary.' Henry remained standing. 'Thank you for letting us wait here, and for the delicious coffee, but we'll be going now.'

'Henry,' I hissed. 'We can't leave her on her own on Christmas Eve.'

'She's not on her own,' he whispered back. 'She's got Ivan.'

I gave him a fierce look. He responded by closing his eyes. 'Please don't make me stay here. I've had about as much *different* as I can take.'

'Here you are. Complimentary hamper. Enjoy.' Polina held out a small wicker basket containing milk, mince pies, a bottle of wine, and a few other treats tucked inside. 'Please don't take the basket when you leave. It is my last one.'

'This is wonderful, thank you so much...' I glanced at Henry's desperate eyes but couldn't help myself. 'I don't suppose you'd like to join us...'

'You suppose correct. Thank you for the invitation but no thank you. I will speak to my family now on the video call.'

'Okay, well, merry Christmas!' Henry was already waiting for me by the door. 'Thanks again.'

'Merry Christmas to you. And don't thank me until you've tried spending a night in that death trap. Don't come knocking back on my door, either. I clean, that's it. Any other problems you speak to that owner crook.'

With that, she slammed the door shut so hard my teeth rattled.

Henry, who had retreated firmly back into robot mode, resolutely plodded back through the snow to the car and fetched our bags. This time, Polina had left the key in the door. It was with some trepidation that we ventured inside.

'At least it's clean,' was the best I could manage, after an initial glance around.

'It's not difficult to keep a virtually empty room clean, though, is it?'

Henry wasn't exaggerating. There were in fact three rooms – the main living space and bathroom on the ground floor, and a tiny bedroom wedged into the attic. The living room included a sofa, a lopsided bookcase containing no books, and a kitchen area similar to Polina's. The bathroom had a basic sink, toilet, and bath, no shower. The bedroom had a bed.

To her credit, Polina had added a vase of pine branches similar to the one in her home, so at least that helped mask the smell of must and rot. It wasn't quite enough, however, to detract from the bare beige walls, mud-coloured carpet and dismal not-a-lot-else.

'It's even worse than the photos.' I marvelled.

'Oh, it gets even worse than that,' Henry said, coming out of the bathroom. 'There's no running water.'

'What?' I hurried over to the kitchen only to discover there was no sink. Trying the taps in the bathroom failed to produce anything other than a horrible squeak.

'Maybe the pipes have frozen,' I worried, while Henry flicked through the information folder on the kitchen table.

'Oh no, it's fine.' He looked at me, and to my relief there was a hint of humour in his eyes. 'We can use the well.'

My relief evaporated. 'The well?'

'It's behind the house. Perfectly safe to drink if we boil it first, and deep enough in the ground that it might not even be frozen.'

While I was still processing the well, Henry carried on.

'Speaking of freezing, rather than having to endure boring old central heating, I get to build my second fire of the day.'

I had a look at the fireplace. 'There's no wood. Or kindling. Even if we can get a fire going, it's hardly going to keep us warm overnight.'

I slumped onto the sofa, as it suddenly hit me. I wasn't overly precious about staying in fancy places with luxuries like running water and heating. I was as up for an adventure as the next person. But it was Christmas Eve, and the Coach House would be aglow with good cheer. Even without the extra family members it would be jam-packed with warmth and laughter and loud conversations. The dining-room table would be bulging with tasty treats alongside Mum's tasteless ones.

There'd be the scent of cinnamon and cloves, cranberry, and onions as everyone pitched in preparing for tomorrow's feast, Nana Joy singing along to the Christmas playlist until eventually everyone else joined in.

The tree would be lit, presents slowly accumulating beneath

the boughs. There'd be candles or bowls of chocolates on every spare surface. We'd gather around the wonky advent scene that someone carved in woodworking class to place the final nativity piece in the manger.

There'd be hugs and bickering and something would get broken, but no one would mind. After dinner those who had the energy would wrap up in hats and scarves and take the dogs for a moonlit romp in the forest, coming home to mugs of extra-thick hot chocolate or mulled wine.

This house was the exact opposite of that.

I pressed my eyes shut but it was too late to prevent a tiny tear from squeezing out and trickling down my face.

'Here.' I opened my eyes to find Henry standing in front of me, holding out a glass of wine and a huge slice of Christmas cake. 'Have some fat-ridden, sugar-loaded, ultra-processed cake.'

'Thank you.'

He fetched a second glass and plate and came to sit beside me.

'I'm okay, really. Just a mild attack of homesickness.'

'I'm not surprised; you've got a first-rate home.'

When I opened my mouth to reply, he shot me a sharp look. 'Don't you dare apologise again for me being here, not there.'

'Yes, but—'

'My choice, remember?'

'I'm not sure you had enough information to make an informed choice.'

Henry laughed. 'No one had that information. And if we did, we wouldn't have believed it.'

He reached his glass out to chink it against mine. 'Merry Christmas, Bea.'

'It'd be a lot merrier if we had a fire going.'

'I'll be right on it, boss.'

'One more thing,' I asked, as Henry started another fruitless search for the non-existent firewood. 'Purely from a scientific perspective, no rush or anything, but how is flushing the toilet going to work?'

\* \* \*

A couple of hours later, things were looking, if not great, then as good as they were going to get. After leaving a lengthy message on the owner's phone, Henry and I had found a tiny wood store around the back of the house, and after using a breadknife to hack off some shavings for kindling, together we'd got a decent blaze crackling.

We'd trudged back and forth through the wind-whipped snow until the kettle, cistern and the two saucepans were topped up with well water, and all that exertion had warmed us up to the extent that we could take our coats off. It was now early evening, and we'd settled down on the sofa to a feast of service-station microwave lasagne, supplemented with the basket of goodies from Polina.

While Henry was clearing up, I checked my phone and found that Dad had sent me photos of the Christmas Eve back home, including messages from my nieces and nephew about how much they missed me and hoped I got home soon. I was able to smile and record a reply with only the tiniest wobble in my voice.

I had a brief message from Jed to confirm that Mum had already questioned his overly long bathroom visit, accusing him of dodging the to-do list. There was no way he'd be able to do any more research before I was back. I replied to say that he shouldn't be thinking about that anyway. The next couple of days were a time to celebrate what we had, not worry about what we might lose.

There were a few more messages from colleagues and old friends wishing me a merry Christmas, which I quickly replied to. And then the inevitable follow-up from Adam.

I was trying to be cool and not ask, but I can't stop wondering whether I need to start planning your welcome tour?

I took a deep breath, squishing down the ache that accompanied walking away from a possible chance for Adam and me to make things work.

Not this time

It seemed like forever until the three dots morphed into a reply.

I'm sorry. You must be gutted.

If you need cheering up, I can be free to talk

Knowing that the one Christmas Eve we weren't together he could be free to talk did nothing to cheer me up. What annoyed me even more was how strongly I still felt the pull to say yes. Adam knew how to make me feel better. That had never been our problem. The problem had been how infrequently he'd been around to do that, and how often that made me feel worse. I was so used to gratefully accepting his crumbs of attention when they were offered, it was hard to turn him down even now I knew that there was no happy ever after waiting at the end of the conversation.

'Is everyone okay?'

I looked up to see Henry with two more glasses of wine. He'd changed into the kind of Henry-ish trousers I was used to, along with a cardigan in the same shade of dark brown as his hair. He'd taken out his contacts and now wore a pair of thick, square glasses. If I'd seen that outfit anywhere else, I'd have thought it dreadful. On Henry, it somehow worked.

I typed Adam a brief reply.

Thanks, but I'm fine.

'Yeah. The Christmas-o-meter is measuring full Armstrong.' I put my phone in my pocket and scooted up on the sofa so he could sit down. 'Have you heard from your family?'

'Not today. They said they'd call tomorrow.' He took a sip of wine and leant back, taking his glasses off and closing his eyes. 'It'll be a five-minute how are you, thanks for the gift tokens and see you some time in the new year. Barely a flicker on the Christmas-o-meter.'

I watched him for a moment. The shadows cast from the bare bulb exaggerated the tired creases on his face. I felt a sudden urge to reach over and smooth them away.

'Most embarrassing Christmas family incident?'

Henry's mouth twitched, his eyes still closed. 'There's no way I'm going to beat you on that one.'

'Oh really? What about your dad's donkey costume?'

The twitch grew to a smile. 'Well, if we're commenting on each other's dads, then how about the Christmas Spectacular when your dad tried doing a rap?'

'Oh no, that wasn't the worst.'

Henry opened his eyes, turning to face me, his cheek still resting on the back of the sofa. 'Now this I have to hear.'

'You must remember, when I was thirteen and Dad first introduced the hairdressing course. He let this girl, Isla, practise on the whole family. Jed got out of it because he was sneaky enough to give himself a buzz cut the day before. Me, Mum, and Dad ended up with exactly the same hairstyle the week before Christmas. Which also happened to be the worst hairstyle imaginable.'

Henry burst out laughing at the memory. 'Oh yes! I remember your identical mops. I thought you'd got matching wigs for an act at first.'

'Believe me, if I'd have got hold of a wig I'd have worn it.'

Henry crinkled his eyes. 'I didn't think they were that bad.'

It was my turn to laugh. 'That's because your hair was almost as awful!'

His mouth dropped open in pretend shock. 'Are you dissing my hair?'

'Well, at least it matched your overall look, I suppose.'

'And for one sweet Christmas you got to match too.'

With nothing else to do, not even the Internet to provide entertainment, we spent the rest of the evening talking, filling in the gaps from the previous few years, asking questions about each other's past, present, and hopes for the future. While I'd once considered Henry to be easy to talk to because I didn't care what he thought, I now found that it went deeper than that. As much as prior to this bizarre trip I'd have sworn that Henry Fairfax and I were different in all the ways that mattered, when it came to our values, what lay at the heart of us, we were far more similar than I'd have wanted to admit.

I felt comfortable with Henry because although he set standards for himself that included stopping to help random strangers in a service station, or driving through snow to help out a not-quite-friend, he never once judged me for who I chose to be. I was used to the people close to me being judge, jury, and executioner. Talking with someone who was genuinely interested in why I might disagree with him, who listened with a gentle furrow of intent concentration, rather than interrupting to explain why I was wrong, was a refreshing change.

Had Adam ever listened to me like this? I wondered while boiling some of our precious water reserves for mugs of hot chocolate, determined to keep at least one Armstrong Christmas Eve tradition. With a twist in my stomach, I realised that conversations with Adam had been mainly about Adam. My life, my work, my thoughts had been a sub-plot in the grand biopic of Adam's future rise to stardom.

The kind of attention I got from Adam made me feel flattered. Henry made me feel *interesting*.

Not that I was comparing the two, given that I'd been in love with Adam for twelve years, and until this weekend Henry had been the oddball kid from my childhood. I did think – or rather, I *hoped* – that this Christmas had maybe realigned our relationship to being friends.

I had no intention of ever mentioning him being infatuated with me. However, we were laughing about a bonfire night where the faulty fireworks started shooting indiscriminately across the Charis House playing field, when I accidentally brought it up.

'Your mum, though!' I exclaimed. 'She kept going on about how you'd thrown yourself in front of me to protect me, and how you were my knight in an orange cagoule. I was so irritated because you'd obviously dived out of the firing line without noticing I was standing there.'

Henry looked sideways at me. 'Given that this happened during the height of my excruciating crush on you, there wasn't a second of that party I didn't know exactly where you were standing.'

'What?' I shook my head in disbelief. 'Are you saying your mum was *right*?'

He gave a rueful shrug. 'Just trying to do the decent thing.'

'I don't know whether to ask about this crush. I feel like I should know about it, but I don't want things to get awkward.'

'I'm surprised you didn't twig at the time.' Henry blew out a sigh. 'It was a standard teenage-boy-with-no-female-friends obsession. You were the obvious target.'

'Except that I had a boyfriend.'

'In a way, that made it easier. It was a great excuse to avoid doing anything about it apart from listen to depressing music while wallowing in my cursed existence.'

'I cannot believe that teenage Henry Fairfax was capable of wallowing.'

'A temporary state induced by the adolescent changes in my brain. I got over it. No need for any awkwardness now.'

'That's a relief. I wouldn't want to be responsible for your broken heart.'

He smiled. 'Top Christmas film?'

Subject closed.

* * *

'That's the last of it,' Henry said, stepping in the front door.

I looked at the pitiful number of logs in his arms with dismay. 'That won't last us the night.'

He carefully placed them on the floor a safe distance away from the fireplace. 'The snow's so deep that we won't find anything else dry enough to burn.'

'So we're now on heating rations, as well as water.' I added it to the list of complaints that I'd be reporting to the letting agents as soon as we had Internet or they were answering the phone again.

'If we keep the doors shut then hopefully we can retain some heat in here.'

'What about upstairs, though? There was ice on the inside of the bedroom window when we arrived. That roof keeps in about as much heat as a tent.'

'I'll sleep upstairs. I can borrow Beyoncé's trick and layer up. Unless you'd rather I had the sofa?'

I handed him his hot chocolate. 'I won't be able to sleep knowing you're upstairs potentially slipping into a hypothermic coma. Could we both sleep in here? If we bring down the pillows and bedding, use the extra cushions, one of us could sleep on the floor.'

'If you're sure?'

'We've already spent two nights as roomies, might as well make it a third if it avoids freezing to death.'

It didn't take long to create a makeshift bed in front of the fire. We agreed that I'd take the sofa, with a duvet for warmth, and Henry would take the floor, with two blankets and assorted clothing.

We added a carefully rationed-out log to the fire, turned off the lights, and settled in, trying to ignore the temperature already dropping.

It no longer felt strange to have Henry's solid presence nearby as I slept, and after another eventful day I found myself dozing off almost instantly. However, when I woke up with a start, every bone in my body shivering, I was disheartened to see it was only two in the morning.

Teeth chattering, muscles clenched as they braced against the cold, I pulled my hat back down over my ears and debated whether I dared brave exiting the duvet to find another jumper.

'You know how you didn't want me freezing to death?' Henry's soft rumble interrupted my fretting.

'That would be my preferred option, yes.'

'I don't suppose you'd be open to sharing the duvet?'

Without saying anything, I slipped off the sofa, bringing the duvet with me. Henry deftly arranged the blankets so that the bedding was evenly distributed and then settled back down on the far edge of the cushions.

The additional layers helped, but not enough. It felt as though my blood had turned to icy slush and I'd never get warm again. After a long minute, Henry rolled onto his back, shifting close enough that I could feel his heat radiating like a giant hot-water bottle. There was no risk of this man freezing to death. I couldn't resist inching a tiny bit closer.

'Come here, then.'

In a smooth motion that brought back vivid memories of the time we'd shared a bed all those years ago, Henry wrapped his arm around me and tucked me up against his chest.

'Thank you,' I murmured, relaxing into the softness of his two jumpers, the darkness creating an intimacy that made me bold. 'I think you must be the kindest person I've ever met.'

'I told you once before, I can't sleep if I can hear your bones clacking together.'

'Happy Christmas, Henry,' I added a short while later.

'Happy Christmas to you too,' he rumbled back, giving me a gentle squeeze.

And lying there in the pitch black, my head resting on the slow, solid thud of his heart, warm, safe, utterly comfortable, I realised that I was happier than I'd been in a very long time.

# 18

When I next drifted into consciousness, the first thing I became aware of was a jarring pain where the cushions had slipped apart leaving my hip resting on the floor. Squinting my eyes open, the second thing was an exposed patch of skin on the side of Henry's neck, a mere inch away. I breathed in carefully, not wanting to wake him, inhaling the now familiar trace of coconutty shower gel mingled with his natural scent. While not yet light, the inky darkness had lessened to a greyish hue that promised dawn was on its way. I snuggled deeper into the duvet, closed my eyes again and, suddenly, my nerves began to prickle, alerting me to the fact that I was lying beside the warm, solid body of A Man.

*It's not A Man, it's Henry!* I ordered my now accelerating heart to stop being so silly. I pulled away to remove the ridiculous temptation to press my lips against that smooth patch of neck and decided that the best thing to do was turn around and wriggle far enough away that I could pretend he wasn't there.

Only, for reasons that sent my mind spinning in all sorts of unexpected directions, my body refused to cooperate. Every sense had sprung to life in acknowledgement of this other person in such close proximity. I should have felt awkward, on edge. Maybe even a bit icky.

That was not how I felt.

I felt alarmingly, incomprehensibly attracted to Henry Fairfax.

Before I could allow *that* thought to develop, I slithered out from under the covers and clambered to my feet, scuttling off to the bathroom without checking if he was awake or not.

We'd left a full saucepan in the sink and I didn't hesitate in splashing the frigid water over my face, rubbing off the remnants of sleep and the unnerving feelings that had seemingly appeared out of nowhere.

I glared at myself in the mirror, straightened my hat, and jabbed my finger to emphasise the point.

'Don't even go there!' I whispered. 'Pull yourself together! It's *Henry*!'

*Ah, but that's the real point*, my traitorous heart whispered back. *It's Henry. And he's not who you thought he was... and once upon a time he was attracted to you, too...*

The only way to shake this off was to keep moving so forcefully I couldn't think. I clattered out of the bathroom, flicked on the kettle and paced up and down alongside the table while it took forever to boil.

'Are you okay?'

I nearly jumped out of my skin at the sound of his voice, despite having to acknowledge that no one would have been able to sleep while I was exuding so much nervous tension. Forcing myself to glance over, I felt a rush of relief. It was only Henry, after all. Sitting up in the pile of blankets, his hair a mess, face dark with stubble and wearing a bile-coloured fleece beneath his cardigan. I continued looking at him for a few more seconds, just to be sure that the disturbing feelings had gone.

*Phew.*

'Bea?'

'Oh! Um, yes. I'm fine. Trying to keep warm. I don't suppose you could get the last two logs burning while I sort breakfast?'

'Have you checked the weather?' He stood up, stretching so that his hands brushed the ceiling, revealing a flash of skin in between his cardigan and the top of his crumpled trousers.

The feelings twitched in interest, so I flipped around and started scooping coffee into mugs. 'Not yet.'

'Wow, is it a special day today or something?'

'I've literally just got up.'

'I'd have expected you to scroll through all the juicy data before getting out of bed.'

'I might have done, if I hadn't been in bed with you.'

Unfortunately, I turned around with the mugs just as I said it, so he got to see my look of horror accompanied by cheeks bursting into flames. Henry flicked immediately into robot mode, kneeling down and focusing on precisely positioning the logs on top of last night's ashes.

I left his mug on the floor nearby and retreated back to the kitchen area, busying myself with opening the packet of crumpets we'd scavenged at the service-station shop.

'There's no toaster,' I said, once Henry had the fire blazing. I walked over holding out a crumpet stuck on the end of a fork. Sitting on the cushions toasting our breakfast was a helpful distraction from the vaguely weird atmosphere still loitering, as if something significant had happened that neither of us wanted to talk about. Using the last items in the hamper, I introduced Henry to cheese and chutney on crumpets, which he initially regarded with deep suspicion, until he tried one and had to admit it was the only way to eat crumpets from now on.

We took our final crumpets outside with another mug of coffee, perching on a stone wall at the back of the house. As Walter had predicted, the wind had settled and the air was crisp and clear. We watched the sunrise streak across the pale winter sky, illuminating the snowfall with a glittering rainbow of gold, reds and oranges.

'Almost as good as the forest.' Henry breathed a contented sigh as a flock of crows danced across the field beyond the wall.

I nodded in agreement. 'Speaking of which...'

'You're right.' He took a final swig of coffee and stood up. 'We need to get you home. First, though, I got you a present.'

I followed him back inside, assuming he must have found something at the service station the day before and feeling relieved that I'd thought to grab something for him, too.

'It's in the bedroom.' Henry had a strange smile on his face that caused me to hesitate. 'There wasn't room to hide it down here.'

Baffled at what he'd been able to sneak out of the service station and up the stairs, I approached them with no small sense of trepidation.

'Hang on, wait!' He then made things worse by squeezing past me and rushing into the room, closing the door until he called out, 'You can come in now,' with what I could only interpret as unbridled glee.

I slowly opened the door, finding the poky bedroom veiled in shadow, and what appeared to be Henry, crouching down in the middle of the room holding out one hand. For a second I thought this was some horrifying proposal, until the light suddenly clicked on. There was an unearthly squeal, as the light revealed a hideous grin, mismatched eyes rolling about in different directions and an outfit even worse than Henry's.

'Aaagh!' I jumped back onto the top step, almost tumbling down the whole staircase until Henry dived out of the doorway and grabbed me. Several uneven breaths later he pulled back to examine me.

'Sorry,' he managed once he'd ascertained that he'd not caused a stroke. It was hard to accept the apology when his eyes were shimmering with laughter and he was unable to stop his mouth twitching.

I shook his hand off my arm and went to examine the elf more closely. 'When did you pilfer this?'

'I thought it was a good candidate for worst ever present.'

'It would have won worst ever Christmas accident if I'd broken my neck on the stairs.'

'Sorry.'

'Sorry doesn't count if you're laughing while you say it!'

'Does this help?' He came to join me by the elf, whose eyes were still rolling about accompanied by the horrible squealing sound. Henry pointed to a small box bouncing in the elf's hand as it jerked up and down.

'I'm not touching it. If that's for me you need to give it me yourself.'

He turned off the elf using a switch at the back and then retrieved the box, which was wrapped in a sheet of A4 paper tied with a shoelace.

'Can I open it away from this abomination?'

'I think you'd better go downstairs before you hurt his feelings.'

Once back in the main room, I fetched the present I'd wrapped in the cover of a Christmassy magazine and we swapped boxes.

I suspected it before I'd even started unwrapping, but it didn't lessen the glow that spread up from my belly and across my face as I removed the paper. Henry had bought me a small gift box of chocolate, on which was printed 'Best Christmas Ever because it's with you'.

He shrugged, ears pink and expression uncertain. 'It was all they had left, and, you know. I thought it might be funny.'

'Funnier than your other present, that's for sure.' I looked at him, feeling fidgety and almost flustered as he opened his to discover the exact same gift.

His eyebrows raised briefly in surprise before he looked back at me, eyes intent, all trace of humour gone though he was still just about smiling. 'Thank you. I love it.'

'Me, too.'

'Duly noted for future presents: chocolate, yes, creepy animatronics, no.'

'Duly noted: Henry is going to buy me future presents.'

'Contrary to all reason and logic, Armstrong Christmases have kind of grown on me. I think I'll stick around for another one.'

'Speaking of which...'

'Definitely time to get back to it.' He picked up his bag and walked over to the door.

'Um, haven't you forgotten something?'

Henry glanced around, momentarily confused.

'My other present.'

'You want to bring the elf?'

I looked at him askance. 'You think I'm passing up the chance to inflict Frankenstein's Elf on my family?'

Fifteen minutes later we were off, our new passenger strapped into the back seat.

## 19

It was a careful crawl on the smaller roads, but once we joined the motorway the gritters had done their job and the only reminder of the previous night's chaos was a thin layer of brown slush. The traffic was quiet, and we soon settled into a steady pace that would have us home in time for a late Christmas lunch.

I was fizzing with anticipation as we headed back to Charis House and the jolliest, cheesiest Christmas playlist would have summed up my mood perfectly. However, I had to acknowledge that, at some point during the past two days, Henry and I had become an *us*, and it felt completely natural to scroll past 'Christmas Bangers' and settle on 'A Classical Christmas'.

For the first hour or so, I focused on my phone. There were more video messages from home, including Frankie and Daisy imploring me to hurry up and get back, because Grandma said they weren't allowed to open presents without me. My social media channels also had numerous Christmas GIFs and greetings from viewers, to which I sent replies ranging from a simple 'like' to a paragraph, depending upon who had sent it.

Mrs Lewinski hadn't got a mobile phone, let alone a Facebook account, but she'd spent the last few Christmases alone, so as per usual I gave her a call.

Strange. It rang straight through to her answer phone. I waited five minutes and tried again, this time leaving a message wishing her a happy Christmas, and enquiring as to whether she was all right, given that she hadn't answered the phone.

'She could be in the garden, filling up her bird feeders,' I speculated, worry tugging at my gut. 'Or in the shower.'

'Asleep?' Henry suggested.

'At eleven in the morning? If it was the afternoon, possibly, but not at this time.'

'She could have gone for a walk.'

I shook my head. 'She can barely manage the garden path on a good day. There's no way she'd have gone out in the snow.'

'Where does she live?'

'Newark. Not too far from the castle.'

'Do you have the address?'

'No. Why?'

'If she's still not answering when we reach the turn-off from the A1, I'll keep on going and we can check in on her.'

'Henry, that's miles out of our way...'

He kept his eyes on the road, face impassive. 'An extra forty minutes, tops. If the roads remain this clear we'll still be back in time.'

'Not if we find her lying on the floor with a broken hip. Or in bed with the flu.'

Henry waited until he'd overtaken a lorry before replying. 'So, on the basis she might be stuck on the floor or ill, you don't want—'

'Okay! Yes. If we can find out her address then maybe we can drop by. If you're really sure.'

'I'm really sure that if we don't, you'll spend the rest of the day worrying about her.'

With a bit of online searching, I had an address for Muriel Lewinski. A mile before we reached the turn-off towards home, I called again. No answer. A prickle of anxiety skittered up my spine. Dad messaged to ask if we had an ETA. I blew out a shaky sigh and told him an hour.

Twenty minutes later, we pulled up outside a shabby terraced house on a narrow street. It was nearly one o'clock. I knocked on the front door with a clammy fist, Henry standing right beside me.

After a few minutes of knocking and waiting, we found a passageway that cut through the terrace a few doors down. This then required us to climb over a gate stuck shut due to a rusted bolt so we could hurry up to the back door, Henry peering through the kitchen window while I knocked again.

'Can I help you?' a suspicious voice carried over the next-door fence.

'Hi,' I blurted, jumping back from the door as though confirming their suspicions.

A youngish man was scowling at me, the trail of a cigarette drifting above his head.

'All right, Dale?' A woman who looked to be his mum appeared next to him.

'These people are poking around Mrs L's house.'

'Oh, yes?' The woman narrowed her eyes at me, adjusting the paper crown sitting on her black curls. 'We were trying to see if she was okay,' I said, stepping closer. 'That's all. I've called several times wishing her a merry Christmas and she didn't answer.'

'Well, maybe that's because she's gone out,' the woman replied.

'Has she gone out?'

'We're hardly going to tell you that, are we?' Dale retorted. 'Skulking about on Christmas Day. Prime time for burglaries. I saw it on the news the other night. If you're targeting a helpless old woman, then I'll—'

'Hang on a minute!' his mum interrupted, her eyes growing wide. 'Speaking of news, I recognise you now. You're that weather woman! The one who reads out all the questions people send in. Begins with a b...'

'Bea!' the man replied.

'Yes, I said it began with a b, didn't I?'

'Bea Armstrong,' I said.

'Yes! Bea Armstrong! Well, why didn't you say?' The woman stuck her hands on her hips.

'Just 'cos she's on TV doesn't mean she's not robbing anything.'

'Oh, shut up, Dale. Get inside and check on the spuds. While you're at it tell the others that the woman from the telly's here. Bring Shannon's phone, with the good camera.'

'Look, it is lovely to meet you but we're late for our own family dinner, and we really just want to check if Mrs Lewinski is okay. Did you say she'd gone out?'

'Said she might have done. I thought I saw a car pull up and her disappear off a few hours ago, but it could have been anything or anyone, really. We should probably call the police to be sure.'

'You don't have a key?' Henry asked.

'Ooh, who's this, then?' The woman straightened up, patting her hair so that the crown fell off. 'Your fella, is it?'

'No. It's just a friend. Do you have a key?'

'Well, that's a shame. Why wouldn't you want a lovely looking lad like that?'

Glancing over at Henry, his navy-blue beanie bringing out the shine in his eyes, I couldn't actually think of any good reason. But before I'd managed to come up with a more appropriate answer, their back yard was full of people, all insistent on introducing themselves, while handing out glasses of Prosecco and bowls of nibbles. There were four generations of Joneses ranging from eight months old to ninety, and every one of them wanted a selfie.

'Eh, Beano!' one of the men called, knocking on the window of the next house along. 'That woman from the telly's here. The weather one. Bea Whatsername.'

Within minutes something akin to a street party began forming along the back yards. Someone set up a speaker playing disco music as kids raced in and out of the adults' legs clutching shiny new toys. There was no way that Mrs Lewinski could have been inside and not heard the commotion. I tried asking a few of the people pressing in for a picture, but no one knew anything.

Another message came through, from Mia this time, asking when we'd be arriving, causing stress to expand like a balloon trapped inside my ribcage. Henry caught my look of desperation and raised his hands, calling for everyone's attention.

'Does anyone know if Mrs Lewinski is inside her house, or has she gone out?' he boomed.

'Mrs L? She's here, int she?' A teenage girl waved her phone in Henry's direction. 'That holiday guy who goes on your weather show just posted. Mrs L went to his for... hang on... goose? What are they gonna do with a goose?'

I quickly found Byron's Instagram page. There they were, Mrs Lewinski, Byron, and another two people I didn't recognise, all beaming out at me. Mrs L was holding a very large glass of sherry.

I couldn't help it, I was so relieved and happy for them I burst into tears.

* * *

There was no way that Henry Fairfax was going to break the speed limit, but I was grateful that he made every legal effort to get us to Charis House as soon as possible.

'Does that happen a lot?' he asked as we whizzed back down the A1.

'No! Only when I'm making a formal appearance, like a community fair or a school visit.'

'How often do you do those?'

'It depends on the time of year. Maybe every other weekend I'll have something on, about the same during the week.'

'People really like you.'

'I really like people. It's one of the best things about my job.'

'I don't suppose Summer spends her weekends at village fetes.'

'Summer probably has more friends than me. It's not like I've got loads of other things to do.'

We left the main road and started heading towards the forest.

'You don't have many friends?' Henry sounded surprised. Which surprised me.

'Ur, hello, remember school? I wasn't exactly Miss Popular.'

'You always acted like you never needed friends. I mean, there was Lucy and that other girl, Rowena.'

I watched the snow-capped trees whizzing past. 'Everyone needs friends.'

Henry cleared his throat. 'I would have been your friend.'

I turned to look at him, finding his eyes firmly fixed on the road ahead. I briefly wondered if the same memories were tumbling through his mind as mine. The shame and regret clogging up my throat made it hard to speak. 'I thought you didn't like me.' I paused, tried to come up with a better way to explain it, because I knew that wasn't completely true, and Henry deserved my honesty.

'At least, I wanted to believe that you didn't...'

'Because then it made it easier for you to not like me?'

I thought a bit harder. 'Okay, so here's the truth. And this is the first time I've realised this, so bear with me. I was jealous of you.'

Henry jerked his head back in surprise. 'What, because I always beat you in the physics tests?'

'No, nothing like that. You know what people thought of me in school.'

'What, that you were clever and nice and were interesting enough to not care about fitting in with the crowd?'

'That is not what people thought about me!'

'It's what I thought.'

'Okay, so to almost everyone else I was the strange kid with the embarrassing parents and even worse clothes. And I *really* cared about not fitting in. I spent so much time and energy avoiding any more attention than necessary so I wouldn't provoke more mean jokes or bitchy comments. It's like I adopted this general air of apology for sullying the school with my dweebiness.

'And then there was you, Sir Henry of Nerdville, hand straight up every time the teacher asked a question, perfect crease in your school trousers, insisting you had no idea who Ant and Dec were. You were far worse than me, and you didn't even try not to be.'

'You were jealous of me being more of a nerd than you?'

'I was jealous that you seemed oblivious to your position in the pecking order. I was angry that you didn't have the decency to be ashamed of who you were, when so often I felt like my shame would consume me.'

'Wow.'

'How did you not care?'

Henry considered that for a while. 'I suppose I didn't care what people thought about my fashion sense, or taste in music, because those were trivial things that said nothing meaningful about me. I did care about being trustworthy and kind. A decent person.'

'And being right,' I couldn't help adding, smiling to soften the tease.

'Yes.' He screwed up his face. 'That, too. Maybe I also considered myself to be above all that popularity guff, and therefore above most of the other kids. Which I freely admit made me a pretentious little twazzock.'

'Do you ever regret not being a normal teenager? Missing out on the parties and the flirting, all the guff?'

'Regret spending years trying to be someone I'm not, forsaking time doing the things I enjoy to hang out with people who I had nothing in common with?'

'Fair enough.' I blew out a long sigh, my forehead vibrating against the icy window. 'I'm still jealous, though. Even if you do wear jeans and ditched the bad hair, you're still happily going through life being completely you, not even realising how much most of us struggle with that.'

He shook his head. 'Are you joking? You've defied your parents' wishes and expectations and taken a job they can't understand. You do that job differently from anyone else, even down to how you dress. You walked out of a fantastic opportunity because you refused to go along with everyone else in the room and say something negative. We're nearly an hour late to an Armstrong Christmas dinner because you had to check on a woman you've never met. I think the only people I know who are as authentically themselves as you, Bea, is your parents. It's really time you stopped beating yourself up about who you think you used to be.'

'Thank you,' I managed to reply after taking a minute to compose myself.

'And I forgive you.' He spoke softly this time, but as always with utter sincerity. 'Even if I was a pompous git, I understood. And I deserved a lot of it. Please forgive yourself.'

I reached over and took hold of Henry's hand where it rested on his thigh. He wrapped his fingers around mine and held them tight, and that was about all we needed to say on the subject. For now, at least.

## 20

The whole of the drive had been cleared of snow, so we were able to wind our way up to the Coach House with no problems. The front door opened before we'd come to a complete stop, and dogs, children and everyone else tumbled out into the cold to give as warm a welcome as if we'd been to the North Pole and back.

'Come in, come in, the food is waiting,' Mum ordered, tutting.

'I'm trying!' I laughed, almost suffocating in Dad's hug, a tiny niece hanging off one leg and a Labrador bumping up against the other.

'Can't we open presents, first?' Frankie whined as Mum herded us into the dining room, decked out in all its Christmassy splendour. 'You said when Auntie Bea got here we could open presents.'

'Yes, well, that was before she decided to take a diversion to a random street party, making us sit and wait for her.'

I glanced at Mia, walking next to me, in alarm. She raised one eyebrow. 'Your parents get a notification every time someone tags you online. It's been non-stop.'

'Since when?'

'Since yesterday morning. I think Nana Joy's speech hit home.'

'I have a very good explanation for the detour.'

'I'd hope so. We've been instructed not to pass you any chestnut stuffing until we've heard it.'

* * *

The rest of the day passed precisely as scheduled by my mother. After we'd lingered around the table until well into the afternoon, the laughter and stories continued in the kitchen while most of us cleared up, Mum and Nana Joy retiring to the living room with the children. Henry and I snuck the animatronic elf inside and hid him in the pantry. I ended up bent double in an uncontrollable fit of giggles thanks to Jed's reaction when he opened the door and found it.

'Funniest ever Christmas moment,' Henry wheezed, once he'd found enough breath to speak. Mia simply raised a suggestive eyebrow at the two of us and dragged her furious husband out of the kitchen.

The reaction to my retelling of the final interview round was as predicted. What else could I have done? Who would want to work for someone like that, anyway? There'd be other opportunities, ones that didn't involve compromising my values or trampling on fellow professionals.

I grabbed onto their encouraging words, held them tight, and tried my best to believe them.

After clean-up, we finally got to open presents. Unlike most years, my parents didn't give each other items made by a student in one of the practical classes. To everyone's surprise, they swapped tickets for a cruise.

'Two weeks in the Mediterranean on a luxury, adult-only cruise ship,' Elana read from the accompanying leaflet. 'Join us on a once-in-a-lifetime adventure.'

'Can I come on an adventure, too?' Daisy asked. 'Please!'

'Duh, it's adults only,' Elana scoffed.

'I'll be very quiet and growned up,' Daisy pleaded, causing Elana to merely roll her eyes and keep reading.

'A cruise?' Jed asked. 'What brought this on?'

Mum tipped her chin in the air. 'We're having our first holiday in nearly ten years. Perhaps we finally got tired and fancied a break.'

'It doesn't look cheap.'

'Well, given that we're half a million pounds short, I don't think a couple of thousand will make that much difference!'

Dad reached over to Mum from the neighbouring armchair and took her hand. 'It's from our personal savings, nothing to do with the school funds. And if you want to know the truth, we felt it was time to focus on something other than Charis House. Something we can look forward to.'

He stopped there, but the unspoken words hung in the air as potent as the scent of pine tree.

*In case we have to close the school.*

Daisy mercifully saved us from lingering on that thought too long.

'Nana Joy, here is your present from me and Frankie and Elana. It's a book that you listen to because Mummy said your eyes are too old to read any more. Nana Joy?'

'I think she's fallen asleep again,' Frankie whispered, almost loudly enough to wake her back up.

The rest of the day was spent playing with new toys and games, snoozing, reading, a short amble with Dumble and Dash and trying to find room to squeeze in some crackers and cheese on top of dinner.

Having Henry there felt as natural as Nana Joy belting along to

*Frozen*. There were the obvious comments, and pointed glances our way, but I was too happy to be home to care.

Once the youngest and oldest members of the family were tucked up in bed, exhausted after such a busy few days, most of the adults went over to check that everything in the school hall was still ready for the Christmas Spectacular. The pupils had spent the last day of term adding the final decorations and checking that the lighting and sound systems were all set up properly, but with the weather so terrible, and the old building not much better, a quick check was sensible.

For some reason, everyone needed to be there except for Henry and me. I had to admit that I didn't care what that reason might be. As the day had progressed it had grown harder to ignore the fluttery feelings that had appeared that morning. Every time Henry brushed past me or ended up squashed beside me on the sofa (which, when I thought about it, seemed to happen quite a lot) I had a flashback to waking up beside him that morning, and, rather than fading away, the attraction seemed to be settling in and making itself at home.

Henry was lovely, I mused while cutting us both a piece of chocolate log. He was kind and thoughtful and I could talk to him for hours without getting bored or irritated. And while not being the most important thing, but definitely one to bear in mind – he was *here*.

So, there were only two reasons for not, as Mrs Lewinski's neighbour so bluntly put it, wanting him to be my fella.

One: I had no idea how he felt about me. After all, with the exception of the brief crush that he'd well and truly got over, we'd both spent twenty years working very hard at *not* liking each other.

Two: my parents would never let me hear the end of it, considering it proof (if needed) that they were always right when it came to my life decisions, and I was not.

I was carrying the cake back to the living room when I remembered the third reason.

I was still in love with Adam.

*Wasn't I?*

It was only then that I realised he'd not messaged me all day, and more to the point I'd not thought about messaging him.

*There you are, then,* I told myself, settling back down beside Henry on the sofa. I broke up with Adam six months ago. Nothing had changed apart from a few brief interactions to show that nothing had changed. If I'd got the job with BWM Today, would I have really wanted to give things another go?

Did I need to work out the answer to that before giving any more thought to my feelings for Henry, given that it was now irrelevant?

Henry, as if aware that I was thinking about him, glanced up from his historical novel and gave me a smile, the shadows from the log fire dancing across the planes of his face. Our feet, both in matching slipper socks that Nana Joy had given us, were only inches apart where we'd each propped them on the coffee table. I could sense the electrical sparks zapping between our toes as my heart started to thump.

Apart from the fire, the only light was the moon shimmering through the window and a soft lamp by Henry's side of the sofa. The dogs were curled up in a furry pile beneath the tree, and the room was scattered with the detritus of the day. I took a slow breath, unable to focus on anything except for one coherent thought:

*I think this is what I want.*

*Like this.*

*No more waiting around for someone who's off chasing impossible dreams. A man who cares about what matters to me.*

The past couple of days I had felt part of a team, not a cheery-faced appendage.

Henry might not be the man for me. I certainly might not be the woman for him.

But maybe I was starting to realise that I didn't want to settle for the kind of relationship I'd had in the past. It was time to move on, focus on the future. Consider whether it was an accident that Henry's toes had crossed the two-inch gulf to mine and now rested gently against the side of my foot.

Only then the doorbell rang, and all the mights and maybes vanished the second I opened the door.

## 21

'Hey.' Adam, despite being several inches taller, managed to somehow look up at me through his thick, dark blond lashes in an expression that conveyed a paradoxical combination of nerves and utter confidence at how well he'd be received on the Coach House doorstep.

'What are you doing here?'

'Freezing to death. The taxi insisted on dropping me at the end of the drive.'

I took in his ripped jeans, battered leather jacket, and sopping-wet trainers and stepped back to let him inside. Before I had a chance to catch my breath or clasp onto the whirling swarm of emotions, he wrapped his arms around me and pulled me tight against his chest.

'I've missed you so much,' he breathed against the side of my head.

I sucked in the scent of his jacket, rested my chin in that familiar spot on his shoulder and had to agree.

Not that I was about to tell him just yet.

Dash and Dumble worming their way between our legs

provided a timely excuse to step away, creating enough space to allow my lungs to start functioning again.

'Seriously, why are you here?'

Adam grabbed hold of my hand, ducking his head to gaze into my eyes. 'I just... I couldn't stay away. I had to see you. When you told me about the job interview, I started thinking about what it would mean. To have you close by again. I was so happy, so hopeful... and then when you told me that wasn't going to happen, I realised—'

'Hello.'

At the sound of Henry's voice, I instinctively started to pull my hand out of Adam's. He responded by holding it tighter, turning to Henry with his wannabe-rock-star grin.

'Hi, hello. Sorry to interrupt your evening. I'm Adam.'

Henry flicked his gaze up from our conjoined hands, his face full on robo-Henry. 'Yes. We've met before. Several times.'

'Oh, man, I'm sorry. I'm hopeless with faces. I meet a lot of different people in my industry.'

'Adam, this is Henry.'

He looked at me, as if none the wiser.

'Henry Fairfax? He was in my year at school.'

'Nah. Sorry, mate. My bad.'

'The boy Mum and Dad wanted me to marry.'

Adam gave an apologetic smile as he shrugged it off, but I'd felt his hand clench in mine for a split second. He knew full well who Henry was, and I couldn't for the life of me fathom why he wouldn't admit it.

'Anyway, let me get you a drink. Coffee? Or Mum's made some mulled fruit thing.'

I was filling up the coffee machine when the others arrived home. The icy blast of air accompanying them through the back door grew even colder when they saw Adam sitting at the kitchen table.

'Adam,' Jed said, eventually, seemingly the only one capable of being polite. 'I didn't know you were coming.'

'Well, of course you wouldn't,' Mum said. 'He wasn't invited.'

'Yeah, I hope you don't mind me dropping in.' Adam stood up, holding out a hand to shake Dad's; Dad reluctantly acquiesced. 'I'm staying with my mum for a few days, sort of a last-minute arrangement, and couldn't resist paying Charis House a visit. When I saw the light on I just had to come and say thanks. This place changed my life. Or rather, you did, Principal and Vice-Principal Armstrong. Probably saved it, given the path I was headed down until you stepped in.'

And there you had it, Adam had not-so-subtly stroked my parents' Achilles heel. Mum pursed her lips, muttering, 'I hope you've offered your guest something to eat,' as she marched out of the room, gesturing for the rest of my family to join her.

'This must be the first time your parents have voluntarily left us alone together,' Adam joked, taking a sip of coffee.

I watched him slouching back in his chair, and knew that this time there'd be no rash decisions made in a moment of passion, no 'love will find a way' mentality, choosing the now and ignoring the heartbreak that came later. It was time to grow up, and if Adam wanted to try again then he had to feel the same.

'You were explaining why you're here.'

'Yes.' He shifted in his seat, for the first time looking genuinely anxious. 'Like I said, I really missed you, and have been thinking about you – about us – and why we went wrong.'

'That would be because you chose your mythical career over me.'

'Yes. That's true, and I wanted to say sorry. Not just for that time, but for all the times I made that choice. Not that I should never have said yes to a gig or a tour, but, well, I could have done things differently. I lost the best thing I had while going after something that might never happen. That was stupid and even worse, it hurt you. I guess I'm here because I wanted to say that I'm sorry.' He shrugged. 'It felt like the kind of thing that needed to be said face to face.'

'On Christmas Day?' It was getting harder to keep up a tough exterior when inside my walls were crumbling. I'd never heard Adam suggest that he might not succeed in music before. Let alone that his choices might not have been the right ones.

*Maybe I wasn't the only one who'd done some growing up recently?*

The tiny ember of hope that I'd very nearly snuffed out a few hours ago began to glow. I couldn't be certain that Adam meant it, that this was any different from any other time, except that it was Christmas Day, and he was here, at Charis House, and didn't actions speak louder than a whole album full of words?

He put down his mug and slid his chair closer to mine, reaching for my hand again. 'It seemed too important to wait. I hope that's okay. I didn't mean to ruin the day for you. I was hoping it might make it better.'

I still had enough wits about me to slide my hand away, despite my pounding heart. 'I'm grateful for what you've said. But you can't turn up out of the blue, offer a quick apology, and expect things to go back to how they were.' I blew out a frustrated sigh. 'I mean, I suppose you can expect that, given how many times it's happened before. But not this time, Adam. I'm not going to get back on this merry-go-round. It never goes anywhere.'

'Okay. I understand.' He nodded, face serious. 'But is it okay if I stay and finish my coffee? Maybe we can catch up? Then I promise I'll leave you to it.'

'How are you getting back to the village?'

He gave a sheepish shrug. 'I hadn't thought that far yet. It was a kind of impulsive, in-the-moment, grand gesture.'

'I'd ask someone to give you a lift, but we've all been drinking.'

'No, it's fine. I'll see if that taxi's still free.'

Ten minutes later we'd established that neither that taxi, nor any other, was available and prepared to come all the way out to the forest for a fifteen-minute fare.

Adam sat frowning at his phone after yet another fruitless call. 'Looks like I'll be walking, then.' He pulled a wry smile. 'It's not like I haven't done it before.'

'Not in freezing snow, you haven't.' I pushed back my chair. 'Come on, she's more likely to say yes if you're standing right in front of her.'

\* \* \*

'On one condition,' Mum announced, after I'd raised the possibility of Adam staying the night. 'You stay long enough to perform at the Spectacular tomorrow.'

'Oh, well... I haven't got my guitar,' he replied, already grinning at the prospect.

'Someone can fetch it for you.'

'I don't think there's a spare slot on the programme,' Jed interjected, stoically immune to Adam's charm.

'Well, he could always do something with Bea,' Dad said, moving the counter a few steps forwards on the new board game everyone was playing. Everyone except Henry, that was. He'd apparently opted for an early night.

'I'm not doing anything, so that would still be an extra slot,' I replied.

'Well, of course you are!' Mum huffed. 'Everyone's doing something this year.'

'No, I'm not, due to this being the first I've heard of it.'

'It was in the itinerary, and at least two of the emails.'

The emails I skim-read, because reading multiple paragraphs of orders and instructions from my mother made my innards shrivel.

'I haven't prepared anything, so Adam can have my slot. A perfect solution.'

'No. What would be perfect is all of the family taking part in the Charis House Christmas Spectacular when it might very well be the last one!'

'Oh, for goodness' sake! How many times are you going to use that to emotionally blackmail me into doing what you want?' I said, my voice starting to rise. 'Because it's only been four days and it's already getting old.'

'Bea,' Jed warned, his expression grim.

'I'm sorry if that's how you feel, Sweet-Bea,' Dad interjected. 'However, we did mention it several times. It'll seem like something's missing if you don't take part.'

'You may have mentioned it several times, but didn't anyone notice that I hadn't said yes?' I spluttered, feeling the force of my family's expectation starting to topple me like a steamroller. 'You can't expect me to stand on a stage in front of hundreds of people and perform something with no preparation. It's not fair. I'm sorry I missed it in the emails, but it's too much to ask.'

'It may well be Nana Joy's last curtain call,' Mia, ever the mediator, said softly. 'Even if there is another Spectacular, the doctor said it's the last year she'll be up to performing.'

That hit me with a wave of sorrow and guilt that caused me to sway on my feet. I felt a strong hand grip my waist as Adam spoke from behind my shoulder. 'Don't worry, Principal Armstrong. I'm sure we can come up with something.'

'I'm not promising anything!' I insisted, but my voice was

wavering. 'If it's going to ruin the show, then I'm not getting up there.'

'Yes, dear.' Mum smiled, her eyes swivelling from me to Adam. 'Whatever you think is best.'

So, somehow, I'd gone from cosy Christmas bliss with my childhood nemesis to contemplating performing with my childhood sweetheart in the space of under an hour.

And that wasn't the biggest twist of the day.

After my parents had sorted a blow-up bed in the study for Adam, and I'd scurried up to the attic to find some much-needed thinking time, I had just settled into bed when my phone rang.

Baffled as to who could possibly be calling me at eleven o'clock on Christmas Day, despite the unknown number I answered it.

'Bea, it's Baxter.'

'Oh! Baxter Bigwood?'

'Do you know many Baxters?'

'Sorry. I'm very surprised to hear from you.'

'You haven't replied to Mel's email. She's off today so thought I'd chase it up myself.'

'I haven't checked my emails in the last couple of days.' What with the storm, and it being Christmas Day and everything.

'I'll summarise. The job's yours. We need official acceptance by the twenty-eighth, so any negotiations in the contract, speak to my legal team before then.'

'*What?*'

'I'm sick of yes-men. Or women. It's time someone stood up to me. Oh, and tell Driver to give me a call. I like him.'

He'd hung up before I'd had a chance to pick my jaw up off the floor.

\* \* \*

So, all in all it wasn't the best night's sleep. Again.

By the time I'd found the energy to shower and drag myself downstairs, Nana Joy informed me that the rest of the family were already at the school hall.

'The man with the swaggery shoulders has gone somewhere else but said he wouldn't be long. The other man, with the sexy smile, gave him a lift.'

I made us a fresh pot of tea and buttered two slices of Mum's banana bread.

'Are you all ready for the show this evening?' I asked, taking both pieces of bread for myself after Nana Joy wrinkled her nose up.

'Which show is it tonight?' she replied, frowning in concern. 'Things have been so busy around here lately I'm starting to lose track. Hang on, I'll call Bernice. She'll know.'

'No, Nana.' Bernice was her agent and manager who had passed away fifteen years ago. 'It's the Charis House Christmas Spectacular, remember?'

'Of course!' She shook her head, the frown deepening. 'I got a little muddled, there.'

'I'm sorry.' Sorrier than I could begin to express. I gave her a moment to recalibrate, then forced a deliberately bright tone. 'What's your song choice for the Spectacular?'

This she had no trouble remembering. 'I'm going to do the first song I ever performed on stage. "I'll be Home for Christmas".'

'That's a lovely choice.'

'And then whatever takes my fancy for the encore, depending on the feel of the crowd.'

'Perfect.'

Nana Joy could make up a song on the spot and it would still blow our socks off.

'It's my swan song, did you know?'

I nodded, trying to wrestle back the smile and failing miserably.

'Oh, don't fret. It's all right to be sad.' She gave me a wry look. 'I was one of the best! But everything has its time, and boy, did I make the most of mine.' She reached out to pat my hand. 'I travelled the world and performed with some of the greats. Oh, the things I've seen! Seventy years getting to do what I loved, and seeing all those people love it too. I can't think of a better way to spend a life. But do you know what my favourite performance was?'

I knew my nana well enough to have a good guess.

'The Charis House Christmas Spectacular. Our friends and supporters in the audience, rooting for us. Sharing the stage with all those children who for one night get to feel the magic of performing. Being up there with my family, who are my greatest legacy, outshining any show. Are you going to join me at my swan song, Beatrice?'

'I wouldn't miss it for the world.'

## 22

I thought about what Nana Joy had said, once Adam had returned with his guitar and we were walking over to the main house to find an empty music room. Not about it being her swan song, although that painful truth was a bruise upon my heart. I thought about her life spent doing what she loved, and how despite the lack of accolades – or money! – the performances she treasured were those spent with the people she cared about the most.

Melody had sent an email containing various forms to complete along with a detailed work contract for me to sign. The salary felt almost criminal. The additional perks were overwhelming. I'd be given the opportunity to research and present various extended features.

I'd be able to do what I was doing now - stroll alongside Adam, each of us content to be lost in our own thoughts - without having to schedule in trains and book days off and stress about last-minute changes of plans.

While it was only sensible to be cautious when it came to Adam, and to take things, if there even was going to be anything, slowly, that should have no bearing on whether I accepted such an incredible job. And Baxter Bigwood offering it to me despite me walking out on him allayed most of my fears about whether I'd be able to be myself or not.

I'd get those forms completed first thing tomorrow.

For now, I had yet another Armstrong-mandated humiliation to prepare for.

\* \* \*

It was like stepping back in time, walking into the Charis House hall that evening. Unlike most school halls, this one had thick stone walls with intricately carved coving and a ceiling covered in geometric patterns rather than fibreglass tiles and ugly strip-lights.

The smell, so uniquely home, awakened a stream of different memories and feelings. Ancient floorboards and musty drapes, the eight-foot spruce tree dominating one corner. This year, the pupils had chosen a sixties theme, in honour of Joy Papplewick. Their retrospective interpretation of this included paper chains criss-crossing the ceiling, masses of shiny tinsel, and multicoloured fairy lights wound around the pillars and window frames. The walls were lined with posters of Nana Joy's earlier musicals, but the high-light was the stage, which had been framed to appear like a giant, retro television, so that the performers would appear to be on screen.

We'd spent the entire afternoon attending to the final details, soothing fraught teenage nerves, and rectifying last-minute costume mishaps. All of the other Charis House staff were there to help with the preparations, including supervising the various student teams of caterers, ushers, and sound and lighting techni-cians. Now, after racing back to the Coach House to get changed, I was hovering in one corner, watching as the guests began making their way to the plastic seats, the buzz of chatter blending with the faint tinkle of background music and the rustle of coats and hats being gratefully removed in the heat of the hall.

It was easy to spot the family members of the students who'd be performing – a mix of excitement, wariness, and full-blown fear on behalf of children who'd previously had the spotlight on them for all the wrong reasons. In between the anxious faces were the usual crowd from the village, along with a good sprinkling of my parents' friends and other supporters of the school.

My heart swelled with joy and pride at being a part of the amazing endeavour that went so far beyond a mere show, while at the same time it ached that this might be the beginning of the end.

'Hey.' Adam appeared at my side, nudging my elbow. 'Strange to be back, isn't it?'

'I'm here every year, so not really,' I said blandly, scanning the crowd.

'Okay. That's fair. I'm genuinely sorry for all the years I missed.' He put one hand on my shoulder to turn me towards him, and as my eyes caught his it was impossible to ignore the crackle of chemistry. Adam's features had roughened over the years, bearing a decade of long days and late nights on the road, but in his eyes I saw the boy I'd fallen in love with.

'Well, I suppose what matters is you're here now.'

'You look incredible.' He smiled, generating another crackle. A lack of options had forced me back into Mia's red dress, so I almost believed him.

'Not so bad yourself,' I conceded. 'Very seasonal.' Instead of his usual jeans and T-shirt, Adam wore a form-fitting, powder-blue suit decorated with snowflakes around the cuffs and lapels. His blue bow tie already hung undone and he had on silver trainers. He looked like a rock star at an awards ceremony. I tried really hard not to swoon.

'Come on, then, time to go backstage.'

Once every seat was occupied, Mum and Dad opened the show, as always, with an upbeat sixties medley peppered with jokes and dodgy dance moves. The next hour and a half was a combination of polished brilliance (one boy performed hilariously accurate impressions of the teachers), raw talent, and good old-fashioned enthusiasm. Jed and Mia sang, and their children performed a magic trick that everyone thought had gone disastrously wrong until Daisy popped out from behind the Christmas tree. However, when it came to the Charis House pupils, the skill level was irrelevant. Most of these children carried scars from the kind of battles the rest of us couldn't even fathom. They'd been knocked down, beaten up, and kicked out more times than they could count. Yet here they were, giving it their all. It was impossible not to be moved by that level of courage and determination, and watching the amazement on the performers' faces as they received their applause, how they literally grew at the audience response, never failed to make me cry.

I, on the other hand, was a local semi-celebrity facing the very real danger of ending up as a viral meme. Not only that, this night meant a lot to my family, and I wanted them to feel proud of me for once. I did my best to quell my jangling nerves by reminding myself that it couldn't be worse than the year Jed bullied me into an operatic duet, and besides, this year Adam was sure to get all the attention.

'And now, we have a special treat for you!' My dad beamed, after it felt as if I'd been waiting in the wings forever. 'Those of you who've been friends of Charis House for a while will remember one of our favourite bands of all time, The Spex. Now, this evening, we have the pleasure to welcome back their lead singer, Adam Wilson, who is going to perform with none other than our daughter and your weather presenter, Bea Armstrong!'

Before I could change my mind and flee for the hills, Adam

grabbed my hand and dragged me onstage, waving and grinning at the cheering crowd.

Okay, this was happening, then. I might as well enjoy it.

With only a couple of hours to rehearse, we'd decided to keep it simple and stick to the theme. Nana Joy's most well-known hit was a cover of the old song 'If I Had You'. She'd declared herself so sick of singing it that she was happy for someone else to perform it this evening. While her version featured a big band and a choir of finger-clicking backing singers, Adam had stripped it back to our voices and his guitar and added a harmony that made my warble sound almost as if I shared a bit of DNA with a West End star.

When he sang the last chorus, he stopped smouldering at the crowd and turned to me, the intensity as he sang about how he wouldn't mind leaving his pals and his old life behind 'if I had you' so startling that I forgot to come in with the next line, leaving him to seamlessly finish the song.

There was a moment of utter silence, as though the whole room held its breath.

Then Adam grinned, leant forwards and kissed my cheek, and the audience erupted.

In that moment, it was hard to remember why I'd ever thought it was a good idea to break up with this man. Head spinning, heart scampering, I really needed time to think.

'Not bad.' Jed nodded as I walked off-stage and Adam went to put his guitar away. 'They loved it.'

'They loved Adam,' I replied, still breathless. 'He's so good he managed to make me not bad.'

'Yeah, well.' Jed shrugged as though trying to dislodge a fly on his shoulder. 'He always was good at putting on a performance.'

I stopped then, as if jerked back by an invisible string. 'What's that supposed to mean?'

Jed looked at me, and in his eyes I saw pity mixed with big-brotherly concern. 'Please make sure you know what's real, and what's part of the Adam Wilson show.'

'While I appreciate you sharing your opinion, I know Adam a lot better than you. I can tell what's real.'

'I just don't want you getting hurt again.'

'It was a song, Jed. Like you said, a performance. And this may surprise you, but I don't especially want to *be* hurt again, so you don't have to worry.'

'Okay.'

'Yes, it is okay.'

It wasn't okay. My head and my heart were mashed up and inside out and I hated Adam doing this to me, while at the same time I felt terrified that I might love him for it. I had the duration of a disconcertingly unpolished knife-throwing act to get myself straight before Nana Joy's swan song. And then to make things even more mind-frazzlingly complicated, Henry stood up and beckoned me over to a free seat beside his.

'Thanks,' I mumbled, sliding in next to him while the crowd clapped with relief that the blindfolded weapon hurling was over.

'Your song was excellent. Especially considering how little time you had to prepare. You and Adam make a good duo.' He was watching the stage, so while I didn't doubt that Henry was being as honest as always, it was hard to interpret how he felt about it.

'I messed up at the end, but I think I might have got away with it.'

'You seemed to be enjoying it. That's the main thing.'

'Did you?'

*Um, what? Why on earth would I ask that?*

'Excuse me?'

'Did you enjoy seeing me and Adam as a duo?'

Oh, help. I'd disintegrated into an emotional mess with no filter. Why was I pushing Henry on this?

His eyes flickered to mine briefly.

'Why wouldn't I have?'

'I don't know. I'm being paranoid. Forget I said anything.'

*Because you need to know how he feels before you decide what to do about how Adam feels,* a sly voice inside my head wheedled.

That wasn't it at all! I'd loved Adam since I was fifteen years old. I'd hated Henry even longer. The recent revelation that he wasn't a total dweeb would have no influence on what happened with me and Adam whatsoever. Pushing Henry for some sort of sign would only end up embarrassing us both and ruining the potential for far less awkward Armstrong-Fairfax get-togethers.

Henry hadn't replied, but a crease appeared between his eyebrows that indicated he was formulating an answer. As he turned to speak, Dad sprang back on stage, and the crowd hushed, in anticipation of the evening's highlight.

'Friends and Charis House family. I could introduce our final act by telling you all about her phenomenal career. I could list her awards, her achievements, her glittering success spanning seven decades. But to me, of course, she is simply the best mother I could have hoped for, who happens to sing rather a lot. Would you please welcome our most truly spectacular talent, Joy Papplewick?'

It took Nana Joy an age to hobble onstage, her favourite purple shoes matching an ankle-length, sequined dress, but when she eventually made it to the spotlight, we were still clapping and cheering her every step. As she lifted her chin, one hand on the microphone, the other on a hip in her trademark pose, the room fell so silent we could have heard her false eyelashes flutter.

And then she opened her mouth, and the years fell away as she spent the next seven minutes doing what she'd been born to do. The tiny croak in her voice, the odd wobble on the high notes meant nothing. We were entranced, believing every word and feeling every note. After a heart-wrenching ballad, she finished off with the liveliest version of 'Santa Claus is Coming to Town' I'd ever heard, bringing the whole room to their feet, stomping, clapping and belting along with her. I'd not known it was possible to smile so hard and cry at the same time.

To those who'd never seen it, calling a school Christmas show a 'spectacular' might seem somewhat over the top, a little grandiose.

That night, the description was perfect.

\* \* \*

I'd helped myself to a mulled wine and was chatting to one of the school governors when Adam asked if I could spare a couple of minutes to talk. Assuming he'd lead us to a quiet corner of the hall, instead I followed him all the way out and down the corridor. To my surprise, we passed Henry and Nana Joy heading towards the main entrance.

'This lovely young man is escorting me home,' Nana Joy said, leaning against Henry, her arm firmly tucked through his.

'She's totally wiped out,' Henry explained. I could see that. Beneath her dusting of powder Nana Joy's face was tinged with grey, her shoulders hunched with exhaustion.

'Are you sure? I can walk you, Nana, let Henry get back to the afterparty.'

'Oh, do stop meddling,' she retorted. 'He offered and I accepted. No one asked Miss Jealous Boots to interfere.'

'Well, that told me!' I leant forward and kissed Nana Joy on the cheek. 'Sleep well. You knocked everyone's socks off tonight. Definitely saved the best 'til last.'

'I did rather, didn't I?'

We waited until they'd resumed their painstaking shuffle, then Adam linked arms with me and continued down the corridor. It was only as we approached the far end of the building that I realised where he was taking me.

The tiny music room had been one of the places we'd escaped to when looking for a quiet spot to meet undetected. It was here, sitting side by side on the piano stool, that Adam had kissed me for the first time. He'd serenaded me with songs that he'd written, and we'd whispered our first, tentative confessions of love.

In addition to the piano, the room was usually bare save for a plastic chair or maybe a couple of music stands and some random percussion. Most of the music students preferred the larger room that held a mixing desk and the other equipment needed to produce digital music. This evening, there was a blanket on the floor, upon which waited a bottle of wine, two glasses, and a vase containing a dark-pink rose.

Adam closed the door behind us, and we sat down on the blanket. After pouring us both a drink he attempted some small talk, but I was far too distracted with why we were here.

'What's going on?' I asked, gripping the stem of my wine glass so hard I was surprised it didn't snap.

'Right. Yeah, Um... perhaps we could stand up?' Adam offered a hand to help me up. He was smiling, but when he took my drink and placed it onto the piano, I could see his hands shaking.

I'd already started to guess what might be about to happen when he slowly sank to one knee.

'Adam...'

'I know.' He released a nervous laugh. 'I know. But please, hear me out, and then you can decide whether to throw me out into the snow or not.'

'There is a wide range of options between... *this* and throwing you out into the snow.'

'Yeah, but having spent six months considering other options, this is the only one I want.'

*Oh, boy.*

I tried to think of something rational and reasonable to say, but my head was spinning too fast to form a coherent thought. Instead, I stood there, muscles frozen, which Adam took as an invitation to carry on.

'I love you, Bea. These last few months have been hell. Everything feels wrong when I don't have you. All those things that I used to live for – making music, being on stage, all of it – are meaningless. And I know that I can't keep putting you in second place. I'm choosing you, every time. Please forgive a total idiot who's finally come to his senses, and choose me, too.' He paused, took a deep breath and pulled a ring out of his top pocket. 'Marry me, Bea. I'm nothing without you.'

'I don't know what to say...' All the words were a jumbled mess, stuck in the back of my throat.

'Say yes.'

'We have a lot to talk about...'

'Say yes and then we'll talk. I'll do whatever it takes to make this work.'

My phone suddenly rang in my clutch bag, adding to my fluster. I let it go to answerphone.

'It's not that simple. Can you... can we... can I have some time to think?'

I lowered myself back onto the blanket, and Adam topped up my glass and handed it back to me.

'Is that enough time?' he asked, eyes glinting to match his smile.

I gave him a stern look before taking a sip of wine. 'What does "choosing me" mean?'

'I've left the band.'

'You've left bands before.'

'This time I'm not looking for a new one to join. I can't promise never to do the odd gig again. I definitely want to be part of the next Spectacular. But I'm retiring from professional music. Like I said, it's not worth it. I'd rather have you.'

'So what are you going to do instead?'

My insides were in knots. Adam had made a lot of promises before, but he'd never once talked about giving up his dream. I'd been waiting for a conversation like this for so long. Now that it was happening, I didn't know what to think.

'Dino offered me a job in his bar. Said he'd promote me to manager as soon as I'm up for it. I thought if you were working the early evening slot in London it'd be perfect; our hours would line up. But then you didn't get the job, so I turned him down. I've not got anything sorted in Nottingham yet, but if this is where you'll be then I'll be here, too. I'm done with being so far away from you.'

My phone rang, interrupting my freewheeling thoughts again. I opened my bag and rejected the call without bothering to check who it was.

'Saying you'll move up to Nottingham, leave all "your pals" behind for me, get some random job that feels crap compared to doing what you love, it won't be long before you start resenting me for it. I wouldn't give up my career, my life, for you. You can't do that for me.'

He shrugged. 'I've already decided. This is what I want. And I'm not being stupid about it, I'll get whatever job I can to pay my share of the bills, but I'm going to take some time and figure out what I really want to do, something that I actually stand a chance of doing.' His mouth twitched. 'I had wondered about teaching music.'

I took a moment to try to absorb some of this, but it felt too big to even know where to start.

'I got the job.'

Adam sat back in surprise. 'The London one?'

I nodded.

'Then I can work for Dino. That's amazing, Bea. It couldn't be more perfect. This is...' He stopped to top up our glasses again. I'd drunk the last one without even noticing. 'To us.'

Before I could decide whether I agreed that there'd be an 'us', my phone rang for the third time. Disconcerted, I checked to see who was calling. Henry. And from a quick glance he'd called the first two times as well.

'Hello?'

'Joy's collapsed.'

'What?' It felt as though every organ in my body stopped dead.

'Ambulance should be here in a few minutes. She hit her head on the kitchen worktop.'

'Is she awake?' I was already scrabbling to my feet, ignoring Adam's questioning look.

'No. But she's breathing.'

'Mum and Dad?'

'I can't get through to them. They probably put their phones on silent for the show. I didn't want to leave her to come and find them.'

'No, of course not.'

'If you're still with Adam, can he let them know while you can come straight over? I don't mind going with her in the ambulance, but I thought that—'

'I'm coming now.'

I hung up, hurriedly filling Adam in on the bits he'd not picked up from my side of the conversation even as I yanked the door open and started running towards the main entrance. I hurtled out of the doors, oblivious to the freezing air biting at my bare skin as I skidded through the slush.

## 23

Nana Joy was on the kitchen floor, a tiny lump under a blanket, a thin cushion from one of the dining chairs propped underneath her head.

She looked dead.

Henry placed one arm around me as I knelt beside her, cradling her icy hand in mine.

'You're freezing.'

I barely noticed the jacket being draped around my shoulders, all of my attention fixed on willing my nana to stay with us.

'The paramedics are here,' Henry said, gently moving me back. 'Let's give them some room.'

'I want to hold her hand,' I insisted, gripping on tighter. 'I'm not leaving her.'

'You need to let them take a proper look.'

'They can do that with me holding her hand!' One part of my brain could hear my half-demented shriek. The other part had decided that holding her hand was keeping my nana alive, and I'd be damned if anyone was going to prise me off her.

I was vaguely aware of hushed voices behind me, and then a

paramedic appeared on Nana Joy's other side. 'Hello, Bea, I'm Danny. We really need you to move away from your grandmother so we can help her.'

'No. No. You can help her from there. I can't let her go! Please don't make me!'

Ignoring my protests, Henry wrapped one arm around my waist and used the other to peel my fingers off Nana Joy's. Even as I cursed him, he simply held on, firmly moving me into the far corner of the room.

'Please don't let her die,' I gasped through heaving sobs. 'Not yet. Not now. *Please.*'

\* \* \*

Dad took one look at my face and said that I could ride in the ambulance. When he arrived at the hospital with Jed and Henry I was still loitering in the corner of an emergency bay, watching the doctors prod and peer at and stick tubes into my precious nana.

'Why don't you find a seat in the relatives' room?' a nurse suggested, squeezing past us with a clear bag of liquid. 'Just while we get Joy comfortable.'

'I'd like to stay with her, if that's okay.' I took a step closer to the bed. The nurse did the double-take that I'd grown used to, taking a second or two to place me before breaking into a sympathetic smile. Before I had a chance to capitalise on my celebrity, a doctor turned and blocked me from moving any closer.

'You need to give us some space.'

'I'm scared she'll die by herself, without knowing we're here.'

'We're trying to make sure that doesn't happen.' He paused to fiddle with some wires. 'Not tonight, anyway.'

'Come on, Sweet-Bea.' Dad reached for my hand. I was still wearing Henry's jacket over the stupid red dress, and he had to burrow up inside the sleeve to find it. 'Nana knows we're here. And how much we love her.'

'Son, why don't you see if you can find us a coffee somewhere?' Dad said a short while later, placing one hand on Jed's knee, which had been twitching up and down with increasing frenzy. 'Come on, I'll walk with you, find a quiet spot to call your mother.'

'Where is Mum?' I asked, once they'd left the waiting area.

Henry moved along the row to sit in the chair Dad had vacated, next to mine. 'She stayed to see everyone safely out of the hall. There were a few kids whose parents never showed up and she was worried they might not have a lift home. Adam's with her, helping clear up.'

'Mia?'

'At the Coach House with the children. Your mum will be here once she's locked up.'

'Thank you for driving Dad and Jed.'

Henry furrowed his brow. 'Of course. The roads are icing up again. They shouldn't be driving distracted.'

'And thank you for... taking care of her, while she was on the floor.' I started crying again. Henry put his arm around the back of my chair and pulled me up against him, letting the awful gulping, gasping sounds get buried in his shoulder.

'I've still got your jacket,' I said after a while, my face pressed into his now damp shirt.

'That's fine.'

'You'll be cold.'

'I'm fine.'

I twisted my head to see Dad and Jed sitting further down the row of chairs, heads bent over disposable coffee cups. There were two more cups on the small table in front of them, and while I really didn't want to move away from the solid reassurance of Henry's chest, the least he deserved was a warm cup of coffee.

Straightening up, I gave my face a good rub, tucked my hair behind my ears, and took a couple of deep breaths. The panic had eased along with my tears, replaced with a sense of resolute calm.

'I've made a mess of your shirt,' I whispered.

'No problem. I didn't want you disturbing anyone. Or being disturbed.' Henry gave an almost imperceptible nod towards the other row of chairs. At the far end were an elderly couple who were both snoring, heads lolling on their chests. Slightly nearer to us was a middle-aged man wearing enormous headphones pretending to be engrossed in his phone. I knew he was pretending because he angled his phone towards me in a move I'd seen far too many times over the past couple of years.

Before I had a chance to turn away, Henry had stood up, taking two huge strides up to him.

'Give me the phone.'

The man shuffled back in the chair, eyes darting frantically. 'What?'

'Give me your phone.'

'Um, why?'

'So I can delete the photos you just took of my friend.' Henry's face appeared neutral but his voice dripped with contempt. 'This is a *hospital*. You should get thrown out for this.'

To the surprise of everyone now watching, the man burst into tears. 'I'm sorry.' He handed his phone to Henry, and then leant past him to look at me. 'I'm sorry, Bea, just it's my missus in there, Marge. She loves you. She always cooks dinner for quarter to seven so we can sit and watch your weather thing. Says it proves there are still people out there who care about each other. Since we lost our Noah, well. It gave her a bit of faith back that the world ain't all rotten.' He stopped to take in a shuddering breath, swiping the tears and other mess off his face with his coat sleeve. 'She's in a bad way, and I thought it might help her, knowing you'd been in here, too.'

'You could have tried asking,' Henry said, his tone notably less annoyed as he deleted the shots.

'Yeah. Didn't want to bother you.' He ducked his head. 'I can see this was worse. I'm very sorry to have intruded on your privacy. I'll find somewhere else to wait.'

He took his phone back and started shuffling off, but before he'd reached the door my heart had taken over my head, as usual.

'Hang on.' I walked over to him, placing one hand on his arm. 'Henry, do you mind taking a picture for – what's your name?'

'Alf.'

'For Alf to show Marge once he's able to see her?'

'I don't mind.' Henry raised one eyebrow. 'Are you sure you don't?'

I stood with Alf while Henry took a few shots, by which time three more people were hovering tentatively nearby.

'Um, would you mind...?' a woman with a young boy asked, holding up her phone.

'Not at all. As long as you can keep them to yourselves, for now. We're waiting until morning to let all of our family know why we're here.'

After taking a few more photos, and exchanging some brief words of sympathy along with a couple of hugs, I sat back down.

'That really wasn't necessary,' Henry muttered stiffly, once everyone had settled back in their own seats.

'Maybe not. But it's better than the alternative.'

'I would have made sure they deleted them all.' Henry blinked, furiously, and I noticed his ears had turned red. I sat back, surprised as I realised that he was annoyed that I'd felt pressured into having the photos, at a time when I was desperately upset.

'Thank you. But I didn't mind,' I said, leaning closer to him. 'If posing for a few photos helps distract them from a horrible evening, then I'm happy to do it. Being on television means all sorts of people want to tell me things or ask my advice, and while I rarely have the answers, I know that when someone they recognise takes the time to notice them or to listen, for some reason it helps. I love that my job means I can brighten someone's day by saying hello. It's ridiculous that it should matter, but I've accepted that it does, so I might as well do my best with it.'

Henry nodded, his forehead wrinkled in thought. 'I guess that's one good thing about not getting the BWM Today job. It would be impossible to manage this if you were famous everywhere.'

'It would make it harder, yes.'

'And I'm sure you'll be grateful not to be moving away from your family now, too.'

'Mm.'

I took a sip of my freezing-cold coffee. Now really wasn't the time or the place to do it, but Baxter Bigwood needed an answer.

'I take your point, though,' Henry added. 'You definitely seem calmer after chatting to those people.'

'Ugh.' I sank lower into the seat. 'I'm sorry I lost it, back at the house. Being home does that to me,' I carried on, feeling the need to explain such undignified outbursts to this man who never seemed to lose his composure. 'Simply walking up the drive is enough to rouse all those unresolved emotions from my childhood. Add to all that being back in the Spectacular...'

'Adam.'

I paused, closing my eyes as the conversation in the music room came flooding back. 'Yes. We were in the middle of an... intense conversation when you called.'

'He looked like a man on a mission.'

I really didn't want to talk to Henry about Adam right then. Even thinking about Adam was too much to handle. Only, at that moment the doors to the waiting room opened and there he was, Mum right beside him.

After everyone had been updated and Jed had gone to fetch more coffee, they settled down to wait. Adam took a seat beside me, tucking a stray lock of hair away from my face before taking my hand.

'How are you doing?'

'I'm okay.'

I was doing okay, until he turned up. I didn't have space in my head to deal with the Adam situation right now.

He bent closer, eyes intent on mine as if assessing whether I was telling the truth.

'It was really kind of you to give Mum a lift, but you don't need to stay.'

His gaze sharpened. 'Of course I'm going to stay.'

I looked away, not having the strength to say that I didn't want him to. That conversation in the music room had been like some teenage fantasy. This was real life. I daren't let Adam back in, start allowing him to be the person I leant on, until I'd had a proper chance to consider what he'd said and whether I was prepared to trust him again. That wasn't fair on either of us.

A few people had left and yet more arrived after Mum and Adam, quickly filling up the chairs. When another anxious-looking family shuffled in, Henry stood up.

'I'm going to head back, get out of the way. Do any of you need anything before I go?'

'Of course, Henry. Go home and get some rest.' Mum got up and gave him a brisk hug. 'We can't thank you enough for helping Joy.'

He blinked a few times. 'I'm just relieved I was there.'

'Make sure you take care driving back. There's a nasty fog settling on top of the frost.'

He nodded. 'Let me know if you want anything bringing. Clothes or whatever else Joy needs.' He gave a small smile. 'I'm good with lists.'

'Don't forget your jacket.' I started to shrug it off.

'No, you keep hold of it.' He held up a hand in protest.

'It's warm enough in here. Please, take it for the car.'

'You'll need it on the way home.'

'Mate, she can wear mine,' Adam interrupted, standing up and whipping off his blue jacket so fast one sleeve caught me on the side of my head.

Okay, this was too much. I had a feeling this conversation was about more than a jacket, and I could not handle it right then.

'You know what, why don't you both go? Henry, would you mind dropping Adam in Hatherstone?'

'What?' Adam looked at me, a mixture of hurt and surprise on his face.

'I need to focus on Nana Joy. You being here... it's not helping.'

'Okay.' He gave a slow nod. 'I'm sorry. And all that we said before, I'm not going to pressure you. I just want to be here for you. Whatever you need.'

'I know. But what I need is to wait with Mum, Dad, and Jed and not have to think about anything else.'

'I understand.' He leant forwards slightly, as though to kiss me, but I gave a brief shake of my head, crossing my arms against my chest.

'I'll let you know when we hear what's happening.'

It was only once they'd both left that I realised Henry hadn't taken his coat.

\* \* \*

At some point in the early hours of the morning, a doctor came to tell us that they hadn't found any evidence of a serious underlying issue. They suspected Nana Joy had fainted and the head injury had knocked her unconscious. They would know more when – or if – she regained consciousness. The next few hours would be crucial.

'You and Jed should go,' Mum said, once the doctor had left us to digest the news.

I started to protest, but she cut me off, jerking her head sharply to where Dad sat hunched on the plastic seat.

'We can't all stay here all the time, or we'll end up collapsing with exhaustion. Your dad needs to be here now. You go on home, get some rest, walk the dogs, and have a decent meal. We'll sit with her once visiting hours are open in the afternoon. Then you can come back later on and take over.'

I desperately wanted to stay. But I also knew that Mum was right; we needed to pace ourselves. After repeated sleepless nights and non-stop days I was also so tired I could barely stand up any more, which was no use to anyone.

We were permitted to briefly see Nana Joy before we left, but all this allowed for was a soft kiss on her papery forehead, a tender squeeze of her hand, and a fervent whisper that we loved her, we were praying, we would be back soon.

Jed drove Mum's car back to Charis House. For the first half of the forty-minute journey we rode in silence, the faint jangle of late-night radio playing carols in the background. All I could think about was those stupid months I'd wasted, hiding behind my job, keeping myself busy doing everything I could think of apart from the most important thing. I couldn't even remember the real reason why I'd avoided home for so long.

The guilt and the shame were like a crushing weight on the back of my head. If Nana Joy died in that hospital bed, and I never had a chance to tell her how much she meant to me, how sorry I was for disappearing, the pressure might just snap my spine in two.

'What was your favourite Nana Joy play?' Jed asked as the Christmas lights of the town began to fade.

'*The Lion, the Witch, and the Wardrobe*,' I replied, without having to think about it. 'It was the first one I went to see. I was entranced by the whole musical, and it wasn't until she started singing that I realised this nasty, sneaky witch was my wonderful nana. I thought she must genuinely be magic to transform herself into another person like that.'

'It was amazing to see her become her characters, but what about that solo show, when she told stories in between the songs? I think I loved her best when she was being herself.'

I nodded in agreement. 'In that case, my favourite has to be my tenth birthday party. I was so embarrassed I could have cried when she started singing that Sugababes song. Then she began the rap and jumped on the table, and all those scary girls from school started clapping along and squealing. For one, sweet day I felt good enough. They were all lining up for her autograph.'

Jed nodded his approval. 'The big shows were great, but nothing beats a personal performance.'

'I'm so angry with myself for missing so many of her last ones.' I pressed my head into my hands, although the pain was lower than that, ripping through my chest.

'You have a choice now, Bea. It's one I talk to my students about almost every day. You can beat yourself up about what's happened. Allow the guilt to keep gnawing away. Or, you can accept that the only thing you can change now is what happens next. Make the most of that.'

'Only she might not have any time left.'

He was silent for a moment. 'Maybe not. But the rest of us do.'

* * *

We found Mia chatting quietly with Henry, having finally persuaded the children to get some sleep after hearing that Nana Joy was sleeping, too. She made a pot of tea and assembled a platter of leftover Christmas Day cheese and crackers. I felt weary down to my bones, but, once I'd hauled myself up to the attic, found it impossible to settle. Instead, I opened up my social media accounts, deciding to work through some of the comments and messages in the hope that it would take my mind off things.

There was a semblance of comfort to be found in reading the Christmas greetings and chatter between the people who frequented my feeds. Mrs Lewinski thought it hilarious that I'd gone looking for her and ended up starting a street party, offering me a formal invitation to have lunch in the new year.

As I scrolled down, responding with a like or a brief reply where appropriate, a realisation started to bloom.

*I love this.*

*I love these people, this community I've helped to build.*

*I don't know if I want to leave them, to give this up.*

What Henry had said was true. While I'd presented Baxter Bigwood with my 'vision' for how I could replicate the success of my local role on a national scale, it would be impossible for one person to manage. There were already so many people actively involved online that it was getting hard to keep track of the different profiles. Baxter had mentioned assistants, media people, but did I want a random intern posting while pretending to be me?

I wanted to turn up to a secondary-school environmental day and shake hands with a teacher who I knew loved paddleboarding with her Irish Setter, but was concerned about the state of the local lake and wanted to know what practical things they could do to clean it up. And I would have an answer, because I knew that lake, knew the head of the charity who managed the nature reserve it was located in, and had in all likelihood invited him to join us for a drink in the pub that evening.

I wanted the work I did to impact the streets I walked every day, the communities I knew and cared about, the forest my family called home.

Was I selfish, wanting to focus on my own neighbourhoods?

Wouldn't it be better to take this wonderful thing I'd somehow started and spread it across the country, get other people involved?

And wasn't the whole point of applying for another job because my current one now required double-dose migraine medication?

*Ugh.*

Now was really not the time to be making a decision like this.

The problem was, I didn't have long left to decide.

And, to be honest, it was easier than thinking about Adam's proposal.

## 24

The exhaustion must have finally overtaken my tumultuous thoughts, because once I'd fallen asleep I stayed that way until the sun was peering around the edge of my curtain. My immediate instinct was to check my phone, but there were no messages. I quickly texted Mum and had a reply to confirm that there'd been no change, which was about as much as we could hope for. Wrapping myself up in a giant cardigan for comfort as much as warmth, I padded downstairs to find everyone else at the breakfast table.

'So, what's on the itinerary today, then?' Jed asked, attempting to smile.

Daisy and Frankie leapt off the bench and hurried over to a laminated sheet pinned on the giant noticeboard hanging beside the back door.

'Um... clear up the hall this morning. Hot dogs on the firepit then—'

'Then free time,' Daisy interrupted her brother, squeezing in front of him so that her face was two inches away from the sheet. She wrinkled up her nose. 'What's free time?'

'A rare and fleeting commodity,' Jed replied, solemnly. 'Enjoy it while it lasts. So, it makes sense to stick with—'

'Wait, I haven't finished!' Daisy glowered. 'Six p.m. is the Christmas trail at... at...'

'Rufford Abbey,' Elana droned, not bothering to look up from her bowl of cereal.

'I was about to say that!'

'Well, now you don't have to.'

'Please!' Mia said, in a voice that brooked no discussion. 'We're all tired and feeling sad about Nana Joy being ill. Let's not squabble.'

Mia's mouth pinched in a way that a less indignant child would have spotted meant trouble. Jed, who'd learnt the hard way not to miss his wife's body-language cues, stood up with a noisy scrape of his chair. 'Come on, let's go and play your new board game while the adults clear up breakfast.'

Daisy and Frankie had disappeared in the direction of the living room before Elana had time to huff out a pre-teen sigh.

'Elana?' Mia asked. 'Are you playing the game or helping us in here?'

'Fi-i-i-i-n-n-n-ne.' She dumped her half-full bowl on the sink with a clatter. 'I'll leave you to talk about grown-up things that a little child like me can't possibly understand and go and have fun as if my own great-grandmother isn't lying in a hospital bed and probably going to die! You can fill me in on the PG version once you've made it up.'

Once it was clear that Elana's angry thuds were heading up the stairs, not in the direction of the board game, Mia offered a hasty apology for leaving me with the mess and went to find her.

'I'm so sorry,' Henry said, pouring a mug of tea and handing it to me.

'It's not that big a mess.' I helped myself to a croissant from a large plate in the middle of the table and added a blob of Mum's home-made, sugar-free jam.

'I meant Joy. It must be even harder when something like this happens at Christmas.'

I shrugged. 'At least it means we're all here.'

'How long had you originally planned to stay?' Henry sat down opposite me.

'I'm back at work on the twenty-ninth, so was heading home tomorrow evening. Jed and Mia are nipping down south to visit her parents but then coming back to stay over on New Year's Eve. It's slightly ridiculous, given that they only live a mile away, but they seem to enjoy it.' I took a bite of my pastry, which was warm and flaky and delicious, followed by a swig of tea to wash away the bitter aftertaste of the jam. 'I'll decide what I'm doing once we know more. It's impossible to think straight at the moment. I shouldn't really miss any more work, but if... well, if things are bad, I'd rather miss work than time with Nana Joy.'

'Could you commute into work from here?'

'I don't have a car so getting there would be a nightmare. And hospital visiting times overlap with my work hours. I'd barely make it to see her in time even if I paid for a taxi.'

'Could you swap shifts, given the circumstances?'

I considered that. 'Given my current reputation, I don't think anyone'll be bending over backwards to accommodate me. To be honest, if it starts to get awkward, that might just help me make a big decision.'

'Oh?'

I took another sip of tea. 'Baxter offered me the job.'

Henry sat back, the immediate surprise on his face gradually replaced with a huge grin. 'So he damn well should have done.' He shook his head, with a mixture of delight and what might have been a smidgin of pride. 'Even walking out on him, you were still parsecs above the rest of them.'

'What secs?'

'One measurement up from light years.'

'Okay. Thank you.' Henry looked deadly serious, so I hid my smile behind another bite of croissant. 'He said he'd had enough of yes-men. Oh – and he also told me to tell Driver to call him. He liked you.'

'What?' Henry rolled his eyes. I made no pretence at concealing my smirk this time.

'I'm not sure if he wants to give you a job or ask you out on a date.'

'Either way, it's a hard pass.' He shook his head, mouth twitching. 'But getting back to what's important... congratulations! What an amazing achievement.'

'Yeah, although not one I'll be mentioning to my family any time soon, given what else is going on.'

'Hopefully you'll be celebrating with them – *all* of them – before you know it.'

'Yeah... maybe.'

Henry quirked his eyebrow. 'Are you worried they'll be upset you're moving away?'

I shrugged, feeling another rush of hot tears start to gather behind my eyes. 'I'm more worried at how upset *I* am about moving.'

'Ah. Okay.'

'Especially now. I'm actually wondering whether I want the job after all.'

'Right.'

'I mean, part of me is like, "don't be an idiot, Bea, remember why you applied in the first place! How could you even think about turning down such an incredible opportunity, especially when working where you are has become a total stress". I mean, it's London, not Antarctica – I can be home in two hours. And being able to do in-depth features, proper news reports, all the amazing things that I've dreamed of for so long. What possible reason could I have for not immediately replying with a massive yes?'

'The fact that you haven't means there must be a reason.'

I pushed my plate and mug to one side and slumped across the table, pressing one cheek against the smooth oak. 'I'm trying to figure out what that is.'

'Which can't be easy when all this other stuff is going on.'

'It's extremely not easy.'

Henry was quiet for a moment. 'What does your heart say?'

I sniffled. 'My heart is wondering if I'm making excuses because I'm a big, fat wimp who's scared she's going to mess this up as badly as her current job. My heart thinks that it's made so many stupid mistakes that it can't be trusted any more.'

'Maybe your heart simply can't bear the thought of being employed by Baxter Bighead.'

That made me smile. 'That, too.'

'You'll figure it out in the end.'

'In the end is tomorrow, so I really might not.'

'Okay, if your heart doesn't help, let's try your head. A list of pros and cons. At the very least it can reveal which pro or con matters most.'

While I poured us more tea he used an app on his phone to create a table with two columns. 'Okay. Pros for taking the job.'

I quickly ran through the things I'd already gone over. The work I'd be doing, the career opportunity... the money and other perks, blah, blah, blah...

'Anything else?'

Yes, there was one more potential pro of taking this job and moving to London. While I was still trying to come up with a convincing way of pretending that, no, there were no more pros, because mentioning this one to Henry would make me feel itchy, there was a knock on the back door and the pro let himself in.

'Hello!' Adam called, stopping dead for a microsecond when he saw Henry and me sitting at the table. 'Oh. Hi. There you are.'

He took a few swift steps over to me, bent down, and kissed the top of my head, handing me the enormous bunch of flowers he was carrying as his face creased in sympathy. 'How are you?'

'Yeah, you know. Just waiting for more news. Um, I'll put these in a vase.' I spent half a minute longer than necessary hunting for a vase in the dresser cupboard, then busied myself arranging the yellow and pink roses and adding water. Seeing Adam still kicked a jolt of adrenaline into my bloodstream.

'Any update on Nana Joy?'

'She's stable, but we won't know more until she wakes up.'

'Right. Wow. Is she likely to do that soon?'

'I don't know. We don't know anything, really.'

Adam looked as though he was waiting for me to say more, but I was wrung out from thinking about it and really didn't want to go over it again.

'I'll leave you to it.' Henry gave a polite nod as he got up and left.

As soon as we were alone, Adam came over to give me a hug. It was a weird sort of side-hug due to me still holding the vase, but that seemed about right all things considered.

'I wondered if you wanted to go for a walk, maybe get a drink somewhere? It could help take your mind off things.'

The temptation to disappear off into the Adam and Bea bubble tugged on my bruised heart. He'd been my escape for so long that the thought of a few uncomplicated hours away from all the worry was almost overwhelming.

'I promise I won't mention the ring in my pocket unless you want me to.'

Ah, yes. With Adam, things could never stay uncomplicated; that was part of our problem.

The simple truth was, I felt too tired to resist the one thing I'd been hoping for since I was a teenager. When he reached out and took my hand in his, more familiar to me than my own, I couldn't remember why I was bothering to even think about it.

Right about the second I was about to give in and run off with Adam for the squillionth time, Jed walked in.

'Bea, are you ready to come and start on the hall?' He paused when he saw Adam, eyes narrowing.

'Um, I need to clear up here and get changed first. I'll see you there in a bit.'

'There's loads to do before we go and see Nana Joy. You know if we leave the building anything less than perfect Mum will feel compelled to sort it before she's able to sleep.'

'I know, I said I'm coming!'

'I'm happy to help,' Adam said, pretending that Jed wasn't giving him a death stare. 'I think I remember where most things go, and I'll definitely never forget Principal Armstrong's high standards.'

'While we appreciate the offer,' Jed said, in a pleasant tone that somehow came across as more threatening than if he'd snarled, 'I need to talk to my sister about some family stuff.'

'Okay. I could see you later on, then?' Adam said, as indifferent as ever to Jed's hostility. 'After the hospital?'

'Maybe. I'm not sure how late I'll be staying.' I started stacking the dirty pots into the dishwasher. 'It's just really not a good time...'

'I know that, Bea. That's why I'm here. I want to help.'

'Thank you. I'll let you know if it's not too late.'

'Any time. Message me when you're free and I'll come over.'

'I'll see you down there.' Jed threw me a sharp glare and abruptly left.

It felt as if I was having to choose between Adam and my family. My career and my family. Being happy and my family. It was a giant mess and I had no idea how to handle any of it.

*Okay, Bea. One step at a time...*

Right. I thought of Henry's pros and cons list. What mattered most, right now, this morning?

I said goodbye to Adam and went to help my brother tidy up the small mess I could handle.

## 25

It was surprisingly therapeutic, stacking chairs and sweeping floors. The hall wouldn't be in use again until term restarted, so Jed and I removed the paper chains and gaudy streamers while the children helped Mia undress the trees. It felt eerily quiet without Mum and Dad there until Elana plugged her phone into the sound system, clicking on 'Joy Papplewick's Greatest Hits', and we sang and danced, laughed and cried as we set about restoring order.

'You said you wanted to talk about family stuff?' I asked Jed as we started winding fairy lights into loops neat enough for my mother to approve.

Jed glanced up. 'This might seem like the wrong time to discuss it, but with Nana Joy being so ill, I think we need to decide what to do – if anything – about finding Dad's father.'

'What, you mean in case she dies?' I choked back the dread scrabbling up my throat.

He carried on looping, face grim. 'Possibly. Or, if she's seriously ill. What do we do, if we find him?'

'You mean, do we tell her?' I used a piece of wire to secure one perfectly even loop in place and started on the next section. 'The chances are it won't come to that. If he's died, or doesn't happen to have a spare half a million pounds to give away, or does have money but doesn't want anything to do with his supposed son.' I stopped to look at him. 'Oh. That's why we need to decide now. Because if we do find him, we'll need Nana Joy to corroborate it.'

He shrugged. 'It had crossed my mind. We can't turn up on an elderly man's doorstep and chuck this grenade at him on a hunch.'

'Crap.' I sat down on a plastic storage crate. 'This is really, really difficult.'

'Yes. But like you said, it's really, really important. We don't need to make any big decisions yet. All I'm saying is that if we do want to follow this through, depending on if and who or what we uncover, it might be best if we uncover it sooner rather than later.' He stopped then, swallowing hard as he fought to control the emotion. 'It's horrible. I feel like a monster even bringing it up. But I know Nana Joy wouldn't want us to lose Charis House if we didn't have to, if she could help...'

'I think when life gets turned upside down, all you can do is take it one step at a time. There's no harm in carrying on the search for now. Like you said, it probably won't lead anywhere, but at least we'll have tried. If we *do* find something, we can worry about it then.'

'So, we keep looking?'

I lifted my head to the grand ceiling above us, scanning my gaze across the carved cornices, the shimmering chandelier, and hundreds of years of Armstrong life and love.

'We keep looking.'

* * *

Once we'd finished clearing up, and rewarded the children's hard work with the promised hot dogs, they settled in front of a

Christmas film while Jed, Mia, and I resumed the search. We had a couple of hours before Jed and I were setting off to the hospital, so we decided to focus on the four large boxes of memorabilia that Nana Joy often opened up when we were younger, which were in Nana Joy's bedroom.

'Remind me what we're looking for?' Mia asked.

'Anything relating to people who Nana Joy might have confided in,' Jed said. 'Or who might have discovered her secret another way. A personal assistant, best friend, her doctor. Or, even better, any reference to the list of potential names from *A Murder in Paris*, on that Post-it. If we put anything that looks promising in a separate pile, we can go through them later when we've got more time.'

It was a small pile. By the time we had to leave we'd worked through two of the boxes. After a brief debate we put those away and carried the remaining two up to my attic room, so we could go through them another time without arousing suspicions from Mum or Dad.

We'd found the name of a housekeeper and personal assistant in an interview about how she managed as a successful, working woman. Joy had declared them to be, 'Absolute pearls! They know me better than I know myself, and I couldn't manage without them.'

A couple of photographs showed her on the arm of the murderer from *A Murder in Paris*, but they were all in the year or two after Dad had been born, and it seemed unlikely that she'd have remained so close to the father of her child while keeping his identity hidden.

There were a few other names mentioned that we felt it worth following up on, but it was all very tenuous and vague, and we couldn't help drawing the same conclusion.

'Maybe we should just ask her?' Mia said, as we tidied everything back into the boxes. 'Being so ill might make her reconsider keeping such a big secret.'

'Maybe, but it seems wrong to bring it up now, considering it's such a forbidden topic,' Jed replied.

'She knows that Charis House is in trouble. What if we came around to it that way?' I suggested. 'We could mention how it's a shame none of the Armstrongs can help, and subtly wonder whether there might be anyone on Dad's side of the family. If she starts getting upset at any point, we can change the subject.'

Jed frowned. 'Dad would flip out if he knew we'd been bothering her about that of all things.'

'I know,' I said. 'But I'm not sure what else we can do.'

'Like you said, one step at a time. We can't ask her anything right now.'

We all went quiet, remembering that not only could we not ask her anything now, maybe we'd never be able to.

* * *

We had a Christmas miracle while we were sitting by Nana Joy's bedside.

Or it felt that way even if the doctor didn't think it was much of a surprise. To see Nana Joy's eyelids fluttering and eventually opening and her clear, albeit bloodshot eyes fix on mine felt about as incredible as the angel Gabriel showing up with a trumpet.

She remained awake for only nine minutes, which the doctor said was to be expected, and managed a few coherent sentences, which was very encouraging, even if she did sing most of them. Given the state of our parents when they'd set off for home we decided not to disturb them with the news until they'd had a chance to get some sleep.

'This family is becoming full of secrets,' I mused, once I'd fetched Jed and me a celebratory coffee and cake from the café.

'Secrets?' a painfully dry voice asked.

'Nana Joy, how are you feeling?' I asked softly, cradling her fingers.

'Awful. Did someone hit me over the head?'

'No, Nana, you fell and hit it yourself on the kitchen worktop.'

'That explains it, then.' After accepting a sip of water, she closed her eyes and appeared to sink once again into oblivion, until piping up a few seconds later. 'You aren't going to sit there watching me sleep, are you?'

'We're reading,' Jed replied.

'You don't have to stay.'

'No, but we'd like to,' I said. 'I've missed far too much time with you over the past year.'

'It's all right,' she said, slurring slightly from the effort, her eyes still closed. 'You've been working hard.'

'Harder than I should have done. You're far more important than a job.'

'It's a good place to hide, though. Work. From irritating thoughts or interfering journalists. Keep busy enough and they might give you some peace.' She feebly patted my hand. 'I'm glad you're here, but don't hang about on my account. Not now. Not ever. You should be spending time on what you love the most.'

'I love you.'

Her wrinkles deepened in the semblance of a smile. 'I love you, too. But don't pretend you don't know what I'm talking about.'

I wasn't sure that I did know. I'd done a pretty good job of trying to love my job more than anything in recent months, but it felt as though the snowstorm had blown everything into a different place and I wasn't sure of anything any more.

She spent the next couple of hours dozing, while Jed read and I tried not to think about the clock ticking towards various different deadlines in my head. At ten o'clock the nurse politely invited us to leave, and we decided to head home rather than loiter needlessly in the waiting room.

'Miss Armstrong?' another nurse called from a side room as we were about to exit the ward. 'Would you be able to take these? Only patients aren't allowed flowers on the ward, and we're running out of space.'

She opened the door wider as I approached, a wry smile on her face.

There were dozens of them.

Flower arrangements, fruit baskets, cards, chocolates. A three-foot-tall stuffed pig.

'These are all for Joy Papplewick?'

I'd trusted the hospital staff when they'd assured us that they would be discreet about their famous patient. I guessed someone couldn't resist a gossip.

'They're actually for Bea Armstrong's grandma.'

'What?' I started to read a couple of the notes and cards.

*Get well soon, Bea's Gran!*

*Hope this cheers you up as much as your granddaughter cheers up my dad xx*

*Sorry you're not well, hope the doctors can forecast a brighter day tomorrow.*

'This is...'

'Yes.' The nurse reappeared with a trolley. 'Let's load them up, shall we?'

'Does this happen to you a lot?' Jed asked, scanning the room in bemusement.

'Usually people just send an email or a card to the newsroom.'

'Usually you're talking about other people and their lives, not sharing about yours,' the nurse said, starting to stack the gifts onto the trolley.

'I didn't share about this, either.'

'Quite a few other people did. Have you been online today?'

I had, but not since arriving at the hospital. My phone had started pinging with notifications as we'd entered the ward, and I'd turned it onto silent and stuffed it in my bag to avoid disturbing anyone and ensure that I was fully focused on Nana Joy.

Resisting the urge to start checking my feeds now, I eyed the pile of fruit and flowers and had a better idea.

Half an hour later, we handed out the last-but-one bouquet and wheeled the trolley back up to the ward. I'd intended to keep a couple more to dot around the Coach House, but seeing people's faces lift as I stopped them in the hospital entrance and handed them a gift proved irresistible.

'Keeping that?' Jed asked, smirking at the pig.

'It's for Daisy!' I retorted, tucking it under my arm along with a box of my favourite chocolates. 'Perhaps. I'll decide in the morning.'

Once Jed was driving us home, I tentatively peeked at my phone, which was inundated with photos from the night before. Once the first hospital visitor who'd taken a selfie with me had broken the silence, the others had swiftly followed. My social media was flooded with well wishes and condolences. There was an embarrassing number of comments about how kind and generous I was to take pictures with people when my own grandma was 'hanging onto life by a thread'. There were plenty also calling me an attention seeker who'd turned a family tragedy into a publicity stunt.

Even as I trawled through the hubbub, I was tagged in a link to a 'breaking news' article on my own work website.

### Weather Presenter Brings the Sunshine to Local Hospital

Below it were more photographs, taken earlier at the hospital, with a paragraph gushing about how 'Our Bea' had selflessly donated all of the gifts from her 'devoted fans' to other hospital patients, visitors and staff. I tried not to wince at my frazzled hair and grey eyebags. They weren't any worse than the previous snaps from the day before.

Jed waited until we were sitting around the table with Mum, Dad, Mia and Henry and then insisted I read it to them.

'Shouldn't we update them about Nana Joy first?' I said, trying to hide my fluster behind a giant mug of tea.

'I called Jed while you were talking to one of the doctors,' Mum said. 'You weren't answering your phone, and now we know why.'

'Come on, Sweet-Bea,' Dad added. 'We're dying to hear it.'

I opened my mouth a few times, but couldn't get further than the first two words. I was still getting used to family showing more than a vague interest in my work. The attention was disconcerting.

'"Despite the recent weather, there was sunshine all round at one of the Sherwood Forest Hospitals late on Thursday night as local BBC weather presenter, Sherwood Forest's very own Bea Armstrong, brought Christmas cheer to patients and staff alike..."' Henry carried on reading the short article, which had clearly been written to squeeze out every drop of festive feelgood possible.

There was a moment's silence once he'd finished, during which time I tried not to slide under the table and hide behind Dumble and Dash.

'When did this happen?' Mum asked, bristling.

'Just now, before we came home,' I stammered. Was she really annoyed that I'd given Nana Joy's gifts away? The chocolates I'd brought back were lovely, and it wasn't as though Nana Joy could enjoy them.

'No.' She shook her head in dismissal. 'When did you become "Our Bea"?'

The article had called me that four times.

'I'm on television five days a week, I'm going to be relatively well known in the area.'

'Beatrice, there is a difference between a face people recognise off the television and someone who inspires them to send pineapples to an elderly woman they've never met! You're clearly far superior to the average weathergirl.'

'You're a local treasure!' Dad blotted his tears on a napkin covered in penguins wearing Santa hats. '*Our* Bea is Our Bea!'

'Maybe we should watch the news more often,' Mia said, frowning at her phone. 'Have you seen all these comments?'

For some strange reason, seeing my family astonished at a few online stories about me, seeing them *proud*, had me fizzing with resentment. I felt as though they were telling me off for being sneakily successful. As if they couldn't have seen it for themselves every evening.

I was brought back from the brink of painful, angry tears by a hand resting on mine, where it clenched the denim fabric of my boilersuit beneath the table. As my fingers instinctively let go, Henry wrapped his around my palm and gave it a squeeze. It was only when he'd taken a seat beside me a few minutes earlier that I'd realised I'd been missing his reassuring presence.

'Bea is way more than a weather presenter.' Henry spoke with a quiet authority that sent goosebumps scurrying up my back. 'Haven't you seen the community she founded? The features she writes? She spends her days off tirelessly supporting local events and organisations and they love her for it. What she's created out of a three-minute slot is utterly unique and inspirational. And given how well those two words sum her up, none of her family should be surprised in the slightest. You should be her biggest fans.' Henry's ears were well past pink and heading for scarlet as his volume increased. I wanted to lean over and kiss the crease of annoyance at the side of his mouth. Only then he went and ruined it. 'Her work is so ground-breaking that Baxter Bigwood offered her a role as his number one national weather presenter, even though she walked out of the interview.'

'She got the job?' Mum barked, eyebrows furrowing in confusion. 'You got the job?'

'Sweet-Bea, that's wonderful!' Dad exclaimed. 'Why didn't you tell us?'

'I...'

'Jed, fetch a bottle of champagne and some glasses. If there's none left over from Christmas you can open one of the New Year stash.'

'Mum, it's after midnight.'

'And? Maybe you should have told us earlier, then.'

'Please can we not do this now...?'

'Why not? Nana Joy won't mind. She's going to be fine, and if she was here she'd be the first to toast your success.'

'Can you listen to what I want for once?' I threw a pointed look at Henry, who had realised too late that in trying to help he'd actually made things worse. 'I haven't decided if I'm going to take it yet, so you can save the champagne until I do.'

'Oh, no,' Mia groaned, sounding devastated about a job offer that was nothing to do with her. 'This is not good.'

'I hardly think that taking a few days to consider it is a disaster,' I huffed, gripping the chair to prevent me running out of the room screaming.

Mia finally looked up from her phone. 'Someone's made the connection between you and Nana Joy.'

## 26

There wasn't a lot we could do beyond phoning the hospital to let them know. Having retired from the spotlight years ago, Joy Papplewick being in hospital was hardly likely to cause a paparazzi frenzy, but the eighty-seven-year old star 'hovering between life and death' might well result in a few news-famished journalists sniffing around. We also agreed to release a short official statement, just in case, so I wrote a couple of sentences about how my grand-mother, Joy Papplewick, was currently recuperating well after a fall and expressed her love and thanks in return for all the kind words and gifts, adding a request for privacy so she could mend in peace.

After posting the statement, I gulped down the rest of my second glass of champagne, Jed having opened the bottle despite the original reason being discarded, and headed to bed for some desperately needed oblivion.

I bumped into Henry at the bottom of the stairs.

'Thank you for what you said back there.' I reached a slightly tipsy hand out before realising that I had no idea what to do with it, opting to give his arm a gentle prod.

'I can't believe your family are so oblivious to your career,' he said, frowning as he zipped up his coat. 'Don't you fill them in on what's going on?'

I shrugged. 'I used to try, but they just don't get it.

'Because they don't *try* to get it?'

I shrugged again, hoping he couldn't see how I was swaying a tiny bit. 'It is what it is.'

'What it is, is wrong.' He pulled on a hat. 'Anyway, I hope what I said helped.' He paused then, fingers still midway through tying a scarf in a regimental knot. 'Apart from what I said about the job offer. I genuinely hadn't twigged that you might not have told them. Given that you told me, and I'm not exactly your closest confidant.'

'You know what?' I leaned a little closer, taking an extra stumble that brought me within three inches of his neck. I breathed in a lungful of his coconutty scent, producing an instant flashback to waking up beside him on Christmas morning, with all the strange and wonderful feelings that had accompanied it. 'Right now, you are, in the most scientific of terms, exactly that.'

Henry looked down, his gaze meeting mine, and for a second I caught a glimpse of the man behind the robot mask. Something flashed deep in the bright blue of his eyes, like an electric eel skimming below the surface of the ocean, and it was dangerous and thrilling both at the same time, sending a shiver across every inch of my skin.

Who knew how long we would have stood there, or whether we'd have moved any closer to each other, if the kitchen door hadn't flung open and Mia taken one look at us before slamming it closed again.

'Right. Anyway.' Henry took a step back, bumping into the front door, his face flinching in alarm before adopting a blank expression again. 'You sound like you need to get to bed.'

'I do.' I nodded. 'I don't know if I'm really tired or a bit drunk.'

'Maybe both?'

'Maybe.' It was then that I registered Henry had been getting ready to go outside. 'Where are you going? It's nearly one in the morning.'

'Home.'

'Home?' I shook my head as if a fly had crawled into my ear. 'This is home.'

'My home.' His eyes were now firmly focused on the tiled floor between us. 'I've been over the stable apartment today and made it habitable. With everything going on I thought it best to get out of the way.'

'You're not in the way!' I said, unable to hide my disappointment. 'You're the nicest person here.'

He gave one, firm shake of his head. 'If you knew what I was thinking when your boyfriend showed up this morning, you'd know that isn't true.'

Then before I could process what on earth that meant, or how to respond, he'd gone.

* * *

I'd hoped to sleep in late on Friday morning, burrowing under my duvet where real life couldn't reach me. My delightful mother had other ideas, stomping up the attic steps and pounding on my door until hearing me croak in reply, which she then took as an invitation to barge in.

'Bea, you're late. We're all getting ready to go.'

'You are kidding me,' I groaned, tugging the duvet up over my head.

'You promised to join in with the itinerary. Surely your grandmother being unwell only reinforces why we need to spend this precious last day together before you disappear off again.'

I slid one arm out and fumbled for my phone, checking for the inevitable mountain of notifications before holding it out to her.

'My goodness. Are all those messages about Nana Joy? I suppose you'd better read them.'

I pushed back the duvet and rubbed the sleep from my face. 'Today is also the deadline for the job, and I have a contract to scrutinise and a load of forms to complete. I'll try to make it to the pantomime, but I won't have time to walk there or have the pub lunch.' It was a good five miles to the nearby village where they put on the same outdated performance of *Sleeping Beauty* every year.

Mum hovered for a few seconds, conflicting thoughts chasing across her face. 'Okay.'

'Okay?' Now that did wake me up.

'I appreciate that this job application is important to you and it requires some focused time and attention.' Mum spoke slowly and carefully. 'And we must shield Nana Joy from all those people. Please handle that however you think best. We will miss you today, but we understand.'

'Right. Okay.' I didn't know whether to laugh or cry. Had my mother actually listened to me for once? 'Well, I hope you all have an amazing time. I'll miss being there.'

Mum snorted. 'You could probably recite the script by heart from here.'

'Yes, that's not the point though, is it? I'll miss being with you, too.'

Seeing Mum's eyebrows shoot up her forehead was like a dagger of guilt between my ribs.

'If I get focused, I can probably be finished by mid-afternoon. I'll go and see Nana Joy if I can get a taxi, then you won't have to worry about rushing back.'

'No need for that. By the time Henry accepted our invitation to stay with us the show had sold out, so he can drive you.'

'Okay, that's perfect, then.' It was unsettling how perfect the prospect of another car ride with Henry felt.

It was only after Mum had clomped back downstairs that I realised Henry could have my pantomime ticket.

I decided not to mention it.

*  *  *

I threw on some recycled fleecy leggings that a local sustainable clothing company had sent me, and the giant cardigan that I'd stolen from Dad several years ago, and hurried downstairs the second I heard the front door close.

'Isn't this lovely?' I asked Dumble and Dash, their claws tapping on the tiles as they followed me into the kitchen. 'Breakfast in peace. We aren't lounging about, though,' I added, flicking on the kettle. 'This is a working breakfast. There's a lot to do.'

I'd brought one of Nana Joy's boxes down with me. I had some sleuthing to do.

First things first, however. Once I'd made a pot of tea and cut a thick slice of stollen, I braced myself and looked at my phone. In addition to the one squillion notifications, most of which were informing me that the bulk of the Joy Papplewick fan club were now following me, I had several WhatsApp messages. All from Adam.

Oops.

Hey, just wondering how things were going and if you know what time you'll be done at the hospital? Did you get the hall back how Principal Armstrong likes it?

I'm still awake, so just let me know what time to come over

Hope everything's ok???

Wow – I just saw you've been busy this evening. I hope you didn't give away the flowers I gave you ;)

The final one was at two in the morning.

Okay, I'm heading to bed now. Call if you still want me to come over, or need to talk. I can't think of a better reason to get a bad night's sleep xx

The truth was that after the encounter at the bottom of the stairs, I'd gone to bed thinking tipsy thoughts about Henry.

I constructed a long-winded apology, then deleted it. I'd never actually said that I wanted Adam to come over last night, because I wasn't sure that I did. This morning, with a quiet house and space to breathe, it was as though having gone over and over all these thoughts and questions for so long, they were starting to solidify into some answers, like butter in a churn. I retyped a short answer saying a quick sorry, I was too tired to talk last night, and left it at that.

Next I whizzed through all the posts, comments, and messages. After finding nothing untoward, I posted a general follow-up thanking everyone again, apologising for the lack of individual replies and confirming that Joy was doing well.

Next, my next job.

In the end, it was easier than I thought to make a final decision. Henry had sent me the table we'd constructed of pros and cons, but when I opened up the BWM Today contract and started reading, I didn't need it.

I loved living in Nottinghamshire. I loved being 'Our Bea'. That the people who joined my online groups and called up the newsroom every day and sent me giant toy pigs felt as if they knew me, that I was one of them. Because I was.

I didn't want to lose that.

It might sound pathetic to some, but I didn't want to be a two-hour train and taxi ride away from my family. I wanted to be here to watch Elana's performances and play games with Frankie and Daisy and sing along with Nana Joy while I still could.

I wanted to watch the same naff pantomime every year and amble in the woods where I knew every tiny footpath and most of the people who walked them.

It was my life to choose, and this was it.

And if I was being really honest with myself, I wanted to stay near enough to build on this accidental new friendship with Henry.

Okay, that wasn't totally honest.

I wanted to see, in extreme private where there was no chance of any of our families ever finding out, whether perhaps we could be more than friends.

Saying no to Baxter Bigwood meant sorting out what the heck was going on with my current job, but for the first time in months, I felt determined enough to tackle that.

I'd just finished sending a brief, assertive, don't-bother-trying-to-change-my-mind email to Baxter when the dogs started bouncing about by the back door, signalling that someone was approaching.

'Hi,' Adam breathed once I'd opened it, chest heaving as though he'd sprinted the whole way here. 'I got your message.'

He followed me into the kitchen, leaning in for a hug when I came to a stop by the worktop, unsure whether or not to sit down.

'How's she doing?'

'Much better, thanks. It's going to be a while before she's back on her feet, but we're hopeful she'll get there. I'm going over later.'

'Excellent! That's really excellent.' Adam grinned, his dark-blond hair flopping over his forehead. 'You'll have time to go out for lunch with me first, then. I thought we could go to that place by the river, with the enclosed terrace. They've got a whole Winter Wonderland thing going on, with roasting chestnuts and a Michael Bublé impersonator.'

'Oh... that does sound nice.'

'*And*, if you need more convincing, there are horse-drawn carriage rides.' He gave me a meaningful look. Adam knew, because he knew practically everything about me, that I'd been dreaming of a ride in a horse-drawn carriage since I'd read *Anne of Green Gables*. Once upon a time, we'd talked about including it in our wedding, before weddings became a taboo topic.

Stepping forwards, he placed his hands either side of my face, gently pushing my messy hair back as he met my gaze. 'I thought this would help take your mind off things.'

I took a deep breath. 'It probably would. But, honestly, I *want* my mind on things. I need to stop running away every time things get hard and learn how to process what's going on, so I can figure out what to do.'

Adam nodded, lowering his gorgeous face closer until his forehead nearly touched mine. 'I'd really like to help you with that.'

When I hesitated, he added, 'You've asked for some space, and I've given it you, Bea. But how are we going to work this out if you keep holding me at arm's length? You're the only woman I've ever loved. After everything we've been through, surely it's worth taking a few hours to give us one more chance?'

Looking into those eyes I knew so well, I had to agree. After all those years, I felt as though I owed us both the opportunity to find out if this time things could be different.

'I don't have time for lunch, but a carriage ride sounds good.'

Might as well have one of my dreams come true while I tried to decide whether I still wanted the other one.

## 27

The Winter Wonderland was wonderful. Wandering amongst the families and other couples, it was hard not to get drawn into the magical atmosphere. It was set in a local forest park and there were various pop-up food vendors and stalls selling Christmassy goods. Seating areas were set around a small stage where a young man crooned big-band classics and in a small paddock, children could pet reindeers.

I continued to resist Adam's offer to buy lunch, but did accept a warm apple cider as we joined the queue for the carriages. It made an enchanting picture, snuggling under a fur rug with Adam's arm around me as the horses clopped down the path, a meadow sparkling with frost on one side, shimmering water on the other.

Only... I didn't quite manage to feel enchanted.

Was it because I was too distracted with everything else going on? Or was it simply that I'd started to realise that if Adam and I were going to stand a chance, it couldn't be based on romantic gestures and starry-eyed dreams. Let alone old memories. I wanted someone to be there for me in the nitty-gritty, ordinary every day. Something that Adam had always shied away from. The big question was, had he really changed to the point that he was ready for a day-in, day-out life with me?

\* \* \*

'I spoke to Dino about the job. He says it's available as soon as I'm back,' Adam said as the carriage began curving away from the river and back towards the park. 'When do you start at BWM Today? If you need somewhere to stay while you find your own place, I can always ask around, see if anyone's got a room to rent.'

I sat up, moving out from under his arm and putting the length of the carriage seat between us. 'Yeah, I would have mentioned it sooner but I only decided this morning.' I tried to ignore the twitch of fear and hope on Adam's face and pressed on. 'I've turned down BWM Today.'

'What?' He quickly twisted his head towards the fields, but I'd already caught his features plummet in disappointment.

I gave him a minute to compose himself before trying to offer an explanation. 'I'm sorry, it's just... my heart is here.'

Adam turned back, clearing his throat. 'Well. My heart is with you, so I guess I'd better start job-hunting.'

We rode on past a family with a young girl who pointed up at the carriage, mouth open in awe as we smiled and waved.

'If we decide not to try again, not to get married, would you still want to live up here?' I asked. 'Because if not, I don't think you should move to Nottingham until we're sure. It'd only put us under more pressure.'

'If *you* decide not to marry me, I'll decide how and where I'm going to live without you then. You don't need to worry about it. It doesn't make any sense for me to stay in London. That was the whole problem before, and I'd only end up travelling back up here every chance I got, anyway. How can you become sure if we're living in separate cities?'

*Because I want to know if you're able to stick it out, even when it's hard?* I didn't speak aloud, but Adam knew me well enough to see it on my face. *Because I'm still expecting you to disappear at the first whiff of a music deal.*

Or, because the thought of this, Adam right beside me all the time, pursuing a passionate, poetic happy ever after, was starting to feel like a scarf that had been wound too tightly around my throat.

Sensing that he'd pushed things too far, Adam switched to more light-hearted conversation, and as soon as the ride had finished, he drove me home as promised. He did ask if I wanted to come and spend New Year's Eve with him in London, but I was reluctant to go while Nana Joy was still so shaky so he offered to take me out in Nottingham instead.

'My mate Zane can get us tickets for this fancy dinner and live band event.'

'Will you know many people there?' I didn't especially enjoy hanging out with Adam's 'mates', or how he tended to ignore me after the first two drinks.

'Irrelevant,' he said as we wound our way through the forest in the car he'd borrowed from his mum. 'I'll only have eyes for you.' He slowed down to allow a pheasant to cross the road before glancing over at me. 'Unless you already have a better offer?'

My other offers were going to a tacky bar selling rip-off drinks with friends I rarely saw any more, or yet another games night at Charis House. I'd been planning on declining both of them, choosing a post-Christmas restorative glass of wine and a good book in my flat instead.

'Let me show you that I'm serious. One night, and after that the ball's in your court.'

It would be a first step to see if Adam had really changed.

'Okay. If Nana Joy is still doing well, I'll come out with you on New Year's Eve.'

'Awesome. It's a date.' He didn't stop grinning until he'd dropped me off at the Coach House door.

\* \* \*

It was nearly one by the time I'd fussed the dogs and grabbed some leftover buffet snacks for lunch. Wasting no more time, I opened Nana Joy's box and dug in. It only took a few minutes to ascertain that this was all memorabilia from far later on in her career, through the seventies and eighties. I had a final quick rummage and decided to go back to the pile we'd compiled the day before. In my brief dabbles in creating news features I'd learnt to spot a possible lead, and there were two here that seemed most promising. One was Nana Joy's assistant, who from what we could gather had been employed for over ten years before she got married and moved away. There was also an interview by a journalist who seemed to have spent a fair amount of time shadowing her, and the level of access he must have had to her life suggested that he might have known more than he'd put into print.

The PA was much younger than Nana Joy, but that still put her in her late seventies, so I wasn't overly optimistic. An order of service from her wedding provided a married name and the location of the church as a starting point. An unusual name meant that it didn't take long to find Zelia Strong via her vibrant Instagram account.

I sent her a message and started hunting down the journalist, Tony O'Dowd, while I waited for a reply. I'd hit my dozenth dead end when my phone started buzzing with a video call – Zelia. I answered so quickly I nearly broke my nail.

After brief introductions – I'd told her in my message that the family were trying to piece together some of Joy's earlier life, for posterity's sake, and she dropped all suspicions that I might not be genuine once she'd seen the family resemblance – I decided to get straight to the point.

'I'm going to be honest with you – Nana Joy has been very ill and it's prompted us to start looking into my father's family.'

It took another couple of minutes to update her before she allowed me to get back to my reason for getting in touch.

'Your father? You mean Jonty?'

'Yes.'

'Ah. I should have guessed. The scandalous secret.'

'That's not quite how we see it.'

'No. None of us who love her ever did.'

'So, are you able to help? You must have had an idea of who my grandfather might be. Or maybe she told you?'

'If I did, do you think I would betray her trust after all these years? You know she still sends me flowers and a handwritten card on my birthday, and a letter every Christmas. Blue hyacinths, my favourites. She paid for my children to have singing lessons for as long as they were interested. Which mercifully wasn't that long, given their lack of talent. However, I couldn't blab even if held at gunpoint, which I think some of those gossip reporters considered. She never so much as hinted.'

'Did she tell you about Charis House?'

'Of course. I visited when it first opened. And I came to the Christmas Spectacular one year, when you were still an infant. I thought it was remarkable what your family were doing there.'

I told her about the current situation, and why we were trying so hard to find this man's identity, however much of a longshot it might be.

'Ah. I see. Well, like I said, I don't know, and if I did I wouldn't tell you. But you might want to try the Brambletons. They had a huge manor house in the countryside. She often stayed there towards the end of her pregnancy, and for the first few months afterwards. I doubt they'll reveal anything either, if they're still alive, but they may be able to tell you if your search is worth pursuing or not.'

I thanked her and went after my next clue. The Brambletons turned out to be a couple who wrote plays back in the fifties and sixties. They had both died over twenty years ago, but I did find a daughter, who had been twelve or thirteen the year that Dad was born, so only around seventy now. After a fruitless half-hour searching online for any contact details, I had a brainwave and called Jed, about to take his seat at the pantomime. Following a hasty explanation, he confirmed that Ursula Brambleton's parents had left a modest amount to Charis House in their will. Their daughter would be subscribed to our newsletter, with her contact details on file. A few minutes later I had her phone number.

After another introduction and slightly rambling explanation, I held my breath and hoped that she lacked Zelia Strong's scruples.

'I'm sorry, I was only a child back then... it was all very discreet. Nobody would have told me anything.'

'Do you remember anyone coming to visit Joy? Either before or after she had the baby?'

She thought about this. 'I really can't recall. She spent most of the time alone, barely leaving the grounds. That sounds terribly lonely, but I think she quite appreciated the peace. And she was so enthralled by her baby she didn't seem to need any other company.'

'No visitors at all?'

'No. Well, apart from that journalist. The one who wrote the big article. He came a couple of times. I remember because I was writing a story for our village newspaper and I asked if he had any advice.'

'Tony O'Dowd?'

'That might have been it. I can't be certain, though. I struggle to remember the names of my own grandchildren these days.'

Tony O'Dowd. A good for nothing journalist, as Nana Joy would call him. I'd always assumed her extreme opinions on newspaper reporters were due to a lifetime in the spotlight. I thought about the tone of the article Mr O'Dowd had written – intimate, verging on tender - and I started to reconsider.

I grabbed a mug of tea and called Zelia.

'What about Tony O'Dowd?' I asked, almost breathless from the hunt. 'The journalist who spent a month with her.'

'What about him?'

'Could he be my grandfather?'

There was a moment's silence while Zelia considered this, fingers fidgeting with her pearl necklace. 'He was in her life about the right time, I suppose. And he was clearly enamoured with her. But so many were, that's hardly conclusive.'

'Did she keep in touch with him?'

'No, quite the opposite. Once the article had been published she refused all contact. I only remember because he tried to approach her at an awards dinner, and she was quite rude in her rebuttal. I just assumed she'd taken offence at something in the article. She could be sensitive like that.'

'Okay, so, looking back, do you think it could be him?' I could hear my heart pounding in my throat while Zelia wrestled with her answer.

'It's as likely as any other suggestion, I suppose.'

'Thank you. Thank you so much.'

She twisted the necklace around one hand. 'Promise me you won't cause her any more hurt than you have to, no matter what you find.'

'She's my nana,' I said, eyes welling up. 'I won't hurt her.'

A few minutes before Henry arrived to take me to the hospital, I struck gold. Tony O'Dowd had written to 'Dearest Joy', thanking her for the time they'd spent together, expressing his sincerest appreciation for her kindness as well as his ongoing 'fondness' and affection.

It could have been a warm thank you from a nice man who warmed to his interviewee but I wasn't buying that.

At the top of the letter was an address in Hertfordshire. The thrill of being one step closer to cracking the mystery buzzed through my bloodstream.

Thrill and also panic. If we'd found Dad's father, what on earth were we going to do about it?

By the time I opened the door to Henry, I had to restrain myself from flapping about like a chicken.

'What's happened?'

I was learning to read Henry's face – the twitch in his jaw signalling apprehension at the possible answer to that question.

'I think I might have found my grandfather.'

'Woah. That's... big.'

'It most certainly is.'

'What did Jed say?'

'The pantomime doesn't finish for another hour. I haven't told him yet.'

'Right. Do you want to tell me?'

'Yes, please. I'll talk while you drive.'

Henry's car was heated to 'cosy'. He carefully unwound his scarf and removed his waterproof jacket and placed them in a neatly folded pile on the back. I tossed my tartan duffel coat beside them and took a contented breath in. It was a very different ride from my earlier trip in the carriage, but settling down into the now familiar seat, the old-fashioned crooner warbling on the stereo, Henry's scent mingling with car polish and antifreeze, was like a soothing balm to my twanging nerves.

He listened while I waffled on about my progress, giving a full blink of surprise when I announced my intention to contact Tony O'Dowd as soon as possible.

'Would it be wiser to sit on it for a day or so, give yourself time to consider this properly?'

'Sitting about considering isn't going to save Charis House.'

'No.' He was kind enough not to add that this ludicrous manhunt probably wouldn't, either. 'Have you managed to find a phone number?'

'No.' I straightened my shoulders, as if rehearsing my argument in preparation for talking to Jed later on. 'So I'm just going to turn up at his house.'

Two blinks that time.

'Are you sure?'

'What else do you propose, other than me keeping this information to myself, doing nothing about it, never telling my own father that I've potentially unearthed the secret of his paternity and watching Charis House slide into closure before some money-grubbing strangers take my family home, one fancy portrait and piece of Armstrong furniture at a time?'

'I'm sure your parents would keep any items that hold sentimental value.'

'What, like the whole house, outbuildings, grounds, and the school they built from scratch?'

'Okay, that was a stupid thing to say. I'm sorry.'

We drove in silence for another mile or so.

'When are you planning on going?'

My shoulders hitched up around my ears as I slumped lower in the seat. 'I'm back at work tomorrow, and I'll need a whole day to get the train there and back. It'll have to be New Year's Day.'

'What are you doing after this? Are you seeing Adam?'

'Once everyone's back from the hospital, it'll be a quiet night in front of the television. Even Mum won't have any energy left by then.' I paused, my voice box suddenly tight. 'I saw Adam earlier on.'

'Let's do it today, then.'

'What?'

I stared long enough for him to give in and throw me a glance. 'I'll drive you there this afternoon. If you like. I'm fairly sure your nerves can't take three more days of not knowing. I'm very sure mine can't handle watching you like this.'

'Henry...'

'Yes?'

I had to swallow back the tearful lump in my throat. This man never failed to surprise me. 'That would be amazing. Thank you.'

'Another road trip with my favourite weathergirl, where anything can happen and probably will? It's my pleasure.' He looked over again. 'Hey, maybe your animatronic elf would like to come, too?'

## 28

Nana Joy woke up as we arrived at her bedside. Her pallor was perhaps a shade less grey than the day before, although her cheeks were still sunken and her eyelids could have been made of lead, the effort it took to keep them open.

'Oh, hello, you're with this one again, are you?' she said, raising one spindly eyebrow. 'I think you made the better choice.'

'Henry gave me a lift, Nana. That's all.' I leant forwards to give her a kiss, hoping it would hide my furious blush. I'd spent a lifetime being teased about Henry, but now that I liked him, it was genuinely awkward.

We spent a few minutes chatting about nothing much, Nana Joy expressing her strident opinions on the other occupants of the ward, the hospital staff, and the 'pig-swill' they'd tried to pass off as lunch. Hearing her sounding almost back to normal, I decided to take a risk.

'Nana Joy, I was reading that feature that was written about you, right before Dad was born. The one where the journalist shadowed you for a few weeks.'

No reply.

'His name was Tony O'Dowd. He wrote a really lovely piece. He clearly admired you.'

'Most people did. I was a star,' she drawled, sounding positively bored by the topic.

'Right. Only... I was wondering if it was more than that. There seemed to be sincere affection there. A friendship. Or... were you more than friends, at all?'

My grandmother pursed her lips and gave a disdainful jerk of her chin. 'I cannot imagine what or who you're talking about, Beatrice. You know how I feel about those word weevils. Constantly trying to burrow into my personal business. I'm very tired now. It's been lovely to see you but I'm going back to sleep. Goodbye.'

She snapped her eyes closed, a fierce furrow creased between her brows.

'Well, that told you,' Henry mused as we took the stairs back down to the car park.

'It told me that she definitely remembers him and has good reason for pretending she doesn't.'

'You're sure you don't want to let this go, at least while she's still recovering?'

'Of course I'm not sure!' I groaned once we reached the main entrance. 'Am I sure that I want to do everything I can, leave no stone unturned in trying to save Charis House? On the one hand it's an obvious yes. But if it could break our family apart – then I'm not at all sure. Isn't a family worth more than a house? Mum and Dad will find a way to keep the school going, even if they have to set up a marquee in the forest or hire a barn from a neighbouring farmer. Won't they?'

'It'd be a major feat, starting again after the devastation of losing the house.'

'Their house, the charity. Mum's history and identity. Let alone having to let all the students down.' I was marching furiously towards the car, driven by agitation and anxiety. 'Right. I've decided. We're definitely going. If it's a dead end, then I'll know. If there's any hope at all, then I can work it out when I come to it. One step at a time, right?'

'Okay.' Henry unlocked the car and we climbed in.

'Unless... except... ugh. The look on Nana Joy's face. Am I going to break her heart? She's in hospital, for goodness' sake! She's eighty-seven!' I leant forwards and buried my head in my hands. 'I need to talk to Jed.'

'How about we stop off halfway and get something to eat, then we can re-evaluate?'

I wanted to reach out and grab onto Henry's calm and level-headed demeanour. Who was I kidding? Spiralling into panic, I wanted to reach out and grab onto Henry.

I looked up. 'Make a list of the pros and cons?'

'If you like. You also might want to figure out what you're going to say when you reach this address.'

'Crap.' Another wave of alarm rushed up my chest. 'Be honest: is this whole idea utterly absurd?'

Henry looked at me, his face serious, eyes gentle. 'How many people in Hatherstone thought that opening an alternative provision school was absurd? Giving these lost kids a chance?'

I offered a rueful smile. 'All of them apart from two. Oh, and your parents. Four.'

'Are you joking? My parents thought the idea was catastrophic.'

'You're not serious? Do Mum and Dad know that?'

'That scar that my dad has on his forehead?'

I nodded, my mouth half hanging open. 'Dad didn't punch him?'

Henry grinned. 'Your mum cracked him on the skull with a cricket bat. She swears it was an accident, but you and I both know that your mum has better aim than a precision laser.'

'So, what you're saying is that madcap schemes run in the family?'

'Or, I'm saying that sometimes it's worth taking a huge risk for something that means so much to you, even if other people might consider it to be foolish and irresponsible.'

'Do you think this is foolish and irresponsible?'

Henry kept his eyes firmly on the road. 'Would I be driving you there if I did?'

The answer to that, I'd realised after spending the past week with him, was probably yes.

\* \* \*

We opted for one of those 'healthy', home-made burger restaurants, a half-mile detour off the M1. I wanted quick, easy, yet not too grim, and a cranberry and chestnut burger on flatbread with sprout salad and parsnip fries was perfect.

'Looks like the kind of thing your mum would make.'

I laughed. 'This is my equivalent of childhood comfort food.'

'Glad you're feeling more comfortable.'

The truth was, that had a lot more to do with being with Henry than it did about the food. Although the festive atmosphere did help: the cosy booth we were sitting in was surrounded by groups of people laughing and chattering, Christmas lights twinkled, and a real fire provided a warm glow. An upbeat tune jingled in the background, and my feet couldn't resist tapping along.

'Ready to talk about where we're headed?' Henry had waited until I'd nearly finished eating before interrupting the good cheer with a blunt reminder of why we were here.

'Not really. But I suppose I'll end up regretting it if we don't.' I put the remains of my burger down, my appetite swiftly vanishing. 'What do I say if he's there?'

'What do you want to say?'

'I want to ask him whether he could be the father of Joy Papplewick's child. Whether he knows that he is, and if so where the hell has he been? Everything else depends on his answer.'

Henry patiently waited while I spent the next few minutes going over my rambling thoughts, winding myself into a tighter and tighter knot until I was back on the brink of a full-on freak-out.

'Hey,' he interrupted eventually, his voice firm. 'Take a breath.'

'I can't remember how,' I rasped.

Henry got up from his chair and slid onto the bench beside me. He looked unsure about whether to hold my hand or give me a hug, but I solved that dilemma by practically launching myself up against his chest, burrowing my face into his ugly green jumper. His arms quickly wrapped around me, and for a merciful long moment I stopped thinking about anything apart from the feel of soft wool against my cheek, and his firm chin resting on the top of my head.

'I've changed my mind. Can we just stay here instead?' I mumbled, once I'd managed to suck some air back into my lungs.

'As pleasant as this is, are you prepared to tell your parents that you ditched them to spend the evening in a restaurant with me?'

'Oh, no. I hadn't even thought of what to tell them.' I pressed my forehead against his breastbone. 'Are we going to have to say we had dinner together?'

'We did have dinner together.'

'Well, yes, but that was because we're on a mission to save Charis House. It wasn't because, well, because we...'

'Because we like each other?' Henry shifted position. 'Speak for yourself. I'd happily spend the evening having dinner with you, purely on the basis that I enjoy your company.'

His voice was as calm as usual, but he couldn't hide how his heart had started pounding against my cheek.

I wondered if he could feel mine, thudding in response.

I closed my eyes, hoping that might reduce the sudden static in the atmosphere, like the air before a storm.

If anything, shutting out the busy room around us only made the tension greater.

Then my phone pinged with a message. Fumbling out of Henry's arms as quickly as possible, I knocked my phone onto the floor in my attempt to grab it.

Henry bent down and picked it up, freezing momentarily when he read the screen.

'It's not Jed,' he said, his face snapping back to robo-Henry as he stood up, placing the phone on the table before brusquely plucking his coat from the back of his chair. 'If you've finished eating, we'd better go.'

'Yes, right. I'll go and pay.'

'I'll pay for my half,' Henry replied, a definite hint of frost in his voice.

'No, you're driving all the way down to Hertfordshire for me. Of course I'm going to pay.'

'Beatrice, has it crossed your mind that if Charis House closes, I'm out of a job? The one I ditched my highly successful career for? It isn't always all about you.'

And with that, he strode off, slapped a note on the bar before counting out what I presumed to be the exact change to cover his bill, along with a 10 per cent tip, then barrelled out of the door leaving me so shocked, it wasn't until much later that I remembered to check what the message was.

We spent the final hour and a half of the journey in silence, with only the cacophony of improvised jazz to drown out Henry's measured breathing and my confused thoughts about what just happened.

\* \* \*

The first indication that this wouldn't be the dream outcome I'd hoped for was the street we turned onto, which was a row of Victorian semi-detached houses towards the outskirts of a small commuter town. They were reasonably sized, well-presented properties but they certainly didn't appear as if the owners would have a spare half a million pounds to give away.

It was nearly seven when Henry pulled up outside the address in the letter and turned off the engine, his eyes fixed on the dashboard.

'I don't know what I've done or said to make you angry with me, but is there any chance you can put it to one side until this is over with?' I paused, trying to control the trembling in my voice. 'I really need you with me.'

'I am with you,' he mumbled, one shoulder twitching.

'No. I need you *with* me.'

He slowly turned towards me, although it took a good few seconds for his eyes to stop darting about. 'I'm sorry. I'm with you.'

I met his gaze, and believed that he meant it.

'I'm not angry with you, either.'

I raised an eyebrow in response.

'I didn't say I wasn't angry. But it's not you.'

'Okay.' I took a couple of deep breaths. 'The longer I sit here, the worse it'll get. Let's do this.'

Then, before I'd even realised that my feet were moving, I was knocking on the navy front door.

The woman who answered appeared to be in her seventies, which was a positive sign. The way her lips narrowed when I asked if I could speak with Tony O'Dowd was not.

'He died in 2004.'

I took an involuntary step backwards, the words – no matter

how hard I'd tried to prepare myself for them – hit me like a physical blow.

'Tony O'Dowd, the journalist?' Henry asked, placing a reassuring hand on my back.

'Yes. Are there many others?'

'But he did live here? You knew him?' I managed to ask, fighting hard to recover my composure.

'We were married.' She scanned me up and down. 'Why are you here?'

'He knew my grandmother, Joy Papplewick.' That produced a definite flicker of interest, so I pressed on. 'Our family are trying to piece together some of the missing chapters in her early life, and we knew she'd become friends with Tony when he spent time with her gathering information for an article.'

'When was this?'

'In 1961.'

'Before I'd met him. He was probably engaged to his first wife, Eliza, around then.'

'I'd love to hear more about him, if you had time to chat for a few minutes?' I asked, plastering on my best TV smile and looking hopefully at the corridor behind her. 'We've come quite a long way.'

She pursed her lips, considering this until Henry interjected with a brainwave: 'I'm sure Joy would be extremely grateful. We'll be sure to tell her how helpful you were.'

'I suppose you'd better come in, then. I'm not making a drink, though. I don't touch the kettle after six.'

'Thank you so much. I'm Bea, and this is Henry.'

'Pat. Please wipe your feet on the mat and take your shoes off.'

She waited while we did just that, then showed us into a modest-sized living room. I wasn't quite sure why I'd asked to come in. Pat clearly didn't know anything about Nana Joy or her baby.

Only – if Tony had known he was the father, there was a chance he'd told his wife. Even if he'd merely had a love affair with Joy, wasn't that the kind of memory people would share at some point?

'Did he never talk about Joy, or mention that he knew her?' I asked, taking a seat on the threadbare sofa.

'He was a showbiz journalist. He knew a lot of famous people. I can't remember him specifically mentioning her, though.'

Could that be significant, that he *didn't* mention her when he'd spent all that time in her company? It didn't feel like an appropriate question to ask his widow, however.

'Was Tony the kind of person who kept hold of items from his past? We found this house because Joy has a letter he wrote her. Maybe she wrote back?'

'Even if he had kept them, after all these years there's nothing left of his now.'

Rather than sitting down, Henry had been ambling about the living room. He stopped now, and pointed at a photograph on a side table. 'Is this him?'

Pat glanced up. 'No. That's my brother.'

'Do you have any photographs we could look at?'

'And then we'll get out of your way,' I added, hoping that would work as an incentive.

'The old ones are in there.' She nodded at a sturdy sideboard, directing Henry to one of the cupboards where he found a neat stack of photograph albums.

'The green one at the bottom. There might be something in there.'

Henry started flicking through, carefully scanning each page. I knew he'd found something when he paused, his entire body going still.

'Is this him?' he asked, moving across to show Pat a picture.

'That was when we were first dating, back in the early seventies. If you keep going there's wedding photos.'

Henry moved across to show me the page.

It was as if the air had been sucked out of every cell in my body. I had to blink to stop my vision dancing before taking a second look, because on the first glance, I'd have sworn I was looking at a photograph of my dad.

'A handsome man,' I choked out, and I wasn't lying.

'He certainly used to be.' It was clear from Pat's sour expression that she wasn't remembering her late husband with fondness, or grief. More like irritation.

'Do you have any children, if you don't mind me asking?'

'I don't.' She shrugged. 'Tony wasn't interested.'

'You mentioned a first wife. Had he any children from before you were married?'

'He wasn't married more than a year or so. A disaster from the start, from what I gathered. So, no.'

'Is it all right if I take a photo of this picture? I'm sure Joy would love to see it.'

'Take it, if you want. I've plenty more.'

'If you're sure?' My hand shook so hard Henry had to gently prise the photo out of the album for me. He also had the presence of mind to ask for her phone number, in case we had any further questions, which she reluctantly provided with the proviso that we didn't contact her after six p.m.

'Now, if you don't mind, Corrie's about to start.'

'Thank you, you've been very helpful.'

'If you say so.'

She had no idea.

## 29

'I can't believe it,' I said for about the billionth time since we'd set off. Jed called when we were about half an hour from home, and I managed to garble out what had happened, including the latest stunning revelation.

'Are you sure?' he asked, his voice thrumming with tension. 'Old photos aren't always that clear.'

'There were several pages of them. It was Dad smiling out at me in every one.' I quickly took a picture of the photo and sent it to him.

'Wow. Okay. What do we do now?'

'Well, we won't be asking his widow for money, that's for sure,' I replied with a weak laugh despite nothing about this being remotely funny.

'Do we tell Dad?'

'How can we not tell him?'

'This might sound insensitive, but should we wait?'

'You mean until Nana Joy isn't here any more?' I gripped the phone harder, nauseated by the whole conversation, my head starting to throb.

'Well, there's no rush, is there, now we know it won't help Charis House?'

'True. But if we do tell him, isn't it better that he still has the chance to talk to her about it? Otherwise it just leaves him with more unanswered questions.'

'That, as far as we can tell, he's never been interested in knowing the answers to.' Jed groaned. 'Maybe the kindest thing to do is keep it to ourselves.'

'As far as we can tell. How far is that though, considering no one's allowed to even mention it?'

'You definitely think we should tell him now?'

'No!'

'You think we *shouldn't* tell him?' I could hear Jed growing increasingly exasperated.

'No! I think that I've no idea what we should do! I was hoping you, as the eldest sibling, would know.'

'Crap.' He sighed. 'I'll talk to Mia.'

\* \* \*

We reached the Coach House at nine-thirty, Jed's car pulling up right behind us as they arrived back from the hospital. Henry declined to come in, saying that he still had unpacking to do. Although he'd not been curt with me on the way home, he'd answered all my comments with robo-Henry politeness, and made no attempt at a genuine conversation.

Mia took the kids up to bed while Jed and I convened in the study.

'There's no question it's him,' he pronounced, after inspecting the photograph in the beam of the desk lamp.

'Me and my stupid ideas.' I shook my head. 'Why didn't you tell me this was a terrible plan from the start?'

'I distinctly remember telling you this wasn't our secret to uncover.'

'Do you also remember persuading me to keep looking, when I was ready to give up?'

'We can argue about whose fault it is for the rest of the night, or we can come up with a plan about what to do,' Jed huffed. I knew it was only the stress making him tetchy, but my little-sister hackles were raised all the same.

'I've told you I don't know what we should do! We were only going to tell anyone if the man we found could help us, but now we've found him, he's become a real person, not simply an idea. I don't know if I can keep this secret. Especially with what might happen now the mission's failed.'

'Then we could tell Nana Joy that we know, see what she has to say first.'

'No!' That suggestion horrified me. 'You didn't see how she reacted when I brought him up. That's not an option. We tell Dad, or we tell no one.'

'Although you've already told Henry.'

'Oh, Henry's practically family, that doesn't count!'

'How convenient that when you want to blab our family secrets to him, he's suddenly one of us. When anyone else mentions him, he's some geek you can't stand.'

'That's not fair!'

'How about Adam? Have you told him?'

'Of course not!'

'Probably only a matter of time,' he snarked.

'Well, that's decided it, then, hasn't it? If I'm such a blabber-mouth, you'd better show Mum and Dad before I accidentally blurt it out on the weather forecast!'

'Blurt what out?'

We both spun around to find Dad standing in the doorway, looking as though he'd caught us setting fire to the Christmas tree. The snowman on his jumper peered suspiciously down his carrot nose.

'Nothing,' Jed snapped, making us appear even more guilty.

Dad moved to pick up the photo that had wafted onto the floor when we jerked around. 'Oh.'

I took an instinctive step closer to my brother, dumbstruck with dread as we watched Dad morph through surprise, annoyance, and resignation before settling on disappointment – quite possibly my least favourite of all parental emotions, despite being the one I was most familiar with.

After the three of us had been standing there for what felt like an eternity, Mum strode in. 'What's happening? Has there been bad news? Is it Joy?'

Dad silently handed her the picture. Mum jerked her head back in surprise before handing it back to him, her mouth set in a grim line.

'You've been busy,' she said.

'Um...' It was the best I could manage, which was one wimpy sound more than Jed, who was far less used to being on the receiving end of a Principal Armstrong glare.

'You'd better explain,' Dad added, lowering stiffly onto his desk chair.

So I began to talk, stammering and cringing at my own words, mainly propelled on by the objective voice in my head that noted how unsurprised my parents seemed.

I finally finished, helped out by Jed chipping in when I got tangled up a few times, and came to a merciful, stuttering stop.

My parents were like twin statues, stark white and every muscle rigid with I daren't discover what... anger? Hurt? Betrayal? Or, most likely, all of the above.

One thing was certain, they weren't about to thank us for our reckless attempt to save their school.

Mum opened her mouth to speak, right about when the atmosphere grew so taut I feared the windows would implode, but Dad gave a firm shake of his head. He was going to be the one to respond.

'What possible justification did you have for involving your nana in this?'

'We didn't... I only asked her...'

'And you were going to ask this man, a *stranger*, for *money*? You were going to tell an elderly man that he had a son, and, if that wasn't enough to send him into shock, you'd then chuck in a request for half a million pounds.'

Dad's hand quaked where he gripped the photo. 'How dare you interfere in something so precious, so private? These are people's lives you've been messing with. How could you possibly imagine this could turn out well?'

I'd never heard my dad sound so angry before. He'd been betrayed and let down and treated horrendously by the people he worked tirelessly to help countless times, and he'd never once lost his temper with them, never shown anything but compassion and understanding. It was impossible to prevent my tears of shock from tumbling out.

'Do you have so little respect for your grandmother that you think she would keep this secret without knowing it was absolutely the right thing to do? Can you imagine what it was like for her, having strangers snooping through her personal papers, trying to blackmail her doctor, sniffing after information that she'd chosen – for her child's sake – to keep private?'

'It must have been awful, but—'

'Then how do you suppose she would feel to know that her own family, her only grandchildren, had done precisely that?'

Dad was almost shouting now, prompting Mum to come and place an arm around him. This was the worst I'd ever felt in my entire life. All the times I'd felt stupid, not good enough, a disappointment, had been nothing compared to this.

'You knew, didn't you?' Jed asked.

'Of course I bloody well knew!' Dad stopped, choking at the words. 'But you had no right to, unless my mother or I chose to tell you.' He threw a withering look at me. 'And Henry Fairfax certainly didn't.'

'I'm so sorry.' It was all I could think of to say.

Dad dipped his chin, face firmly turned towards the window. 'I'm sure you are.'

After hovering there for another anguished minute, Jed took hold of my arm, nodding towards the doorway. I mutely followed him to the kitchen, sinking into a chair while he helped himself to a beer.

Mum found us another bottle of beer and a glass of wine later.

There were more tears, more apologies, garbled half-baked explanations until she silenced us with two raised hands.

'Of all the times for this to come out. We're already under so much strain. Your father is worried sick about his mother. And now this.' She paused. 'As if he wasn't feeling useless enough.'

'Dad isn't useless.' I shook my head in dismay.

'No. But Tony O'Dowd was. The reason Joy never told him about Jonty was because after he'd proposed to her in secret, she caught him with another woman. Having realised she was pregnant, she'd decided to forgive his dreadful mistake when a different fiancée he'd forgotten to mention turned up. Tony O'Dowd was a lying, cheating charmer. Even worse, he was a selfish coward, equally careless with friends and family as he was with women. Your grandmother was only glad she found out in time. He pursued her, still hungry for the second-hand fame and fortune.

Once she made it clear that wasn't happening, he married the original fiancée.'

'He must have known he could be Dad's father.'

'He didn't want to know, so didn't ask.'

Jed took another swig of beer. 'Would you have told us, if we'd asked before we started looking?'

Mum shook her head. 'I might have persuaded your dad to, if I failed to convince you the search would be fruitless.'

'Well, at least we managed to avoid upsetting Nana Joy.' I stood up, beyond ready to crawl under my childhood duvet and stay there for a very long time.

* * *

Once in bed, I opened my laptop and turned to the comforting ritual of my weather websites and social media groups. Scrolling through the data, I offered brief replies to those messaging with queries about their upcoming events, and made a note of those I'd be highlighting in tomorrow's broadcast. Getting lost in my passion wasn't quite enough to dispel the crushing regret, but at least it helped.

I was nearing the end of my notifications before I remembered that I'd had a text message back in the restaurant. I checked my phone and saw that it had been Adam.

I'm so happy you said yes. Can't wait for the big do!

What the hell?

I presumed Adam was talking about New Year's Eve, and hadn't somehow invented a fantasy acceptance to his proposal, but the heart, champagne and clinking-glass emojis conveyed a completely false impression.

I shuddered to imagine the response if someone else had spotted this.

And then I remembered how Henry's mood had changed after he'd picked my phone up off the floor.

Various thoughts tumbled into my head in rapid succession:

Henry thought I'd got engaged to Adam, and he was angry about it.

Was he angry because he didn't like Adam (which I knew to be true) or because... because he *did* like me (which I knew to be far less likely)?

And if he did, then what?

It was times like this I wished I had the kind of friend I could call at eleven o'clock at night to talk about a text. Instead, after pacing up and down my bedroom floor a few times, I paced all the way down the attic stairs and tapped on the door of Jed's old bedroom.

'What?' he growled, flinging the door open, hair already sticking out in a hundred different directions. 'It's nearly midnight.'

'Is Mia still awake?'

'No.'

'What's happened?' Mia appeared behind him, knotting the cord of her satin dressing gown as she blinked the sleep from her eyes. 'Or, should I ask *who's* happened, given that you're asking for me, not your brother?'

'Eh?' Jed mumbled as she firmly nudged him out of the doorway.

'How big is this? Living room?' She gave me a quick once-over. 'I think we'd better go upstairs. Via the kitchen.'

\* \* \*

I dragged the ratty old armchair over so that Mia could sit with her feet resting on my bed while I leant up against the headboard. Pyjamas on, bowls of ice cream balanced on our laps, we looked prepped for the kind of late-night sisterly chat we might have enjoyed as teenagers, if Jed hadn't fallen for someone six years older than me.

'So who's the problem, Adam or Henry?'

I scrunched my face up. 'Sort of both?'

'Go on.'

Wanting to get an unbiased opinion, I showed her the text.

'You got engaged!' Her eyes went round with shock. 'To Adam?'

'No, I didn't.'

I briefly explained about the carriage ride and New Year's Eve.

Her shock switched to focus. 'Did he send this on purpose, hoping someone would jump to the wrong conclusion?'

'That seems a bit far-fetched. It's not like anyone usually reads my phone. And if they did, I could explain. I think he's probably just been overenthusiastic as usual and hadn't realised the connotations.'

'Or he's sending a subliminal message, in case he ever does propose.'

'Well...' I then went on to describe the conversation in the music room.

'I want to say I'm surprised, but it was clear that he'd come back meaning business. That song at the Spectacular. Turning up the hospital. That's a bold move, though, given that you broke up six months ago.'

'He's all about the grand gesture. I think he knew I was serious about moving on this time. Flowers and yet another song with my name in it wasn't going to cut it.'

'I know you haven't said yes... but I get the impression you haven't said no, either, if you're hopping into a horse drawn carriage together.'

I put down my spoon. 'I'm so confused, Mia. It's been going round and round my head, driving me bananas. With everything that's going on, I can't think properly.' I picked up the cushion I'd embroidered with a picture of our previous dog, Pickle, and gave it a squeeze. 'That's why I thought a proper date with him might help confirm my decision.'

'Which is a yes or a no?'

'I don't know...'

'I think deep down you've already decided.' She took a deliberate mouthful of ice cream.

'It's been twelve years, Mia. Twelve years of loving him, waiting, and hoping that one day he'd choose me over his stupid music. My dream came true.'

'But he might not be your dream any more.'

'It seems wrong to walk away without being sure.'

'And to make things even more complicated,' she drawled, scraping out the last of her bowl, 'enter Henry Fairfax.'

'Um, what?' I pressed my spoon against one cheek, hoping the cold metal might prevent my skin from melting.

'You said it was Henry and Adam... ooh!' She leant forwards, eyes lighting up as the pieces slotted together. 'Henry read the text and thinks you're engaged to Adam!'

'Possibly...'

She sat back, settling in for another story. 'What did he say?'

'Nothing. He just went quiet.'

'You know by Henry standards this means he's probably in love with you?'

'We've become sort of... really good friends over the past week. He hates Adam and it's more likely that he doesn't want his friend to get hurt again.'

'You're right. The man's an enigma. I wouldn't be surprised if he's got a wife and kids somewhere he's not mentioned yet. What I'm really interested in is that, for the first time ever, you care what Henry thinks.'

I'd invited Mia up here to get her honest opinion, but discussing Henry in this context still made me want to crawl inside my duvet cover.

'Like I said, we've become friends...' I said slowly.

'And you want to be more?'

I hesitated. That was the big question.

'I don't know.' I rested my forehead against the pillow. 'I've only ever had feelings for one man. I always knew who'd be in my happy ending. As flawed as Adam and I were, I know him. The thought of being attracted to someone else is terrifying enough. But *Henry*? I spent my whole life loathing him, and now I find out he's nothing like I thought. And on top of this awkward history there's our parents, his job at Charis House... it's a lot to think about, even without a marriage proposal peering over my shoulder.'

'Then don't think about it.' She shrugged. 'Go with your gut. Or your heart. Whichever one says you should be with Henry, listen to that one.'

'But it's virtually impossible to gauge what Henry's thinking or feeling. Should I turn down a man who I know I can love, who I know loves me, on the off chance that a man who I barely know might be interested in giving it a go? This is marriage. Versus... nothing.'

'I don't think that's how you should be looking at this.' Mia spoke quietly now, her eyes meeting mine. 'It's not one or the other. You need to figure out for certain if you want to marry Adam, so you can commit to him or commit to moving on without any risk of him popping up and derailing whatever you might have in the future. And then, once you've decided that, you can start thinking about whether you want to see how things go with Henry. It doesn't have to be a big decision now. Whatever your parents might think or hope for, you can keep it casual, try a few dates. There are worse people to dip your toe back into the dating world with.'

'Are there? It's *Henry*!'

Mia smiled. 'Tell me when your first date is and I'll corner him in the staffroom and give him firm instructions on what to wear.'

'You seem fairly convinced on which way this is heading.'

'Bea, I've known your parents for many years now. They've not once been this wrong about anything.'

'Or if they are wrong, they somehow force it to happen, anyway.'

She got up, coming to give me a hug before she left. 'You seem to do a pretty good job of holding out for what *you* want. It's one of the reasons they're so proud of you.'

Now, didn't that bring back the evening's earlier turmoil like a punch in my chest?

I'd have expected another night flipping about like a stranded fish under my covers, the various issues fighting each other for which one was going to stress me out the most. Instead, mercifully, I must have reached overload, because the next thing I knew my alarm was going off, and I had two hours before heading back to work.

I dithered about in the attic until I was dressed, my bags packed, and the room tidied. Finally accepting that I'd run out of excuses, I trudged downstairs to face my parents.

'Ah, Beatrice,' Mum announced. 'You can join the war committee.'

Pouring myself a mug of tea, I chose to stay leaning against the counter rather than sit at the table until I'd worked out what was happening.

'Your determination even to the point of moral treason has inspired us,' she continued, sliding onto the bench beside Dad, who offered me a small smile. 'Time for the orchestra to stop serenading on the deck of the *Titanic* and start figuring out how to build a lifeboat.'

'Okay?'

'Instead of putting all our focus into one final Charis House Christmas, we're going to come up with a way to save the school,' Jed added, helpfully.

'Right. That's amazing. But I have to go to work.'

'Yes, of course you do. We'll fill you in with the plan as soon as we've come up with it.'

'Unless it's six-thirty, because then we'll be watching the weather,' Dad said.

I looked up, my eyes meeting his, and we both burst into tears in the exact same moment.

'Ugh,' Jed grumbled as Dad came and wrapped me up in a hug. 'I'm so relieved I take after the Armstrong side of the family.'

## 30

I instructed the taxi to take me home for a quick change and a couple of deep breaths before heading into work. I'd just about managed to shake off my disappointment that Henry hadn't appeared to say goodbye when he sent a message saying that he was thinking of me and he hoped it went well.

'Well, what does that mean?' I muttered, while yanking on a pair of patterned tights. 'Thinking about me how? A quick, *ooh, Bea goes back to work today, I hope she doesn't get fired.* Or, *I think about you all of the time*?'

I was prepared to be extra-early, showing that the organised, efficient, capable Bea was back, and then while waiting at the bus stop I received a notification confirming a meeting at eleven with the studio head, Mike Long, who I'd last seen one arm casually draped around Summer at the Christmas drinks do.

Even sprinting through the security barrier and up the stairs to Mike's office while mumbling frantic prayers couldn't prevent me tumbling through his door eight minutes late.

'Ah. Bree. I'd decided you'd stood me up.'

'I'm so sorry,' I wheezed. 'I only got the notification about the meeting twenty minutes ago. I'm not due to start work until eleven-thirty so I was still on my way in.'

'Always pays to be prepared, Bree. One of the first lessons of broadcasting.'

What, always turn up at work half an hour early in case the boss decides to have an unscheduled meeting with you for the first time ever?

He stood up, indicating that we should move to the meeting room that adjoined his office, where I was momentarily thrown to find Summer Collins already sitting there. She'd got new glasses, which were so large they almost hid the monstrous smirk on her face.

Once I'd sat down, Mike launched straight in.

'I hear you're leaving us. Thought it best to discuss the handover sooner rather than later.'

'Um, excuse me?'

'Summer will take your slot on an interim basis, starting from tomorrow. While working your notice you'll be mentoring her through the transition and responsible for the content she puts out. Train her up in all that extra stuff you do, so we keep hold of the viewers. She'll attract a whole new demographic, but I don't want that cancelled out by losing your lot. I'm prepared to reduce your notice to four weeks. Don't want to drag it out longer than necessary. HR say you've still got two weeks' holiday owed, so you can clear your desk in a fortnight.'

'Wait, what?' I sat back in the chair, beyond stunned while at the same time very aware of Summer right beside me. 'Are you firing me? Because I've not resigned.'

'Yet.' His smarmy smile sent a shiver of revulsion down my spine. 'Nothing gets past the boss, Bree.'

It didn't seem the right time to point out that my correct name had still got past him.

'I'm not planning on resigning at all,' I gabbled, while my brain frantically tried to work out how to get me out of my own non-resignation. 'Quite the opposite. I actually had a proposal about how I could develop my role further. Have you seen the online engagement stats for the Christmas period? I think now's the perfect time to take things to the next level, if I could share some of my ideas with you?' I stuck on my television smile, steadfastly avoiding Summer in my peripheral vision. 'Although, I'd be very interested to know where you heard that I was leaving, given that it's completely untrue.'

'You haven't been offered a national role with BWM Today?'

I swallowed, hard, and tried to resist squirting my water bottle in Summer's smug face, just in case Mike had heard straight from Baxter.

'I have, yes.'

Summer gave a minuscule flinch that I wouldn't have picked up if I hadn't been on hyperalert.

'I turned it down.'

'*What?*' Summer screeched, losing all composure as she spun to face me. 'Why the hell would you do that?'

'Yes,' Mike added, giving Summer a hard stare that confirmed his information source was sitting in this meeting room. 'Do explain.'

'I didn't want the job, for various reasons. Attending the interview only cemented how much I want to stay here, working on local stories with local people. I know it seems like I lost some focus over the past few months, but I am fully committed to seeing East Midlands Weather grow even bigger and better.'

'That being the case, Bree—'

'It's Bea.'

'Excuse me?'

'Bea Armstrong is a household name across the region. It probably doesn't look great if you can't get the name of your top weather presenter right.'

'Right. Bea. That's what I said. Anyway, as I was about to explain, we've already started the ball rolling for Summer to step in. Like you mentioned, we have a standard of excellence here that you've consistently been failing to meet. To be honest, you resigning saves a lot of inconvenience.'

'What are you saying?' I knew full well what he was saying, I just couldn't bear to believe it.

'He's saying resign or be fired. Either way you're leaving,' Summer chipped in, scrunching her nose in fake sympathy.

Okay, now I was beyond upset and galloping headlong into blind fury. 'Mike, you know I'm the best, most dedicated – not to mention *accurate* – member of the team. You can't fire me because I missed a couple of deadlines due to my email not functioning properly. That's an IT issue. Fire them!'

'I know this isn't what you wanted to hear—'

'What do the producers say about this?'

'The producers feel annoyed that you've yet to bother mentioning your new job.'

'I don't have a new job!'

'Well, if it's too late to accept Bigwood's offer then I'm sure you'll find something else, soon enough.' Mike stood up, as if the discussion was over. I remained firmly seated, and not just because my legs had turned to mush.

'You're sleeping with her, aren't you?' I blurted, my outrage overriding my sense.

Mike threw me a contemptuous glance. 'Your point is?'

'Bit of a coincidence.'

'I've slept with most of the women in this building. Law of averages says that some of them are going to get promoted. Have your resignation on my desk by five.'

The second he'd finished speaking, the door flew open and Jamal burst in.

'Mike, you need to see this.'

'No. You need to make an appointment with Hailey and then wait to be invited into my office.'

'You need to see this before you fire Bea.'

'I really don't,' Mike sneered. 'I don't care how many followers she's got. I haven't got time to deal with incompetence. She couldn't even turn up on time for this meeting.'

'That's because Summer hacked into her email account.'

'Um, excuse me?' Summer said, her laugh of disbelief tinged with panic.

Jamal was a first-rate engineer and Mike knew it. With an exasperated sigh, he nodded at Jamal to continue.

'I started tracking where Bea's been logging into her account, only it turns out half the time the logins were from places where Bea wasn't. Like at six-thirteen this morning, for example,' he said, turning to Summer. 'When Bea's email account was accessed from the computer at the desk where you were working, Summer, and the email about this meeting was deleted.'

Summer stared at Jamal for a long, painful moment before bursting into more laughter, verging on the hysterical this time. 'I went to drama school. I know nothing about computers. Are you seriously accusing me of being some sort of hacker?'

'No, but I am accusing you of being a good guesser.' He looked at me. 'WeatherGirl1? If you'd told me you had such a stupid password it would've made this a lot easier.'

'I knew it was you!' I sprang up, every nerve in my body quivering. I didn't consider myself to be an angry person, but having to deal with this, on top of everything else, the stress and humiliation Summer had put me through... nearly sabotaging the job I loved so much. I was a frothing cauldron of I'm Not

Taking Any More of This Crap and on the brink of a full-scale eruption.

Mike was already on the phone to HR. He took one glance at me and ordered Jamal to get me 'the hell out of here and come straight back'.

I spent the next hour stubbornly getting on with my job, updating the webpages and putting together the daytime bulletins. Mike's office was the floor below me, so I couldn't see what was happening or who was going in or out, but neither Summer nor Jamal had returned by the time I finished the lunchtime broadcast.

I was adjusting the graphics for the early evening forecast when Jamal finally appeared, the rest of the newsroom straining their ears towards us while pretending to be engrossed in their tasks.

'She's caved.'

A sigh escaped me that I hadn't realised I'd been holding in for months, and I slumped back into my desk chair, unable to prevent a tear from spilling out. 'Thank you.'

'You're welcome.'

'Is she coming back?'

'I've been asked to take you out for a coffee. By the time we return, Summer Collins will be a bad memory.'

'I'm not sure I can walk as far as a café.'

'I'm not carrying you, so you'd better rustle up some of that Bea Armstrong grit.'

'What Bea Armstrong grit?' I let out a weak laugh, which was probably his point, and headed out to celebrate my non-resignation with caffeine and a very large piece of carrot cake.

And so, a horrendous morning and nerve-wracking afternoon evolved into a pretty great evening. As soon as the newsreader cued me in, it was impossible to hide the joy at being back, free from the burden caused by Summer's shenanigans.

'You should go home more often,' Mrs Lewinski advised me

when she called at six forty-five on the dot. 'It looks like it's done you a world of good.'

I didn't correct her by saying that it was being back at work that had put the spring in my step, rather than time spent at home. For one thing, I wasn't sure if that was completely true this time.

The evening was crisp and clear so I decided to walk the two miles home. It would give me a chance to savour being back in my neighbourhood as I strolled past the pretty lights and warm glow of the familiar shops and houses along the route, and provide ample time for me to pop in my headphones and call Henry to tell him how Summer Collins got busted.

'Bea, I was about to phone you,' he said as a greeting, automatically increasing the flutter of happiness in my stomach. I had already analysed why I wanted to call Henry, rather than Adam, to tell him about my day. It could be because Henry already knew about Summer's possible sabotage, and had seen her in action at the interview. It could be because Henry had no personal interest in where I worked.

Or, it could simply be because it was Henry.

Hearing he wanted to speak to me nudged all thoughts about work to one side. I was acutely aware that Henry might believe I was back together with Adam. Was he about to say something?

'I just found a couple of guys lurking around the back of the house.'

'Charis House?'

'Yes. Your parents are at the hospital so I didn't want to interrupt their visit. Jed and Mia are already at her parents'.'

'Intruders? Have you called the police?'

'Journalists. From the *Chronicle*.'

I stopped dead on the footpath, causing a man to swear as he almost stumbled into me. As I moved to one side out of the way of other pedestrians, an icy fog of dread descended, its tendrils wrapping themselves around my chest.

'What did they say?'

'They were looking for Joy. Or her son.'

I started moving again, hurrying towards home.

'I pretended I was interested in answering their questions to keep them talking. Someone has sold them a story revealing your dad's paternity.'

'Oh, no. No, no, no!'

'I told them Joy wasn't living here at the moment, but it's not hard to find out that she's still in hospital.'

'Thanks to my stupid publicity stunt.'

'They've given me their card. They're aiming to hit the Sunday paper.'

'That's tomorrow!'

'Yes. If someone offers to do an interview, they'll postpone.'

'Someone being Nana Joy or Dad?'

'Or a local television personality who's a close relative, and happens to be the one who solved the mystery.'

'This is a nightmare.' I was practically running now, my rucksack bouncing against my spine. 'I'll be home in five minutes, then come straight over. I'll try and think in the taxi.'

I turned the corner onto my road, just as Henry replied, 'I'm already here.'

The flood of relief was almost enough to dispel the freezing-fog dread when I saw him standing beside his car, fifty metres down the road and right outside the little path that led to my front door.

Never in a zillion years would I have thought I could be so happy to see Henry Fairfax.

I ran right up to him, skidding to an awkward stop when I got there and wasn't quite sure what to do.

Henry took one look at my face, took a step closer and pulled me into a hug.

'It's all my fault,' I mumbled into his ugly brown coat. 'I've ruined everything. Nana Joy will hate me.'

'She's going to be upset,' Henry admitted, as reluctant to offer an empty platitude as always. 'But you're the Armstrongs. You'll get through it.'

Five minutes later I was once again in Henry's passenger seat. Weaving through the traffic at a steady one mile below the speed limit, I was finally able to think.

'There's no way we can hide this from her if it gets published. It's not fair to have it out there and her not know.'

Henry waited to change lanes before answering. 'At least your dad already knows, and Tony's dead so no one can bother him. It's a mildly interesting story if you know who Joy is, but there's no big scandal here.'

'No, but Nana's not rational when it comes to journalists. For which we can probably thank the delightful Tony. She'll be distraught that they've printed something she's kept secret for nearly sixty years. And of all the times for it to happen...' I shook my head. 'How did they find out?'

'Who did you speak to about it?'

'Her assistant, Zelia. Ursula Brambleton, who she lived with when she was pregnant, and then Tony's wife, but we never mentioned anything about a baby to her.' I pressed a hand against my forehead at another unpleasant realisation. 'I'm going to have to tell Pat O'Dowd that her husband had a love child.'

'If she doesn't already know, was lying the whole time, and decided to spill the story before you did.'

I thought about that. 'I can't see it. Why invite us in, let alone give us the photo, if she was lying? I don't think it's Zelia, either. She loves Nana Joy and they still keep in touch.'

'So Ursula Brambleton?' Henry concluded.

'Only one way to find out.'

Before I could decide whether or not it was a good idea, I'd called her, hiding my number.

'Hello?'

'Ursula, I'm Henrietta Fairfax, journalist with the *Mirror*. I hear you have an explosive story about Joy Papplewick.'

A brief silence.

'I might do.'

'Care to share?'

There was no hesitation this time. 'If you make it worth my while.'

I hung up, too appalled to say anything else.

'She must have put two and two together after I spoke to her.' I swallowed back the nausea churning in my stomach. 'I shouldn't have been so obvious. It was stupid to think she'd have any loyalty to Nana Joy. How am I going to explain being such an idiot?'

'You can't undo it, and you've already spoken to Jonty and Cora about how sorry you are. What matters now is what we do next.'

I sucked in a shuddering breath. The city was behind us now, the forest mere minutes up ahead.

'What *are* we going to do next?'

'We tell your parents and let them decide. Although, you do need to contact Pat O'Dowd as soon as possible. Before the journalists get a chance to.'

It was well after six o'clock, but the journalists would show no respect for her evening curfew, and that meant I couldn't either.

'Who is this?' she snapped, answering after almost a minute of rings.

'Pat, it's Bea Armstrong. I visited you yesterday to talk about Tony's friendship with my grandmother, Joy Papplewick.' *Was it only yesterday?*

'I told you I don't know anything about that.'

'Yes, and I really appreciate your help. Only, I'm sorry to say I have some news that might come as quite a shock.'

'What's he done?'

'Do you remember all the interest in Joy's son, and who the father might be?'

'Not really.'

'Well, it was Tony.'

I waited a moment to allow it to sink in, but Pat didn't seem to need one.

'Is that it?'

'Well, um, no. Somebody's sold the story to the *Chronicle*. They're planning on printing it tomorrow. I'm afraid it's quite likely they'll be in touch asking you for a comment. I'm so sorry, I know this must be upsetting.'

'They can ask away!' she said, with a laugh verging on flippant. 'And why would I be upset? I hadn't seen that waste of space since nineteen eighty-seven. He'd charmed two more fools into marrying him since me. Sounds like Joy Papplewick had her head screwed on right, not telling him he was a dad. Or maybe she did, and he wanted nothing to do with the baby. He wasn't a man to stick around if there was nothing in it for him. Tell your granny not to worry, though. I know what it's like to be caught up in his mess. I'm saying nothing to nobody. Now, if you don't mind I'm watching *The Chase: Celebrity Special*.'

## 31

It was nearly nine when we arrived at the Coach House. To my surprise and trepidation, my parents' car was in its usual spot and the downstairs lights were competing with the Christmas decorations in the garden.

'Beatrice!' Mum exclaimed when she answered the back door. 'How did you know? It's like being surrounded by spies,' she went on, striding towards the living room. 'Those online groupies of yours are everywhere.'

'Know what?' I asked, following her, Henry right behind me. 'I thought you'd still be with Nana Joy.'

She turned to me with a triumphant flourish. 'We are!'

It was a flurry of mixed emotions that accompanied the sight of my nana, huddled in her favourite armchair, cradling a glass of sherry with a blanket tucked around her knees.

'Why it's... you!' She beamed automatically, although I could see her mind fumbling for the right name.

'Sweet-Bea, what a lovely surprise.' Dad got up from the sofa and came to give me a quick kiss on the top of my head. 'You were wonderful this evening. Did you see her, Henry? Nana Joy insisted the whole ward watch her granddaughter on the television.'

'I did.' Henry offered a quick smile. 'She was brilliant.'

I didn't have time to feel pleased that my family had watched my broadcast, or that Henry had, and he thought it was brilliant. While overcome with relief that Nana Joy was home, this was going to make the ensuing conversation even more difficult.

Dad filled me in on what the doctor had said while Mum fetched a pot of tea and granola squares.

'I'm presuming the two of you aren't here to announce your engagement, given the general air of gloom when you walked in. What's happened?'

'I'm not sure I should say right now...'

'If this is about Tony O'Dowd, your nana knows what happened,' Dad said, taking his mother's hand. 'We aren't going to keep anything from her, so now's as good a time as any.'

With trembling heart, eyes anywhere but on Nana Joy, I told them.

There was a stiff silence once I'd finished. Mum, a myriad emotions flickering behind her eyes, opened her mouth to speak, when Nana Joy beat her to it.

'Well, I hoped those bloodsuckers wouldn't work it out until I was dead. But they have, so that's that. Ursula Brambleton always was a greedy thing. I'm not pleased about it, but I'm not going to waste what precious time I've got left getting upset. Besides...' her wrinkles deepened in thought '... the leeches could end up proving useful.'

And so, a plan was formed. There were plenty of objections about exploiting Nana Joy, but she poo-pooed them all, insisting that she'd put up with that for seventy years, she might as well be exploited for good reasons for once.

'I can put up with the bottom-feeders if it means we save Charis House.'

It might not mean that, but she was determined to give it a try.

We called Jed and told him our idea before I dialled the number on Henry's card. My heart would have been somewhere in my mouth, but it was so weighed down with love and pride for my incredible family, it had to stay right where it belonged.

* * *

I had another call to make, but, things being complicated enough, I waited until Henry had dropped me home.

'Hey, how are you?' Adam seemed totally unfazed that I'd called him on the brink of midnight. He'd sent me a few messages throughout the evening about nothing much, to which I'd sent a brief reply that Nana Joy had been discharged and I'd speak to him properly later on.

'Yeah, it's been an eventful day.'

Without going into any detail about how or why – I was far too tired for a long conversation – I explained that we were launching a campaign to save Charis House. We were hoping he could help...

'How long have we got?'

'I'm being interviewed tomorrow, printed the day after, New Year's Eve, so we'll need to be ready for the TV shows by then.'

'No problem. It'll be ready.'

'Are you sure? I know you're a perfectionist when it comes to music.'

'Bea. Charis House – your parents – *you* – saved my life. It's about time I returned the favour.'

There was nothing to do now until morning except worry, panic, freak out, and pray that this plan would be enough.

I took Mia's fashion advice and went full 'Bea' the following morning. It was 30 December, still well within the acceptable date range for Christmas accessories, but I wanted the pictures to be hanging around far beyond the season, so I went for my favourite dress, printed for me by the husband of a local conservationist who I'd interviewed on several occasions. It had a bright blue background, covered in weather symbols and finished off with a rainbow belt. I added a pair of mustard tights to complement the suns and laced up a pair of boots crafted by a Sherwood Forest designer, Grace Tynedale, embroidered with tiny leaves, nuts, and woodland berries.

We'd arranged to meet in the Charis House library. The deal was that Joy Papplewick would appear for photographs, and make a short prepared statement. I would be answering questions and trying not to throw my drink in anyone's face. Unlike most school libraries, this one had been designed to be as appealing a space as possible. There were rocking chairs, beanbags, and other cosy seating options. Despite its age, the room was airy and bright with teal walls and plush rugs on the wooden floor. Several desks repurposed from old doors were tucked into corners, or pushed together for collaborative working, and neatly stacked in a far nook were weighted blankets, waterfall lighting, and other items designed to support those struggling with sensory processing or attachment issues.

There was no heating on while school was closed for the holiday, so four armchairs had been set around a roaring fire. I sat with Nana Joy, sipped a glass of water, and tried to soak up some of her cool composure.

Henry showed the reporter and photographer in. We'd decided that my parents would stay well away this time. He waited, the only hint of tension a slight hunch to his shoulders, until Nana Joy had finished posing beside me like the professional she was. Her dazzling smile and confident posture detracted beautifully from the shadows that still lingered from her fall.

The reporter chattered easily with us while the photographer did his work, throwing in seemingly offhand questions that didn't fool Nana Joy for a second. She tossed her thinning hair, batted spindly eyelashes, and once the photos were taken she looked him straight in the eye and recited nothing more than the barest facts.

'Thank you very much, gentlemen,' she concluded, using Henry's elbow to heave herself up. 'I trust you'll comport yourself with more integrity than Tony O'Dowd ever did.'

She rested her hand, light and frail as a tiny bird, on mine as she walked past me. 'Over you to, my lovely. Time to do what you do best.'

'Tell them tomorrow's weather?' I asked, trying to conceal my anxiety behind a joke.

'Win their hearts and minds!' she retorted, and, with a wink, hobbled off.

The next hour required every ounce of my broadcasting training and experience. I did my best to lay a trail of juicy bread-crumbs, giving nothing away that any of us would regret later, but enough to lead them towards the real reason I'd agreed to talk.

I had the facts and figures all ready, thanks to Jed. More impor-tantly, I had the stories, sprinkled with humour, drenched with heartbreak and ultimately providing the much-needed happy ending. I had the passion, and the motivation, and by the time I'd finished, both of the journalists had contributed to the relaunched Charis House fund themselves.

'That was outstanding,' Henry said, once I'd provided a tour and then seen them safely down the drive. After escorting Nana Joy home he'd returned to the library, leaning on the wall with his arms folded like some sort of self-appointed bodyguard.

He'd smothered the fire and locked up while I was showing the reporters the grounds, so we now started walking back towards the Coach House. The air was murky, with wisps of fog lurking at the edges of the forest, and the grounds felt unnaturally still, our boots scrunching on the gravel the only sound.

Despite the pressing issue of Charis House, an undercurrent of uncertainty hovered alongside us. Henry had been nothing but pleasant since yesterday. His actions were as kind and considerate as I'd grown to expect. But the easy warmth that had grown between us over the past week had reverted to the lukewarm politeness of the years that had preceded it.

And it was only now, when Henry felt so far away, hidden behind his robot mask despite walking right beside me, that I realised how much I missed him.

I missed him nudging me with his elbow and giving a sidelong look that confirmed we were thinking precisely the same thing.

I missed knowing he'd got my back, and if I needed it he'd take my hand, too.

I wanted to drag him back to the library, relight the fire, grab one of the blankets, and curl up with him on the plushest sofa, spending the rest of the day telling him everything in my heart and my head.

And as he held the garden gate open, walked behind me as I made my way through all the shimmering decorations, I knew that he was the one I wanted.

Only, the way he jerked his hand back when we both reached for the door handle at the same instant and our fingers brushed, it appeared that Henry had decided he did not want me.

I didn't have time to think about that now, though. I had ten short minutes to summarise the interview for my parents, trying to provide reassurance while painfully aware that the journalists could spin and edit things into whatever nightmare story they fancied.

'That won't happen,' Henry said, when he followed me out of the door to where hopefully a taxi would soon appear to take me to work. 'You sold it to them, Bea. Literally, judging by the two donations they made.'

'Maybe so. But I know how it works. There are editors to impress and the rest of the day to forget how amazing the cause is and start thinking about how they can make it as sensational as possible.' I shuddered. 'And I dread to think what my producer will say when he sees whatever article they come up with. He's only just unfired me.'

'He fired you?' Henry gave me a sharp look. 'Was it Summer?'

I gave him a brief overview of the previous day's pre-journalist drama, the furrows deepening on his forehead until I'd described Jamal's perfectly timed entrance. The taxi pulled up the drive just as I finished.

'Have you reaccepted the job? I mean formally, signed a new contract?'

'I don't think I was ever formally fired.'

'Even so. He's lost his two top weather presenters in one day. All those ideas, the vision that you presented to Baxter. Maybe you can still make them happen.'

'I don't know. Mike Long is not my biggest fan.'

'Maybe not, but all those other fans have to count for something. You convinced Baxter Bigwood.' Henry's mouth twitched up as I opened the taxi door and climbed in. 'You're pretty hard to resist.'

Then he'd closed the taxi door and left me heading off in the opposite direction wondering what on earth that meant, and whether my lungs would be able to catch a proper breath before I had to stand and speak for three minutes straight in front of four hundred thousand people.

My innards did settle in time for me to spend a good fifteen minutes contemplating Henry's actual point, which was about my career, and he was right – if I was going to incorporate some of the things I'd loved about the potential BWM Today role into my current position, then surely there couldn't be a better time to broach the subject than when my boss owed me a giant apology.

Mike had messaged first thing that morning asking me to drop by his office once I arrived, which I dutifully did, on time and donning my new bad-ass attitude.

'Ah, Bea. Please take a seat. Can I get you a coffee? Tea?'

'No, thanks.'

'Right, well. I wanted to fill you in, in person, about yesterday.'

'Jamal told me Summer's been fired.'

'With immediate effect.'

I said nothing, allowing Mike ample opportunity to offer an apology.

'So, we're moving Grant into mornings, and Katie will cover weekends for now. I'm sure you and Grant will make a great team.'

'Okay.' I sat back, adopting a bland smile. 'I've worked with Grant before so there shouldn't be any issues in working together for a couple of weeks.'

He picked up his phone and started typing, as if to signal that the meeting was over. 'No, Grant'll be a permanent move.'

'Yes, but I'm working two weeks' notice, as ordered by you.'

Mike glanced up, about to offer a blithe correction that, no, I was also back permanently, but then he spotted the glint of steel in my eyes. He put his phone down.

'Oka-a-a-ay. Have you already been in touch with Baxter Bigwood?'

I raised one eyebrow. 'Would you have been, in my position?'

'You know we can't match him on salary.'

'Money isn't everything.'

Twenty minutes later we'd agreed a regular news item, covering the region's environmental and community issues, a weekly catch-up on some of the people who I mentioned in my forecasts and how their events or activities had gone, as well as several other features online, and a promise to cover the Charis House funding campaign.

'What time do you finish this evening?' Mike asked, once we'd shaken on it.

'I usually leave by seven-thirty. You should really know that.'

'We can sign the contract over dinner.' He threw out a smirk and a wink that had every muscle in my body clenching in distaste.

'Emailing it through will be fine.'

'Your loss,' he muttered, back on his phone before I'd had time to stalk out of there.

*No, Mike, it really isn't.*

\* \* \*

I spent a good portion of the evening posting messages about a big announcement the next day in between follow-up conversations with various people I'd contacted earlier on. The rest was spent alternating between pacing up and down and sprawling on the sofa with a cushion over my face while trying not to agonise about the two men who'd so rudely invaded my head space over the past week.

Tomorrow was New Year's Eve, and once the planned dramatics were over, I was going to stick to my commitment to see if there really was anything worth salvaging with Adam. But I knew my heart wasn't in it. My heart couldn't stop wondering what Henry would be doing to celebrate the New Year, and whether he would be wondering about me.

## 32

I caught an early train the following morning, and Dad picked me up from the Hatherstone bus stop.

'Any new additions to the schedule?' he asked as we bounced down the drive.

'No, still *BBC Breakfast* at eight-twenty, *Lorraine* at nine-fifteen and then back to the BBC for the lunchtime news. I'll need to catch the two o'clock train to be in time for work, but Jed should be back not long after that.' I checked my phone for the hundredth time that morning, but so far there was no breaking news about Nana Joy, or the school. 'Have you managed to persuade anyone else to be there?'

'You could say that. Things have been rather hectic since you left yesterday.'

'Oh?'

He merely nodded up ahead, where the main house was coming into view around the corner. A huge banner had been strung between the pillars flanking the front door, 'Save our School' emblazoned across the background. There were numerous cars spilling out of the car park and into any other space they could find, along with two news vans. I spotted a few of the other staff members, along with dozens of pupils, past and present, accompanied by various family members, milling about in the grounds.

'What's this?' I asked, utterly dumbfounded.

Dad smiled. 'One of our alumni has been extremely busy, and things sort of snowballed.'

I climbed out the car and wound my way towards the house, nodding hello to some of the ex-students I recognised, including a solicitor from a top law firm, a woman who employed several other Charis House graduates at her haulage company, and the most recent winner of a prestigious design award.

I could see the news reporters chatting to different groups of students, and wondered why Mum wasn't here to supervise it all – until I stepped inside.

The huge entrance foyer had been transformed into a showcase for the school. There were dazzling displays crammed along every wall. Fashion, art, and other creative pieces jostled for space with science and construction projects. Mum was zipping from one exhibit to another, encouraging, adjusting and barking instructions.

The evidence of my parents' tireless work – which was of course lives changed, wounds healed, faith restored – was all here, in the chatter and the smiles and the serious intent as those who believed Charis House had saved them did all they could to return the favour.

'It's eight-thirteen, Bea, why aren't you in position?' Mum called, spotting me from across the room. Glancing at my watch, I realised she was right.

'I don't know where in position is,' I replied, causing her to abandon the cake she'd been adjusting and hustle me back outside and down the main steps.

'Under the banner is best.' She stopped and looked at me then. 'Unless... I mean... you're the expert.'

'Under the banner is perfect.' I smiled, hoping to ease the anxiety in her eyes. 'Who do I need to talk to?'

'Bea, is it?' a man asked, who was pure BBC from grey side-parting to his sturdy shoes. 'You're well used to this, so we'll just cue in and get started. Two minutes with you, then a couple of questions with Harley and Cairo, ten seconds of the video, and back to you for a final statement.'

Then, before I could ask about the video, or check whether my weather-vane bobble hat was straight, we were live on national television.

The second we'd finished, I checked my social media feeds to find comments appearing faster than I could read them. I'd set up various posts to appear automatically at eight twenty-five, and my followers were responding in their droves.

Henry called me a few minutes later. 'We've already hit twelve-thousand pounds.' No hello or well done, but I guessed he was firmly in business-mode. Henry was overseeing the funding page. He'd also been specifically requested by Nana Joy to keep her company in the Coach House while all the chaos was happening out here. 'Eight of that is from Charis House alumni, but the rest are either viewers or your followers. SaveCharisHouse is trending.'

'I can't believe this. Who managed to get all the old pupils involved so quickly?'

'It was the video,' Henry said. 'You must have known?'

'Known what? I haven't seen the video. All the students were blocking the screens.'

I was beyond grateful that Adam had agreed to record a song for the campaign. He'd written one for his graduation, eight years ago, expressing what Charis House had meant to him, and how it'd helped him to believe in himself. I'd asked if he'd have time to record a version that we could then overlay with images of the house and some of the students from the twenty-seven years it had been open.

'Take a look. You need to start sharing it on your feeds.'

'Where's Adam?'

'You're more likely to know that than me.'

I hung up and did a quick online search for the song, 'Outside the Box'. It wasn't hard to find. As the last notes faded away, I began hurrying down the hall, sure that he'd be somewhere around his old hangout.

'Hey!' Adam's face lit up when he saw me in the entrance to the music room – the upgraded, high-tech one this time, full of wires and buttons and other scarily expensive equipment. 'Well done! Your interview rocked.'

The gaggle of young people clustered around the main screen chimed their agreement.

'What's this?' I held out my phone, ignoring them. The interview was nothing compared to the three minutes I'd just watched.

'You don't like it?' an older girl blurted.

'Are you serious?' I couldn't help it, I burst into tears. 'Adam, this is... it's... how did you...? *Thank you*,' I sobbed, standing there holding my phone out like a total chump. 'It's the best video I've ever seen. How on earth did you manage this in twenty-four hours?'

'Well.' Adam tried to be cool, but he looked like a little boy about to explode with pride. 'These guys helped. And the rest of them.'

The rest of them being students and alumni, all of whom had contributed a line to the song, often in groups, either appearing together or on a number of different screens that Adam had somehow synced together in between images of school life. Every person also held up a sign that stated their job title, or a more profound accomplishment such as, 'despair to hope', 'no longer lost', or 'from trash to treasure'.

The final chorus ended with what must have been a hundred tiny screens, no instruments, just the voices of those who meant every word they were singing.

It was perfect.

Glorious.

I hardly dared to believe it, but I thought Adam might have saved Charis House.

My phone beeped with a message from Mum summoning me to the next interview. I took another precious few seconds to throw my arms around Adam and try to convey quite how much this meant, then dashed back down the corridor, my heart soaring up somewhere in the Charis House turret.

\* \* \*

The next couple of hours passed in a frenzied blur of hugs, hellos, and trying to keep on top of my social media. Two local newspapers turned up, and I had to be ruthless about which calls I accepted and which I sent to answerphone to deal with later. I'd just been handed a mug of tea and a muffin from the school cook when things ramped up to a new level of surreal.

Dash and Dumble heard it first, ears pricked, noses to the sky. A few seconds later the distant rumble gradually grew to a roar as a helicopter appeared above a distant treeline and the various cameramen and photographers still hanging about swiftly pointed their lenses at the sky.

It was soon apparent that the helicopter was aiming for the empty sports field behind the house. A crowd of students rushed as one to see who was inside it, but once I'd made out the logo on the side, I knew exactly who was making this dramatic entrance.

Spotting Henry striding down the path from the Coach House, his eyes roaming about until they came to rest on me, I could tell he knew it too.

'What do you think?' I asked as he joined me in following the throng around the side of the house. 'Is this going to be brilliant, or disastrous, because there's no way it'll be anything in between.'

'Perhaps he's come for his robot elf,' Henry mused, before coming to a stop to watch the helicopter door open and Baxter Bigwood climb out, waving like the returning hero.

Another man followed him onto the grass, carrying a briefcase. This person waited for Baxter to adjust his coat and then pointed towards the onlookers. I wasn't surprised that his finger was aimed straight at me.

'Bea Armstrong!' Baxter bellowed, marching towards us, the man hurrying alongside him. 'You've proven yourself once again to be a force to be reckoned with. I've decided to reject your job rejection. Mannering here will oversee the negotiations. Ah, Driver! Marvellous. You can rustle up a private room where we won't freeze our bits off. If there's a whisky decanter and a bacon sandwich I'll make it worth your while.'

'Baxter, I don't want the BWM Today job. I was very clear about that.'

'Ah, you see, now that's where we disagree,' he said, coming to a stop about six inches into my personal space and peering down at me. 'It's not that you don't want the job, merely you think you want this little one here more. It's simply a matter of priorities. I believe today's performance demonstrates you want something else most of all.' He stopped and glanced around, noticing that Henry hadn't moved. 'Are we doing this here, then? Fair enough. It won't take long.'

He nodded to his employee, Mannering, who took a folder out of his briefcase, opened it up, and handed me a slip of paper.

It was a cheque.

One with lots of zeros on it.

Enough zeros to complete all the repairs and help keep Charis House going for a fair while after that.

'Mr Bigwood, are you bribing me to come and work for you?' It was only Henry's firm hand coming to rest on my back that enabled me to sound anywhere close to normal, compared to the gibbering wreck flailing about on the inside.

He smirked. 'You're an intelligent woman. You work it out.'

'Do you know this man, Beatrice?' Mum asked, appearing at my shoulder, Dad right behind her.

'It's Baxter Bigwood.'

'And who might that be?' she replied, no more impressed by a man landing his helicopter on her lawn than if he'd arrived on a rusty bicycle.

'He owns the news corporation that offered me the job I turned down.'

'So what's he doing here?'

Baxter's face flushed violet at my mother's blatant disregard for the billionaire standing right in front of her.

'I'm here to make her an offer she can't – or *won't* – refuse,' he barked, without taking his eyes off me.

I showed Mum the cheque, my head spinning even as my heart plummeted. If I'd had any trace of lingering doubt about wanting to work for BWM Today, this brazen, arrogant attempt to force me into doing what he wanted had obliterated it.

But scanning the eager faces all around me, these faces who had been let down so many times, how could I be so selfish?

For most of the children who came here, Charis House was their one chance, their only hope. How could I refuse this incredible opportunity, the kind of chance it took years at this school to even dare to dream of, simply because I preferred to stay in my nice, comfortable, stress-free job?

I looked at my mother, on one of the highly rare occasions she actually appeared rattled, and then at my father, blinking furiously as he tried to contain the tidal wave of emotions that accompanied a cheque of that size.

'We've hit thirty-five thousand,' a warm, firm voice spoke right beside my ear.

I swallowed, shaking my head. It felt as though the whole world had shrunk down to this moment, these people. This choice. 'It's not enough.'

'Sweet-Bea,' Dad said, cutting through the tornado raging in my head. 'Don't you dare say yes unless you want the job.'

'But Baxter's right though, isn't he?' I said, twisting to face him. 'How can I *not* want the job if it means this gets to continue? How can I enjoy going to work every day if I know that Charis House is empty, or converted into a tacky spa hotel, and my family are heart-broken, never mind homeless?'

'A very good point,' Baxter chortled.

'Oh, do be quiet!' Mum snapped. 'No one was talking to you.'

'How do you think we would feel, knowing you were working for that bully because of us?' Dad asked, choking on the words.

'It's my decision,' I declared, sliding my hand back to grip Henry's, because even though it was my decision, I didn't have the strength to make it alone.

The second my fingers reached his, he spun me around and took hold of the other one, bending his head to bore his eyes into mine. 'Bea, you have to trust in the right thing, here. Trust this.' He jerked his head towards the house. 'Trust almost two hundred years of fierce, fearless Armstrongs. Trust your parents, what they built here, and how much this means to people. Trust yourself, and the powerful community you created.' The corner of his mouth quirked up. 'Trust Adam, and that bloody amazing video he's made. You don't need to sell your soul to Baxter Bigwood. You – *we* – can do this without him.'

'It's not my soul though, is it?' I asked, struggling to see him through the blur of tears. 'It's just a job. It's just me, compared to all these others.'

'But this is your life, and however noble and valiant and in line with the Armstrong tradition it might be to sacrifice it for the sake of others, you don't need to do this. Just trust in the people you love.'

There was a rigid silence, while the world – or my world, at least – hovered in its orbit; my heart hung suspended between beats. Then I blinked, my vision cleared and I focused on the face in front of me.

'I don't know about any of those things,' I whispered. 'I certainly don't know if I can put much trust in me. But you know what? I've always trusted you, Henry.' My voice grew stronger alongside my conviction. 'Even when I pretended to myself I couldn't stand you, I knew that every word you spoke was true.'

I let go of his hands, turning to face my would-be employer. 'Thank you for the offer, Mr Bigwood. But my previous answer still stands.'

'Good on you, girl,' I heard Mum mutter.

Baxter took a long, slow look at me through narrowed eyes. 'If you change your mind, don't bother getting in touch. Mannering?'

And that was that, he whirled around and swaggered off.

'He forgot his cheque,' Mum huffed. 'How can you become so rich if you're that careless with money?'

'Baxter Bigwood is never careless about money,' Henry said, watching as the helicopter veered behind a stretch of distant pine trees. 'And he's not about to completely lose face in front of a crowd of people and countless cameras, some of them broadcasting live to the nation.'

'You don't mean...?' Dad asked.

Henry's face gradually broke into a beaming grin. 'Looks like we're getting a new roof.'

## 33

It was torture leaving the impromptu festivities behind and catching the train back to Nottingham. A few people had already left, having other places to be on New Year's Eve, but most had stayed. After all, where better to celebrate a new start than at the place where new starts were mandatory three hundred and sixty-five days of the year? Ignoring the remaining answerphone messages and online comments, I spent the journey losing myself in the weather apps, catching up on the morning's broadcast and cutting everything I wanted to say into the brief two minutes I'd been allocated in the shortened New Year's Eve news programme. Oh, and I did watch Adam's video three more times, not caring if the other passengers heard my sniffles.

I'd seen Adam only once since the music room, in a rare breather in between journalists and phone calls. Someone had set the video up on the big screen in the library, and everyone had squashed in to watch. I'd taken a moment to scan the audience, soaking up the joy and excitement shining on their faces. Adam was lounging up against the wall on the far side of the room, and his gaze caught mine, holding me there with a warmth that only someone who'd shared his heart over the past twelve years could fully comprehend. In his battered jacket and ripped jeans, jaw bearing the stubble of a musician's all-nighter, he looked like a thousand memories, a million dreams. Affection ballooned inside my chest, making it hard to breathe, until the boy beside him nudged his arm, causing him to look away, and I resumed my sweep of the room.

Henry had found a spot on the opposite wall. Arms folded, pinning his burgundy tie to his chest, he stood straight as a flagpole, eyes on the screen in front of him, any emotion that might have been generated by the song carefully hidden behind an air of polite interest.

I couldn't help glancing back at him as the video finished, the room breaking out into cheers and applause. With a jolt I found his eyes like laser beams, fixed straight on me. A shiver rippled across my skin, but when I offered a smile he merely frowned, quickly turning to a nearby teacher.

Work finished, I caught the bus just after seven, and was home by half past. That gave me an hour to shower, change, sort my hair and make-up, and flap around squawking about why on earth I was spending New Year's Eve with a man who was eagerly waiting for my answer to his proposal.

It had been a stressful few days to say the least. All I really wanted was a long bath, a good book, and a greasy pizza.

However, glammed up maybe not quite to the nines, but at least a solid seven in a shimmering, mint-green dress, I was ready and waiting when Adam knocked on the door.

'Wow,' he breathed, leaning in to kiss my cheek. 'Every time I see you it bowls me over again.'

'You scrub up pretty well yourself,' I said, which was an understatement. It wasn't simply the dinner jacket combined with floppy hair swept back and smooth skin freshly shaven. Adam was glowing with an energy that I'd not seen in him for years. I felt a prickle of unease that this might be due to me, even as I half hoped that by the end of the evening I'd be feeling it too.

There was only one way to find out. I took hold of his offered hand and followed him to the waiting taxi.

We spent most of the evening talking about the events of the day. I sensed that Adam was deliberately keeping things off the topic of our future, which I appreciated. We ate the fancy five-course meal at a table for two in a discreet corner of the glittering room, although various acquaintances did come over and offer their complicated fist-bumps of congratulations for the video, which had now gone stratospheric. Some of them I recognised, but all of them Adam introduced me to, making it clear that he was with me as he laughed off invitations to join them at a poker game, or for shots at the bar.

'No, thanks, mate.' He grinned at a guy called Cisco who'd tried to talk him into joining the band onstage to perform 'Outside the Box'. 'Bea and I were about to dance.'

Cisco was almost as dumbfounded as me.

'You can do the song,' I said as Adam pulled me onto the dance floor. 'I'd actually love to hear it live.'

'Not tonight,' he said, wrapping one arm around my waist and gently drawing me closer. 'I want to spend every minute of this evening with you. Besides,' he added, starting to move in time with the soft jazz number, 'after the past two days I've kind of grown sick of it.'

It should have been perfect.

Twinkling lights, exquisite decor. Champagne and slow dancing to beautiful music. A gorgeous man who'd given up his dream to be with me.

For the first time ever, I genuinely believed that we could make it work. No squashing of deep-down doubts or cheerily glossing over our issues. Adam had finally grown up. Become the man I'd longed him to be – had *known* with an increasing sense of frustration that he could be. And here he was, making it clearer than ever that he was serious this time, mine if I would have him.

The whole point of this evening was to give Adam a chance to show me that he'd really changed but as we swayed beneath the chandelier I knew with utter certainty that it wasn't going to make any difference.

Not because Adam wasn't good enough. I didn't need or expect him to be anything more than who he was.

Because I couldn't stop thinking about Henry.

Adam had been the beating heart of my past, and I would always, always love him for it.

But I wanted Henry to be my future, and even if that never happened because he didn't feel the same, I couldn't say yes to Adam now Henry was stuck in my brain.

Without realising it, I'd come to an unsteady stop.

'Are you okay?' Adam said, leaning back so he could see my face.

I took a couple of steady breaths. 'We need to talk.'

'Right.' Adam's hand automatically went to brush back his hair, forgetting that gel already held it firmly in place. 'You sure you want to do this now?' He gave a cross between a grin and a grimace. 'Because from the look on your face I'm going to wish I'd made the most of this dance by the time you're finished.'

Instead of replying, I walked back to our table, his other hand still in mine, but as we approached it Adam steered us away. 'Let's find somewhere quieter.'

A short way down the corridor we found a small alcove containing a leather sofa along with a huge vase full of gold and silver branches. Adam kept hold of my hand as we took a seat, his eyes refusing to leave my face.

'You know I've been thinking a lot about what you... about your proposal.'

'It doesn't matter,' he interrupted. 'It was far too soon, I get that now. I'm... I'm withdrawing my proposal. We can pretend it never happened. Let's just enjoy being together for now. It's been good, hasn't it? The carriage ride, the Spectacular. This evening has been awesome.'

He leant closer, resting his forehead against mine, his eyes brimming with fear and hope. 'We're good together, Bea. Without any more crap getting in the way. We're special, you and me. We've been through too much to—'

'No.' I shook my head, my fringe creating static against his skin. 'The past can't dictate whether we stay together in the future.' I gripped his hand tighter. 'Whatever happens, it'll never take away from what we meant to each other.'

'*Mean* to each other,' Adam said, his voice choking up. 'Bea, I love you more now than I ever have. Please give us this chance. Please, just a bit longer...'

He tipped his chin up, mouth desperate as it found mine, knowing precisely how to position itself so that we fitted seamlessly together.

For one bittersweet second I allowed his passion to press against my lips. The scent of him like a touchpaper to my skin, I breathed in and once again fought the temptation to take the easy route, at the very least to delay breaking the heart of this man, knowing the agony of what it had felt like every time he'd broken mine.

'I'm so sorry,' I whispered, pulling away and ducking my head. 'I have to say no.'

'No to marrying me, or to all of it?' he asked, not bothering to wipe away the tears.

'We can't drag it out when we know what the outcome is going to be.'

'You might change your mind,' he pleaded. 'I'm happy to take that chance. To wait, no pressure. You're worth waiting for, Bea.'

'You know I can't string you along like that,' I said, my resolve strengthening. 'I'm sorry, Adam. This is goodbye.'

'What changed?' he asked, voice breaking.

'Me, I suppose.' I shook my head. That wasn't quite right. The least I owed him was honesty. 'Or, maybe I simply got a clearer idea of who I am and what I want.'

'And that isn't me.'

'I'm not the right one for you, not really.' I took his hand again. 'That song. It's been watched by millions. People love it because it speaks to them. It hits right to the heart of their own fears and the dreams they wish they dared to believe in. You can't give that up for me.'

'I can. I already have! Don't make it about that, Bea. I can live without music. I can't live without you.'

'What if I can't live with myself, forcing you to make that choice, when I *can* live without you? When you're my easy option, not the dream I could have had if I'd only dared to believe it.'

'Wow. Don't sugar-coat it, will you? It's only my guts you're ripping out here.' He twisted away from me, rubbing his hands over his face as he tried to pull himself together. On the one hand, I was as shocked as him at my own brutal honesty. On the other, after so many goodbyes, I owed it to him to be clear that this was the final one.

'I guess I'll be making some changes to my new tattoo,' he said, trying to smile as he pulled his shirt out of his trousers and lifted up one side.

'I cannot believe you did that.' I gasped, while at the same time completely unsurprised at the letters spelling out my name in elaborate font across his side. 'I guess you could add some more letters? Turn it into beautiful.'

'I was thinking something with bear. Or beaver.'

'Beagle?' I giggled, releasing some of my stress. 'Beans?'

'Ah, I'll figure it out.' He dropped his shirt with a rueful smile. 'Are we going back in? I think the least you can do is give me one last dance now that you've ditched me.'

I paused before replying.

'Actually, I think I'm going to go home. To Charis House. After everything, I should be with Nana Joy.'

Adam frowned. 'I think Nana Joy would want you out enjoying yourself rather than feeling obliged to stay in with her. You've got a lot to celebrate.'

'You're right. But that's not what *I* want. Nana Joy would want me to be happy. As surprising as it might sound, I think being at Charis House with my family will make me feel that.'

## 34

By the time I managed to find a taxi, Adam was up on stage with a whisky in one hand, microphone in the other, the whole room his backing singers. I slipped into the freezing-cold night, dodging the spray from a residual slush puddle as the taxi skidded up to the kerb.

I'd failed in my private promise to be completely honest.

Nana Joy was a huge reason to be skipping out on my final date with Adam. The urge to catch up on all the time I'd missed with her over the past year, to ensure that there was nothing lingering between us after the Tony O'Dowd hunt, was a physical ache.

But of course, she wasn't the only person who would be partaking in the Armstrong New Year's Eve Legendary Grand Tournament. While the need to be with my family was deep, the desire to see Henry, to look him in the eye and see what I found there, to know whether there was any part of him that felt the same way as I did, was deeper.

Having accepted how I felt, I didn't think I'd be able to sleep, eat, or stop this frenzied fidgeting until I knew.

It was the longest taxi ride ever. Even the late-night shipping forecast wasn't enough to settle my nerves.

Finally, we pulled up beside the Coach House, where I flung myself out of the car and up to the front door.

'Okay,' I muttered. 'What do I do now?'

'Sweet-Bea!' Dad cried, answering my question as he opened the door in a flurry of ecstatic dogs and the warm glow of home. 'This is the best possible surprise! Come in, come in, let me take your coat and we'll find you a drink.'

After hugging me as though it had been months, not hours, he propelled me towards the living room. Standing in the doorway, I had to lean against the frame, almost overcome with emotion.

Mia and Jed were curled up on the smallest sofa, limbs entwined and paper hats tilted towards each other. They'd fully embraced the Grand Tournament historical-themed dress code, in spotty bow tie and a champagne flapper dress. Elana was sprawled beside the waning fire, her outfit a WRENs uniform from the Second World War. While I hovered in the doorway, the dogs squeezed past me and went to curl up with their chins in her lap.

Mum was standing beside the sparkling Christmas tree, her sixties shift dress covered in tinsel, baubles, and other decorations dangling from every possible body part, a gold star balanced on top of her beehive wig.

In the oldest, cosiest armchair was Nana Joy. Daisy and Frankie had squeezed in on either side of her. Frankie held two more baubles, while Daisy was resting her head on Nana Joy's shoulder, absent-mindedly twirling a lock of her great-grandmother's wispy hair.

And on the largest sofa, with a vast, lonely space beside him, sat Henry. My heart nearly scrabbled out of my chest at the sight of him, looking completely ridiculous in billowing shirt-sleeves, lavender waistcoat, dark-brown trousers tucked into riding boots and, of all things, a top hat, as if he'd dressed up as Mr Darcy. Two weeks ago I might have considered his attire ridiculous. This evening, he was perfect.

Perfect for me, anyway.

'Bea, finally, we thought you'd never make it!' Mum cried, trying to keep her head steady so nothing fell off, ending the game.

'Which would make sense, seeing as I told you I wasn't coming,' I said, wading through the piles of wrapping paper, old photographs, and other detritus left over from the previous tournament rounds. This one, a favourite, was the Armstrong version of a festive Buckaroo.

'Look, there's a seat next to Henry,' Dad cooed, when I stopped in the middle of the room, unsure of whether I could cope with sitting on the same sofa as him.

I masked my hesitation with a swift detour to kiss my grandmother, nieces, and nephew, hoping the delay would give me time to stop quaking by the time I sat down. The way Nana Joy pressed her fingers into mine as I leant down pushed a solid weight off my shoulders.

'Bea.' Henry nodded at me.

'Hi.' I offered a wavery smile back.

'How was your evening?'

Did he know I'd spent it with Adam? If so, he must surely be wondering why at a quarter past eleven I'd turned up here, alone.

'It was... nice. Thanks. Lovely food and the band were great.' I paused, slightly disconcerted to see the whole room staring at me, several questioning eyebrows raised. 'But there's no place like home, right? After what's happened the past few days, I wanted to be here, with all of you.'

No one said anything, instead they carried on gawping as though expecting me to keep talking, so I did. 'I feel really, really awful about staying away this past year. There were all sorts of complicated reasons, but it wasn't you, it was me. And I'm sorry, and I'm going to make it up to you by hanging around so much you all grow sick of me.' I had to stop and swallow back the lump expanding in my throat.

'Sweet-Bea, you're a grown woman, with a life of your own. We don't expect you to be here all the time,' Dad said.

'*Some* of the time would be nice,' Mum added.

'You didn't bring Adam?' Mia asked, never one to let tact stop her digging for information.

'No.' This time I wasn't about to fill the ensuing silence with further details. 'Is there anything left in that bottle?'

By the time I'd been handed a full glass of wine and helped myself to a scoop each of Mum's beetroot nachos and Dad's cheesy doughballs, Mum had wobbled, causing a carved wooden angel to fall off her shoulder and ending the penultimate round.

'If there's none of the usual messing about we can squeeze in the final round before midnight!' she announced. 'It's two points to each team. Bea, you can join Henry and your father. Here we go. Time to play Which Armstrong Am I?'

The fancy dress wasn't simply for fun. Every year they dressed up as past members of the Armstrong family. If the other teams guessed the identity, they scored a point, with plenty of bonus points to be had for extra random facts, the more bizarre, the better.

Jed and Mia went first. We all wrote down our answers, although only Mum managed to guess that they were Gordon and Cordelia Armstrong, virtually unheard-of distant cousins to her grandfather. They had such a tenuous link it caused a good five minutes of arguing about whether they were a valid entry until Jed distracted us with the interesting fact that they'd ended up in prison for robbing a casino.

It was six minutes to midnight when we reached the final guess, all of us scrunching our faces, genuinely mystified at Dad's beige jumper, jeans, and dark brown tie.

'This is impossible,' Jed grumbled, only one point behind Mum and determined to catch her. 'There's no historical context here. You could be any member of the family from 1940 onwards.'

'He couldn't be you,' Frankie said. 'Or Mum. Or Nana Joy...'

'He's not Tony O'Dowd, is he?' Elana blurted, before slapping one hand over her mouth when she realised what she'd said.

'I know, I know!' Daisy sang, bouncing about on Nana Joy's knee so hard I feared she might cause an injury. 'It's *obvious*! You're all so silly.'

'Okay, let's have your final answers, then,' Mum said, inviting us one by one to name one of her cousins or uncles, deliberately asking Daisy last.

'It's Henry, of course!' She squealed, pointing with glee. 'Grandad's even brushed his hair into the same style and is sitting all straight like a statue.'

'Got it in one!' Dad laughed, pulling a face that did look uncannily like Henry.

'What?' Jed sprang to his feet, face turning pink with indignation. 'Henry isn't an Armstrong.'

'Unless you've got a seriously juicy fact to win the extra point,' Mia murmured.

'Not yet, he isn't,' Dad said, waving his hand as if to say, *so there*. 'But we all know he will be.'

'What are you talking about?' Jed said, practically yelling. 'That's ludicrous. Even if Bea does eventually wise up and marry him, this is a *historical* round. I might as well dress up in jeans and a T-shirt and say I'm Elana's future husband!'

'Ew, gross!' Elana squealed in disgust.

'Why don't we vote on it, then?' Dad asked.

'Does Daisy still get a point?' Frankie asked, eyes wide with worry for his teammate. 'She did get it right.'

The whole time this conversation had gone on, Henry and I had remained frozen in horror on the sofa.

'We aren't going to vote!' Jed growled.

'It's four minutes to midnight,' Mia said. 'Let's just vote so we can get it over with before the gongs. I don't think you need to worry which way the result will go.'

'Fine.' Jed stuck his hands on his hips. 'Who votes that Henry is a member of the Armstrong family and therefore acceptable as an entry?'

'No, we need to do it in two stages,' Mum said, with a glint in her eye that only increased my mortification. 'Firstly, can we allow future Armstrongs to be included, if we are in a majority agreement that the person will one day be a family member. Secondly, do we believe that this is true for Henry?'

'Two minutes to go!' Elana said.

'I vote that this family is not normal,' Mia muttered.

'Right hand up for the first, left for the second,' Mum barked.

I couldn't bear to look, but at the same time couldn't stand not to. Only Dad, Daisy and Frankie had their right hands up. Every single person in my eyeline had their left one pointing straight in the air. And the only person not in my eyeline was Henry.

'Bea, Henry, are you abstaining or voting no to both?' Mum asked, the words dripping with consternation.

'No to both,' Henry said.

At the exact same moment I blurted, 'Abstaining!'

'Happy New Year!' Elana shouted, jumping up off the floor as the grandfather clock began to chime, quickly joined by her brother, sister and then the rest of the family.

Everybody except me. Face burning, blood roaring in my ears, practically drowning in my own humiliation, I clambered up off the sofa and fled.

## 35

'Bea.'

The voice startled me. I'd headed straight for the garden, hoping the icy air would help clear my head. Now, huddled on a bench beneath a fir tree, I was starting to wish I'd had the presence of mind to grab my coat as I raced out.

I twisted around to see the shadowy figure of Henry coming to a stop a few feet away.

'Are you okay?'

I attempted a watery smile. 'Oh, you know. Every time I decide my family aren't that bad, I've been unfair and I need to chill out, they do something like this.'

He came over and sat down next to me. 'Our families have been making insensitive references to us getting married our whole lives. It's never got to you like this before.'

'Maybe that's because things are different now.'

*Maybe that's because you voted 'no' to it ever happening, when suddenly it's the only thing that I want.*

'You mean Adam?' He sighed. 'If you told them about being engaged, they'd probably stop.'

'Firstly, they wouldn't stop and you know it. They'd probably start referring to him as my "first husband". Secondly.' I stopped, took a deep breath, and dared to sneak a look at him through the darkness. 'We aren't engaged. Adam asked me, and I said no. We aren't anything. Which is why I'm here.' Another deep breath. 'And why I abstained from the vote.'

For an endless, heart-wrenching minute, Henry said nothing. Eventually, at the point I was about to get up and run away again, he cleared his throat.

'Are you... do you... you abstained from the vote because you aren't ruling out the possibility that I become a member of your family one day?'

'Yes,' I managed to squeak. Then, emboldened by the darkness, knowing that I had to do something about these feelings or I'd simply implode, I carried on. 'Via marrying me.'

The shadows prevented me from seeing his expression, but I could hear the familiar frown in his voice. 'You mean you don't not want to marry me, one day?'

'I mean that I'm definitely up for exploring the possibility of our parents being right.' I let out a weak laugh. 'They're right about practically everything else, after all. Worth giving it a go, perhaps? We could, I don't know, try a few dates?'

'Except there's Adam.'

'What? No, there isn't Adam, I just said that.'

'Bea. There's always been Adam. At the Christmas party, the Spectaculars, even sharing a room in Scotland he was there, with his flirty messages. You've broken up with him, what, half a dozen times before? And every time.' He paused to swallow and catch his breath. 'Every time, I felt that twinge of hope. That stupid, pointless hope. That maybe, this time, your whole world would stop revolving around him long enough for you to see me. I can't go back to that. I'm working for your family now. I live in the stable block. Initially, part of the reason I applied for this school rather than anywhere else was because I actually fooled myself into thinking he was out of the picture for good this time. And then here he is, Christmas Day, knocking on your door. I can't go on a few casual dates with you, as if it's not that big a deal. As if I haven't loved you since we were six years old. Like when he turns up again with some new song about your hair or your smile or how this time he's finally stopped being a selfish git, and you go to him, it won't destroy me.

'After all these years, we're finally friends, which is the best thing that's ever happened to me. I can't let myself dare to believe we could be more than that, then have to go back to seeing you with him, shrinking yourself to fit his life, trying to be interesting and fun and cool enough for him to put you first this time. It kills me to say this, when you've just told me that you don't hate the idea of marrying me, but please don't ask me to be the thing that makes you feel better in between Adam.'

I sat back on the bench, in utter shock. It was impossible to process this when my head was spinning, my heart galloping inside my chest.

I took yet more deep breaths.

'For a long time, I was in love with Adam. At least, I loved how he made me feel. Beautiful. Precious. Not like the family misfit. But for a while now, probably a lot longer than I realised, what I loved was the memory of how we used to be. The dream of what we could be. And, especially these past couple of weeks, I've realised that none of those things were that great. You're right, about me making myself smaller so he could fit me into his life, while at the same time never feeling quite enough. And then you turn up and... and make me believe that who I am is already enough.

'I can be myself, without ever feeling scared or ashamed about what you see. And I want you to be completely and utterly yourself with me. The you that loves order and compassion and sensible trousers and who hides behind that robot mask because you've learnt that too often people don't understand you, and so they don't even bother to try.

'I want to understand you, Henry. Because the more I see of you, the more I find myself falling in love with you. You are the best man I've ever known.

'Adam couldn't come close to you. And even if he did, he's not the man I want. Every second I was with him, all I could think about was you. To be honest, every second I'm not with him I can't stop thinking about you, either.'

I reached out and fumbled for his hand. 'I literally just sat there in front of my family and *abstained*. You are way too much of a super-science-genius not to figure out how serious I am.'

'Okay.' He turned towards me, giving my hand a reciprocal squeeze. 'That speech was very lovely, but you're right, I can't deny the significance of the vote.'

'So I've convinced you we're worth a go?'

He shuffled along the bench until his thigh bumped mine. I got a glimpse in the garden lights of those breeches and felt a crackle of electricity. 'You've convinced me that a revote would be a good idea.'

'Oka-a-a-ay. Do you vote yea or nay when it comes to allowing future members of the Armstrong family in the Which Armstrong Am I? round of the New Year's Eve Legendary Grand Tournament?'

'Yea.' Henry leant closer, so close that I could feel the warmth of his breath against my face as he spoke. It took everything I'd got not to pounce on him. 'But that wasn't the vote I was referring to.'

'I might need reminding of the other one,' I whispered, bridging the gap between us to mere millimetres.

'Do I, Henry Fairfax, believe that one day I'll be a part of this weird, wonderful family?' He paused. Swallowed. Reached up one hand and gently stroked the side of my face. 'Via marrying you? With everything I've got, I hope so.'

'I hope so, too,' I started to say, but before I'd finished his mouth had brushed mine. He hovered there for a brief second, and then when I returned the kiss, he wrapped his arms around me and for a blissful moment we expressed everything that had been filling up our hearts, that our words had so clumsily tried to convey, with a passion and a tenderness that I'd been waiting for my whole life.

'I love you,' he breathed, against my cheek.

'I love you too,' I sighed into his neck, still in awe that I was here, in the Coach House garden, kissing Henry.

I would have quite happily stayed there and kept on kissing, only neither of us had a coat on, and the first few flakes of the new year had begun to drift down between the pine branches.

'It's snowing.' I blinked, a larger snowflake landing on my eyelash.

'You could have warned me.' He gently brushed another one from my face.

'I did, at six twenty-five. Didn't you watch?'

'Bea, I have watched every forecast you've ever presented. Some of them more times than I will ever admit.'

'So you were warned.'

'I was probably too dazzled by you to concentrate on what you said. Did you also mention that it would be freezing?' he added, starting to vigorously shiver.

'No, because it's two below that.'

'Whatever it is, I think it's time to go inside.' He bent his head then, and kissed me again. 'Or maybe I can stand it for another few—'

I knew the back door had been thrown open because a pair of hot, happy dogs came bounding up and planted their paws on my lap. The second clue was my mother's voice blaring through the dark, her tall frame silhouetted by the kitchen light.

'Henry, are you out there? Your parents are on the telephone. They tried your mobile but you didn't answer.'

Henry gave an impatient sigh, but I could feel his body preparing to move.

'I told them you're fine, just kissing Beatrice in the garden, but they wanted to say a quick happy New Year anyway, if you can tear yourself away?'

He stood up, tugging me with him. 'I'm not facing them without you.'

'You don't have to face anything without me any more, as far as I'm concerned,' I replied, almost delirious with happiness as I wound my arm through his.

'Thanks, Cora,' he mumbled as we reached the back door and found both my parents, Nana Joy as well as Jed and Mia all clustered in the doorway, wearing grins the size of watermelon slices.

'Oh, phooee,' she said, flapping an overexcited hand. 'You might as well call me Mum.'

'Happy New Year, sis,' Jed said, giving me a nudge as I squeezed past him into the kitchen.

'Happy New Life, more like,' Nana Joy declared, patting me on my freezing cold cheek.

'Happy old life, I think,' I replied. 'Just with some added extras.'

'So now you're finished proving Mum and Dad right, can we find out who won the tournament?'

So the Armstrongs saw in the new year cosied up in the living room with hot chocolate and marshmallows, a toasty fire, and a heated argument that resulted in Dad declaring a draw.

Sitting in the heart of my family home, leaning back against the man I loved, who I now knew loved me, my Nana Joy belting out Auld Lang Syne, my parents' creases of worry replaced with laughter lines. Knowing Charis House was safe, I had to agree that for that one, sweet night, we were all winners.

My future forecast? It was going to be spectacular.

# ABOUT THE AUTHOR

**Beth Moran** is the #1 bestselling author of novels including *Let It Snow* and *Just The Way You Are*. She regularly features on BBC Radio Nottingham and is a trustee of the national women's network Free Range Chicks. She lives on the outskirts of Sherwood Forest.

Sign up to Beth Moran's mailing list for news, competitions and updates on future books.

Visit Beth's website: https://bethmoranauthor.com/

Follow Beth on social media:

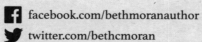

facebook.com/bethmoranauthor

twitter.com/bethcmoran

bookbub.com/authors/beth-moran

## ALSO BY BETH MORAN

# Boldwood

Boldwood Books is an award-winning fiction
publishing company seeking out the best
stories from around the world.

**Find out more at www.boldwoodbooks.com**

Join our reader community for brilliant books,
competitions and offers!

Follow us
@BoldwoodBooks
@TheBoldBookClub

### Sign up to our weekly
### deals newsletter

https://bit.ly/BoldwoodBNewsletter